I0651397

H Slade

The Life and Labors of the Late Rev. William Stevens Balch

With an Outline of His Writings and Discourses

H Slade

The Life and Labors of the Late Rev. William Stevens Balch
With an Outline of His Writings and Discourses

ISBN/EAN: 9783337209049

Printed in Europe, USA, Canada, Australia, Japan

Cover: Foto ©Raphael Reischuk / pixelio.de

More available books at **www.hansebooks.com**

Yours Fraternally,
Wm. S. Balch.

GEO. H. WALKER & CO. LITH., BOSTON.

THE LIFE AND LABORS

OF THE LATE

REV. WILLIAM STEVENS BALCH

WITH AN OUTLINE OF

HIS WRITINGS AND DISCOURSES

AND

BIOGRAPHICAL SKETCHES AND RECOLLECTIONS OF INCIDENTS,
TRAVELS AND CORRESPONDENCE, DURING
A HISTORY OF MORE THAN
SIXTY YEARS.

———

BY

REV. H. SLADE.

———

" His youth was innocent, his riper age
Marked with some act of goodness every day ;
And watched with eyes that loved him, calm and sage,
Faded his late declining years away.
Meekly he gave his being up, and went
To share the holy rest that waits a life well spent."
                                        —*Bryant.*

CHICAGO:
PRINTED AND BOUND BY
DONOHUE & HENNEBERRY.
1888.

THOSE FOR WHOM CHRISTIANITY CAME INTO THE
WORLD TO DO ITS WORK OF HEALING AND BLESSING;

IN FAITH AND HOPE ARE BORN, AND PRAYER IS HAD,
AND PRAISES SUNG, AND SYMPATHY AND
CHARITY EXPRESSED;

SORROWING ONES OF EARTH, THE UNFORTUNATE AND
BEREAVED, THE SICK AND THE DYING;

AND

THE CATHOLIC UNITY OF THE CHRISTIAN FAITH;

THIS VOLUME IS

RESPECTFULLY AND AFFECTIONATELY INSCRIBED

BY THEIR SINCERE

FRIEND AND BROTHER.

PREFACE.

In presenting the record of the personal history of the Rev. William S. Balch, and selecting and arranging events and incidents for holding up the mirror of the deeds of him whom we seek to bring prominently to your notice, that others may be induced to follow his example and feel the influence of his many virtues, it will be the aim, as far as possible, to let the subject of this memoir speak for himself. We have found ourselves chiefly encouraged in these labors from the fact that his was a life uncommonly eventful, and from the great number of stirring incidents and occurrences calculated to enhance the intrinsic value of the volume. His friendly suggestions of wisdom, strung like pearls through all his writings, calculated to arrest every class of minds and awaken them to the vast importance of virtuous living, is what must make this work dearer to the reader than aught else beside. We would not speak in any strain of studied eulogy, and may not claim for any person on earth that he is perfect, for perfection does not belong to this world.

It is but justly due that I should, before passing, express my most sincere and unfeigned thanks for the varied assistance rendered me by many friends who have kindly aided me in my work.

I much value the words of the one dearest to me (now passed to the spirit home), who in her absence writing me, says: " I am sure if you could gather the inspiration to do justice to so good a man, you have no need to go further to write up one of the grandest lives the world has ever witnessed. You have almost worshiped him, and your fault is likely to be the coloring of the picture. What you need to do is to write a candid memoir, that will throw his virtues

uppermost; his strong mind, his strict integrity, his humility, his
loving sympathy with the weak, the poor and the oppressed. He
has always felt that truth was mighty and must prevail, and therefore was tireless in maintaining what he deemed to be right. Aye,
indeed, such a noble life can be written from material so truthful,
so beautiful, so substantial, that even his enemies (if he had them)
would be obliged to say, 'That is Brother Balch.'"

Nothing is truer than the above. And I shall endeavor to be
truthful in my utterances, and trust that the reader will be enabled
to form some partially adequate conception of the character sought
to be portrayed. And we tender our work to all who shall care to
peruse it, in the hope that it will be valuable to many who are pur·
suing the chart of life's voyage, in being a solace and comfort, as
well as an inspiration to fortitude and courage and manliness of
mien. We have no wish or desire more holy than that the gift we
here bring you, in the thoughts evoked from our subject, shall fill
your souls with all beneficent feelings and impulses, as they have
glowed and burned in our own during these months in which we
have pondered and written.

CONTENTS.

CHAPTER VI.

CHAPTER X—Continued.

CHAPTER XI.

CHAPTER XII.

CHAPTER XV.

THE LIFE AND LABORS

OF THE LATE

REV. WILLIAM STEVENS BALCH

CHAPTER I.

PASSED ON TO THE HIGHER LIFE.

On the 26th of December, 1887, there appeared in the local papers of Elgin, Ill., worthy notices of the death of Rev. William S. Balch, occurring on the day previous, and the following tribute of deferential respect and esteem by the pastor of the Universalist church, Rev. A. N. Alcott:

A NOBLE LIFE ENDED.

"On Christmas day, not far from noontide, almost while the Christmas songs and services at our churches were in the air, Rev. W. S. Balch quietly and without suffering breathed his last. The morning hymns and prayers had gone before, as incense, as it were, to prepare his way. He followed quickly these spiritual forerunners to the land of beauty. The day commemorated as the birthday of the world's Redeemer, proved to be also, as we trust, the second birthday of our old and much esteemed friend and long-tried comrade in the battle for holiness in the earth — his

13

birthday into the realm of glory to wear the crown of righteousness for evermore.

"Thus has closed a long and remarkable career. He has been known throughout the East and West, and everywhere had a host of acquaintances and friends. His spirit was large and generous, and his heart was very tender. His mind was accustomed to broad, comprehensive views on all subjects. He sympathized with all ranks and conditions of men, and no one stood more clearly, consciously and heartily than he on that plane of intellectual hospitality which is as wide as the race. He was an ardent and practical lover of all that was noble and good in man, and an ardent and practical hater of selfishness, greed, hypocrisy and pretense. His influence has been great and wide. He has lived a consistent, noble, energetic, good life. We may all thank God for him. He has been an ornament to the Universalist denomination, an able and eloquent workman in it, and continued to feel as keen an interest in its well-being in his recent months and days of failing strength, as when he first consecrated his young manhood and loyal heart to its service. Nothing in his life will ever cause regret or shame to any of us; but rather his whole life and work will ever be a cause for gratitude and pride. His work has been true, open, devoted, self-sacrificing, grand. And those who now mourn his loss—and there will be many of them—may be partially comforted by the reflection that though his bodily form and genial presence and words of cheer will be with us no more, yet his excellent example will remain to us as an indestructible inheritance, and worth more than rubies."

Perhaps no one of our ministers had enjoyed a fuller or more intimate acquaintance with our excellent brother, in the later years of his life, than brother Brigham, who had been a recent pastor of the church

at Elgin—and he is pleased to speak of him in the
following manner:

"In the death of Rev. W. S. Balch, D. D., the
Universalist church loses one of its oldest and most
respected ministers, and the church universal one of its
most devout and saintly characters. He was widely
and favorably known in all parts of the country, and
his name was a household word in all Universalist
families. His eminent services to the church and
cause of righteousness entitle him to be ranked as one
of the foremost preachers of his generation. His active
and able participation in the temperance cause, and all
other moral questions brought before the American
people for the past sixty years, clearly rank him as one
of our most worthy and highly respected citizens. He
was closely identified with the history of our church,
and his life and labors did much to obtain for us a
recognition and to lay the foundation for our prosperity as a Christian church. This generation cannot
fully realize the difficulties under which he labored,
nor overestimate the value of his services on behalf of
our church. Dr. Balch was born in New England, and
inherited the rare, intellectual and moral gifts which
have distinguished his ancestry. His pronounced convictions and firmness in maintaining them, with his
bold and fearless hatred and denunciation of evil, are
characteristics of the old Puritan stock. He was such
a man as might be looked for in the case of such an
ancestry. He was one of a company of remarkable
preachers who gave new character to the Christian
thought of the age and religious life of the country.
His labors extended over a period of more than sixty
years. During his ministry our church passed through
a period of sharp controversy, with which Dr. Balch
was closely identified and became an able defender of
the faith. He was not merely polemic in his methods
of work, but a preacher of the gospel of righteousness,

and a valiant soldier of the cross, reflecting in his own life and character the beauty of holiness. My acquaintance with him, beginning under pleasant circumstances some years ago, ripened into a lasting friendship. He always exercised a kindly judgment and a fatherly spirit that irresistibly drew me to him for counsel and sympathy, and never was I sent away empty. His wide and varied experience with men and affairs of life, combined with a wonderful memory and large amount of common sense, made him a wise counsellor. Dr. Balch was an eloquent speaker, and though somewhat diffusive, never failed to interest and hold his audience. Every word and attitude of the man expressed his devotion, sincerity and earnestness. Honest in thought, sincere in purpose, loyal to his friends, openhearted and plain spoken, he could tolerate no hypocrisy or pretense. To him Christianity was more a life than creed, a character rather than profession, and the preaching of righteousness more than organization. His life attested the sincerity of these convictions, having lived a consistent Christian, and passed to his rest crowned with glory and honor. Dr. Balch had a commanding presence, a strong and active mind, a lofty ideal and a tender heart. He maintained a pure heart and a spotless example. His life work remains as a priceless legacy in our church, and his successful career as a Christian minister becomes an inspiration to all who labor for the advancement of God's kingdom.

" My more intimate association with Father Balch was during my pastorate of the church in Elgin. His friendship was steadfast and his support cordial and liberal. His spirit was gentle and his judgments charitable. I learned to place implicit confidence in the man, and always found him unwavering in his faith, steadfast in his adherance to Christian principles, and every way worthy of confidence. He was, indeed, a model ex-pastor. My words and methods were never subjects of adverse criticism before the public, but whatever criticism or advice he had to offer was always given in private and in a kind and fatherly spirit. I dearly loved the man and can not realize he has left us forever, and that I shall never again look upon his bodily form, feel his genial presence, and listen to his words of cheer. I recall now his last visit to the ministers' meeting when I was present.

" The subject under consideration was the relation of the church to the Sunday-school, and Dr. Balch spoke feelingly regarding the little children, and the necessity of giving them good advantages and early religious training, admonishing the brethren to care for the little ones. We mourn, but not as those without hope, for life is continuous, and there is a ' restitution of all things,' and we believe that this man, so richly endowed with native and acquired gifts, so faithful in his friendship, so illustrious in citizenship, so true and sincere in religion, and eminent in the Christian virtues, is not dead, and that we shall meet again. Farewell, my dear and venerable friend, having passed the stormy period of life, rest thou in peace! Thou hast passed to thy reward ripe in years and experience, respected by all men, and with the priceless gift of an untarnished name, bright as the stars. Thy life hath enriched the world, which will hold thee in loving remembrance."

Truly we may say a great and good man, full of noblest deeds, occupying largest places, and doing most faithful service for his denomination, and for every good cause, with a hold on the hearts of vast multitudes of people, as but few have ever held, has passed from earth to a better home than any of the homes of earth can afford. He has been called to a higher and wider sphere of honor and effort, being lifted up through this life to that which is ampler and better. He has been gathered to his fathers, having the testimony of a good conscience, in favor with God, and in perfect charity with the whole world. The pulpit and press throughout the country have been quick in vying with each other to bespeak his praises, and to lament his departure with tenderest testimonials of their sorrow at the loss of one who has been so widely known, and so honored and loved in the hearts of so many. We may well say, as in the beautiful lines of Miss E. J. Stickney:

> Thy work on earth is done,
> The day has dawned for thee,
> A Christmas day unending,
> For God has called thee home.
>
> For thee no more earth's pain and care,
> But gain surpassing human thought.
> *   *   *   *   *   *   *
> Thy efforts grand to raise and lead
> Mankind to better deeds,
> And broader thought of God's great love
> And mercy, and man's brotherhood,
> Remains a priceless gift.
> *   *   *   *   *   *   *
> Thy path of duty followed long,
> And purity of purpose gave
> A recompense of peace.
>
> Heaven's deepest joys be thine,
> My father's life long friend and mine,
> With reverence from childhood felt,
> As one of many who will say,
> "My life was blest by him."
> This tribute to thy faithfulness
> I lay upon thy grave.

And now commences the endeavor to sketch as faithfully as may be the life and labors of the hero of this story, which may the good God direct to His own wise ends and purposes, as the prayer of so many will be. And in tracing here what he whose history these pages will disclose has to say of the object of this

work, as I gather it from manuscript placed at my
disposal, and other sources to which I have applied,
containing many interesting and teeming events, allow
me to quote from what his own hand has recorded:

'To-day I am just half way across my eightieth year,
and I begin a work which has often been urged upon
me by many friends. I do it hesitatingly, in part to
gratify them, but chiefly to convince young people
that an earnest and constant endeavor to do right in
all things will surely secure for them fair success,
prosperity and happiness, however humble their birth,
strong their temptation, and great their difficulties
which may seem to hedge their pathway before them."

"The young need encouragement, example, faith
and hope. Those in mid-age who have patience to
read the record of a plain, humble, active life may
find something to instruct and entertain. The aged, I
am sure, will be reminded of conditions and events in
the long past, and, by contrast with the present, be
thankful for what they have seen and enjoyed."

Then as he proceeds he speaks of the general character and object of biography, and says:

"Biography truly written is to be regarded as
among the most interesting and profitable reading. It
becomes a study to the thoughtful in the formation
of character. The novels and romances so much read
are little else than personal biographies, painted in
gaudy colors, so intermingled as to excite and please;
sometimes real: too often imaginary, extravagant and
impossible. What is history but a narrative of personal
and associated desires, purposes, plans, actions and results, or successes and failures, for the good or injury
of mankind?"

He speaks of autobiography after this manner:

"An error in biography, written by another, is,
that the author too often writes himself instead of

his subject. At best he accounts for facts, and colors them by his own or others' impressions and feelings. He cannot know, except by inference, what were the serious thoughts, real principles, controlling motives and outside influences which led to the conduct and character he attempts to describe. He makes an ideal hero to adorn his book, or dresses in rags an honest man to gratify a grudge. Every man, the deeds and needs of whose life are worth recording, can best write his own Biography. To do so may by some be thought egotistic. There is the danger that he may magnify his virtues beyond their true measure, and be blind to his own faults. If honest he will do neither. Conscious of his race on the earth being nearly run, his work nearly finished, and his actual record made, it would be a shameful sin, and a deserved disgrace, to write his own hypocrisy, and leave it to witness against his memory. Better that he repent, and leave silence behind him.' "

Then as he continues, his words are :

"I have done no great or marvelous deeds whereof to boast. Born and bred in comparative obscurity, I have never coveted wealth, or obtained it. Nor have I preferred the honor that comes from men to that which comes from God. My chief battles have been fought with myself. Though earnest and active in what was clear to me as being right and duty, in the minutest as in the greatest, I have aspired to live an honest, a useful and honorable life, mingling my own good with the good of my fellow men, my prosperity and happiness with theirs, as a common brother in a common humanity. With these principles I have pursued the even tenor of my way as far as possible, as I have advanced from childhood to old age, and I have found favor and abundant reward all the way, far above my expectations. Having been so prospered and blest in my humble career, I now sit down to detail, briefly as I can, some of the fruits consequent upon such a course of action, honestly begun and steadily pursued for the benefit of those who are and those who are to be. I do it that they may be persuaded to shun the way of evil which inevitably leads to trials, disappointments and misery, and often to untimely death; and to choose and follow the open path of sincerity, purity, honesty, fidelity, humility and duty, which certainly leads to honor, peace, plenty, happiness and long life, with flowers freely scattered all the way from the cradle to the grave, and bright hopes of a brighter future always before them."

It seems that he could not have always been careful to keep a diary or journal of his life, for in speaking of the difficulty of knowing what to write, and what to leave unwritten, we have the following from his pen :

" It is from fragmentary memoranda, jotted down from time to time from the age of sixteen onward, and from the help of a strong and clear memory, that I gather material for what I write. I shall be compelled to condense much, and to erase more, lest the book be so large that but few will have the courage to read it."

He states again the purpose for which he writes:

" My first and leading thought will be to help educate the young, and prepare them for the life before them, but also to give symmetry and strength of purpose to manhood. To do this for the higher attainments of a rational, reasonable and true life, however humble its origin, or great the obstacles which hinder it, is the object of this work. To this object the study and main purpose of my life has been devoted."

His final remarks are, that:

" Having lived in one of the most interesting periods of the world's history, from 1806 to 1886 (it was

in that year he was writing what he here pens), I must
have been a dull observer indeed not to have noted
some of the wonderful events which have transpired
between these years worth describing for the benefit
of those whose duty it should be to go forward in the
highway of progress toward the perfect, in all that
helps to broaden the views, deepen the convictions, and
warm the soul into a clearer apprehension of the wise
and benevolent purpose of Him who created man 'to
glorify and enjoy Him forever.'"

Mr. Balch, I am sure, ought to be able to speak out
of a ripe experience, and we can not doubt that everything of the above is judiciously conceived.

CHAPTER 11.

I continue to quote largely, and to give this account as much as possible in the language of Mr. Balch himself; and it will be perceived that he never fortified his claim to the popular regard by allusions to any illustrious ancestry, but on the contrary avoided courting the favor of the worldly great. Much of what he says is calculated to remind one of what Nathaniel P. Rogers once told of himself: "That he was well enough descended, but had nothing of uppish blood in him; that he believed one of his progenitors was hung, and back farther one was burned at the stake, so that he could not help seeing equal humanity in any living creatures, however neglected or despised."

Mr. Balch opens on this subject by saying:

"Biographies are usually introduced with a grand overture, detailing the good and wise and great traceable in the lives of a long line of ancestors. The attempt is made to find some taint of genius or excellence which must have descended by force of natural heredity through many generations, and centered finally in the hero of the narrative. Success in this direction is thought to be the augury of continued greatness, and bespeaks a favorable reception boy careless readers, under the promise of an enticing book. It fell to my lot to come into the world with no such prestige to help me through it."

"The knowledge and example of great and good

deeds, and eminent virtues in parents, may inspire a
noble ambition and beget a feeling of responsibility in
children, sufficient to lead them to untiring effort to
live worthy of the name they bear.   And so the influence of good society may awaken in children, born in
low and degraded conditions, a desire and a resolution
to rise out of it, and become worthy to associate with
the good in the truer walks of life.   But it will never
do, in this age and country of democratic feeling and
public schools, to plead the purity and nobleness of an-
cestral blood to exalt our virtues or cover our vices.
Every person is self-dependent to form for himself a
character to be respected ; to weave for his own brow a
chaplet of honorable distinction or to sink into obscurity or deserved disgrace.

" I never tried to learn much about my pedigree.   I
knew my paternal grandfather, for I was often at his
house when a boy.   He used to tell me what he did and
suffered during the war of the revolution; how on hearing of the fights at Lexington and Concord he left his
home with several of his neighbors; shouldered his
musket and started for Bunker Hill, reached Charles-
town Neck just in time to cover the retreat, while balls
from the British ships went whistling over their heads ;
how he was at the battle of Stillwater, and Saratoga,
and was hurt by a limb falling on his head, cut from a
tree by one of Burgoyne's cannon balls; how he win-
tered at Peekskill on the Hudson, and at Valley Forge,
deprived of every comfort, at times almost starving,
and continued to serve seven years, till that war was ended, and then returned home half clad, with some almost
worthless bits of paper, called Continental money, in
his pocket.   Sometimes he would take down his old
musket, which lay in two wooden hooks nailed to a
beam overhead, and show us boys the drill of Baron
Steuben.   It was enough for me to start from such a
grandsire, without going farther back to trace my
genealogy."

"I did once, however, ask him about his ancestors when grown to manhood, and he over ninety. It was one of his 'bright days,' as my aunt called them. He was in a very happy mood, talkative, and even merry. He had made many inquiries about my condition, my family, how it fared with us, and what our prospects were. I finally ventured to tell him that I had sometimes been curious to know something about the history of our family—where we had come from, and what we had done that was worth our while to know.

"The old gentleman roused up, and said rather seriously, 'What is that to us? We have only our own conduct to answer for, and honors won by others might not set well on our shoulders.' 'That is very true.' I replied, 'in a certain sense. I have no desire to share honors or emoluments which I do not deserve. Still it is some satisfaction to know something of one's forefathers.' 'I have good reason to desire no such thing,' he said in a somewhat subdued and grave tone, 'for I have always thought it a disgrace to accept property or honors not gained by ourselves but by others;' to which I replied that property without industry and praise without merit do more harm than good. He told me I was right, and he would gratify me as far as he knew, and began, saying, 'I was born in the Old Bay State, town of Newbury, and I lived when a child with my mother in Boston. My father I never saw. I was told that he was a sea captain, and was lost with all his crew when on a voyage to the West Indies.'

"After some explanations of my aunt, what she had learned, he added, 'yes, my mother left me when I was young. She was married to a British officer, and went to live in Halifax, the home of Tories in those days. I have been told she died there, and left me several hundred dollars, which I never received, and it is just as well. So you see that you have nothing to boast of or expect on that score."

"I may say that there are now two diligent persons, working on different lines to search out the origin of the name. Both have followed one branch back as far as Scituate in the Plymouth colony, and mixed it with the early Pilgrims. One has traced it as far as the southwest of England, where the ancient Britons retained their last hold on English soil, and found it there. I have once or twice found the name in England, I think in Bath or Bristol. I saw the name with one letter changed in Wales. I have seen it also in Germany with the plural "*en*" added, Balchen. I have read of it in 'Prideaux' connections, as the name of an important city in Bactria. But all these are trifles, as the predicate of a renown that is ever to be sought after. Self-reliance on the eternal Good and Wise and Just and Holy, and obedience to His perfect and universal law, is the basis of all true honor, prosperity and happiness.'

He would not acknowledge that blood counted for anything, or that ancestry was any help to a man, only so far as it inspired him with noble purposes.

CHAPTER III.

PARENTAGE.

Bro. Balch tells us that "a man has a right to speak of his parentage and childhood, and tell the truth, that others may know how he has come forth into life, what his outfit has been, and what the course has been that he has pursued. How else can an account of his experiences and character be complete and of use to others?

"My father, Joel Balch, was the oldest son of Hart Balch. His mother's maiden name was Priscilla Holt. Among the earliest things I remember of my childhood was the visit of her mother, my great grandmother, at my father's, when I was less than four years old. She had just been married at the age of eighty-four, and rode from Crown Point, N. Y., sixty-four miles on horseback for a wedding tour. My mother's maiden name was Betsey Stevens. Her mother's name was Greene, a relative of General Greene of Revolutionary fame. Her father's name was William Stevens, from which I took my name. He was a soldier of the Revolution, and one of the first Justices of the Peace in Andover. My mother taught the first school in Andover.

"So far as I have learned, my parents and grandparents were esteemed as good neighbours, and honest and respectable citizens. There were no social classifications in those days in that region; but very little now, so far as personal merit may go. None were rich; few were poor. One did not esteem himself above another. He was best who served most, and interfered least in other people's matters, by industry and economy, obtaining an honest and comfortable living. To be an office-seeker was scarcely a grade lower than a sheep-stealer. My father was entrusted with a full share of public business. He served many years as one of the Selectmen, Justice of the Peace, Representative to the Legislature, and in other public positions. He was often consulted in the settlement of public and private affairs. He was a strict domestic disciplinarian, kind and generous, but always setting before his children the duty of obedience to parents, respect for superiors, careful self-government, self-respect, and right behaviour toward companions. He inculcated the right of personal liberty, and a feeling of mutual responsibility."

At a memorial service held in Dubuque, Iowa, on the occasion of the death of Bro. Balch, Judge Adams, who at an early day had his home in that section of the country where young Balch had been raised, says:

" Dr. Balch's father was one of the representative men of Vermont. He was not a great man as the world counts greatness. He was a man of simple ways, strong common-sense, and rugged, sterling character. In property, like his neighbors, he was not rich. The town indeed never had a rich man, and probably never will have. And I think it is equally true that it never produced a beggar. Most of its inhabitants have trodden closely on the boundary line between comfort and want, generally enjoying the former. Their condition, at least, was not very attractive to the casual observer, but amid their humble surroundings, they never failed to cherish a blind discontent; not that which would pull down, but that which would build up. They had in their minds a grand ideal, for which nothing in their outward circumstances seemed to afford very much warrant. "

Bro. Balch recalls matters of his mother's death, occurring when he was very young. The following are his words:

"My mother died before I was four years old, and I remember two things distinctly of her. She was lying on her bed, sick and pale with consumption. My older brother and I had done some mischief, and we were taken to her for correction. In loving words, she told us that it was very wrong to do such things, and she hoped we would be good boys and do nothing that was improper, for it made her unhappy, and would make us so. When she was about to die they took me to her bedside, and said 'This is William.' She turned her eyes upon me with a look that I have never forgotten; then laying her hand upon my head she looked up to Heaven, and moved her lips as if in prayer to God that He might be my protector and guide.

"It was the winter before this that my parent took me to the funeral of an uncle, the earliest thing that I have treasured in my memory. It was the house of my grandfather, and the yard was full of teams, and the house full of people. My father lifted me up to the face in the coffin, and many were crying. Not long after my mother's death my sister Susan, younger than myself, died, and two years later my oldest sister, Priscilla, aged sixteen. This was to me a sad event, for she had loved and cared for me during my father's widowhood with every proof of a sister's love. These events cast a shadow over my young life which left a tinge of sadness that never quite faded from my memory."

Having written thus far, the thought crowded on Bro. Balch's mind something after this fashion, that it was a great piece of vanity, and opinionated confidence, that his life had been worthy of any considerable place in the annals of time.

If this work he was engaged in was ever to be done
at all, some one else who should see him with other eyes
than his, must paint him as he was, and the pen was
thrown aside only to the taken up after six months had
passed, when his eightieth birthday had transpired. in
which many friends of his thought well to notice so
memorable an event and gave him his reception in
Chicago.

It was now that his more partial sympathizers began once more to importune him to leave to the world
the memoranda, at least from which could be compiled
important lessons of his history, for his life had been
too valuable to be passed over in silence. He gives expression to his thought, saying.

"So far I had written, when the capital 'I' looked
so prominent, suggesting self and egotism, that I hesitated, faltered and gave it up. Since then I have crossed
the limit of active manhood into the realm of old age,
and no longer have aught to hope or fear from the
praise or censure of the world. The manifestation un-
dreamed of by me, bestowed on my eightieth birthday
by numerous friends and many strangers, has so stimu-
lated, strengthened and cheered me, that I have taken
courage and again given heed to the renewed advice of
those who have known me best. and start to write in
brief the story of my life and labors."

He now sets out with seemingly a more steady purpose to do what he had been so reluctant to attempt.
His first work is to give an account of his birth and
childhood.

CHAPTER IV.

BIRTH AND CHILDHOOD.

But very little need be said under this head, and that little we will let Mr. Balch furnish himself.

" I was born," he says, " in the obscure town of Andover, Vt.. April 13, 1806, in a house of two rooms, partly of logs, and situated on a road that was afterward given up, and the house allowed to go to ruins. It was when I was only a few months old that my father moved from this house to where he had charge of a grist and saw-mill, afterwards returning to Andover, where he lived and died. My childhood was spent like the childhood of most poor farmer boys, in a comparatively new and sparsely settled town in those days of rural simplicity, not as they were and are in villages and cities at the present time, rather more strictly perhaps than many of my playmates.

"The first lesson I learned was the First Commandment with promise, a lesson I never forgot. It was well for me I did not; and I think it would be well for every child and parent, and for the world at large, if it were strictly enforced in kindness in all cases, never in anger, always in love.

"In the family we were never allowed to speak, but always taught to listen while others were talking. We never sat at table until we were able to work, but sat upon a low bench in the chimney corner, with our pewter basins of bread, or hasty pudding and milk. Our food was always plain, but sufficient, and served to nourish and build up strong constitutions. The fine art of spoiling food by cooking to tickle the palate

31

and create a false appetite was not much known in that region at that time. Our clothing was very plain, all home-spun. The tailoress came once a year to cut, baste and fit coats for the elders, and the cobbler to make and mend the shoes and boots; but home talent cut and made dresses for the girls, and frocks and trousers for the boys, patching them when necessary. Truckle-beds were fashionable in those days, and the boys went bare-foot in the summer.

"While I was yet a child, wearing a frock, I went with my three sisters and older brother to school, a mile from home, by the abandoned road leading by the old house where I was born. I looked upon that ruined shanty with a reverence scarcely exceeded while wandering among the ruins of Baalbec, Karnock and the temples, tombs and ruined cities of the East. We had few playthings with which to amuse ourselves. Broken bits of crockery we converted into dishes, and on two great bowlder stones not far apart, away up in the pasture, we used to play house-keeping, go visiting, keep school and hold meetings, and thus imitate the ways of our elders. It was a great joy afterwards to sit upon those rocks and gaze upon the bold romantic scenery spread all around save on the west, prevented there by the ridge of Mt. Terrible, Markhams and Globe Mountains. Wide over the hill country the view extended to the grand Monadnock in New Hampshire, Wachuset in Massachusetts, and along the granite ridges which were seen as far as the eye could reach. I was a great admirer of Nature, and loved the hills and valleys of my native State. And it was then that I drank in my uncontrollable fondness of natural scenery and the desire to travel over the earth's surface." A fondness that seemed to remain with him as long as he lived.

CHAPTER V.

BOYHOOD AND YOUTH.

" At the age of seven, if not earlier, we were all taught that we had something to do in the way of work. This we understood was to be our lot when out of school: the girls to do housework, knitting, sewing, spinning, weaving, etc.; the boys to do chores, running of errands, picking up chips and stones, bringing in wood, riding on horseback to plow out the corn, and, indeed, doing many kinds of light work which we were capable of."

At ten years old our boy began to use the axe and spade, and the scythe some, and to keep busy in whatever was to be done. At fourteen he strove to do a man's work, and succeeded fairly. It is easy to perceive that he was occupied with work far beyond the great majority of boys of our own times. He tells us that he was never called lazy but once ; that, when about ten years old, his father wanted something done, and he did not fly around quite as quick as he desired, and he said :

" I thought you were going to be a good smart boy to work, but I am afraid you will be a lazy lout." " I have never," he says, " been accused of laziness since. I have heeded his lessons to do a thing when it ought to be done, or not at all, and to do it well ; not delay lest I should hinder others ; never to ask another to do for me what I could do for myself ; and always to be

33

on time : to put everything in its place, and never to
go where I was not wanted. I learned these lessons
early and never forgot them. They have been constantly impressed upon my mind in all the matters of
my after-life. Looking upon life," he says, " as a serious responsibility, presenting prospects of good or evil
requiring much thought, and much self-denial, as well
as constant care, and involving duties which must not
be trifled with, it became a leading object with me to
find out what I was in the world for; what the purpose, possibilities and end of my being ; and the source
and means of a useful, honest, honorable and happy
life."

He speaks of his opportunity of learning from books
as being very limited. " Never but a single book," he
tells us, " Hale's History of the United States, was ever
bought for him to study, as the younger of the family
always used the books of the older." The school
which he attended was always taught by a woman in
the summer, and was twelve weeks in duration. That
in the winter by a man was eight weeks. After he
was eight years old he had no privileges of schooling,
except three months in winter and on rainy days in
summer. By the laws of Vermont only a few of the
most common branches were taught, and these he had
mastered when he was fourteen. As he had no means
of advancing his studies beyond this number, he continued to review them for two winters, and so became
thoroughly familiar with them. There were but very
few books to read in those times, among which he
names " the Bible, the New England Primer, Watts'
Psalms and Hymns and The Columbian Orator."

There was a small Town Library, out of which he procured The Scottish Chiefs and Chalmers on Astrono-
my. The latter he read at fourteen with intense interest while making maple sugar in the woods. This
opened to his young mind a vast region for thought of
which he had never dreamed. He says :

"It lifted me out of the grooves of common thinking, and set me on the edge of a new world for explor-
ation, and I felt that I must not neglect my work, and
so toiled the harder for time to read and meditate.
On that high eminence, in the midst of the native forest, while alone, with the broad heavens over me, and
silence all around, was just the place for a mind like
mine to read such discourses, and drink in the spirit that
pervaded them. It was of immense service to me, in
opening a broad field for mental and moral cultivation,
and especially in enlightening me in regard to Christianity."

The other work he tells us he read evenings while
his father was from home, which gave him a better
chance to the light. This he read as a fiction, and wondered how much of it was true. But his mother's Bible furnished his chief reading, which was only Sundays, rainy days, short noonings and evenings, and as
he had to work hard he was often too tired to read, put
in his time to the best advantage.

"I never liked to read," he says, "about bloody
wars, and some of the wicked transactios recorded in
the Old Testament. In fact I must say I have never
in my life enjoyed hearing, or reading about the quar-
relings, fightings, and bickerings which have made
miserable, and disgraced men and nations in past ages.
From my earliest thinking it has seemed strange that
men should make a business of studying how to kill

their fellow men: how to make widows and orphans, and fill the world with misery and mourning. As reasonable beings they should find better employment than studying the arts, the refinements, and heroisms and horrors of war. In this they are more ferocious than any of the lower animals. They are not brutish, they are more than brutish, for brutes never study the arts and contrivances to kill. In seeing cats, dogs and children fighting, I always want the weakest to conquer. I never had any courage to fight. I never thought it brotherly or Christianly to do so, for men or for nations. I can not say that I ever admired Amazons."

"In my earlier classical studies (what little I had) and in later years, even to this day my soul had revolted at the vivid descriptions of the ancient historians and poets, who tell us of the jealousies and dark deeds of the gods and heroes they paint so glowingly; quarrels in heaven, and sin and shame upon the earth, and vengeance and tortures, and disorders generally. It seemed to me a great waste of time and talent, to study dead languages to learn what evil thoughts and vain desires are leading men and women to pursue lives of sin and shame, which so sadly disgrace human nature, and make a polluted wreck of what the good and wise Creator must have intended for His rational offspring. Equally unpleasant and odious seemed the wranglings and divisions which worldly ambitions, selfishness and pride brought into the Christian church in the early centuries, which continued to increase down through the dark ages, and still linger in diverse forms, despite the light and freedom of the present day. The ante and post Nicene fathers never had much attraction for me. The glorious gospel of the blessed God, which told of one God the Father, one Lord the Savior, one Humanity, a Brotherhood, and one final, holy, happy destiny, all of which was contained in my mother's Bible, and is fully sustained by my purest desires, my best reason and highest hopes, is much more to my mind: and I saw little good in trying to follow the savage trails through the vast wilderness of the dismal past. I was early impressed with the conviction that it was the duty, and should be the business, of every man and woman to live in love, peace and good-will toward all men, and do all the good possible."

"I may say that so vivid and strong were my impressions of the grand scenery, historic events, pure and lofty sentiments, and poetic descriptions found in the Bible, lifting the thoughts of people above the grosser matters of common life, that I was early inspired with a living desire which grew into a purpose, to visit those lands, and see where patriarchs and prophets, Jesus and His disciples lived and labored to bless and save the world from sin, sorrow and death, a thing which seemed almost impossible I ever should do in my humble condition, but still dreamed of by night and by day, and has since been accomplished to my great satisfaction and profit.

"When quite a small boy my father bid off, as the fashion sometimes has been, one of the town paupers, an old lady called Aunt Polly, to take care of at ninety-two cents a week. She was a quiet body, but very pious after her kind, and wonderfully notional, even to being whimsical. She had the only plastered room in the house, with fire and furniture all to herself. I used to bring in her wood and do little chores, for which she allowed me to read in her large New Testament, much larger than our Bible. Sometimes I read to her aloud. One day she asked me if I understood what I was reading. I thought I did, and so answered her. But she then and afterward talked to me about different matters, as to how we were all poor, depraved creatures, odious in the sight of God until we were converted, and would be sent to hell when we died to suffer forever in a lake of fire and brimstone, unless we repented and believed in Jesus. It frightened me and I asked my father if it was so.   He said indifferently, 'I hope not.'

" I asked her one time what it meant to be con-verted.   She said I was too young to understand it.   I asked her how I could get converted.   She didn't know; I must wait and learn.   I asked her if I should die before being converted what would become of me. She feared I would go to hell.   I afterward inquired if my mother and sisters were in hell.   She was afraid they were, for she never heard they were converted.

" I pondered over these things with much anxiety, and was very sad whenever I thought of them.   I grew afraid of the dark, for I did not know what evil crea-tures there were lurking about to catch me.   I was de-tained at a neighbor's one afternoon a little later than usual, till it was beginning to be dark, and was to re-turn by a way where the dense shade of the trees would make my path difficult to follow.   Observing fire-flies darting here and there, I could imagine the eyes of imps watching me, to catch me as I crossed an old bridge close at hand.   O, the horrors that seized me !   I think my hair must have stood on end. I looked neither to the right nor left, but walked straight on. When over the bridge, and past a dark spruce woods I ran with all speed into my chamber, jumped into bed, covered my head and felt safe.   No language can de-scribe the misery I endured while trying to be good, but thinking I was all bad, and could do nothing to help myself in any way.   Aunt Polly told me the more I tried to be a good boy the worse I was off, for only God could convert anybody.   I could not understand it, and the more I tried to, the worse it all seemed.   I did not ask others about it, for I did not know any but her who were converted.   My father was a dilligent reader of the Bible, but not a professor of religion. Often I used to go away by myself and think of these things, till, almost frightened out of my senses, I would tremble all over.   When I thought of my mother and sisters, where they were, I wished I had never been born."

"When I was nearly twelve years old Elder Manning, the only preacher in town, preached a sermon from the text, 'By grace are ye saved, and that not of yourselves.' In it he argued the sentiments of Aunt Polly very emphatically, making salvation depend upon the election of grace according to the foreknowledge and determinate council of God, and not on personal effort, for the creature could do nothing of himself but evil. A few months after it he gave another sermon from the text, 'Where is boasting then? It is excluded. By what law? Of works? Nay; but by the law of faith.' During the sermon he drew a line, and said substantially that the sinners were all on one side and the saints on the other, and asked, 'How shall the former get over to the other side from where they are? They can do nothing to set themselves over, for if they could they could boast. Here I am over, and why won't you come? You cannot pray to get over. You cannot pray to pray to get over. It is faith that takes them up, and sets them over upon the other side.'

"As we walked away from the church I asked a boy older than myself respecting the matters of the sermon. He could tell no more about it than I could. We concluded that it was all over with us, unless we were among the elect, and that we were or were not of that number was not for us to know. And still do what we would, do something or do nothing it was all the same for God was going to bring everything about to please Himself, not us. The conclusion was not very satisfactory, but so it was.

" In the afternoon it was quite a common custom with Mr. Manning to improve upon the morning service as it was called, and he preached a full hour and a half from the same text, rehearsing in part what had occupied an hour before, and closed the whole with a fervent exhortation, that, as 'he had that day set before his hearers the way of salvation, the way of life and of death, the way to heaven and the way to hell; it was now left with them to choose which road they were going to take. If God was God he told us, 'serve Him; but if Baal then serve him. I have cleared the skirts of my garments from the blood of your souls. It is for you to decide what you will do— be saved or be damned, forever and ever.'

"On our way home that afternoon we were sad and anxious. At the forks of the road, where we were to part, my young friend and I sat under a tree where we had often sat to discuss more important subjects, and talked over the sermon we had heard. All seemed more dark and incomprehensible than ever. We had often been told that we must not use our reason on religious subjects, and so concluded that there was no use in trying to do anything. We could only wait, take things as they came, and abide the consequences. We proposed to give it all up, and let it go; for turn whichever way we would nothing would be changed, and, of course, nothing would be gained by it.

"Upon arriving home I found my father discussing the sermon with a neighbor. I listened to them, and discovered that their conclusions were much like ours. My father said with emphasis, 'Well, after all, it amounts to just this: You can and you can't: You shall and you shan't: You will and you won't; and you will be d—d if you don't.' I was horrified. My father doubt Elder Manning who is a converted man, and a student of the Bible? He is not a Christian. He is nothing but a natural man, and "the natural man receiveth not the things of the Spirit, for they are spiritually discerned'— a passage of Scripture which I had often heard the Elder quote till I had it by heart, and did not know why it was not as plain as anything of a mathematical character."

The son makes the statement:

"My father was called a Freethinker, as most in the town were, which the Elder said meant 'Infidelity of the worst kind, for the moral and benevolent man who had never been converted was more dangerous to the souls of men than the most rebellious sinner, since he is looked upon and respected, and thus his influence is detrimental to religion.' He also tells us his own thought, that his father, like a great many others, mistook in one thing, for he found as he grew older that he had always been a believer in Christianity, but with the least confidence in the forms, and pretensions, and special tenets of sectarians; for by the fruits of their conduct otherwise, in the realities and duties enjoined by the Gospel, they were really no better than those they condemned. His neglect was, that he did not explain these things to his children, and help them understand what was a more rational, truthful, and essentially practical explanation of Bible teaching. Had he done this I should have been saved much most anxious suffering. But he believed young minds should not be biased, but left free to examine and decide for themselves—not a very helpful manner of youthful training.

"You can be assured that the things to which reference is had in the above, were a great deal in my mind and I dwelt upon them long and anxiously. I wondered if other boys were troubled about them as I was. They did not seem to be, and my young companion, I thought, treated them rather lightly. It is more than possible that they thought the same of me, for with them I was often gay and jolly like themselves. God has so made us that we cannot always be of one demure cast of mind.

"Not far from this period it was that three young ladies professed to be converted, and were to join the Baptist church. This seemed a time for us boys to learn something and we went. The Baptists required a public confession. After the sermon they were asked to stand up and relate their experience. I gave all attention, thinking now it would be told us how to get

converted. Two were very bashful and said but little,
but in answer to the leading questions asked them, such
as: 'Did you feel that you were a sinner? Would God
be just in damning you? Is it through the grace of
God and the sufferings and death of Jesus that you hope
to be saved? Do you pray often in secret? Will you
be faithful to our church?' To all of which they
nodded affirmatively. The other was more bold and
spoke up plainly. What I remembered was that she
continued to sin till she saw herself on the brink of a
burning hell when she resolved to turn about and get
religion, and now she had found her Saviour and was
happy. Many years after I saw that person fallen
far from the character of a practical Christian believer.

"My mind caught more particularly upon the burning hell. I thought if I could see that, I might hope to
be saved. Many a time I laid my head upon my pillow
and tried to see it. I could see soldiers marching and
fighting at Plattsburg, and various imaginary scenes,
but caught no glimpse of what seemed necessary to my
conversion, according to the scheme of the preacher.
All was so dark and incomprehensible that I surren-
dered to what seemed the inevitable, and resolved to
avoid all thought upon the subject. I still continued to
read my Bible as carefully as ever, and many things
respecting the will and pleasure of God: the object of
Christ's mission, and the requirements of duty seemed
plain enough but for the creeds, and I resolved that I was
going to trust in God, obey the commands, do my duty
as I found it to be as far as possible, and abide the consequences.

"With my mind in all this flurry, there came the
Methodist to preach in the Union Meeting House, and
Elder Manning attacked them with great severity, de-
nouncing them as 'noisy brawlers, disturbers of the
peace, misleading the people, and said they ought to be
put down by law.' A quarterly meeting was ap-

pointed to be holden in a short time, and as my father
was a member of the Legislature, and he would be
away, he told me to attend and invite persons home
with me, as there would be but few persons to entertain
them. I did so, and we had six come to our house, five
of whom were women. They sung and prayed, and
being in charge, I entered into conversation with them
and tried to state to them some of my difficulties.
They sought to enlighten me by explaining the doctrine
of free will and personal responsibility, as opposed to
the ideas of the Calvinists, that God had ordained whatsoever comes to pass.

"I listened attentively, and it seemed to me far more
consistent to hold people responsible only for what they
can do, and that they should be so held after requiring
them to avoid evil and do good. But the method and
means of conversion, and the beginning and resultant
of the divine government, as taught by them, remained
as dark and mysterious as ever. Their singing delighted me, and their preaching and exhortations were
very much more earnest and affectionate than those I
had been accustomed to hear. But darkness was still
over me and in me and all about me, and I found no
deliverance. I still kept to the reading of the Bible,
and thought as seriously of my reading as I had done.
The duty of right feeling and living was plain and
reasonable, but the dogmatic teaching most strenuously
insisted upon, as the most essential part of experimental
religion, I could not understand. 'In all my gettings'
the wise man taught me to 'get understanding.' And
as Aunt Polly questioned me I did not dare to shut my
eyes, call it all plain, and leap in the dark. I preferred
to use my reason and rise into the light, rather than to
sink into deeper darkness of ignorance at the bidding
of others.

"Our church structure was for all denominations,
of which the Baptists and Universalists were the most
numerous. The Universalists were the most pros-

cribed. They were always preached against, and denounced as infidel. I remember going to church one
Sunday to hear one preach. It was Mr. Loveland
He read from the Bible and Watts' hymns. When he
came to pray I was astonished. What, Universalists
pray? This was not as I had been told. What had
they to pray for? They don't believe in God in the
Bible or religion, and yet pray as devoutly as Elder
Manning or anybody else. There was always one sentence in Elder Manning's prayers that was forever
troubling me, for it seemed to accuse the Almighty of
injustice. It was this: 'O Lord, if thou hast been
just to mark iniquity in us, we should long since been
in the grave with the dead, and in hell with the
damned.' The prayer of Mr. Loveland was more rev-
erential and devout. I somehow came to the conclusion that it was all for effect, to make it appear that
he was religious as well as others: that it was put on
and that it was studied and superficial.

"At home I ventured to ask my father about it,
whether Mr. Loveland could be honest and sincere in his
prayers; and he asked me 'Why not?' He said, 'The
difference between him and Elder Manning was that
he prayed for the salvation of sinners according to
God's will, and believed his prayers would be answered;
while Elder Manning prayed for what he believed
and preached never would be answered.' I then asked
him if Universalists believed in God, and reverenced
His laws? 'Most certainly' he said, 'and they believe
that he is good and kind to all His children; that He sent
Jesus to save the whole world, and that He is going to
do it; that before He yields up His reign He will see of
the travail of His soul and be satisfied.' This greatly
surprised me, and I feared that my father was falling
into dangerous heresy, and became anxious about
him."

It was at this juncture of affairs that one or two
things transpired that shook Bro. Balch's faith in per-

sons of high standing in Church and State. First Elder Manning sued two members of his own church for defamation of character, which brought a great deal of scandal along with it, as well as hatred and discord. And then after this he himself was prosecuted for perjury; and the State's attorney who was brought forward to defend him, who stood high in his profession, and appeared very much of a gentleman, met with a most fatal fall. And in losing confidence in two such persons it began to creep into his mind regarding the opinions these men stood for, that perhaps this might account for so much indifference to religion, and so much want of faith and character in the Christian church. And finally he comes to tell us in just so many words, " Careful observation, study and inquiry of a long life have convinced me that the difficulties encountered in my youth, when earnestly seeking and praying to know the truth, and learn and do my duty in the exercise of my best faculties, is a leading cause of the indifference, irreligion and practical infidelity so prevalent at this day. What is irrational, contradictory and absurd, serious, thoughtful and honest minds can not accept as truth and duty in religion and morals more than in anything else." " Children ," he tells us "should be taught to use their reason, the distinguishing attribute of man, in what they see, hear, read and think, and employ it freely in the conduct of their lives. It is a great wrong, a sin and shame to attempt to restrain or misdirect it. Conscience will bear witness, and experience will teach the value of such a course, and every day will they be blessed in pursuing it." He tries to impress it, that along with the prevalent errors of the religious teaching of his early years came innumerable evils which made his young life unhappy, and prevented the expanding of his mind.

I think there is one thing in all this that is quite clear, that he made uprightness of conduct a sort of governing principle, so that but few persons, even of saintly worth, are privileged to look back upon a boyhood more singularly pure and well spent. I am told that when a boy he always stood aloof from being engaged in bad scrapes, and counseled his associates to avoid all disreputable young people or places of resort. Once, however, we are informed that in marauding a neighbor's lemon-patch, he was sent by his father to work out the damages the next day. He attributed his success in life to the training of his will, his energies and his self-control by his parents at home, to whom he owed everything as it were.

CHAPTER VI.

Brother Balch informs us that having gone through the lessons and mastered all the studies taught in the district school the fall after he was sixteen, his father told him that he might go to Reading, twenty miles away, and study with the Rev. Mr. Lovel and, who was a Universalist minister, and who took a few private scholars on very favorable terms of board and tuition. Accordingly he set out with everything he had for an outfit tied up in a handkerchief. He thought it altogether in vain that he attempt to describe his thoughts as he went forth, but says that

"If ever a stricken soul prayed devoutly, he did, in view of the responsibilities that would be resting upon him as he started out into the world alone. Not in spoken words, but in profoundest thoughts and most earnest desires I prayed," he says, "to be kept in the right way through my whole life, and to follow it, let it lead where it might. I had faith it would never lead me wrong, with God and the religion of Christ as my guide. Four miles from home," he tells us, "I dropped into a farm house to warm myself, and though strangers we entered into a free conversation. The man knew my father, and said : ' He heard he had a son who was a teacher,' referring to my brother, Aaron, who had fully prepared himself for teaching. We

47

talked of the matter, and he persuaded me to go to a neighbor of his and take their school, which he was sure I could do. I went, finding the man in the woods chopping, and without asking me scarcely any questions, he offered me $7.50 a month with board for eight weeks. I engaged the school and went on to Reading, staying two weeks, renewing my studies, when I returned home and received a severe reprimand for my rashness in not minding what I had been told."

It was now time for his school to commence, and he entered it, all going well to the end. He tells us that he "made pleasant acquaintances, and gained much useful knowledge: and a few days before closing, a committee from an adjoining district came to engage him to finish out their school term, which had been broken up by the teacher being turned out," as they informed him. The price agreed upon this time was $8 per month, for six weeks, and when the six weeks had expired he returned home with $27 in his pocket, the first money he had ever earned for himself, and feeling as proud as any young lad could.

His brother was now twenty-one years of age, and was leaving home to engage as teacher in a private school in the city of New York, called St. John's Academy, being near St. John's Church. The money was all given to him, that he might be properly manned for the new undertaking, and William settled down again to doing the work that is always accumulating on a farm. The brother had not been at his post long before he wrote for William to come and be an assistant in his school, which he was reluctant to do, dreading to appear in a great city like New York.

But it was thought best, and " the 19th of August," he says, "was the day arranged for me to set forth on my journey. My father purchased for me such an outfit as he could, and gave me $8.00 in money, which, with the few dollars I had earned by working late and early, sometimes by moonlight, I took all I had in a bandana handkerchief and started. As I bid good-by to my home I noticed that my father's voice trembled, and tears glistened in his eyes as he said, " God be with you, my son."

" The first night I spent with my sister, three miles from home, and the next morning my brother-in-law took me to the top of the crossing of the Green Moun tains, where he left me to go on alone. I cut me a cane from a shrub, and looking east over the Connecticut Valley to the Granite Hills, and the grand Monadnoc. I bowed reverently and turned westward, and journeyed forth into the great open world, a pilgrim and a stranger. I stopped for the night in Dorset, at the foot of the Rupert Mountains, where I met parties from Andover returning from a visit to Saratoga Springs. In the morning I climbed the mountain on foot, and the second day pursued my journey with blistered and bloody feet. After arriving at Greenbush and crossing the Hudson to Albany, I had gone but a mile or two when I was overtaken by a gentleman with whom I struck up a bargain to ride with him quite a distance on my way, he to receive four shillings; but one of the shillings to be in talk. We were chatty all the way. I found he was a lawyer and a member of the Legislature. He inquired of me, and finding I was a teacher, he offered me $150 a year and board, to teach the school in his village. I told him 'I was a minor, and my father had engaged me in New York, where I was then going.' 'I see you are an honest young man,' he said, 'and you are right in obeying your father.'"

Coming where the roads parted and their directions would diverge, he was told the road to take to
reach the place to which he was going, and, having
agreed to pay him a few shillings for his ride, he took
out his wallet for that purpose, when it was answered by
the stranger that he was well paid, and he should refuse anything in the way of money.

At Albany he engaged passage on a sloop to the
city for three dollars, arriving there on Sunday morning, the third day, so ill-clad that the brother did not
think it proper that he be seen upon the street till furnished with a suit that should better become him.

It should be told that he remained in the city only
three months at this time. The confinement in his
close schoolroom was undermining his health, and he
could not become reconciled to the artificial distinctions
and extravagance of the city life. He tells us of being
greatly dissatisfied, half sick, and homesick the whole
time. The man for whom he worked was a broken-
down merchant from Boston, who sought to make a
living and keep up appearances in a way that did not
meet his mind. The meals were in a dark, dingy base-
ment kitchen; the front a miserable, green painted
grocery, kept by a haggard old woman, and the place
for lodging in a garret no better than the rest. The
schoolrooms were in the second story, only one of
which, the parlors could be accounted decent. Outside
appearances somewhat disguised the reality, a condition
of things which he had never been taught to respect.
But he says: " He bore it with patience, and with what
fortitude he could, but in sadness all the while."

He speaks of " seeing but very little of the city, but
enough to make him despise its fashions and false-

hoods." It appeared to him that life here "was a sham, a pretense, and a wretched wronging of humanity. The rich, the poor, the good, the bad, the gayly grand and miserable, were all brought conspicuously together, and the widest extremes were jumbled in the most careless and reckless manner. Even in the churches there was a costly array of worldly pride that did not at all comport with the teachings and example of the humble Nazarene. And if all this was to be found in religion, where were they to look for plain, honest, sober realities in everyday life, or in character? They did not instruct or edify, and everything was so unlike the meekness and simplicity of his rural home that he cared not to know or find out farther about it."

I again quote his own words, in which he tells us:

"I had fully resolved that I was going to leave the wickedness and worthlessness of so dismal a place to me, when as yet I had said nothing to my brother, or to my employer, of it all, and I only told them a week before leaving the city. Every persuasion was made use of to induce me to remain. It was Saturday evening when everything was in readiness for me to leave the next morning, and my brother said to me that he had persuaded father to let me come to the city that I might learn something of the world and be a man among men; and now that I should return to be a nobody and a nothing, among the stones and stumps of Vermont, the rest of my days, he did not know how to be reconciled to it. My answer was brief, but plain. I shall never pretend to be what I am not. I will not play false with myself or with others. We were both sad at parting. Nine years after this my brother came and studied with me in preparation for the ministry, which he entered and pursued till his death."

While passing up the river there came a proposition
from the Captain that he become a mate for his vessel
the next season, which he was almost persuaded to accept, and told the Captain that he would take the advice
of his father on reaching home and allow him to decide
the matter. But the company into which he was
thrown, and an attempt to compel him by force and
threats to settle up the voyage with them in a drinking
frolic, put this all by, and made the dark world as it
was to him seem even darker than ever, till he tells us
he was "frightened at himself." It was a mere hap-
pening, or chance event, that delivered him out of their
hands only to confront him with still another proposition to become a partner with his uncle in his meat-
market, to which he had hesitatingly consented. But
no sooner was he expected to assist in slaughtering an
animal than his heart entirely failed him, and he pulled
off his frock, retiring from the yard, leaving others to
do the work which he could not do, and for which he
was laughed at, and told that he was "sighing for an
opportunity to be back in the mountains when it was
right in hand for him to achieve a fortune." And indeed it hardly seemed to him now that anything was
left to him but to return to his home and devote himself to the kind of work which he had so recently left
in going to the city.

On a most beautiful afternoon when he had ascended
out of the valley of the Hudson, and from an eminence
from which was presented to him a grand view of a
wide region from the Green Mountains over all that
vast intervening country to the Catskills and the Mo-
hawk—the November sun shining splendidly upon the

beautiful scene—he waited, and wondered, and admired
—almost worshiped; and forgetting himself in his
reverie he was happy again. He grew more and more
calm, and as he reflected he said to himself:

"Why all this uncertainty and unsatisfactoriness of
life? Here is nature robed in splendor. The hills and
dales, the mountains and rivers, the fields and forests,
are here as I passed this way before, looking as smil-
ingly as they can. Yonder is the sun, moving majestically in his glorious chariot of light, steadily pursuing
his course from day to day, scattering beauties and
blessings upon all the earth, and why should man be
unhappy? With all else fulfilling some benevolent
mission, why should not man, the noblest and best of
the Creator's work, have some high purpose as well?
There must be somewhere a place, a work, a duty, for
every least creature of His."

Then his thoughts rose to a higher realm:

"He who made all things made me. I am the work
of His hands, and He loves me with all the ardor of an
infinite affection; loves me as His child, with a boundless, perfect, everlasting love, and this should reconcile
me to the methods of His government. Nowhere
could I look but I beheld the most convincing evidence
of His impartial beneficence. Reflections of this character brought me to the gate of a new world, and fixed
a determination in me to do my duty as it was made
plain to me, to love all men and work for their welfare
as opportunity was afforded me; to make the best of
everything, not being anxious about the future, but
submitting myself to the will of God.

"This was a crisis in my life. I rose in strength,
full of faith and hope in God, and resolute to pursue the
path marked out for me, lead where it might. A little
way on I came to a rill making down from the mountains, beside which I ate of my last spare loaf and drank

from the stream, and no meal ever relished better. My
journey homeward, though wearying to the flesh, confirmed in me the resolutions I had formed. Much did I
reflect on the passage, ' It is good for a man to bear the
yoke in his youth.' Often carriages passed me with
empty seats, but no one asked me to ride, and I asked
none. Nor did I ask for food, though suffering greatly
from hunger. Frozen apples served for my breakfast
on that last day, and then I resolved that never while
riding, with means to carry him, would I pass a lone
and weary traveler by the roadside. That resolution I
have kept."

He tells us of being lovingly received, with no censure when he related his experience and gave the reason
of his return. He remained at home but a few days,
when he went to Ludlow and engaged to teach the
same school he had taught the previous winter.

"There were two Quaker families in the district,
from whom I learned," he says, " the simple principles
and habits of that people, and admired them : they
seemed so consistent with the spirit of Christianity. I
have profited by them ever since."

Two days before that school closed a person came
to him from an adjoining town and engaged him to
teach a school where the teacher had been turned away.
He was offered an advance of wages to commence the
school at once, and he did not hesitate to accept of the
terms made him. Returning home and relating to his
father what he had done, it was thought that he should
not enter it, as it was a large and bad school, always in
trouble with its teacher, and if he had won a reputation he was now sure to lose it. The son could only
answer that " he had agreed to go, and if he did his
best he could not be blamed, as he would be if he failed

to keep his engagement ": when the father told him to "go and try it, but be careful." At the opening of the school the son explained to the scholars what had been told him of the school, and that "he had hesitated to undertake to be their teacher, lest he should bring himself into trouble and get a bad name : but if they would agree to do their best to change this opinion, he would help them, and he thought by working together they would succeed to the advantage of both. If they favored this idea would they take their seats and books, and they would begin. There was nothing that looked like trouble during the whole term."

Returning home, his father was given his wages, and they talked over the matter of future prospects. The father thought it better that he fit himself for teaching, and perhaps go to Kentucky, where he had heard teachers were wanted at fair wages. If the son chose he could take what money he had earned and expend it in studies with Mr. Loveland, which was the same proposition made him before. And the son tells that such encouragement raised his ambition, and he decided at once that he would do so. He borrowed of a schoolmate some Latin books he thought to study, and started in pursuit of an education. He was a whole day making the distance through snow and mud, and reached his destination at 9 P. M., tired and hungry.

The next day, March 29, 1824, he began his studies of Greek, Latin and Mathematics. As a change from his books he resolved to read the Bible through in course, noting such passages as related plainly to the will, pleasure, purpose and plan of God, in the cre-

ation and government of the world; and the relations, duties and responsibilities of man to his Maker
and fellow-men, and find if he could the ground of
hope for a future life.

We pass now to April 13, 1825. He is this day
nineteen years old. It is the annual fast, and as
there is no public services in the place, the day is
spent in reading and thinking. He comes to the conclusion that what he is doing is at least a dull business,
and wonders what it is all for. It may have a meaning, and be useful; but it looked to him not very
needful to find out by such a round-about way of
quirks and turns, what the ancients were desirous to
express, seeing we had enough written in a much
plainer way that could be made of practical use in
this living age. But having begun to be learned he
supposed he must go forward, believing that the darkest time is always just before day. By request of Mr.
Loveland, he went with him twenty miles on foot to
hear him preach, he telling him that he wanted to
teach him to walk, for the good of his body as well
as his mind.

He had been from home only a month, and now
returned to help his father in some of his spring
work. After another month worn and weary he re-
commenced his studies, pursuing them as he could
under greatest difficulties; but considering that it was
fortunate if there was any honest way for the poor to
get an education. Sundays, as they came, he would
try and hear somebody preach, though frequently by
going quite a distance away.

The month of July was spent in helping his father

hay it, when he packed up his effects and returned to his books again. Soon after this he heard a sermon preached from the text "Satisfy us early with Thy mercy, that we may rejoice and be glad all our days."

"The preacher was not a person of much learning, but his soul seemed to overflow with the love of God, and kindred humanity. He applied religion to the young, as a guide and safe-guard of life, sure to bring a daily blessing. It was a great lesson to me. It was the first sermon I ever heard which took a deep hold on my feelings, and aroused in me the conviction of the obligation of obedience to God for his great mercy, as a fitting preparation for the life that was before me. I was now happy.

"As Mr. Loveland was to be absent during the fall, I now went to my home remaining but a single night, when I left for Chester Academy to fit for College. Three months were spent there in hard study. I had not been in the school long, before a fellow student, a charity scholar preparing for the ministry, came to my room to catechise me on religion, especially in the matter of faith. I told him I believed in God the Father; in Jesus the Savior; and in the moral responsibility of all men, according to their ability to know their duty. He asked me if I believed in prayer? I told him I did—especially in secret prayer. He asked me to pray, I did so—the first I had ever made in the presence of any person. It was in the words of Jesus. He then began to press upon me certain dogmatic tenets, as essential to salvation. I told him I had formed no doctrinal theory, but had nearly finished my first reading of the Bible in course; had noted important passages, but had not arrived at any definite conclusion; that I was not prepared to accept for doctrine the commandments of men, however ancient or popular. He was afraid I would be led astray, and become an heretic. I said I might be from the sects; but I hoped not from God

and truth and right and duty; that I was not prepared
to enter in controversy on matters of opinion; nor
willing to be dictated to by any one. He retired, perhaps not satisfied. During the term the students were
required to declaim. I tried it with the rest, having committed, as I thought correctly, a part of one of Adams'
orations. Mounted on the rostrum, my knees trembled
like Belshazzar's, and all was cloudy around me. I
started out and stumbled, making a complete failure,
bowing myself off of the stage, and resolving never to
attempt anything of the kind again. But by the earnest entreaty of the preceptor I consented to make a
second trial. This time I took Cicero's oration against
Cataline, and succeeded fairly with two or three pages.
I mention these things to say that I never had a faculty
of committing language in a way to recite it. My mind
has run more on facts than on words.

"At the conclusion of the term my room-mate and
self were assured that another year would fit us for
college. But my brother, with a second person,
had now bought St. John's academy, and desired me to
be an assistant teacher. As I had no means to go
through college, I consented to their proposition, provided they could make arrangements with my father.
He was too poor to help me, and I knew of no one of
whom I could borrow the money, and besides I had no
disposition to do so. " Owe no man anything, but to
love one another," was my Bible motto. I would in-
volve no man with a risk on my success. I had read in
Poor Richard's Almanac, " Let every tub stand on its
own bottom," and the Book said, " Despise not the
day of small things." Terms were agreed upon, and
I was to be there soon after the termination of my
school.

" I attended a funeral at this time where Mr. Loveland officiated. When I witnessed the grief of the
mourners, the thought struck me that I ought to be a
preacher, and help, teach and comfort my fellow-men. It

soon vanished, however, when I thought of my unfit-
ness for such a vocation. I had need to be taught and
be more fully established in the principles of Christianity. No! I could never think of being a preacher,
lawyer or doctor. I would be a teacher, for all had
need of being taught, and in that profession I could be
of some service.

"March 17th, in company with a particular friend,
I started in a wagon for New York. This time I had
$15 for expenses. The roads being bad, we were three
days reaching Albany, as long as I had been in walking it before. From there, by steamer, the passage
was quickly made in twelve hours; being a third of the
time it took by a sail vessel, and by rail three hours at
present. So hurries the world on its way."

Mr. Balch commenced his school, he tells us, with
feelings very different and everything much improved
from his former visit. All was cheerful and happy,
and he started with a firm resolution never to complain, but to do his duty and hope for the best. On
the 13th day of April he could say, "I have closed my
twentieth year." And here I condense from his journal the following:

"One year more to prepare for manhood. Calmly do
I review my past life, and find many errors and mistakes, chiefly the waste of time which might have been
better employed. These I shall never be able to recall,
but will try and make them lessons for future improvement. My opportunities have been limited for intellectual culture, but not for the more essential moral
education which forms character in every condition and
period of life, and tends directly to open the way to
future happiness, and honorable success in life. I see
now how much precious time is wasted, which with
proper means might be profitably employed in gaining
useful knowledge that would conduce to the highest
interest of all. I have not had such means, except

from the open volume of nature spread out before me, and from the Bible, which I have found in agreement with what is more important to the welfare of mankind. There is much in both I cannot comprehend, and it is about these I have heard preachers and people talk and contend most earnestly. I have thought it better to hold fast, and make improvement from, what is plain, practical and immediate, than to be urgently seeking to find out what is difficult, and vehemently striving to convince others of what is not clear in one's own mind. I am now resolved to devote all spare time to study; to continue to search the Scriptures with free and untrammelled thought, and to persevere in the way of well-doing. God guide me and keep me in the path of duty, keep me from evil and make me useful while I live.

"Soon after commencing my school I was induced to join a literary society in what was then Greenwich village, composed mostly of teachers, and returning late one night from this Society, the moon shining uncommonly bright, portions of Hudson street open to the river, vessels were silently drifting with the tide. The hills on the shore stood up in bold relief. The streets were quiet, save the tread of watchmen on their rounds, and an occasional passer. It was a grand silent, solemn hour for meditation. In this great city, small in comparison then with what it has come to be, how different everything from what I had been accustomed to look upon in my own rural home. All was marked with change in the outward, and yet God and goodness, truth and duty, did not change. The inward, the real, is the same everywhere, and always, but, oh, the pit-falls that one has to shun. Wise is the man who is not overborne and caused to depart from the strait and narrow way by the glittering temptations that lie in wait to deceive the unwary. 'The Lord preserve me from evil' was my fervent prayer. Had I stood before the multitude then, it seemed as if I could proclaim

REV. WILLIAM STEVENS BALCH.

aloud the greatness of Him who has made all things,
made man what he is, and what he is capable of; and
could warn convincingly my fellow-men to beware of
the insidiousness of sin, which surely leads to misery
and moral death. I almost resolved that I would
attempt it at some future time."

He found that his landlord was a Presbyterian, and
started in with the family in attending that church.
"The pastor, Mr. Patton," he tells us,"was very loyal
to the creed, and defended all the severer parts of it
with the greatest alacrity possible; election and reprobation, effectual calling, final perseverence of the saints,
once in grace always in grace, endless misery, &c. &c.
On the latter especially he placed the greatest importance, and described with vehement eloquence the
tortures of the damned in the style of one-hundred
years ago. On one occasion he described heaven, with
God and Jesus seated on a great white throne with
the chosen ones, the elect, kneeling before them, among
whom doubtless would be some of his congregation,
while the great majority of them would be weeping
and wailing and gnashing their teeth, in the flames of
a never-ending wretchedness, fit only to be in the
society of the damned."

At home he was asked by the family how he enjoyed the sermon, to which he made answer, "not at
all, and if he believed the Bible taught the existence
of such a God, he would never wish to read it more,
for he could conceive of nothing worse of an almighty
demon." He was told that his "remarks seemed very
severe for a young man," and remarked that "young
or old, it was all the same, for he could not love and

5

worship such a being, which it seemed to him that
neither the Bible, reason, nor the purest and noblest
desires of the human heart taught." And he added
that he "could not understand how a man could pray
so fervently for the salvation of the whole human
family, believing that his prayers had necessarily to
go unanswered, since it was unalterably decreed that
the greater portion of them all would be damned.'
The very tame answer was, "God does not act to
please us." Again he replied that he "was glad of it,
that he acted to please himself, and we might always
therefore put our trust in Him and not in human creeds."

It is just about impossible to understand the horrid
views that were preached from the pulpits of those
days, and the dark pall that hung over the world upon
these subjects ; and we little know how much it meant
to stand for truth against the falsehoods of men when
the fathers stood for it fifty and sixty years ago ; a vast
deal more than now. Our people and ministers could
not see why those views were not grossly immoral in
their tendency ; especially when sinners were told that
there was vastly more present happiness in sin than in
righteousness, and the only motive for loving and
serving God was the selfish fear of being punished forever.

Bro. Balch tells us that much more was said, not
the most edifying ; though he did not think that any personal feeling grew out of the conversation. But as
silence ensued for some little time, he was becoming
frightened at what he had said, when it was remarked
that he would see things differently when grown
older. But he confesses that he never has ; that the

world has greatly changed in the last half century upon all these subjects, till we never hear the pleasures of sin talked of; the rolling it as a sweet morsel under the tongue; and the pursuing it with a zest so long as there are no evil consequences to be experienced in the world to⁓come.

CHAPTER VII

Our narrative has already anticipated, in the order of time, some things that are now to follow, in showing forth the leanings of Bro. Balch's mind at this early period ; and yet, it is quite likely that he is to pass through trying experiences, and most important changes, before he shall become perfectly established in views that shall bear the scrutiny of his most approved judgment. But it is now he is resolved that he will seek instruction and edification from some other altar ; and he tries several places, to see if he can not find some more consistent teaching to which his mind and heart can give credence.

He first goes for a time to a Unitarian church, and is somewhat pleased; but is not instructed concerning those subjects which he had been taught as truth, but could not believe, and yet must accept, or he could not be saved. He next goes to hear a Rev. Mr. Mitchell, an eloquent preacher, but with a mystical way of treating his subjects which he could not understand, more especially some ideas of a substitutional theory, and a crucified Savior, in which God is pleased with the sacrifice of His own Son as an offset for the sins of the world. No sinner was to suffer for his own sins. Sin was of the nature of a debt, which called for satisfaction or payment, and Jesus was to pay this debt, excusing the sinner from all suffering on his own part. Young Balch could not see how there was any justice in such a transaction.

After this he tells us a patron of the school invited him to go and listen to still another preacher and says:

"I went and the sermon was on the Atonment. The preacher defined the word as reconciliation; that God was in Christ reconciling the world unto Himself, not Himself unto the world. It was, in effect, making the sinner at one with God, and placing him on terms of friendship with Him. It was this that opened to me a train of thought which made the matter plain, and harmonious with strict justice; the natural law of cause and effect; holding each and every man responsible for his own conduct, the same after as before the death of Christ. I saw that what the law demanded was obedience, and employed punishment as a means, and not as an end, in the method of the Divine, as it should be in all human, governments. My thoughts of God henceforth as the great and good Father, governing the world for the ultimate good of all his children. and his own glory, were of course immensely exalted; and it removed from my mind a burden of anxiety, and a cloud of doubt, and drew me into a closer unity and reverence, and a more filial trust and confidence, than I had ever felt before. My heart rejoiced, and I was exceeding glad at what I had heard. I continued to attend that church for many months, and was greatly comforted.

"One evening, sitting alone, and knowing no one present, the communion service was celebrated. The preacher explained it, much to my mind, as a memorial of the love of God and the self-sacrifice of Christ, as set forth in the gospel; and when the emblems were offered me I partook, with the silent prayer that I might feed on the substance and spirit of the truth as made known to me, and that God would thus approve

the act and bless it, to my lasting good. I went to my
home that evening feeling that my conscience approved
the act, and with firmer resolutions to do my duty in
life as it should be open before me, and to shun whatever might have a tendency to lead me into evil. I felt
that I had more closely allied myself, and was identified
with the Christian religion, and it was a step full of
sacred emotions that I never saw cause for regretting.

"The summer wore away, and in pursuing my my
studies alone I went but little about the city, except for
exercise. I spent much of my time, in cool evenings,
on the roof of the house in meditating upon life, its
lessons and duties. With the end of July came the
summer vacation, and I was for a time a good deal at
a loss to know how to spend it. Country resorts and
seashore recreations were not so common events as now,
and I had no means to spend on such indulgencies. The
passage out of the city over to the Jersey side was but
a shilling, and being in search of cheap board I decided
on my first journey among foreigners, as the Jersey
folks were called. And as I inquired for board, and
told who I was and what I wanted, the woman thought
she could take me, but would go and see her man and
let me know. Returning, she would take me at $2 a
week, plain board. I found it a quiet, Jersey-Dutch
family, myself much at home, the husband keeping a
small meat market and two daughters helpful about the
house.

"Devoting much time to books, the old lady soon
asked me if I was studying to be a dominie. I had not
then learned the meaning of the word, but as I supposed
that it was something about books, I told her I was, and
immediately I was the object of a great deal of attention. I found that they were all good Christians after
the Reformed Dutch type, and regarded me as one of
them. As names and titles were of but little value in
religion, as I was disposed to think, I took no pains to
correct my innocent blunder, and we mingled our ideas
in perfect harmony.

"One evening the conversation of the good lady turned on her brother, who lived some miles in the country, for whom she felt a great anxiety, for he had become a Universalist. 'Indeed,' said I, 'what does that mean?' 'Why, he believes all men are going to be saved.' 'I suppose, then, he has become a very bad man, hasn't he?' 'Oh, no, he is one of the best men I ever saw; always doing good, and trying to help every-body.' 'He never reads the Bible, does he?' 'Oh, yes, he reads it all the time when he can. I can't quote a passage but he tells me all about it. Well, I must confess that there are many passages which lead us to hope that doctrine may be true: such as "God will have all men to be saved, and come to the knowledge of truth;" and Jesus "gave Himself a ran-som for all to be testified in due time," and "As in Adam all die, even so in Christ shall all be made alive." Yes, he quotes them, and it does say so, but it can't mean so.' 'Jesus tasted death for every man, and became the propitiation for the sins of the whole world.' 'Yes, that says so, but it can't mean so.' 'He will swallow up death in victory, and there shall be no more death.' 'God shall be all in all.' 'Yes, that says so, but it can't mean so.' Numerous passages I quoted, to all of which she had the same answer. Finally, the old gentleman interrupted: 'What do you think such Scriptures do mean, Margaret, if they do not mean what they say?' 'I don't know,' she answered, but I believe our Dominie knows more about them than Brother John does. What do you think, mister?' 'I have not yet studied far enough to explain them differently from what you think they say. I am not caring any great deal about doctrines and command-ments of men which are not taught plainly in the Bible, and are not agreeable to reason and the best desire of the human soul. Such passages, if there are those that cannot be understood, I leave them till we shall have some further revelation. It appears to me that it is more Christian to obey the plain commands of God, by doing the duties of to-day, and so being prepared for those of to-morrow and each day through life, which is the best approach to a more reasonable and hopeful future.' 'That is my religion,' said the old gentleman. 'I think if we practice it, it will be well with us now and forever; much better than worrying ourselves and others in getting ready to enjoy the blessings of the Heavenly Father hereafter. Jesus taught us to pray for our daily bread and to be delivered from evil. Is our Dominie better or wiser than He?' This ended the matter of our conversation.

"It was a short time after this, of a Sunday afternoon, my host invited me to go and hear a Methodist, and a real ranter he was. He labored very hard to frighten his hearers, describing hell as a place of literal fire and brimstone. He said If you could put your ears to the windows of hell you would hear sinners, and among them some of your dear friends, probably, screeching in infinite agonies, lamenting that they are not having the same opportunities you are privileged with, to repent and get religion; warning his hearers to do so, and to save their souls before it was everlastingly too late; and much of the same sort. Going home, the good man said: 'He gave it to us pretty hot to-day. When I hear such things I wonder why the good Lord keeps these souls alive, and these fires burning for the mere sake of torturing them, as it can do Him nor no one else any good. I think pure religion has more to do with daily duties, love to God and love to men, even to our enemies, serving one another, and thus fulfilling the royal command of doing as we would be done by.'

"At home he described the sermon, and discussed the matter with his wife, much to my satisfaction, if not to hers. He was a man of good, practical common sense, plain, honest and benevolent, in nothing vain or pretentious. My weeks there were full of practical instruction, by which I was greatly profited."

REV. WILLIAM STEVENS BALCH.

Mr. Balch has told us that of the errors which per-
plexed and darkened his young mind, the first and worst
of which was the perversion of both the letter and spirit
of the teaching of the Bible, and the bold contradiction
of reason and experience by those who profess to accept and defend the truths of religion, viz., that sin in
the present brings more happiness than holiness; or, in
other words, the wicked are blessed beyond that of the
righteous. He declares most emphatically that this
was the sentiment taught as an essential truth of a
saving faith, and that it was predicated on the necessity of a future judgment and retribution in the eternal
world, where we are to look for the rectification of the
mistakes of this world and the complete reversal of the
plan of administering of the divine government as at
present. He was reminded of many positive declara-
tions of Scripture to the effect that "God will by no
means clear the guilty," but "will render to every man
according to his deeds;" that "he that doeth wrong
shall receive for the wrong which he hath done, and
there is no respect of persons;" so that "though hand
join in hand the wicked shall not be unpunished." He
could recall passage after passage, such as "Verily he
is a God that judgeth in the earth," that "His judgments are abroad in the earth," and that "the righteous
shall be recompensed in the earth, much more the
wicked and the sinner." He was coming to think that
for all who obeyed there were rewards, and all who
disobeyed there were punishments: results which inevitably followed as effect followed cause. It seemed to
him that the order of God's government was this order
of indissoluble, eternal and connected causes, and from

the operation of it there could be no escape. In this
was seen the essence of duty, making it consist in obedience to the natural, healthful and God-established
relations and necessities of our being, in works of piety
and benevolence, or in loving God and man. That
which we were forbidden were actions and excesses
which were wrong, and that which it was commanded
us to do were actions which were right and proper, and
not to be denied by us save to the wronging of our
own souls. This was to place all duty on a natural
basis, or to found it in nature and the fitness of things.
It was to say that in the regulation of the world God
had established certain laws—pure, perfect, and permanent rules—from which He never deviated ; laws which
regarded the best happiness of His children, and in obedience to which we always find peace and prosperity,
but when we violate or infringe them, disease and sorrow and wretchedness are our portion. But in all we
mark the perfect righteousness of God's government,
and on the permanency of this principle rests its whole
structure.

Bro. Balch never sought to be nice in any matters
of this character, in a speculative way. It was enough
for him that the good receive good, and the evil evil ;
so that a man's character made his condition ; made
his heaven and his hell. We can not do wrong and
feel right. Punishment always follows disobedience,
and there never can be anything but wretchedness in a
sinful course of conduct. The neglect of duty would
as surely be punished as putting our hand in the fire is
punished ; in finding ourselves just so much the worse
off for it. Following in this train of thought, and seat-

ing himself to a careful study of the Scriptures without
note or comment. seeking no other man's interpretation, he was not long in coming to the conclusion that
there was no disagreement between the laws of God
written in the folds of nature and the leaves of the
Bible as regarding this one subject of duty and interest. He soon found that nothing could be stated
plainer than that "there is no peace to the wicked,
that they are like the troubled sea when it cannot
rest, whose waters continually cast up mire and dirt;"
while " great peace have they that love God's law, and
nothing shall offend them;" that " the way of the
transgressor is hard, " while " wisdom's ways are ways
of pleasantness and all her paths are peace." It was
from this that the appeal was made, that goodness was.
happiness, and therefore we should do good; that
nothing is ever gained by sinning; that sin is the worst
thing. the hell of the universe, and holiness the best
thing, the heaven of God and eternity, even as it is.
told us by the Preacher in the book of Ecclesiastes
that " Though the sinner do evil an hundred times,
and his days be prolonged. yet surely I know that it
shall be well with them that fear God. But it shall
not be well with the wicked ; neither shall he prolong
his days, which are as a shadow, because he feareth not
God."

According to this view punishment was the natural
evil consequence of our wrong or sinful doing, which
was a most bitter thing in the experience of it; and the
purpose of Christ's mission was to save us from sin by
saving us from sinning. Salvation in this sense was not
anything purchased for us by another; nor was it an

escaping from hell and going to heaven when we
die. No; it was character, Christain character; man
hood and womanhood perfected.   Jesus does not
save us in putting forward a substitute for our obedience, but in leading us to obey the law of God.   Men
are saved just as far as they accept and act out the
Christ spirit or principle and follow the teachings
of this sublime life in their souls, and no farther.   And
grace does its work only by leading to voluntary obedience.   Of course this was a wholesome and salutary
view, that sin involves punishment, and as long as it
continues punishment will necessarily follow ; and that
whenever and wherever men become holy, reconciled
to God and to duty, they will be happy, and not before.
Believing this sincerely, we should no more rush into
sin than we should rush into the fire.   Brother Balch
speaks of this as one of the strong incentives to virtue,
and wishes that it may always be understood that we
are required to live virtuously in order that we may
live happily.   His adorning of virtue was always in a
light that made it a great blessing to be achieved for
the individual welfare, and, viewing it from his stand-
point,

> " It was as easy then for the heart to be true,
>   As for grass to be green, or skies to be blue.
>   It was the natural way of living."

As yet Brother Balch had constructed no creed for
himself, to which he had thought to surrender his convictions to the exclusion of anything new that might
seek to come in from without and to claim his hospi
tality.   But finding an organization entertaining views

so much like his own, the question naturally arose in his mind, should he not join his interest with theirs and receive from them what assistance and sympathy, and fellowship they could give him?

It was here in New York in 1826, listening to different preachers of our faith, and while occupied in teaching, that he received the right hand of fellowship from Rev. Abner Kneeland, and was admitted a member of the Universalist Church, of which he was pastor at the time. It was not till the next year that he received the rite of baptism by immersion, at the hands of Bro. Warren Skinner, pastor of the Universalist Church at Cavendish, Vt. It is no light thing for a young man to break away from the theological principles to which he has tacitly subscribed, and which he has learned to regard as sacred from his church association during his whole early life. Having a mind and character of his own, marked by courage and decision, it was but natural, perhaps, that he should come to conclusions very different from those that were entertained by many of his friends. We can be sure that he was one who took great pleasure in the investigation of truth, and, finding it, he embraced it with the full ardor of his nature. And being no slave to mistaken dogmas, he accepted like an honest man what his reason approved. The person who can thus think for himself, and has the courage to do it, who feels that necessity is laid upon him to go wherever truth shall lead, is greatly to be commended.

He was now to return to school duties and engaged at twenty-one to continue teaching a year for $150. But in less than a month a schoolmate came to the

city seeking a situation, and Bro. Balch offered him
his place if he would lend him twenty-five dollars
for three years, the first without interest and the
remaining two with interest at six per cent., providing
his employer would agree to it.   The offer was accepted
and was satisfactory all around.   With that sum he procured his first outfit and started out as a lecturer on
language by the recommendation of Daniel H. Barnes,
the founder of the high-school system, and W. S. Car-
dell, the author of a new system of grammar.   His
first attempt was in Poughkeepsie, and very successful ;
he realizing enough to take up his note and leave him
with means to help himself on his way, besides a very
flattering   recommendation   from   the   chief   men
of the place.   In Hudson, Greenbush, Albany and Troy,
he met with good success.   In Troy he had a very large
class engaged, and was giving private lessons to a Mrs.
Willard, of the female academy, when sickness made
him abandon this employment sooner than he would
have otherwise done.

In alluding to this afterward, he says: "It seemed
to me an open door into manhood life.   It overcame in
part my natural bashfulness, and made me conscious of
a responsibility resting upon me to pursue an honest
and humble endeavor to deserve the confidence of those
among whom my lot should be cast, and employ what
talent I had in making myself useful to my fellow men.
I have always had to regret my preparation being so
small, and yet all I could afford.   Except a fitting for
college, which after all I had not the means to enter,
my studies had been chiefly pursued alone, much the
larger part before and after the hours of school from

four to eight A. M., and four to ten and a half P. M., and
Saturdays, shut up in my little room."

He stops to tell us how he had entered life "without so much as one cent of money, or a decent suit of
clothing;" but as he left New York in this lecturing
tour he was resolved as soon as able to enter the ministry; for his heart was on fire for the love of the Universalist faith. He assures us that the wilderness before
him had seemed " dark and almost impenetrable."
But he entered it now " with a stout heart and reliant
upon God." He would not relate all his "trials and
misgivings, sometimes almost yielding to despair."
Now the ministry was impressed upon his mind as the
plainest and most direct course for him to follow. His
experience had convinced him that there was " need
of plain instruction in various departments of common
life;" and he came to the conclusion that " religion
practically presented was the most needful of them all. It
laid the basis of all right living, and, properly understood
and faithfully followed, led to the best success and truest
happiness which God had designed for His children."
Under this conviction fully matured, he resolved to
begin at once a more thorough preparation for the
work. It seemed to him " the truest avenue in which
he could be of service to his fellow men." And so
after returning to his home, and remaining only a
couple of weeks, he started on foot for Reading with
the few books he had managed to collect, to prosecute
his studies with the Rev. Mr. Loveland.

I have but little doubt that the father thought of
making a Universalist minister of his son long ere this,
and before the son had conceived any such purpose, for

it will be recollected that he had sent him away from his home at the age of sixteen to go and pursue his studies with this same Mr. Loveland, a plan which was defeated by the son engaging himself as teacher in the public schools, and afterward of a new system of grammar, in which he became so deeply interested as to publish books of his own upon the subject.

Bro. Balch tells of having pursued his studies in company with Otis A. Skinner at this time for the space of only three months, at which time his money had been exhausted, and at the advice of Bro. Warren Skinner, and his invitation, he took a seat in his wagon and they went on a preaching tour to Saratoga, Bro. Skinner doing the preaching, he tells us. It was here that Bro. Warren Skinner applied for fellowship in his behalf, and it was granted September 20, 1827. We have his description of this in the following language: "I was compelled to pass a rigid, and I thought a needlessly severe, examination, by a committee of the convention, of which Rev. Paul Dean was chairman. A spirit of sectarianism was at work in the denomination at that time on matters of doctrine, made more intense by another spirit, which had alienated some of the brethren. On the regular subjects I felt quite assured; but when it came to Trinity, Pre-existence, Future Punishment, Divine Sovereignty, Free-will, Bodily Resurrection, and some other subjects, presented metaphysically, and with a manifest feeling that did not belong there, I stumbled, and deemed my case hopeless, till Bro. Sebastian Streeter came to my relief, declaring that it was wrong to pursue such a course in reference to matters that had

always been in controversy, and never had been settled by the wisest of heads. 'Why,' it was asked, 'do
you bother the young brother with questions that you,
nor I, nor anybody else can answer? If he wants to
preach why not let him try? He seems to be as well
qualified as we were.'" He was fellowshiped, and
was glad to get through with such an ordeal.

He tells us of having preached four sermons previous to this time. His first was in the study of Father
Loveland to twelve of his associates from the text,
"The Spirit made me go with them, nothing doubting."
His first public sermon was given at Lempster, N. H.,
the text, "Every valley shall be exalted, and every
mountain and hill shall be brought low, and the crooked
shall be made straight, and the rough places smooth;
and the glory of the Lord shall be revealed, and all
flesh shall see it together." He, it seems, was for bringing everything to a level. Being once told that such
was the case, that his was the leveling spirit, his reply
was that he leveled up as well as down. He sought
first for the elevation, and then for the equalization of
sunken and sorrowful humanity. He had no higher
purpose than to unite all men as brethren, and to league
all in effort for the elevation of all.

He walked on foot thirty-nine miles to preach this
sermon. His pecuniary resources were so scanty at the
time that he started off in September without any over-
coat, and with but $5 in his pocket. Much of his
preaching for the time was for $5 a Sunday, and he
felt well paid, if he could only get an audience to hear
him.

6

CHAPTER VIII.

CHARACTER AS A PREACHER.

In speaking of Mr. Balch as a preacher, let me say as a first requisite that the work of the ministry constituted his chief delight, and was the leading purpose of his life, to which his whole soul was given. From the time he made the choice of it to the time of his death he became fully consecrated to its service, never allowing outside business or personal ambition to interfere with the main object to which he sought to devote himself. If other matters engaged a portion of his time, yet none inconsistent with this, or to be made secondary to it for a moment. Every high and worthy cause awakened his interest and received some share of his attention, but never to the forgetfulness of his calling or the neglect of one of its duties. Peace, temperance, freedom, education, he spoke and wrote and labored for them, but no one ever identified him with either of these, or supposed him to forget the character or office of the Christian ministry. In talking, in reading, in journeying, in health and sickness, in labor and rest, his heart seemed ever to turn to it, and he could say, as did an apostle, "This one thing I do, forgetting the things which are behind, and reaching forth to those which are before. I press toward the mark for the prize of the high calling of God in Christ Jesus." If this same apostle could say, "I am determined to know nothing among you, save Jesus Christ, and Him crucified," so Brother Balch could say. I am determined to know nothing among you save my preaching, and the application of it to the sins and sufferings of the world, and the promotion of truth and righteousness among men.

He tells us himself that "from the time he entered the ministry he had given himself to it as to the first and chiefest of all duties. He had never neglected intentionally any obligation of the gospel in his power to perform, for secular business, or personal ease or gratification." Everything else he had made subsidiary to that one thought, "to serve the Lord by doing good to mankind," as his language is. After having preached fifty years we have these words from him : "I have ever felt that I was not my own, but the servant of Him who put me into the ministry. I have had many tempting offers, which gave almost certain promise of worldly wealth and positions which men call honorable, but I have preferred the motto of my life : 'Shoemaker, stick to your last.' Hence I have kept to the work of the ministry, and in it outlived by several years, as a settled pastor, all who entered it with me, and many who came into it several years later. I love it still as ardently as ever, and see as much need of its active and energetic operation as in years gone by ; even more urgent, as sectarian walls are crumbling fast away, and new and purer crystallizations are forming around grander truths, sublimer hopes, and broader charities."

None will deny, who ever heard Mr. Balch preach, that his whole heart was in his preaching. If he has gone abroad, it has been to fit himself for the higher

duty of proclaiming the unsearchable riches of Christ,
and for the sake of being more efficient in this, his one
calling. If he has given lectures on his return, it has
been with a view to the same end—of making it helpful to him in his preaching. He has gone to gain valuable lessons from the country and people and institutions where the feet of the Savior had trod, and not, as
so many had gone, for the mere pleasure or name of
having been abroad. He could hardly stand before an
audience to speak upon the most common subject without doing more or less of preaching in some portions of
it. He could not write you a letter or engage you in
conversation for a half hour but you felt, before he
reached the end of it, that he had preached you quite a
sermon. Everything with him was made to bear upon
the improvement of the people's morals or religion.

And then again it is to be observed that Bro. Balch
preached sermons—he did not preach essays. You
never found him delivering mere philosophical disqui-
sitions from the pulpit, as so many do. He may have
written and delivered essays, sometimes, but this he
did not consider was his calling or avocation. His were
always sermons, for he preached the truth of God in
such a way that it was made to sit in judgment upon
men's sins. He did not deal with truth as alone, but
with truth as it affected duty.

Many persons have never learned to distinguish
properly between what is a sermon and what a lecture,
a speech or essay. There is at least this difference:
The one is concerned more with the exposition of the
subject in hand; the other with the treatment of it in
reference to its application to conduct. A sermon has

intimate relations with character. It does not partake of the nature of a speech, or, if so, it is a religious speech, spoken by a religious man, who is seeking to promote religion in others. There may be such a thing as a decorous handling of the great subjects of religion which is no preaching at all, because more intellectual than religious or moral, and because engaged in for the entertainment of the hearer, much more than to persuade and influence to the doing of good. With Bro. Balch, however, there was always the faithful speaking, and reasoning, and entreating for the essential rights and duties of humanity, in the application of Christian principles to the wrongs and evils and sins of the world.

I risk the statement that he has done more earnest work in preaching in a direct, plain, simple, common-sense way that was calculated to reach men's hearts and homes, and purify and sweeten their daily lives, without being a dealer in men's endless distinctions and speculations; and that he has converted more persons to the great truths of Universalism, and worn off more prejudice against our blessed views than any other person living or dead in the Universalist ministry, if I may except, perhaps, Father Ballou. With no systems of metaphysical theology, and no coldly elegant moral essays did he occupy the minds of his hearers; but with highest duties pressed urgently home upon all as rules of practices. He made everyone see and feel that a genuine, upright, holy life was the one most needful thing. It will not be said that he ever sought to imbue men's minds with particular views and sentiments respecting this or that entanglement or perplexity; or to cause any number of speculative opinions, termed articles of faith to be received. No—good principles he insisted upon, and fundamental doctrines he preached : but with the abstractness of theology as is at present, and has been for many centuries in controversy, he had very little if anything to do. To him the general duties of men were plain and palpable. They were such as result from what are the known dependence and wants of humanity, and a desire to benefit, and make the race of mankind loving and happy. And he felt that he was deserving of praise, and was laying others under obligation to him, so far as he promulgated a true idea of life ; an idea of life as it ought to be, and was designed of God to be, and was instrumental in the establishment of a practical goodness in all its purity and excellence in the earth. All his teaching was to the effect that God was to be loved and worshiped by us only in the exercise of affection, and in just and kindly offices performed out of regard to our fellowmen.

He held that the great fundamental principles of Christianity, its essential teachings, were all of the simplest character, and not of any dogmatical import ; that they were those great regenerative principles of truth and love, and of a conservative power and influence by which the world was to be saved and blessed, and mankind made Christians indeed. He esteemed all metaphysical questions as foreign to the purpose of the Gospel, and accordingly his preaching was level to the capacities, and met and satisfied the wants of the humble and unlettered. It was this that gave him such access to the commonest minds, which constitute the greatest share of our churches and congregations.

His was exactly the kind of religion which the people needed; not intricate, but within the easy comprehension of every one, and consequently the people were enthusiastic in listening to him. He could preach great, grand, glorious truths in a way that the common people, the uncultivated, heard him gladly, and wondered at the gracious words that proceeded out of his mouth. His power lay, as much as in anything, in the full sympathy of the people to whom he preached, and they listened the more attentively because he was one of them in education and position, and never disowned his condition, or was ashamed of it, and because at the same time he made every one feel that their fraternity was honored and exalted by his belonging to it. You find him always identifying himself with the lowly condition in which the masses of mankind are born. As he went among the people he went as a friend, and so was received as a friend.

He himself tells us of having been charged by Father Ballou, standing in a pulpit at Watertown, Mass., to be "simple in his preaching, preach so that children can understand you, and then the old folks can." And in his reflection upon what is here said, he remarks: "It is not the glitter of fine essays, rounded periods, and studied postulations that is needed. The church is cursed with too much of that stuff—chaff, in which occasional grains of wheat are found. The preacher of to day needs good, square common sense, a knowledge of men and things, and experience in the real more than in the fashionable world; a heart full of zeal for God, truth, purity and humanity; an aptness to teach plainly and practically what he knows: to

meet and mingle with the lowly, and help them to rise
from their low estate ; and to show a humble, sincere,
devoted demeanor, that ' his good be not evil spoken
of.' He need not dogmatize when he preaches, nor
need he fail to produce in the mind of the hearer a profound conviction that the chief object had in view is
the advancement of the interests of humanity, and the
people's welfare and happiness."

And it was this that made him effective for doing
the will of the Father in heaven, and commended him
to so many of his brethren. He continues to tell us:

" In prosecuting this work, the controlling thought
and purpose of my soul has been to present truth
plainly and practically before the people; to avoid all
metaphysical, dogmatical and philosophical questions,
the discussion of which would not convince and edify
my hearers. I have never shunned to preach or
to do what I thought practically important, nor allowed personal feeling or party attachments, the fear
or favor of anybody to swerve me from my convictions
of what was true and right and suitable to the ministry of Jesus. In many things I have erred in judgment, as I afterward saw, and have come short in
many more, but I never intended to flatter, fawn, sup-
pliantly obey or purposely offend. In the rapidity of
extemporaneous speaking I may have said many things
and in many ways which a more calm and deliberate
preparation would have avoided. But I have tried to
keep my heart to meditate no evil, and therefore to
risk less in such cases I have no doubt that a more
studied and fastidious style would have won more admirers, but I doubt if it would have reached more
hearts. In a play-house where amusement is the chief
aim it may be appropriate to ascribe prominently, ' We
study to please,' but never in a Christian pulpit. To make
plain the path of duty, to convince of sin and show

how to shun it, to guide the young, counsel the erring, comfort the afflicted, and persuade to the exercise of faith. hope and charity, are the higher aims to which I have aspired, and sought God's help to achieve."

And most surely this has been so.

And Mr. Balch was a great preacher, if to be estimated by the eminent services he has rendered in behalf of our Zion or the cause of righteousness among men. He was a great preacher, because a great teacher. He not only occupied a high rank, but he stood in the foremost rank of large numbers which were acknowledged to be great. I do not know why he was not intellectually great. I am not meaning that he was so very learned a scholar, with a mind developed and disciplined by severe training. enlarged and enriched by varied culture in all the multiplied departments of human thought and study. He never claimed to be learned in the technical sense. But his was no common order of talent. He was richly endowed by native and acquired gifts. His mind was penetrating and comprehensive in its grasp and discriminating in its judgments, moving rapidly through the processes of thought, and with a quick and clear perception, seeing readily the resemblances and differences of things. which made him prominent in the walks of literary and professional life. There was never any distrust of his ability to gather up all the principles and bearings of his theme into one comprehensive view, and bring the whole field of observation directly under the eye of his auditor. He never made you feel that he was deficient in the breadth of discussion of deepest questions; and you deemed him a master, fitted for the largeness of even philosophical criticism.

He was a student by nature; and if his sermons were not always the most orderly, they were rich in earnest thought and in originality of conception. There was thought written all over every one of his features. There are but few who will not allow that he had great strength of thought, largeness of desire, constant activity of mind, which enabled him to multiply the resources of his later years. He was a man of remarkable endowment of head and of heart, no more marked for energy of character than for vigor of intellect or power of expression.

I recall the words of Dr. Sawyer, who in writing me says, "If I am to speak of him intellectually, I must accord him great abilities. His education was not obtained in any college, and I do not know whether a thorough college training would have improved him, or rather whether he would have submitted to it. His perceptive faculties were very large, and he gathered in through them a vast amount of knowledge. He had such stores of general information that he could not talk to an audience without saying many things of interest and profit. With wholly extemporaneous sermons he could not have maintained himself for seventeen years in New York City, without having had a good deal of genuine preach in him." After stating this, with much more, he is pleased to add; "This I am sure is a very imperfect sketch of my old friend. I know him well, but I have not done him justice, I fear."

You were forever made conscious in listening to

him of greatest depths of research, that opened into
vaster fields of knowledge and wisdom, and which carried your conceptions, if not your aims, far above your
powers of execution.

We are accustomed to speak of men who have
acquired valuable information by dint of their own
exertions as self-made men, and this was true of
Brother Balch, only as God made him ; that is, He
gave him the sacred instinct of thought, and the thirst
for knowledge, that by a wise, faithful and constant
use of his powers he should be successful, as much as
he made the bee to extract the honey from the flowers
of the field.   If success was a thing which he had to
work out for himself, yet it was God that " worked in
him to will and to do of his good pleasure."

A very marked peculiarity of his preaching was its
intensely practical character.   With most men religion
does not take form with them so as to find a lodgment
in the heart, and so does not rise to the dignity and
strength of what religion is designed to afford.   It is a
vague hope or fear, which is not without its influence ;
but not fitted to guide, or too feeble to become controlling in human affairs, to rule the purposes of life,
or shape its ends.   The larger proportion of pulpit
effort has had but little relation to the particular needs
of the people, its chief aim being to give an expose of
the preachers' system of divinity.   But with the subject of our narrative religion was instinct with a moral
vitality in every feature of it.   It was something to
work in the individual bosom, and in society at large,
and to improve and bless all those who were serviceable
in the active duties of life.   He preached his heart

truths, and to the heart, till the people were obliged to
accept them, in the love of them.   He was an "able
minister of the New Testament; not of the letter
which killeth; but of the spirit which giveth life."
If he preached doctrine, it was in its practical phases.
Who ever heard him preach in any other manner?
His idea was to preach and practice the Christian ethics
with a minimum of doctrine and ecclesiasticisms.   The
faith of the Christian as it seemed to him was a vital
principle of action; a living sentiment of the heart
and affections, that always went hand in hand with
good works.   There might be professions which were
a mere pretense, and any amount of hypocrisy might
be practiced.   There might be self-delusion; but no
true. Christian faith that did not prompt to good works;
that did not manifest itself in good works.

Such a thing never entered Brother Balch's mind,
as the separation of Christian doctrine from Christian
practice.   He sought rather to unite them in the closest
bonds of attachment, making them parts of a complete
whole, each essential to the other.   A man's principles
were what he did; not what he said, and it seemed to
him that he only believed in Christianity who lived it.
A man must have Christian principles: and, having
these enshrined in the heart and affections and in-
wrought in the living soul, he would act upon them;
and this was what, to his thought, made any man a
Christian.   Religion was precisely this active principle
of love to God and man in the soul, to be made to act
in the toil of life, for the glory of God and the salvation of his children.   It was to be carried out and exemplified in the conduct, and in striving against the

world's evils, and for the world's good. And for this did Mr. Balch prize it. He was in all the tendencies of his nature and principles a reformer, a helper in every good cause, in every prominent charity, in every leading interest of the community in which he lived. The service of humanity was his highest aspiration.

Always a reformer, Mr. Balch was in the front rank of every movement, tongue, pen and hand ready to relieve. His temperance work began with his public life; and later he was one of the organizers of the Washingtonian movement, continuing persistently in his warfare against this great foe of intemperance till the time of his death. He was temperate in all things, even to abstemiousness. You could sit at his table, and while drinking your tea and coffee, he would be drinking nothing but water. He was a rank hater of every evil, and never failed to raise his powerful voice against public or private wrong, and especially upon the evil of intemperance, was he always ready to talk and bestow active energy. Listen to his own words as we find him uttering them in 1878. "Into the temperance cause I entered fifty years ago, on the ground of strict total abstinence from all that intoxicates, including tobacco, and I have worked in it ever since. In the various humanities I have taken part ; such as moral reform, prison discipline, anti-gallows, and aid to the poor and oppressed of every name and clime." He showed a brotherly interest in every kind of work that needed the heart of true sympathy, and did not shrink from bearing solemn witness against the wrongs, the injustice, the heart-breaks and miseries of his fellow-men, and championing the cause of the weak and defenceless everywhere. An Abolitionist of the early time, he was a personal friend of Garrison, Phillips, Whittier, and their compeers; and stood valiantly for the victimized sufferers of unutterable wrong. And thus did he proclaim abroad, and to the world, the divine method by which we are to win our battles against the strong and the mighty for the overthrow of all sin, wretchedness and misery. He tells us that he had but "one rule and purpose by which he was governed in all the affairs of his life. It was to adopt all real improvements, and fearlessly maintain them; to do all the good he could, and as little harm as possible, and to teach that in purity there is peace, and in holiness there is happiness."

And what could be grander than such a life, lived out in all the relations in which he was called to act toward his fellow men in his intercourse with the world? What could be said more, or better, than that he was ready always to resist the wrong, and to maintain the right at all hazards? His influence was always on the side of the right, and you never found him advocating a wrong principle. And how should it be, but that such a life of itself alone, without any teaching of the uttered word, should speak powerfully, and should be a priceless legacy to the world?

But when, in 1840, Brother Balch preached what I will call his great sermon, at the United States Convention of Universalists, holding its session in Auburn, N. Y., from the text in John's Gospel, Chapter xiii, verse 35, "By this shall all men know that ye are my disciples," it seemed as if it went like an electric shock all over this broad land. Men were startled at such incisive utterances as awoke them from a sort of lethargy. in which they were reposing, and being held as spell-bound to a mere mode of faith. If I have heard this sermon referred to once, and indeed from the lips of the preacher himself, I have heard it twenty times from the lips of others. Persons have declared to me that it was the most memorable sermon that ever came before that honorable body. It was this that brought Mr. Balch more prominently before the world, and gave him that wide-spread popularity which he has fairly won for himself. It has been said that it secured for him his invitation a short time afterward to preach as a candidate to the Bleeker Street Church, in New York City. But along with that invitation came a difficulty. Mr. Balch had never preached as a candidate, and he did not believe in being placed in rivalry with others of his brethren to be promoted over them. to their great discomfort, and so he informed them that it would not be agreeable for him to visit them in the manner they proposed. And now what was to be done? Well, if he could not come in their manner, then he might come in the way that should be pleasurable to himself, and they would engage to settle him without his being heard by the society at all.

But what about the sermon that had obtained for him all this astonishing notoriety? Understand, he was going to give them the test by which they might know whether they were the disciples or Christ or not; and he stopped to make some comments first on the word "know" which was in the text. "By this shall all men KNOW that ye are my disciples." It was not any matter of guess-work, or mere imagining; but of

absolute knowledge; when from a right experience the
reality of it should be brought home to their hearts;
as when "the spirit of God bears witness with our
spirits that we are the children of God." Then as he
proceeded with his subject, it was to tell them in what
manner they were to "know" it. And he was very
sure that it was not by the adoption of any credulous
theory that left the whole matter in a still deeper mystery, that no one was able to tell you anything about.
Well if not this, was it from believing in any of the
man-made creeds of the day? A person might say that
he believed in the Trinity, and you could not well
doubt his doing so; but did that make him a disciple of
Christ—or a Christian? Another might tell you perhaps that he believed in Election and Reprobation; or
in Total Depravity; or in Endless Misery; or in Universal Salvation; and the query was again, did that
make any man a Christian? We could know that it
did not, for very bad men had not unfrequently believed in every one of these doctrines. "By THIS shall
all men know that ye are my disciples." By what?
He here brought in the context, which he had kept
back for a purpose until now, "that ye have love one
to another;" and asked his audience to take particular
notice how plain and reasonable the whole matter was
to the simplest understanding of even a child.

A person listening to Mr. Balch's handling of this
subject upon another occasion, at a subsequent time,
informs me that he had so adroitly managed the development of the theme till he was ready to spring the
answer upon his audience, that when he said, "Now,
see how simple all this is, as Jesus taught it, they

were literally struck with amazement and delight, so that it became a matter of marvellous wonder and conversation with all who heard it. The people almost rose from their seats at the grandeur of the annunciation of so important a truth as that the loving and serving of our fellow-men is to be the test of discipleship." That single sermon, giving such remarkable prominence to the practical side of our religion, and the work which Brother Balch has done through a long life, making him such hosts of friends and such a favorite preacher with so many, have done more than we can tell to shape and mould the thought of the denomination, and to put jewels in his crown that shall shine as long as there shall be any memory of the order to which we belong. The supreme interest of the life of Brother Balch has lain in the fact that it has been so much ethical, and of such practical utility to our people, and that his religion has been made to embrace every form of philanthrophy.

It is truly lamentable how much of our time, and of every time, has had no very perceptible relation to human salvation and improvement ; to regeneration, or to any human interest whatever. There are those, the whole tendency of whose efforts is to make the world a painful desolation, whereon it would seem as if the sun might refuse to shine. Borne up by the faith of the gospel, he was always hopeful, if sometimes sadly so, keeping faith in the perfect goodness of God through all changes and vicissitudes. Most people are prone to grumble. They are pessimists in practice if not in principle ; but in the darkest and most trying circumstances he believed that God reigned, and that

7

the world moved on with regularity, for which we ought to be grateful.

It is true, he chided himself sometimes with being sedate; thought he was too much so for a man of the world, and that his profession had made him more so. To me he always seemed like a man that was subdued beyond all gay and passionate exuberance; a man that didn't quite know how to laugh in a natural jolly way, without its being a little forced. He sometimes wished, he said, that he could "get out of such a habit, and talk and laugh at nonsense, seeing no evil, no wrong, no misery anywhere;" but then he tells us he "was never made so, and had never been converted to it."

But while he was conscientious, seeing so many of the evils of the world, and taking them to heart to be burdened with them, yet he was moderately cheerful and playful, to be accounted for partly by what he tells us, that "experience had taught him to think kindly of his fellow men, and that the longer he lived the better he thought of their hearts, while he might think less of their heads." You could know that there was something of humor about him, though not a humorist. It is told by Dr. Sawyer that "he was preaching one day, and repeating the remark of some merchants, that a man could not make a living and be rigidly honest; he stopped and said in the dryest kind of a way: "I do not think people ought to say such a thing till they have tried it." It will be agreed that Brother Balch could tell a good story, but he was hardly at home with a story in the pulpit, and never with a witicism. If he may be said to have treasured a fund of anecdote from being blessed with a retentive memory,

yet he always considered that it was to be used spar-
ingingly, and barely for the sake of illustration, if
needed ; and he knew how to adapt his stories to that
end, so that every one would say that there was an aptness about them, if nothing else. If not chosen with a
studied refinement they were never of an exceptional
character, and no one was ever left to feel that they
were privileged to indulge in his presence in any im-
proprieties of speech. I recollect my telling a story at
one time in a Sunday school where I had been given a
class, and he came to sit in it. It was something transpiring in my boyhood days. I was going by the canal
through a part of the State of New York, and we came
into a lock. There were seated out on one side of the
lock two men, and one said " You stole my wool."
The other did not deny it, but simply retorted, "I did
not do it till I came to you, and went to others to get
work ; and it was not given to me. And I did not do it
then, till I went through the town to beg, to keep my
family from starving; and some of the very persons
who refused me work, called me a lazy lout, and told
me to go to work. I then took your wool, and sold it
to buy bread for my family." Just then the noise of
the water disturbed my hearing further ; and I was remarking to the class that " it seemed to me at the
time, so far as I heard, the man that stole the wool
had the best of the argument "; when Brother Balch ex-
claimed " Why, Brother Slade ! " I always deferred to
him, and whatever else I might have said, I pursued
the subject no farther.

No one ever got ahead of Brother Balch. He was as
quick to answer, and as ready at repartee as he was to

perceive the right and wrong of a matter. Professor
Standish, of Lombard University, has contributed the
following, as told by Brother Balch himself, that he
was at one time desired to preach at a State Convention in Vermont on the last afternoon, when the cars
would take most of the people to their homes at an
early hour; and he agreed that he would do so, if they
would be present promptly at 1 o'clock, to commence
the services. He did not fail to appear at the time;
but as yet there was no congregation or choir.
Shortly, however, the choir presented themselves, and
the congregation began to come in very scatteringly.
Brother Balch did not wait for congregation but gave
out the hymn as soon as there was anybody to sing;
and as soon as the hymn was sung he offered a prayer.
A last when the sermon was proceeding in a very satisfactory manner, and nearing its end, one of the clergymen, more tardy than the rest, came in and took his
seat immediately in front of Brother Balch; and lean-
ing back in his chair, he took his watch from his
pocket and held it in a manner that his attention might
be attracted to it. As soon as it was brought to his
notice, he stopped short and remarked, 'I would have
the brethren understand, that I am not preaching for
time, but for eternity.'"

Dr. Sawyer writes me that he often told Brother
Balch that if he wanted to get his best sermon, it
would be on some very important public occasion when
the person chosen to preach would fail to be present.
He would go to him and say, "Balch, Smith has not
come, and the people are all here waiting, and you must
preach," and that put him upon his mettle, and he

would do his best. But this confidence in his ability would sometimes betray him, and I have seen him, at some conference meeting perhaps it would be, talk against time, but he would go on until he caught a thread of discourse, and then for ten or twenty minutes rush forward like an orator with electric effect.

It is told that at the United States Convention held at Boston in 1845, Brother Chapin was to preach the occasional discourse at the School Street Church, Father Ballou's, and there were a great many more people than could get into the house; when Brother Otis A. Skinner arose and said that Brother Chapin would repeat his sermon from that same pulpit in the afternoon, and begged those that were present not to occupy the seats, that others might have a chance to hear it. Then he added that Brother Balch would preach at his church at that very hour, and those who were unable to gain an entrance there would repair immediately to the Warren Street Church, for he knew that Brother Balch was always ready with a sermon prepared for any occasion.

This recalls a circumstance which occurred at the time of my own ordination in 1842, in Pawtucket, R. I. The occasion was one of more than usual interest, for it was the meeting of the State Convention, and their new church was to be dedicated; and the charge and delivery of the Scriptures would be by Father Ballou. There had been a church before this, but Jacob Frieze was the preacher, and he turned infidel, the consequence of which was, that we lost our church, by its going out of our hands into the hands of the Baptists. The very great crowd of people that were

brought together made it necessary to seek other
quarters for preaching, and this Baptist Church of our
own erection was procured for Brother Balch to preach
in; he taking for his text the words found in Haggai
ii: 3. "Who is left among you that saw this house in
its first glory? and how do ye see it now? Is it not
in your eyes in comparison of it as nothing?"

Brother Balch was always prompt in meeting all
kinds of occasions, and sick or well he would go to fulfil
all appointments. In those days he was sick a great deal.
At one time he was to go to a place called Manville,
fourteen miles north of Providence, to preach of an
evening. In the morning he came down from his room
with his terrible dyspepsia that destroyed much of the
comfort of his life, regretting that his appointment was
out. And now came a call that he go as far the other
way and attend a funeral at 12 M., and his return
would be not directly through Providence, but by the
way of Pawtucket, and I thought it would give pleasure to Brother Balch if I would go out to Pawtucket
and go with him to his evening appointment, and accordingly I went. Brother Balch was very glad to see
me, and gave me to understand right away that I
must drive his horse for him. As we jogged along, he
remarked that he felt wretchedly, and that I would
have to do the preaching. I had scarcely preached a
sermon then, and gave him to understand that it would
not do at all, remarking at the same time that I supposed they would think that "those that turned the
world upside down had come there also," to which he
made reply, "Why, that is a good text." We then
turned to talk about different matters, and sure

enough, when Brother Balch rose to take his text, that
was it. And I recollect how he laid his subject out.
He said he never learned but what Paul plead guilty
to the charge. He was sure the world was wrong side
up then, and it was wrong side up now, and he was
ready to contribute his mite in trying to turn it over.
And I thought before he got through he had forgotten
all about being sick, and I never saw such a turning
over of the world in its theories and practices.

I have said much as Dr. Sawyer says, " Wake Brother Balch up in the night, and ask him to preach a sermon upon any subject within the range of Bible teaching, and in two minutes he would have it all thought
out and be ready to begin, and words filled with eloquence would flow glibly from his tongue sufficiently
thrilling to stir the hearts of any people." He was one
of your minute men; and his mind was quick to see all
the bearings of a subject, and he could be relied upon
in an emergency. He had a rare faculty of seeing things
at a glance. He could reach a conclusion by orderly
processes, but if necessary could do it intuitively.

Mr. Balch had taken high ground upon the reform
character of our religion from the very first, and it is
but just to his memory to state that when many of his
brethren began to talk of "a new departure," he found
that he had taken it along with his vows to preach
Universalism, which was nothing different from
New Testament Christianity; and long before many of
them were born. Providence seems to have raised him
up for the fulfilment of a special mission to our denomination; and he began immediately upon his entrance
into the ministry to emphasize the all-vitalizing spirit

of Universalism; and to turn the thoughts of many
minds into the more practical ways of thinking and
doing.

In April, 1832, he removed to Claremont, N. H.
and in September, 1832, he commenced the publication
of the new paper called the "Impartialist." I find the
motto he employed as a heading to his sheet is composed of two texts of Scripture, "What is truth?" and
"Speaking the truth in love." On the first of these he
remarks, "We are willing to receive truth, let it come
from what source it may, even though it shall termi-
nate in the entire overthrow of our present faith."
And then at the head of the editorial department he
places Paul's words, "Doing nothing by partiality."
In addition to this we find him quoting the words of
St. James which tells us, the wisdom which is from
above is without partiality," and he hopes that
he may be governed by this wisdom. He designs
to make his paper what its name purports; an
"impartial paper, for the free discussion of all great
subjects of a doctrinal and moral character." In setting forth the reason for publishing the "Impartialist,"
he assures us that "it is for advocating the simple unvar-
nished truth of God; humbling the pride and arrogance of the self-righteous; teaching sinners the folly
of sin, and persuading all to hope and wait and work
for the salvation of men."

We have a further expression of the same sentiment
from him in the following: "We are happy in the belief that a paper is now established in which all important subjects shall be treated with candor. Our
cause is the cause of truth. Our object the happiness

of all men. And the means by which we hope to accomplish it, the extension of light and knowledge by free investigation among the people. We have no creed to support from which we dare not depart. We have no forms, usages or traditions, too venerable or sacred not to be repudiated when shown to be wrong. Hence from us the public may ever expect fair and honorable treatment in relation to every subject that concerns the welfare of humanity."

And from that time to this, counting the long years of his life, he has stood more than any other at the very front of all the great practical questions which we are found discussing in our own times; and has done more in evening up our Universalism; and making it, and keeping it, a thing of the life (not in the role of a sectarian, but as a teacher and helper in all good works), on the broad principle of universal love and good-will; devoting himself to truth, right and humanity; and never to creed, or sect, or party, as allowing them to conflict in any manner.

Brother Balch was a Universalist, and preached it everywhere, in all so-called Evangelical churches as well as our own. He did not know how to preach without making it the basis of his sermon. It was the staple of everything he said and did. It was warp and woof and structure, and organization, and all, from foundation to capstone. But while preaching Universalism he did not preach it in a sectarian way. I find an article in his scrap-book taken from a paper published nearly fifty years ago, entitled "Universalism against Sectarianism." It is almost a lament. He says. " Universalists are often regarded as sectarists;

and they may sometimes be so in truth ; but when they are they depart from the principles of their profession. They acknowledge no particular mode of faith as indispensible to Christian character. They approve the good, the true, the useful in everything. Having no creed, which they regard as of binding authority, they have nothing with which their own, or other minds, should be checked in thought, unless it shall be a mere name. I am sorry to say that there is too much pride of name, and love of party in the world ; and everything of a partisan or selfish character should be kept away from us. We ought to take a high stand in these matters, and rise above the slime in which sectarians move. We ought to present the true principles of Universalism to the world ; not its abstract doctrines as they have been understood ; or as they are explained by this or that man, this or that sect. Let us maintain the broad faith of our religion, and avoid partisan feeling, and we shall be measured by a new standard." He asks to know " What evil, sect or party has not wrought in the world ? What evil are they not working all the while ?"

It will not be said that there was anything narrow or sectarian about Mr. Balch. His sense of truth, his love of truth, his reverence for truth all pointed in anther direction. Universalism he regarded as a comprehensive name for good-will toward man. It was a spirit of benevolence, and kindness, and sympathy ; originating ,with the Universal Father, and reaching out, and embracing all men, and laying them under its high, and everlasting obligations. Christianity to his mind was hospitable, inclusive rather than exclusive, and from sectarian and party strifes he always kept aloof. He was never a bigot to name, sect or party, and would have none of that belittling, partisan spirit which holds so much sway in all our churches. And only a short time previous to his death, when too weak to write it himself, he caused it to be penned by another, that he might leave it as one of his last messages that "Christianity will never triumph, until sectarianism, and dogmatism are excluded from it, and the fruits of the spirit are accepted as the proof of faith and fidelity. When these differences, and bigotries, dissolve away under the warm sunshine of divine and Christian love, and we begin to live like brethren — the true disciples of Jesus — the world will be speedily converted, and never before. The true Universalist can be no bigot, no enemy of his brethren, can desire and do no wrong, oppress no man, reject no truth, refuse no good, neglect no duty. If men will stand fast in true liberty, and labor in love for the good of the whole race, in preference to building up a sect for sectarian and selfish ends, the Lord will bless them, and prosper their work."

Brother Balch had the true view of liberality. It was not looseness, nor license, nor liberty to do wrong, in any manner. He was no anarchist, or non-government man; for with him "every thought was to be brought in subjection to obedience to Christ." But he was large-minded in the support of everything good; everything his heart told him was right and true. He had a mind which dared to think for itself, and a tongue which knew how to speak. He applauded investigation; not only tolerating, but encouraging free inquiry.

He counseled original research, bidding every seeker after truth keep his eyes and ears open, that he might learn all God had to teach. He did not draw the lines about certain opinions and say, "Thus far shalt thou go, and no farther." He was positive in his convictions with well-defined logical sentiments, being fitted by nature, rather than by education, to follow out a clear and well-sustained argument; to weigh conflicting testimony, and compare the results of actual experiment. With views thus clear, he ever thought to definitely express them. He vindicated the right (as in duty bound) to reason without prejudice, to examine, think, judge and act for himself as unto God, and not answerable to any who should usurp the privilege of dictating what the course of another should be. No man was to be the keeper of his conscience. Neither the scorn of men, nor the petty rules of fashion, nor the bounds they set to propriety or expediency, could deter him from searching out the mind of God, in his endeavor to know the truth that he might be made free; in the assurance that "if the truth should make him free he would be free indeed."

Thinking accurately he acquired a decision in his opinions, and was brought out of the darkness of other men's dim and guessing thoughts, into the fulness of persuasion, and with his emphatic utterance he may have seemed to some as being dictatorial in spirit. But nothing could be farther from his intention. He sought to apply good sense to theology, to reconcile knowledge with belief; reason with revelation; to humanize the church; yet retaining therein all that was divine. In his hands religion was more humane, more

natural, more rational, more liberal. He had a few
great fundamentals to which he held with the greatest
tenacity; but beyond that the largest liberty was
accorded to everyone. He always wanted the kite-
string well in hand, and then he cared not that the
kite itself should float broadly to the breeze. If he
entertained some views peculiar to himself, it was not
that he sought to take away any liberty of others. He
was as willing that everyone should entertain and defend
what seemed to him right and good, as to do it for
himself. It was not then that he was seeking to inveigh
against any man's thoughts or opinions, but that he
might better commend and encourage virtue and the
right in all matters of well-being and well-doing. He
acknowledged no responsibility to any body of men,
or any system of theology, for his manner of thinking,
or for the opinions he might entertain, and he could
not for the sake of policy or to suit the circumstances
of the occasion in which he found himself placed, fal-
ter from strict duty from the principles of Christian
uprightness, or the law of eternal and all-binding morality, which encompassed him about.

He was the friend and disciple of what was true,
and he would have scorned himself had he shrunk in
any presence from avowing and defending the thing
that seemed to him most right. He would be true at any
price in making a manly defence of coveted sentiments,
but he ever impressed you with entire ingenuousness
and sincerity, and would stand so unabashed and nobly
before you, that often he made you greatly ashamed.
You could not meet him without feeling his earnestness of purpose, his loyalty to his convictions, and his

determination to work hour by hour and day by day
to accomplish all the good he could.

There are those who never do aught to merit the
resentment of their brethren, or draw down the dis-
pleasure of friend or foe upon their heads. But there
are those as well who can not be made to swerve from
their soul's integrity. They had rather die than turn
back from a principle of right. They are fearless and
independent in their thinking, and having once made
up their minds for themselves, they know nothing but
to go forward, and the prospect of favor if they remain
silent can not beguile or entrap them. The agony of
sharing in the battle that is to be waged to give triumph to justice and righteousness gives but a nobler
daring, and consequently carves for them a nobler life.

Now there is honor in all this. We can be assured
that manhood is a thing which is much wanted in the
world; and the minister needs to be wise, if may be,
above the majority of men; independent, but consider-
ate; fearless without rashness; firm without obstinacy;
honest and faithful to assert his convictions when
others may shrink from doing so; not believing that
he has the right to sacrifice the great boon of his religion for worldly esteems. The fact is, that wordly
honors—that worst of human evils—has forever played
too great a part in men's religions. Wherein, let it be
asked, consists the manhood of a man? Is it not in his
interior thought, and not in anything merely outward?
A man's proper personality lies in the character of his
thought; and he is true and self-respecting only so far
as he is true to his inward thought, scorning to com-
promise it through outward conformity where any

cardinal point is involved. In the common affairs of life manly men do not favor pretence, nor encourage an outward conformity that belies the inward conviction.

The whole truth here, then, if it were told us, would be that Brother Balch sought to live faithful to his own convictions, and would never consent to sacrifice a principle for the love of popularity, or for what the greater number might think to affirm as right. It is not too much to say that he stood to his integrity as resolutely as ever martyr stood at the stake. He was one of your imperturbable souls; and nothing moved him from the stateliness of his tread. He believed that he had reverently to obey the divine voice that speaks to us from the heavens; that the thing for us first of all is to do right; and if we cannot live by that, then we can die; and the wise thing for us to do under such circumstances seemed to him that we should die.

Now it is these things we have been saying that furnishes us a clear reason as to why Brother Balch was ever opposed to too much creed theology, and by his incessant opposition to the narrowing process was frequently brought into strife with his brethren. With his enlarged views of what Christianity meant to teach, and his breadth of humane sentiment, he could not brook the methods by which so many minds had been brought in subjection to the hierarchy of sects, and there seemed to be no other way for him, if he would be true to himself, or true to the truth, than to stand unyieldingly just where he did stand. He professed before God, and in the sight of men everywhere, to accept with thankfulness all the great essential doctrines of

the Christian religion, and trusted that he was a sincere lover of the precepts which Christ inculcated;
and yet as a brotherhood of believers we might not
agree altogether as it respected many a non-essential,
and each was to be his own judge in matters of this
character, and no one had the right to say, "Why do
ye so?" He did not regard it as strange at all, that
there should be all those differences of opinion respecting modes of faith and administration of church government; but, that such differences should be made a
bar to Christian fellowship, and to prevent good men
working together in a worthy cause was thought by
him to be plainly anti-Christian and reprehensible.

He was not presuming that we could ever frame a
form of belief that would meet the exact thought of
any great number of persons in its minute details, for
no two persons could be found anywhere to think just
alike—not if they thought at all. He deemed it more
or less the fault of every system that writes its creed,
that it fixes the limits of inquiry, and harnesses thought
to a circle; and so puts the powers of the mind to sleep.
It substituted the forms of truth for truth itself; gave
authority instead of reason, and sought to tempt or
force the mind into subjection. In this way it appeared
to him that creeds often became fetters and restraints,
whereas the minds of men should be kept upon the
alert, when new principles were being inculcated and
new plans and institutions recommended, to explore in
all fields of progress lying in advance of them. His
rule was the one thought, that

"We must upward still and onward,
Who would keep abreast of truth."

And a creed, of course, then, to meet the wants of any considerable number of reasonable minds, and to be a bond of union among them, had necessarily to be very general and comprehensive in its statements, in order that it might not become what other creeds had been in other churches; something to bind the conscience, a yoke of oppression, a chain to fetter the soul's freedom. This was his main objection to creeds and confessions—the use they made of ecclesiasticisms to bind thought and restrain conscience, hindering the truth, and preventing the soul's progress in its upward aspirations for the absolute, the infinite, the eternal, the universal. He would have no man's intellectual being dwarfed by the claims of the church to provide and enforce a dogma. He had too much faith in reason, too much respect for the rights of individual judgment, too much confidence in our common humanity, too much tolerance for opinions. Protestantism, he held, begun in a protest against the rejection of reason; being a way of thinking and not a conclusion of thought; a progressive work of investigating and growing, rather than a dictum or a dogma. Give it up, and all that has been won in the religious progress of the past three and a half centuries, is gone.

Brother Balch had none too high an opinion of the church, so but what he was always jealous of its encroachments upon individual liberty. Nothing with him had reflected so great disgrace upon humanity, and made integrity itself stand abashed, as the false assumptions of some who were large in their professions and little in their deeds, and really stole the livery of heaven to serve the devil in. He had not to go far to find

8

many sad examples of the backwardness, and even be-
trayal of the clergy of too many of those good causes
that stood posing most grandly before the world. He
had a caustic tongue for all such as were forever holding themselves in the back-ground, and no faith at all,
and scarcely more of patience with them, in arraying
themselves in opposition to everything but the old,
the ancient, the venerable, regardless of its being right
or wrong. He almost hated your cautious. timid, time-
servers, as traitors to humanity; believing that they
wrought more enduring damage to the race than all
other enemies put together. He could not think that
we were to parley with evil, or to temporize in any
manner, sealing our lips, and stifling our thoughts.
We were not to become recreant to our honest convictions of duty. but to stand out boldly, speaking and
acting in the defence of the right, the true, and the
holy. This was his radicalism. to purge to the bottom
of things; to make a clean sweep of all error, laying the
ax at the root of the tree; leaving no one particle of
diabolism to curse or cure any longer.

No severer strictures are anywhere found than those
pronounced by the Prophets upon the shepherds of
Israel; that they "did not feed the sheep, but fed
themselves; that they ate the fat, and clothed themselves with the wool; that they killed them that were
fed, and did not keep them from becoming a prey to
every beast of the field." And it is in this same strain
that the Savior followed on, when he said, "I am the
Good Shepherd. The Good Shepherd giveth his life
for the sheep. But he that is an hireling, and not the
Shepherd. whose own the sheep are not, seeth the wolf

coming, and leaveth the sheep and fleeth; and the wolf
catcheth them and scattereth the sheep. The hireling
fleeth because he is an hireling, and careth not for the
sheep. ''

Permit me to quote in this connection the words of
Brother Balch as touching this subject. He says:

" That the church has been backward and dilatory in
its movements, often in the wrong, and opposed to
progress, cannot be denied. This has been its great
mistake, and a chief hindrance to its universal spread
and triumph. Although directed and controlled by
those who claim to be of the elect, the converted souls,
it has failed to demonstrate the spirit and power of
truth committed to its charge. The frailties of human
nature have found place in its counsels and conduct,
and misguided its decisions and doings. Its management has not been unlike other public bodies, gotten
up in the same manner, maneuvered by selfishness for
personal interest and party gains. Indeed, how much
like the rest of the world has been its methods of working, and rarely has it shown more wisdom or less personal ambition and worldliness. Its boastful pretensions
have never been well sustained. Hence divisions and
dissensions, oppositions and strifes, have come down to
our day, and still exist among the professed followers
of our Lord, the Master, the Teacher, the Saviour of
the world. The diverse and numerous sects that began
with Paul, and Peter, and Apollos have continued to
multiply, each claiming to itself superiority over every
other, in the measure and distinctness of the opinions
defended, or in the perfection of its mode of government administered. Very small differences have often
led to very bitter controversies, and lasting alienations.
And thus the church militant has failed to become the
church triumphant "

His whole life was a protest in this same direction.

He did not believe that it was for our church to become narrow, sectarian and dogmatic, like other sects, copying their plans, and adopting their methods, or in placing ourselves in rivalry with them; but to try and manifest the spirit of Jesus as exhibited in the earlier days of Christianity, or even in our own earlier days.

The church, with him, was the expression of the life of religion—or the working of brotherhood from the heart of humanity. He had seen too much of the illiberal and persecuting spirit of these older sects to make him in love with their policy—and when our own profession of belief came before the Illinois State Convention, met in Mendota, in 1865, I think, for interpretation and handed down to the different State Conventions from the United States General Convention, he looked upon it as being a limit of faith, and as if truth was something to be determined by vote, and men must be left in nothing to think for themselves, but must have it dictated to them what they were to believe; and it met with his unqualified disfavor—and requiring the approval of two-thirds of the States to ratify it, the measure was defeated. In aiming to put somebody's else interpretation upon the creed, and making it authoritative with him, he could not see where it was going to stop, and his mind at once took the alarm, and revolted as if by instinct. He claimed that he had been charged in the most solemn manner, and accepted the charge at the hands of Father Ballou, "to search the Scriptures in the light of reason rather than of creeds; to not suffer himself to be misled by human and sectarian authority; but to beware of all such tendencies," and he was sustained by conscious integrity when brethren found fault. Some had called our Profession of Belief a Confession of Faith; reminding him of some kind of priestly, or Catholic confessional, which had for him no savory meaning that would pave its way to his acceptance, and he caught at it. It was too much, and he would have none of it. He was so stirred as to return to his pulpit in Galesburg and preach a sermon upon it, by which some declared that he took himself away from the denomination. But the sermon was in effect, saying that if Universalism was not Universalism, then he was not a Universalist. To say that Brother Balch was not a Universalist, was about equivalent to saying that there was not any Universalism in the world, and never had been any. He was the very incarnation of the thing—Universalism made flesh among us.

Brother Balch tells us that his objection was not to the interpretation *per se,* but to the assumption of power to give it authority by a body elected for no such purpose. He could not see how one man, or any set of men, had any right or business, to interpret authoritatively the evident intention of somebody else in drawing up a declaration of principles for the denomination. It would hardly seem that our allegiance to a prescribed faith could be greater than our allegiance to the Scriptures, for it did not exist only as it was believed to be a rescript of the essential doctrines of the Bible; and then of course as open to investigation and interpretation as the Bible itself. "My objection" he says to the Declaration, "was, that it introduced a new and wrong principle, and made a general to meet an exceptional case, which it did not meet

when applied; that it attempted a precedent which un-
rebuked must be fatal to religious liberty, and personal
responsibility; that it prescribed a new test, a mere
submission to authority, where no new truth was given,
no change was made, no new principle was pretended—
a mere interpretation. To such a test I did not, do
not, and God helping me will not, submit. I deny utterly, emphatically, and continually, the right of any
man, or council of men, to exercise lordship over my
faith or conscience, to decide by vote what I do, or
may or shall believe. God never made, nor gave to
councils, synods or conventicles, to popes, kings, priests
or laymen, a mold in which to cast forms of truth for
all time; nor indicated a system of patchwork to repair and interpret old and obsolete doctrines of men,
to keep them respectable, and preserve them from oblivion. The true Christian rises above all this, and
thankfully receives the light of truth, come whence it
may, and where there is found an honest confession
of the spirit of Jesus, and a sympathy of heart to do
good to fellow man, there is a willing fellowship of
hands to work in all good causes.

Some have thought Brother Balch too beligerant and
contentious, ready to enter the arena of controversy
or join in the affray of polemics with a war of words
that did not always conduce to harmony in the denomination, and they have attributed to pugnacity
what had to be charged to his loyalty and fidelity.
Firm in what he deemed the course of right and duty,
he wished no occasion to pass without defending his
honest convictions. Thinking for himself, he deemed
it no less a duty to act for himself, and his wisdom and

convictions did sometimes compel him into a heartfelt
and honest opposition. But hear him, "I do not like
to find fault with brethren whom I love, and with
whom I have worked so long and I think faithfully—
I know honestly and religiously. But it does seem to
me that we have made a wide departure, not only
from the habits and usages of our fraternity, but from
the principle, broad, generous and loving—embraced
in the very name of what we profess—and are in the
ruts of preceding sectarians. Especially have we departed from the simplicity, the zeal, the humility and
patient working of a half-century ago. It were a great
satisfaction to live in peace and good-will with all, but
not at the sacrifice of truth. I can not yield the truth
for any cause, nor shun to defend the right." It will be
acknowledged that Brother Balch was not one of those,
who thought it necessary to inquire how the rulers and
Pharisees and chief priests believed, for fashion and
custom, and tradition and pride went as little way
with him as almost any man you ever meet. But he
does not scruple to say of himself. "We suppose we
love popularity well enough—as well, perhaps, as anybody else—but we love honest principle and manly
integrity better. Shall we refuse to tell the truth, and
a truth which regards the public welfare, through fear
of losing the good opinion of others, or the affection and
esteem of brethren. How could we do such a thing?
If others esteem us the less because we have told
them the truth, we are certainly sorry for it—not that
we have said what we have—but that their esteem has
not been founded on some better principles. We prefer
the respect of our own conscience to the flatteries of

all the people in the world." There are certainly enough
that will flatter you; but the numbers are too few that
will tell you the important things that it most concerns
you to know. We must understand that it is a great
thing to be a man of sturdy principle, and that Brother
Balch always was. He felt that in standing in a religious attitude before the world, it was as though he was
standing in the presence of God, and he must not dis-
simulate. It is, indeed, mortifying in the extreme, to
see such weakness and pusalanimity in those who have
education and influence, and who ought to be leaders
in the cause of truth and the right. How many are
incapable of any opinions of their own, and less capable
of expressing them. They have no real reliance upon
themselves, and no ambition except to be with those
who are high in authority. If our brother was ambitious at all, it will not be said that it was in this direction. And still, in not always agreeing with his brethren
in regard to some measures of denominational management, we may be sure that it arose from his heroic
fidelity to truth and honesty; and though his language
may not always seem to some to be couched in the most
respectful manner that could be, yet his purposes and
motives, and the main drift of what he aimed to say
and do, was never very far out of the way. I will vouch
for it, that he has been nearer right, upon the whole,
in all these years, than most of those who have sought
to oppose him.

It is a satisfaction to know that he was always
aboveboard in everything he did. His nature was
frank and open as the day, and there was that in his
countenance and bearing that bespoke your confidence,

and commanded your respect. His was never an intriguing spirit, acting under a mask,and seeking sinister ends, but with a heart outspoken in words of unmistakable import, he pursued with clear and steady aim, the course which seemed to him wise. He believed less in human contrivance than almost any man you might encounter. There was nothing to be carried by trickery, or by artifice and scheming with him. Too many are apt to place reliance upon management and maneuvering more than on principle and merit, but he scorned to resort to any extreme tactics, or any unconscionable methods to carry a point. He hated meanness and strategy, and could be fully relied upon never to do aught to gratify petty, personal ambition, or to advance his individual fortune, that was not straight forward as between man and man. His methods were all simple and plain, as in the advancement of the cause of truth, and the practical power of knowledge for the elevation of mankind in virtue and happiness, and his means gradual but sure as for the righting of every wrong, like Christianity, displayed in the moral teachings and pure life of Jesus, which is admitted to be the clearest demonstration of the power and value of truth in reference to the needs of man. It may be said that

"His armor was his honest thought,
And simplest truth his highest skill."

He had no other method than to compass right ends with right means, and wait patiently for the issues of his cause; and so spoke the truth and left it to battle for itself. He had such confidence in its capacity to vindicate itself, and make its unobstructed way to the hearts and consciences of all who prize and love it, that he would dare trust anything to it. All right and true principles were everlasting, and to his mind nothing could shake or destroy them.

Mr. Balch has never written many books, but the bulk of what he has written has been of a character to do honor to his religion. Among the number, to which he always referred with more or less pride, were his "Lectures on Language," in 1838, and his "Grammar of the English Language,"in 1840. About the time of these publications he also published·· A Manual for Sunday Schools," and some other smaller works. At a later date, after his first visit to the Old Country, he brought out " Ireland as I Saw It ", and then last of all his "Peculiar People". Several of these have already received notice in what seemed the more proper place for them. Of the last mentioned I give it here. It was mostly written in leisure hours after Brother Balch's last return from Europe and the Holy Land, though not published till a considerable later date, and was designed to illustrate in practical life certain great moral principles of Christianity. In a review of the book by Dr. Thayer, among other excellent things, he says of it, "The entire narrative is of that pure moral character that it cannot fail to open the well-spring of affection and love in the hearts of all who read it."

The following is what we ourselves said of it at the time it was first brought under our eye:

" It is one of the books that is not written to while away an idle hour, or make money without the consideration of doing the world a valuable service. It is crowded full to repletion of the noblest sentiments to which the heart responds as if by instinct, and it is impossible that a person should rise from the reading of it without being made better and more manly by it. Every page almost from beginning to end evinces what ought to be the spirit and workings of Christianity when carried out into real life, and yet it is of the story kind — fresh as any novel. The reader need not expect to find any foolish sentimentality in it — for it is just such a book as we might suppose Brother Balch would write if he was going to try his hand at making something that should be both readable and instructive. From the moment you sit down to its persual you feel that you are taken possession of, and no other impulse is as strong as that of being hastened along toward the end. He who has read any of Brother Balch's narratives, or travels in the East, knows, without being told, that he could not write anything of an uninteresting character. I will acknowledge that I have never looked into such a storied mirror of the Christian religion, so fully dis-playing what Christ aimed to do for the world, were the world but willing to profit by his teachings and example. It gives one faith in the Millenium, to look at so genuine a people as he describes : a community of such simplicity of manners, modeled after the pure and loving spirit of Christianity, without anything of the world's vain distinctions and extravagances. In regard to the world's selfishness and oppression, it sets off in strangest contrast with the so-called Christian practices of to-day, in the midst of so much of parade and pre-tensions, and sham ceremonials, and sectarian ambitions and strifes, that have done so much to destroy the religion of the world."

A donation was made of this work by Mr. Balch to the " Universalist Woman's Association," of Illinois, with the copyright and plates, of which honorable mention was made at the time of his death by the directors of the board, in a set of resolutions, the first and second of which were :

"*Resolved*, That we will respect his memory for the good and useful life of four-score years just closed.

"*Resolved*, That we honor his name for the generous gift to the the Universalist Woman's Association for missionary purposes."

Brother Balch always felt a great interest in missions. It was his ruling passion, in accordance with the prayer of faith, "Thy kingdom come, and Thy will be done on earth as is done in heaven," and he was unwearied in his exertions, traveling far and near to visit the brethren, and attend associations and conventions as far as would consist with the discharge of his home duties. The spirit of missions is everywhere the same, whether developed in the home or the foreign field, and he responded with high and grateful enthusiasm to every Macedonian call; yet the moral desolations around him claimed his first effort.

It will be acknowledged that his whole life was missionary in its spirit and labors, though he was of opinion, and says: "We can rightfully claim a better gift to bestow on what we call heathen nations, than sects who have been engaged in foreign missions for many years. The true history of these missions would reveal facts and results little understood. It has been mine to visit many stations in Greece, Turkey, Syria, Palestine, Egypt and Mexico, and I know whereof I affirm." He thought we had heathen enough all about us, and should begin first to help them at our very doors. He asks to know, "Where are crimes more common, thefts, robberies, murders, drunkenness, gamblings, every degree of extravagance, folly and shame, more common, good and wholesome laws less regarded, justice more outraged, than in America? Talk of 'heathen Chinee.' Are they not more industrious and less complaining and quarrelsome than other laborers? Do their opium dens breed more mischief, or lead to more crime and misery than the thousand rum-holes in our large cities that we license to keep open?"

He did not feel sure but the people of those countries could be of service to us if sent from that way. He supposes a case, that a delegation "should come from some heathen center to our most cultured Christian cities, with a Chunder Sen at their head, to inquire the way of salvation, and asks, "Where would they learn the true, pure, plain principles which Jesus taught, or who were his disciples? What evidence would be given them?" A London journal (quoting statistics to back it up) presents as a moral paradox the statement that the most poorly paid working girls in that metropolis are those engaged in the work of sewing and binding Bibles. It adds that for every heathen abroad who can be induced to use the sacred volume for anything else than gun wadding, a dozen of these girls are driven to peredition at home.

There are great numbers to doubt if the teachings of these sects have any greater morality in practice among them than have the heathen allowing that their theories are better. An, educated paganism presents peculiar features in a daily paper which is being published in Japan, in which some rather free criticisms are offered on the Christian religion. It wants to know among other things, "Whether a Christianity

which allows liquors to be sold at every street corner
and licenses gambling houses, is any better than a
heathenism which simply tolerates these things, and
asks no impertinent questions?"

We mistake in many respects about these peoples.
A large share of the descriptions given of them are
scarcely honest from the fact that, instead of relating
things just as they are, we shuffle all the centuries
together and present the old pictures of Grecian,
Roman and Egyptian debaucheries, as though they
were photographs of existing facts. The evidence,
however, is constantly accumulating through the
descriptions of competent and trustworthy travelers,
that their moral condition is far better than is generally represented, and that their average standard of
morals is not so much lower than in many portions of
Europe and America.

I find the following among Brother Balch's preserved
matters:

Dr. Albert Leffingwell, a man of wide travel and
fine culture, says, in *The Laws of Life:*

" Not only are the laws better obeyed in Europe than
with us, but we are surpassed by the people whom we
are accustomed to regard as only half civilized. ' Better not go down that street this time o' night,' said a
London policeman to me one evening, within sight of
Westminster Abbey; 'it isn't safe for strangers.' Yet
I have wandered on foot and alone throughout the by-
ways of Tokio and Osako late at night, without the
least apprehension of danger, though surrounded by a
people who could hardly understand a single sentence,
I might say. Even India, with a population the most
poverty-stricken on the face of the globe over which a
civilized flag floats, is one of the most law-abiding

countries in the world. In proportion to numbers comprising the population, the criminals of India are far more often foreigners than natives, strange as they may seem. While in Bombay, I learned that the authorities had discovered the strange fact that increase in criminality was almost exactly in proportion to adoption of European ideas. In other words, the heathen were more law-abiding than the whites who governed them."

Henry Ward Beecher once asked questions like these:

Do you know that in China there are 2,000 colleges, and that their libraries outnumber ours ten to one? Do you know that in that country there are more than 2,000,000 highly educated men, and that out of that vast population of 400,000,000 there is scarcely one who cannot read and write? Do you know that in good manners, for which there is an ample market in this country, China leads the world?

We go to these foreign countries, carrying our boastful pretentions and rivalry of sects; puting ourselves in a kind of exceptional independence to them; mistaking and traducing their characters as though they were not combining in themselves any of the virtues of Christianity, while in many things it were not strange if they were far our superiors, and better behaved than ourselves. The term heathen is always used in a way that implies condescension and contempt. Brother Balch believed in missions at home and abroad, but saw many things to modify our too urgent zeal in sending large sums of money away to the heathen just now, as our people are circumstanced: our societies struggling for existence. And not the least of those was his objection to importing the evils of Christian dissensions and sectarianisms, and historic quarrels into those countries. It isn't as though we were necessitated to go abroad, because we cannot spend all the money we have in educating heathen at home.

If we are desirous to learn respecting Brother Balch's missionary spirit, we must follow him up in his different settlements over churches and parishes, and his rambling over State and Nation. He was ordained May 28, 1828, and the next day found him on his way to fulfill an appointment in a distant field, to which he was invited by a stranger whom he never saw before. He himself gives this account of it:

"The morning following, I was standing on the piazza of the house where we had been entertained during the convention, with Brother T. J. Sawyer, then a student in college, waiting for the stage which was to take us to Troy, where we had planned to start on a tour of lecturing, neither of us having money to pay our board for a week. A strange gentleman came up and addressed Brother Sawyer, as the elder and better-looking man, asking him if he were not a preacher. He answered him no, but that I was. 'Well,' said the man, 'I have but a moment to say that I am going to Newfane, Vt., where there is a small society that wants preaching. I will take you over, and you can preach next Sunday, and if they do not want you I will bring you back.' 'Go,' said Brother Sawyer, 'and I will go to Troy and stay with Brother Willis till you come back.' 'But what if I do not come back?' I asked. 'Then I will go back to college, and you go to work.' Just then the stage drove up. He entered, bade me adieu, and I started off with a man I had never seen, and whose name I did not learn till two days afterward. We were till the third day at noon passing over the Green Mountains, and reached Newfane on Sunday. It was immediately noised about that Captain

Carter had brought them a preacher, and a meeting would be held in the school-house that evening, on going to which when the time came, I found was crowded full. You can depend upon it that strange thoughts rushed into my mind as I entered there as a preacher. I shall not try to tell you my feelings. I was devout. I was humble and in earnest, and God helped me."

It was here Brother Balch spent his first three months, preaching usually three times on Sunday, as was the custom then largely in all parishes, and three or four times during the week, for which he was paid less than \$25 for his entire services. In the winter of 1828–29 he went back to teaching school, preaching occasionally in different places, and continuing his studies with Father Loveland. As the spring returned, he returned to Newfane, engaging to preach half of the time at \$5 a Sunday. The other portion of his time he preached in surrounding towns, and in Winchester, N. H., traveling on foot twenty and forty miles to reach appointments, and received the same pay of \$5 per Sunday. He remained in these places, preaching in nearly every town in that region, till he married his wife in August, 1829, and was invited to his first real settlement in Albany, N. Y.

He continued to work just as hard in Albany as he had done in his former field, and as he says ,"not knowing how to take care of my health, I became worn down with over-exertion and was obliged to abandon my charge." He had formerly preached at Watertown, Mass., to which place he had been invited before going to Albany, and it so happened that Dr. Williamson was having under consideration the matter of settling in Watertown, when it was proposed by

9

Brother Balch that his friend come to Albany, and let him go to Watertown, and it was thus arranged. Brother Balch would afterward refer to it as " A swapping of societies." After going to Watertown his health somewhat improved for a time. But again it failed and after two years he was induced to remove to Claremont, N. H., in 1832. Dr. Adams to whom I am indebted for several of the above facts, says in his " Fifty Notable Years " that " he preached there half the time, and supplied in Hartland and Springfield Vt., and Newport, N. H., until a new church in Claremont was finished, and that here he was very actively employed, not only as pastor, but as doing missionary work in every direction."

Brother Balch never knew when he had done enough, or when to give himself rest from his labors. It was in the spring of 1833 that Brother S. A. Davis, now of Hartford. Conn., became a student in the home of Brother Balch, and he tells us that he was " a young man, only twenty-seven years old, but did a great work for our faith in that section of New Hampshire, and in the adjoining towns of Vermont, and did it at that early day when the prejudices of men ran very high." He is speaking after his death in the *Gospel Banner*, and is pleased to add. " No minister in our church had a larger share of my love and confidence." I find in Brother Balch's journal that he had " seventeen preaching stations," and that he was the means of bringing " several ministers into the State, and no less than three or four into the ministry." A large portion of the time he established and edited the paper called the " Impartialist." writing generously for it. He assisted in forming the New Hampshire State Convention of Universalists. A then present citizen of Claremont, and a member of his congregation, writes me that "the church which was dedicated by Brother Balch in 1832 was remodeled and rededicated in 1883, and that Brother Balch was present to assist in the exercises, reading the original hymn which he composed for the first dedication fifty-one years previous."

It may not be amiss to reproduce the hymn in this place.

To Thee, O God, who hearest prayer,
    This earthly temple here we raise;
May we Thy choicest blessing share,
    And dedicate it to Thy praise.

Here may Thy humble offspring bend,
    And worship Thee, Thou Great Unknown;
And may Thy quenchless love descend,
    And seal, and fit us for Thine own.

May we Thy ancient truths dispense,
    Thy sacred will and power proclaim
The faith once given to the saints,
    The hope that's found in Jesus' name.

May we Thy holy Sabbaths spend
    Within these consecrated walls;
And round this altar lowly bend,
    While Thy good spirit on us falls.

Here Lord we'll sing, and preach, and pray,
    While we Thy sanctuary throng;
And when we're called from earth away,
    In heaven we'll raise a nobler song.

In going from there to Providence, R. I., in 1836, his labors were scarcely lightened in any respect, for he still had a wide field in which he was constantly employed outside of his parish work.

It was the same in all the years of his ministry. He was very popular, with hosts of friends, and was always going here and there and everywhere. He was most truly the people's friend, and therefore did they hear him gladly. It is told that he took the greatest interest in the progress of the cause, and was reaching out and building up the faith in every direction. In a short time the large church was crowded, and a second society was formed in the city, which, because of the troublous times on account of the Dorr movement, did not prosper very well at first, but having survived that terrible struggle has moved steadily along to the present time. A letter from Brother Cushing says, "The period of Brother Balch's ministry seems to have been a period of great prosperity in the history of the old First Church and Society. It was marked by important events in the history of our little commonwealth, and his eager spirit made him an important factor in the public concerns of the day. Leaving here nearly fifty years ago he left a deep impression upon the life of the parish, and the life of this whole people. He is pleasantly remembered by many of the oldest citizens, who when he was present to preach for me on a recent date, took the greatest pains to listen in large numbers to their friend and leader of long ago. I learn that during the years of his stay in this city no less than sixty persons united with the church, and on its record to-day, there are the names of at least six who became Universalist ministers, and who, I presume, pursued their course of study for the ministry with him." [The preparer of this volume being one of the number.] He adds, "You can imagine that he kept something like a primitive theological school during his Providence pastorate." And this was so. His life has been to train men in the ways of religion and for the same useful and honorable work to which his own many years had been devoted. But little less than thirty have been in his family at one time or another, seeking his assistance in preparing themselves for the ministry.

It was while in Providence that I became acquainted with BrotherBalch. in first hearing him preach at Fall River, Mass. I may be said, like many others, to have grown up with a terribly dark pall hanging over me, calculated to embitter my childhood and youth. and darken the whole future of my life. Just about everybody in those days shared these severer views, which had been a chief element in the religion that so generally prevailed. There was no such Heavenly Father as now conceived of, who was an unchangeable Friend. by whom we were kept and blest; who loved us. and loved all men, with a boundless, perfect. everlasting love; no tender, beneficent Providence, the highest possible motive and purpose for infinite welfare. I almost hated the very name of God, though not the God that ever lives and loves, but the stiff idol of men's creeds and worship. The very works and ways of God had all been perverted to me. I knew indeed that theology, as I had been taught it, was an ill-woven tissue of absurdities. I had heard a single Universalist sermon previous to this, which, though it produced something of an impression upon my mind at the time. had been nearly effaced from my memory. And it was left for Brother Balch in that first sermon of his to which I ever listened to give a turn

to my life which has made me so much what I am, that
I am claiming but very little responsibility for my religious belief. I confess to have been taken out of a
slough of despond, and my feet placed upon that Rock
of Ages that has been cleft for us all, and is so much
higher than we are. And let me tell my readers that
I would rather part with every grateful association I
have ever formed, than to lose from my soul one feature or lineament of that excellent faith connected with
the name of Universalism, as I first learned it from
this father and friend, with whom I have lived on such
intimate terms from that time to this.

Let me try and summerize the sermon if I can.
The text was I Peter i. : 3–4, " Blessed be the God
and Father of our Lord Jesus Christ, which according to his abundant mercy hath begotten us
again unto a lively hope, by the resurrection of Jesus
Christ from the dead, to an inheritance, incorruptible,
and undefiled, and that fadeth not away." He said
that his subject was the Christian's "hope," and that
he should go to his text for all that he should attempt
to prove that evening.

He next declared that it was " a lively hope," an
animating and rejoicing hope, and further, it was the
hope of "an inheritance, incorruptible and undefiled,
and that fadeth not away," and that we were " begotten
to it by the resurrection of Jesus Christ from the
dead," as the proof of our resurrection. Notice the
four points which he makes: The Christian's hope; a
lively hope; the hope of an inheritance, incorruptible,
etc., and our being begotten to it by the establishment
of the fact of the resurrection. He had read each of

these right from his text, and under the head of each
he had devoted more or less extended remarks.

But now he turns to notice the first part of his text,
which reads " Blessed be the God and Father of our
Lord Jesus Christ, which, according to His abundant
mercy, hath begotten us to " this hope. Under the head
of God he shows that He is the All Good, the infinitely good Being. And then He is the Father, infinitely more tender than any human parent can be. And
besides all this He is abundant in mercy—which, of
course, is no less than infinite—and the Christian's hope
to which the God and Father of Christ has begotten
us is according to this infinite mercy. He means to
hold us to this statement. He tells us what a chord in
music is—that it is where the notes all harmonize together, or are at agreement with each other—and a
discord is where there is no such agreement. He then
takes a pair of scales and makes use of them by which
to illustrate his subject—putting the Christian's hope
into the one, and the infinite mercy of God into the
other, making them exactly balance, so that the first
is "according to" the last. Not, mind you, according
to anything that is in us, but according to God's infinite mercy and fatherly care for his children. He
now quotes his text once more : " Blessed be the God
and Father of our Lord, Jesus Christ, which, according
to His abundant mercy, hath begotten us again unto a
lively hope—by the resurrection of Jesus Christ from
the dead—to an inheritance incorruptible and undefiled,
and that fadeth not away," and declares, that if you
ever find him preaching any other gospel than that of

Universalism—set it down that he is either insane or dishonest.

I saw no other way but to accept his conclusions, and from that moment it seemed to me that I was in a new world, with everything assuming a new aspect. There was nothing in my whole life but was entirely changed. I saw with new eyes, and understood with an enlightened mind. Heaven and earth, and sea and skies, were filled with evidences of the unbounded benevolence of the All-wise Creator. O, how my heart did bound. It was the happiest hour of my life. I rose on my feet and shouted it to the great congregation, for it was impossible that I should keep from telling of it. From that day to this it has been my joy and my hope, the inspiration and glory of my being. I consider that I owe it to Brother Balch that I am what I am to-day, and it is out of my everlasting gratitude that I am engaged in writing the life of the man who preached that sermon. I recollect once asking him, "Do you remember that evening?" "Remember it? Why it was one of the most startling events of my early life, and I said to myself, if I never made a convert before, I have made one now." There are thousands I doubt not in this land, and in other lands, that are under like obligation to Brother Balch. I should not dare even attempt to estimate the immense amount of good he has been instrumental in accomplishing, in opening the blind eyes, and turning men from darkness to light, and from the power of Satan unto God. I deem that man most noble of all, and as having placed himself in the high role of honor, who is trying to set good examples, and do good, and who is leading men into the light of truth, and the love and practice of virtue.

It was in November, 1841, that Brother Balch went from Providence to New York, and here again he was greatly respected, being acknowledged as one of the first preachers, and standing as high, and sought after as much, to assist in every good cause, as any minister in the city. He was a felt presence in all that great metropolis. Dr. Bolles, one of New York's most eminent preachers at present, writes me: "Mr. Balch was a power in this city, and the affection with which he is remembered by old friends finds no diminution to this day. His ministry was a great success." One of his successors in the ministry, settled over his society after twenty odd years, says: "I followed him in the Bleeker Street Church, and found that he had done good service, made many true and lasting friends, and left an influence in favor of liberal Christianity which can never be exhausted." Still another, and a woman this time, wants to tell us, that 'while in New York he worked hard for the cause of religion, and was a friend of the poor, and held in greatest esteem by every one. He seemed like a father to us all." The Bleeker Street Church became at once very prosperous upon his going there. They were not only highly pleased with him as preacher, but as pastor as well, and his general popularity was such as to frequently fill their large church to overflowing. He may be said to have always drawn large and interested congregations. Dr. Sawyer gives us an illustration of his popularity in the portion of New York where his church was located:

" He was engaged to deliver a temperance address
in one of the orthodox churches in the neighborhood,
but had advised the person having charge of the meeting that he had a wedding to attend, and could not be
present till late, and he must keep the audience patient.
When he reached the church it was packed, and the
manager was waiting at the door for him. The moment
he discovered him he seized and pulled him through the
crowd, remarking, with an oath, 'G——, Balch, you
draw like a blister.'"

"If the parents of Brother Balch," as is told us by
the before-mentioned Judge Adams, " were always kept
in humble circumstances, yet what they despaired of
for themselves they hoped for their children. And
when the favored son packed his scanty wardrobe and
went out from the old homestead to try his hand in the
great world, neither the father nor mother thought that
the world had anything too good for him, and they
always believed that the world's best was entirely possible to him. I imagine," he continues, " that when
the report came to the old Balch homestead that young
William was making his mark as a preacher in New
York City, among the ablest divines of the country, the
fond father and mother thought that it was a mere
matter of course. Had ever a young man gone to New
York with a truer purpose, a warmer zeal, or a grander
conception of human destiny? It is true he did not
carry to the city any extensive learning of the schools.
No Yale or Harvard had accredited him with its diploma. But it is not probable that either William the
son or Joel the father wasted any regrets over that
matter. The young preacher carried the learning of
the heart, and those graces of speech which are born

not of the schools of rhetoric, but of the heartfelt devotion to all that is noble and good."

It was while here in New York that a great change
came to him, in the death of the wife of his early choice,
who, as a prudent housekeeper, and in the faithful discharge of her responsible family duties, filled a large
place in his home.

*   *   *   *   *   *   *

In leaving New York it was to part with a great
many friends, and a good strong society, in order that
he might retire to a long desired quiet of a rural home
near his native place. But here he worked harder if
anything than ever before, for he was literally all over
the State of Vermont preaching and lecturing. "For
seven years," he tells us "calls were more frequent and
numerous, labors more pressing, opportunities for rest
and study far less." So far as work was concerned, it
was as here stated in every place in which Brother
Balch was ever settled. There was never any rest for
him as long as he lived.

Let an old friend from among his parishioners at
this period speak of him, who says that "he knew him
for thirty years.

> "And knew him but to love him,
> And named him but to praise."

He tells us that during his residence in Ludlow he
"took a great interest in temperance and all public
improvements, especially the public schools, and that it
was largely through his instrumentality that the graded
school system was established there; that he represented
the town in the Legislature two terms, and was a very

efficient member, but was too honest in his own convictions of right and wrong to be very popular among that class of men who usually control such bodies. I thought of him as finding always the better and tenderer side of human nature, and seeing something to admire in the rough, uncultivated man whom many would pass by unheeded. " Brother Balch," he continues, " was greatly beloved by all classes of citizens, and sorely missed when he left us. His ministry was a benediction, and his memory will long be cherished by generations to come. I cannot find words to do justice to the memory of such a man, and so gifted a preacher, who was such a true and sincere friend, and whose life has been such a worthy example for us all to follow." In the reception given to Brother Balch in honor of the eightieth anniversary of his birth, there came a communication that "In the esteem of the people of Ludlow parish, none has a warmer place in our hearts, and none a warmer welcome in our homes today, than Brother William S. Balch. Our best wishes are with him."

*   *   *   *   *   *

It was now,after leaving Ludlow in 1865,that Brother Balch came West. He had long entertained the idea of removing to this western country, and talked about it from quite an early period in his ministry, so that Dr. Thayer got off the following hit upon him :

Man never is, but always to be blest,
Balch never goes, but is always going West.

Mr. Balch's most intimate companion, J. C. Havemeyer, of New York City, tells of his being very fond

of travel, and that he accompanied him with others
on a journey to Hennepin, Ill., in 1842 or 1843, when
thirteen constituted their party. He says, "When on
our way through the lakes to Chicago, he preached on
a Sunday morning to the first-class passengers on the
upper deck of the steamer; and in the afternoon to
the second-class, or the emigrant passengers on the
main deck, much to their delight, and showed himself
to be one of them." He had a sister and family living
in Galesburg, and here he spent five years of his ministry, from 1865 to 1870, in full charge of a society,
with much outside labor, during which time 124 persons connected themselves with the church. One person writing me from there, says, "I do not think that
any too much can be said of him as a model pastor for a
society. As a neighbor and friend, as also a preacher, I
am sure that I have never known his equal." He attached himself very closely to the students of Lombard, and gave them greatest pleasure by his interesting and instructive manner of lecturing and preaching. He was, moreover, of important service to any
who were seeking the ministry as a profession.

From here he again retired to a nice, quiet home,
with good friends, in Hinsdale, near Chicago, preaching and working as before; settled as he supposed permanently and for life. But an urgent demand was
laid upon him to remove to Elgin, where any amount
of work needed to be done. It was here that his home
was kept, and his last days mostly spent, prepared for
quiet and comfort in his declining years. He succeeded
the writer of this in 1871, and for nearly six years remained pastor of the society, greatly beloved till the

Rev. Mr. Boynton came, when he again thought to retire, with a visit planned for himself and wife to California.

It was at this time that Dubuque, Iowa, had lost
their preacher (he going out from among us) and they
desired that Brother Balch might come and supply a
Sunday for them, and he accordingly went. Out of
this grew another three years' ministry, with no less
good effects than in previous fields. He retired from
his labors there with just as cordial friends as any one
needed to have. He was able to count on many warm
admirers in that church, who were ready to speak of
him as one who was known only to be greatly loved
and honored as a faithful friend and pastor. Indeed
he always made friends wherever he went, for he was
pre-eminently a friend of the people, and a friend of
everybody. This was his last pastorate, from 1877 to
1880, at the expiration of which time he returned to
Elgin to remain (with the exception of visits made from
his home and travels abroad) till the time of his death.
Here he preached more or less during a period in which
they were without a regular pastor, and officiated at
funerals and weddings up to the last.

I will give but few words in this connection, of how
his life was regarded in Elgin, reserving what farther I
may say till I shall come to the chapter on "Home
Life and Varied Employments." My first words
are from the nearest neighbor Mr. Balch had during
all the years he kept his home in that city. He says :

"I have lived a near neighbor to Mr. Balch for the
past fifteen years, and cannot speak too highly of my
esteemed friend. He was a true man. His aim in life

was to do good. He was an excellent neighbor, and as true and noble a friend as I care to have. He was especially a friend of the poor, an advocate of temperance in all things, and always interested in every good work tending toward benefiting mankind. Such in brief is the man I delight to honor, and when such a man is taken from us we deeply feel our loss."

Another testimonial from a close neighbor (Judge Wilcox) is the following:

"Brother Balch was endowed with great intellectual ability, yet he was plain and unpretending, free from ministerial airs, faithful to duty, honest, exemplary, unselfish, and ready to aid in every good work. His clear exposition of Christ's teachings (with which he was wonderfully familiar) and kind words, have brought peace to many troubled souls. Measured by the beneficent and far-reaching effects of his labors and example as a preacher, he is justly entitled, I think, to rank as a good and great man, and by his death the Universalist denomination looses one of its most successful, useful and noble ministers. He was certainly a manly man, for he had the heart of a true man in him."

I cannot forego the chronicling of words so pregnant with meaning as the following, by Judge Ranstead, making a triplet of names, which might be much added to if space did not forbid. He says:

"Mr. Balch was a neighbor, and intimate friend of mine for many years, and I knew him well. He impressed me as being one of the ablest and strongest men mentally I ever met. Yet he was very simple in his character, and adapted himself readily to all kinds of society, and recognized men of all callings and creeds as brothers. He was a positive man, with strong convictions and expressed his sentiments fearlessly, and still was charitable, forgiving and kind. To those who knew him, it is needless to add that he was eminently a good man. He carried his religion into his daily intercourse with men, and lived up to the standard of his preaching, which I always deemed first class. I think it may be said of him, as I have often heard him say of the Great Master, " He went about doing good."

*   *   *   *   *   *

It has been objected sometimes that Mr. Balch preached long sermons of a rambling character, and that his labors in being spread out over a broad field did not tell effectually for organization. But I doubt if it will be claimed that he did not work heartily and untiringly with his brethren, in all general methods for promoting the cause of our Zion. He took the greatest interest in the progress of the faith always. His whole life was devoted to this one thing, he seeing his way clearly, and never running into any of the multiplied vagaries of his time. It should be told that he was very active in helping to organize the United States Convention of Universalists, and that while Father Ballou, Brother Streeter, Whittemore and others, uttered warnings against usurpations of power, the claiming of authority over others, and the danger of becoming sectarian, he fully believed in an organization that should be wisely adapted to the end of the denominational existence, and to a general statement of the leading and distinguishing features of our faith, looking to the law of growth, but not to an inflexible creed, answering to all time, and articles of belief so numerous and specific, that no variety of opinion could be tolerated.

There is no depreciating the work Mr. Balch did for our cause, assisting to organize societies, and helping to plan churches, and train ministers for the service, almost equal to any minister in the denomination. His was the freest form of religious organization, with nothing of ecclesiastical tyranny. He believed in an organization well equipped for doing all right things; just as he believed in the church, that we might give and receive assistance, and by combined effort better do the work which the Master requires at our hands. Of course there is wisdom in having some kind of working plan for doing everything that is sought to be done. Who does not see the reasonableness of what another has said, that, " Our work is to make Christians, and to make churches ; to multiply our ministry in numbers and effectiveness; to carry our glorious faith to multitudes who are losing faith all for the want of it; to mass and drill our forces, and to march boldly forward in all the socialities, moralities, reforms and philanthropies."

It is to be understood, however, that the more spiritual religion may not reveal itself chiefly in conferences and conventicles, and corporations ; worshiping God neither at Jerusalem or Gerizim, but in spirit and in truth, and in the beauty of holiness. And its progress is not always to be determined by ceremonials, and statistical tables. It is a kingdom that cometh not so much by observation, and may be felt more in being seen less. It has been said truly that "It is to the dissemination of just ideas, and to the bringing of men into true life, that we are to look for the evidence of real service on the part of any form of religion that claims the attention of the world." Great good is done in scattering the seed of the kingdom in numberless hearts, even though the instrument or means for propagating itself

10

is not seized hold of and prosecuted with vigor. It is
so that the hymn runs:

> Sowing the seed by the wayside high,
> Sowing the seed on the rocks to die,
> Sowing the seed where the thorns will spoil,
> Sowing the seed in the fertile soil.

It was the silent leavening that the great-souled
Chapin wrought, as did the Master, in tempering the
hearts and passions of men, and achieving unspeakable
victories over individual sin and sorrow. It is
Chapin himself who reminds us that " Jesus wrote no
huge volumes, nor framed any specific laws; but love,
mercy, compassion, tenderness, sympathy, good will to
men: He kindly taught these to the world, sowed
them, precious seed, in the few hearts that would receive them, and calmly went His way—His way of
healing and blessing." And in this he made a defense
of his own course. Brother Balch's ministry was of a
missionary character. He rambled in sermon, and
travel, and went everywhere, over State and Nation,
scattering the seed, and waiting patiently, but hope-
fully, for the harvest to spring and grow. Nor did he
deal in commonplace matters, and glittering general-
ities, as if attempting to cover the whole sphere of duty
in every sermon, and regenerate society at large, but
always had some definite practical aim, as when a great
many years ago " The Divine Revelation of Nature " as
it was called, was producing a good deal of a sensation
in the community, and he was to give the charge at
the ordination of Brother Biddle. He did it after this
fashion: " I charge you to preach Jesus Christ, and
Him crucified, and not Andrew Jackson Davis, and

him mesmerized." It is true that Dr. Sawyer writes
me that he "used to compare him to a shot-gun which,
as it scattered broadly, was, therefore, pretty sure to hit
somewhere, while a rifle, unless very skillfully directed,
was almost sure to fail."

I once heard Brother Balch tell this same story (I
think it must have been), though somewhat changed, upon himself. As it has been written out by another hand,
I may allow him to give it in his own manner of relating
it: He said, a father and son once went out hunting and
came to tree in which was a squirrel; whereupon the
son said, "Give me the gun and I will bring him down."
The young man took long and steady aim, but somehow
the squirrel remained in the tree, and did not come
down, when the father said to the son, "Here; you let
me have that gun; you are no good at a shot." So
the father took the gun, but being afflicted with
shaking palsy it was difficult to follow the weapon
with the eye, so violent were its gyrations. However,
the discharge was effected, and down came the unconscious rodent. "There," said the victorious parent, "when
you want any shooting done you can call on me." "No
wonder you killed the squirrel," replied the young man,
"for when anybody takes aim at a whole tree at once,
if there is anything there it has got to come down."
And so concluded Brother Balch, whenever I preach or
lecture, or do anything else, I take aim all over, and if
there is any game anywhere about I expect to hit it.
And the fact is he generally did hit it. Now this we
may consider his own answer to his being diffusive and
rambling, and not always connected in his ideas. His
was not a fragmentary gospel, and he had preached it

till it became so important in his mind that he wished
to get the whole of it into every sermon, for he did not
like to do things by the halves, and this made his
sermons frequently long. And then, too, he went upon
the principal of "line upon line, precept upon precept,
here a little, and there a good deal."

Of course his sermons were oftentimes purposely
long. But I wonder if he is the only man that ever
did such a thing as preach long sermons, and if we
who do this are sinners above all those who dwell at
Jerusalem. Why, I never knew that there was any
particular length for a sermon. I have listened to sermons that it seemed to me that they were very long at
ten minutes, and then I have listened to sermons that
were short at two hours. There is an old adage that
says "Circumstances alter cases." It is said of the
apostle Paul, that on one occasion he continued his
preaching till midnight, "and a certain young man
seated in a window sank down in a deep sleep and fell
from the third loft, and was taken up dead." It depends
very much on the question how important the subject
is that is being treated at the time, and who is treating
it. In Brother Balch's generally interesting and rest-
ful manner I have known him to preach well on to
two hours, and his audience reluctant to have him
stop at that. I saw him try it once, however, when
but for three or four large persons having been crowded
into one seat which was never meant to hold more than
four common persons, he might have got along well
enough, but he preached a whole hour that time, with
the house very warm and closely packed; and when
I supposed that he was right at the point of saying

amen. he struck off on to a new lead and talked half
an hour (which to be sure was a fit illustration of what
he had been saying before), but as he stepped down out
of the pulpit into the main aisle a friend chanced to
remark to him that his sermon was long, or he preached
a good while. "Yes," he remarked, "he got upon the
everlasting gospel," when a second remarked "I thought
as much." This seemed to trouble him a little, for he
hardly expected the first remark to be followed up
with a second, which should drive the matter home so
close upon him. So when he arrived at the house of
this last lady with whom he was to remain over night,
he had to tell a story to take off the point of her remark, which was a famous way he had of doing sometimes. His story was of the preacher in earlier times,
when the custom was to treat sermons under a great
number of heads, and as he came to his eighteenthly,
and chanced to use the expression, "What shall I say
next?" some one in the congregation cried out, "For
God's sake say amen."

Another story which he told, was of an intemperate
man, who, coming home in the evening in a state of in-
toxication, thought it necessary that they have prayers
(as their custom was) before retiring. and standing up
at the back of a chair to sustain himself, he notwithstanding fell upon the floor right in the midst of his
prayer. and looking up very tenderly into the face of
his wife, inquired of her "If it hurt her," and she answering that it did not, and desiring to know if it hurt
him, he replied: "No, but it was a terrible clap."
Brother Balch said his sermon "was a terrible clap,
but it did not hurt anybody." I once knew a minister

to hurry up a funeral sermon beyond any decent propriety, because he was anxious to go a fishing with
some young friends. I would think that too short a
sermon. And it seems to me that a sermon is as often
made long by the fault of the hearer as by the preacher.
There are a great many things in these days that take
people's attention; the dinner is waiting, or there is
something else it is thought, needs to be done very
much. I knew something like this once to change the
location of a church from where it was first voted to
have it. It so happened that there was a card party
on hand the same evening the church was to be located,
and two or three were in haste to get home to join in
the game. In their haste to leave as soon as the vote
was declared, it was supposed that they were offended
at what had been done; that they wanted the church
which had been burned down located on the old
site, which was very much nearer the dwelling of these
two or three, and thereupon the vote was reconsidered,
and the house located where it was first decided not to
locate it. The feelings of an audience is not always
the standard for judging the length of a sermon.

*   *   *   *   *   *

No adequate conception of the character of Brother
Balch as a preacher is had, without considering him in
the sphere of a natural-born pulpit orator. He was
possessed of most shining and brilliant qualities, and
had the flash and sparkle of ideas, and a very superior
quality of voice—clear, rich, mellow, musical—which,
with his natural enthusiasm and earnestness of manner,
not only gave a fine effect, but stirred and thrilled his

auditors to the highest pitch of fervent feeling and
rapturous delight. People delight to tell of the music
of his voice, and how in the pulpit, while he plead for
truth and goodness, he seemed transfigured with the
soul of true eloquence. A great attractiveness of his
manner as a speaker lay in his agreeable intonations,
and in the deep, spiritual expression of his voice. And
this, connected with the peculiar simplicity and beauty
in which his thoughts rose and clothed themselves in
words, established a perfect communion between him and
his hearers. His ideas took graceful and engaging form,
and there was nothing he wrote but possessed a peculiar
charm which was certain to secure for it attention. It
was because of this that the minds of the people were
ever plastic under his hand, and he could mold them
for the time being to almost any shape required.
They would hang on his glowing speech for hours,
and as he sat down there would be nothing but
praises, and this not only in his palmiest days, for he
was "The old man eloquent." He was conspicuous in
any gathering as soon as he rose to speak. You might
announce him to address the people from any platform
of our ministers, and each should have been heard for
a score of times, and he would not suffer in the number
that would flock to hear him. There was nothing more
engaging and impressive than his reading of a favorite
hymn, and he would do it with such rare felicity and
power, that it would seem equal in pathos to many an
unctious sermon preached from our pulpits.

Perhaps I should make a distinction here between
eloquence and oratory, for I recognize a difference.
An orator, it has been said, is one who makes a some-

what elaborate speech, and particularly an eloquent
public speaker who stirs men by his bursts of utterance, whereas eloquence is the art of clothing thought
in an earnest, fluent manner (it may be quiet and rest-
ful), which makes it effective with the hearer. Somebody has described eloquence as "the utterance of great
truths, so clearly discerned. so deeply felt, so bright and
so burning, that they can not be withheld, and that
they create for themselves a style and manner which
carry them far into other souls." It is this same
thought that the poet has expressed in the lines which
follow :

> Eloquence is the deep, impassioned fervor
> Of a mind deep fraught with native energy,
> When soul and sense burst forth embodied
> In the burning thought;
> When look, emotion, tone, are all combined;
> When the whole man is eloquent with mind;
> A power that comes not at the call or
> Quest of vice, or of ignoble birth,
> But from the gifted soul, and the deep-feeling breast.

The Saviour was most impressive and persuasive in
address. He spoke with a commanding power of authority—"spake as never man spake"—and yet I do
not know that ever any one thought to call Him an
orator. A person might be eloquent in common conversation, but it would never be said of such an one that
he was an orator. The Christian Union seems to me
to have rightly distinguished in what it has recently
said, that "an art which rises by natural climax out of
the conversational mood into lyric earnestness and
beauty is superior to the more stately and ornate
model which so often passes for eloquence."

And I will say that I have heard Mr. Balch when he would be speaking in the most natural, easy manner, and he would commence to warm up, and would rise higher and higher in the pathos of his subject, till it seemed as if he was perfectly inspired, and his audience would rise and cling to him, till they were obliged to stop and catch their breaths. I claim nothing for him of studied oratory as in the schools, but for real, fervid, pulpit eloquence, I can not think him excelled by any other person I ever listened to. Persons may smile at what I am saying, but I must be allowed my own opinion, and I speak as my heart prompts, and do not hesitate to say, that no one has ever moved me more than he, when in his best moods words of kindling energy have poured forth from his lips like a mountain torrent, swaying the hearts of his hearers like a mighty rushing wind.

And I am not alone in what I am saying. People tell me of having heard others speak who were called the world's greatest orators, but have never felt the power of eloquence as sometimes at the speaking of Mr. Balch. Dr. Emerson says: "I first heard him speak nearly fifty years ago, at the Akron United States Convention, when my youthful ears got the secret of his success. He was in look, bearing and manner every inch the orator." A person hearing him in Chester, Vt., in 1870, on the occasion of his visiting that place, says, "I would be glad to give a synopsis of this brilliant discourse, for I have never listened to anything delivered from any pulpit in the town that would equal in eloquence, in lofty sentiment, pure logic, and scholastic ability, what I heard Sunday evening, and I be-

lieve all who were so fortunate as to be present would
fully endorse my statement.   He is unquestionably one
of the ripest and most gifted orators of modern days."

Permit me to quote once more and this time from
the *Vermont Standard*, published at Woodstock, that
State.   The editor is speaking, and he says:

"Mr. Balch was a native of the adjoining town of Andover, and always made it a point to visit his old acquaintances, and what few distant relatives lived there, whenever he came to Vermont.   On such occasions he never
failed to preach, and such preaching (as we venture to
say) will never be heard again in that rock-bound town
to the very end of time.   As an extemporaneous speaker, but few, if any, could excel him.   He always
appeared humble and wholly devoid of pride, and in
the devotional part of pulpit exercises (if such are
proper subjects of comment) we think no person on
earth could be happier.   It was truly a benediction to
listen to his soul-satisfying orisons.   It was our privilege to be present on the occasion of one of these visits,
not very long after he had buried his first companion,
and vividly recalling the fact that not a few of his
former associates had also gone up higher, he was sen-
sibly affected . but not to the extent of hindering the
richest flow of subdued eloquence we ever listened to,
either before or since that time.   This is saying very
much. as we are well aware. for we have heard about
as gifted, and eloquent pulpit orators as this country
has produced, but we cannot alter our estimate notwithstanding all this."

Brother Balch never could preach a written sermon
in what we would call a half decent way, for he wanted
to be allowed to go off in those flights occasionally
that would raise you right off your feet, and he felt
hampered, much as if you had him pinioned in a

straight-jacket. And I think this accounts for the reason of his being sought after to go in every direction, and preach and lecture, and attend funerals and weddings in greatest number. He may be said to have gone almost everywhere, preaching in school-houses, churches, halls and dwellings : in barns and groves and fields ; on the sea and on the land : wherever people could be gathered to hear the word, and be benefited and blessed with the great salvation, ever " ready to give a reason for the hope that was in him, with meekness and fear."

It fell to him to officiate at a great number of funerals, and his consoling words on all such occasions have done not a little in bringing him nearer to the hearts of many persons. It is worthy of mention his being called on one occasion where the husband had committed the dreadful deed of violently killing his wife and then taking his own life. He left his home with no knowledge of the circumstances being related to him, and proceeded on his way till, nearing the place where the funeral was to be attended, the full particulars of the strange event were narrated. He had no time left for any careful preparation to meet the great responsibility that was so suddenly thrust upon him.

As he reached the house a large concourse of horrified people, of all persuasions had gathered, watching, and wondering what disposition was to be made of a case like the one in hand. How was the minister to get along successfully this time without meeting with a terrible discomfiture of his creed ? The calmest one of them all was Mr. Balch, for he knew in whom was his trust. He selected for his text the tenth chapter of Jer-

emiah. and the last clause of the twenty-third verse. "It
is not in man that walketh to direct his steps." We are
left to imagine in part what the discourse was from what
it naturally would be from such a text, and such a
preacher as we have known him to be. Suffice it to
say, he told them what a weak and fallible creature
man was, that there never had been but the one perfect
one. and how we often had to wonder why our lot has
been, to be led in such ways as we are led: that the sins
we all of us actually commit are of a character to demand the utmost of compassion from our fellow-men
as well as from Him who is the God of infinite purity
and perfection.   He instanced Paul in his great sin of
breathing out threatening and slaughter against the
Christians. compelling them to blaspheme, and when
they were put to death giving his voice against them,
and how little he had to do with the being arrested in
his course.   Were it not for the underlying providence
of Him whose thoughts of kindness toward us are infinite, we do not know into what dark paths we might
wander.   It is God's infinite mercy that is holding us,
as it were, every one of us, in the hollow of His hand,
and but for it what wretched creatures we all should
be.   It was true that many of the ways of Providence
were dark and mysterious to us, and the heart grew
weary at times over these vexed problems of life, but
it would seem by reflecting upon the indulgence we desire for our own short-comings we might refrain from
judging others of our brethren too severely; for was it
not enough that all the innocence and peace of the vicious had fled, without their being obliged to endure the
rough censure of those who shared a happier fate?

Why should we not allow our own desires for ourselves to measure to others the debt of love that is due them. Could we not well afford, in our own short-sighted understandings, to leave those who go from us, in the hands of God, in the assurance that He is competent to take care of them, that each going to his proper place, the place that heaven has designed for him, he goes to the best place there is for him? And shall we not rest in the confidence, that

> Blind unbelief is sure to err,
> And scan his work in vain;
> God is His own interpreter,
> And He will make it plain.

It was evident, that when that large audience returned to their homes they found nothing to cavil about. The preacher had won upon the hearts of all, and spoken words that every one felt to respond to.

And so it was always with him. People were greatly interested in his matter and manner. They would go greatest distances to hear him preach one of his commonest sermons, and no one ever heard him once but they were anxious to hear him again and again. They have said to us, that he was the most instructive preacher that ever they heard; that he was always saying something that made it profitable to listen to him, and they did it with the heartiest delight. They will tell you of having met him only once or twice in their lives, and how they were impressed with his wonderful gifts, and the almost exhaustless fountains from which he drew to instruct, and gladden and comfort his auditors. He came to be so widely known at last that he could scarcely go anywhere but he was warmly greeted. It would be impossible to recall the number of times when traveling on cars, and mentioning Elgin, the question would be asked me, "Do you know Brother Balch? He married me, or he attended the funeral of some member of my family, or my father's family." And when I would tell them my long acquaintance, and intimate relations with him, it would be to make answer, " Well, do please give him my best regards." Everywhere it has been our lot to go since entering the Universalist fellowship, eyes have brightened and countenances have lighted up at the mention of his name. Surely, a faithful, unselfish ministry has its compensations.

Well, Brother Balch has gone, and has done his preaching here on the earth. His last sermon was preached in Galesburg, Ill., on the 25th of September, 1887, where he went to attend the wedding of his grand-niece the Thursday before. He was ever faithful as a minister, and could say, as he laid off the harness (only as he never did lay it off), " I have finished my course with joy, and the ministry I have received of the Lord Jesus, to testify the Gospel of the grace of God. I am now ready to be offered, and the time of my departure is at hand. I have fought a good fight; I have finished my course; I have kept the faith; henceforth there is laid up for me a crown of righteousness," conferring upon him the undying honors of the Christian name; enabling him to live in the affections of all good people, with a halo of glory that shall encircle his fame as long as any memory of our cause shall exist or any wholesome, helpful thing shall be done.

CHAPTER IX.

MR. BALCH was of a wonderfully social nature, and always entertaining in conversation. He would in the shortest time attract attention, and gather around him those who were delighted with his instructive communications and charming address. His ready talent made him conspicuous in any community, while his modest simple manner, so earnest and sincere, won our hearts at once, and we felt drawn to him with an unusual degree of affection and the kindest confidence. Being in his social relations without reproach, respected, beloved and honored by all who knew him, without the least effort on his part, or thought of becoming so, he could not help being the center of any circle in which he moved. Amiable in his intercourse with his fellow men; respectful of the rights and feelings of others, and attentive to all who had claims upon him, he stood high as neighbor, citizen, friend and brother; and no one shared in a larger happiness of friends and friendships than did he. None could boast a closer attachment to his kind, and yet he employed no arts for winning their friendship. He always made friends wherever he went, for he could be counted as among the foremost helpers of the world's joys. There was right-heartedness and kindliness of feeling, which served as links of affection and made him regardful of the necessities of friends and foes. He was large-minded, generous and liberal, and believed that pure spiritual friendship, Christian love, was the essential to make society what it should be, as desirable and as happy. It did seem as though he was loving towards every one; and sympathy was about the first and last thing in his character.

There are those who love themselves so inordinately that they have but little regard for those about them; but the whole lead of Brother Balch's religion was in the direction of humanity, for he could not understand how he who "loveth not his brother whom he hath seen, could love God whom he hath not seen." There was thoughtfulness and kind consideration, which made him throw himself heart and soul into the work of instructing, consoling and relieving his fellow creatures of every earthly woe, exerting his utmost effort to help them in all ways, socially, morally and spiritually. All duty with him implied a practical goodness on his part, the neglect of which could not be atoned for by any mere excess of feeling, or show of zeal, or strictness of formal observance. that did not tend to that result; that did not go to increase the sum of blessing, virtue and happiness in the world. It was to him a joy unspeakable to be found among his fellow men, making efforts to reclaim them from their vices; to alleviate as much as possible their sufferings and their sorrows; to enlighten their ignorance, and to raise them up to a virtuous, a holy and happy condition. Whether it be strictly true or not (as some one has remarked) that to be saints we must live among saints, Brother Balch believed it to be true, that to .be men, fully developed, whole Christian men, we must live among men—and there was no good cause engaged in for the furtherance and promotion of truth and righteousness and human happiness in the earth but met with his ready and hearty sympathy, and if anything was to be done, his hearty co-operation. Oh, to have a heart full of love to kindred humanity; to feel for it in its lowest estate; to bend in sympathy with the oppressed, the meanest and humblest child of sorrow; to have a mind eager always to think right concerning the unfortunate of our fellowmen; and a brother's hand to stretch out in mercy, ever ready and desirous to labor for the ignorant and degraded, the suffering and the lost; is a great thing. It constitutes the only true greatness of humanity, and the almost unexampled glory of Christianity. And Brother Balch had this heart in him to sympathize with all suffering ones; to weep with those that weep, and to rejoice with those that rejoice.

We too often narrow down our sympathies to a certain small set of exclusive ideas, but he had a large congeniality with every class of minds, to enroll them within his sympathies, as though born with him, under the same roof, and never thought he was losing an immaculate reputation for character, by practicing the gospel of brotherhood.

We do not think of it enough, that Christianity seeks to establish such a principle of goodness in every individual heart that it shall be ever ready, impelled from no motives from without, but only by the work-

11

ings of a true, loving nature, to seize all the opportunities for doing good that offer themselves daily and
hourly in the experience of every human being. You
may think this not a very important matter, but
human happiness is an aggregate of little satisfactions
and enjoyments, and the good which we can do each
other is the sum of numberless little attentions and
kind offices, which for the very reason that they are
small and common, and frequently called for in the
familiar intercourse of life, are likely to be omitted.
But let no one say that he cannot speak some kind word,
or perform some kind act, which shall find an entrance
into the comfortless heart, and bless him that gives,
and him that takes. He can, if he will, and he certainly
will, if he shall reflect but for a moment on God's
great purpose in sending him into the world.

Being of a warm social nature, Brother Balch took
this practical view of things, regarding everything with
reference to its uses; to the more sensible and wholesome purposes of life. And Christianity found his heart
chiefly, as it gave energy and direction to those principles and affections which render us useful men and
women, sincere friends, earnestly devoted to each
other's welfare.

Many a man goes through the world giving scarcely
one bright, cheerful, encouraging word, taking no pains
to lighten the burdens of any soul, but he sought to
enter into relations of love and good-will with every
one, and it gave him a cheerful welcome in all society.
It was his constant wonder that there should be those
to take so little interest in that which promises to be
of service to the race, and neglect the calls of humanity

in laboring for the good of their fellow-men. He could not see how they could behold all the terrible evils that bind down and destroy the souls and bodies of our kindred, and yet remain indifferent, their hearts unimpressed and they unconscious of the spirit by which they are made to feel it their duty to strive for the blessing of their brethren and their kindred. We think of him with sympaties so true and responsive, with helpfulness so great and charity so broad that we will not allow any other to hold a deeper place in our heart of hearts. His presence was a blessed benediction, and his welcome tread was ever heard where was darkest grief and anguish. Distress never failed to find an answering voice in his heart. Woe enlisted all his feelings, and he ever delighted to assuage human grief. He hushed the sigh of despair in the bosoms of the sorrowful, and gave unto them " beauty for ashes, the oil of joy for mourning, and the garments of praise for the spirit of heaviness." He was ever sought after both far and near in that supremest moment when life had become extinct, or when it was found hanging by a slender thread, showing that the silver cord was to be loosed and golden bowl broken. It may be truly said of him as was said of that singularly upright personage, given us in that partly allegorical story of the life of Job, putting words into his own mouth for him to say them, " When the ear heard me then it blessed me ; and when the eye saw me it gave witness to me, because I delivered the poor that cried, and the fatherless, and him that had none to help him. The blessing of him that was ready to perish came upon me, and I caused the widow's heart to sing for joy. I was eyes to the blind, and feet was I to the lame. I was a father to the poor, and the cause I knew not I searched out."

The heart of Brother Balch was full of pity because he loved, and he loved because underneath all that was dark, and strange and dreadful, he saw that which was to be loved; and notwithstanding the mysteries and shadows, the misfortunes and struggles, the unrequited toils and bitter tears, that make up so much of human life; there was that which was capable of being developed into everlasting good.

And so it was that the orphan found in him a father; the widow and the aged a support, and the stranger a hospitable friend. And the afflicted—he could speak to them in those affectionate terms that temper the bitterness of tears. There are no sufferings which sympathy will not soothe. All the sorrows of life are dissipated by the rays of fraternal love as the frosts of winter are melted by the rising sun of morn.

We cannot better close this chapter than by introducing the very beautiful and appropriate poem of Mrs. Caroline A. Soule, tendered on the occasion of the celebration of the eightieth anniversary of his birthday; and in which she tells how Mr. Balch came to her home shortly after her husband's death, when she knew him only by name, and when her heart was so near to breaking that she could not shed a tear; and what a Godsend it was to her. The title of it was:

A TENDER, REVERENT MEMORY.

REV. WM. S. BALCH.   1852

My life was in its summer time,
  Blossoms over, fruitage rare,
And all the bells did sweetly chime
  Upon the scented, golden air:
Bells of bridal, bells of birth,
  Sweetest bells upon the earth,
And my heart was keeping time,
  To the joy bells' chime !

My life was in its summer time,
  Ripest fruit within my hand,
When suddenly the bells did chime
  Saddest tones in all the land;
Tones of sorrow, tones of death,
  Tones that hushed my joyous breath,
And my heart kept dirge-like time
  To the sad bells' chime !

Then quickly came the winter time
  With its storms and snow;
And all the bells did sadly chime,
  In tones of weary woe;
Bells of dying, bells of biers,
  Saddest bells to loving ears,
And my heart was keeping time
  To the death bells' chime !

Tears I could not shed, O no,
  All too sudden was the woe !
Like a frost in June it fell,
  The wild ringing of that bell !
All my life seemed gone and dead,
  Buried in that cold, white bed.
All my summers seemed now spent,
  Why, O why, was death thus sent ?

To my home a friend then came,
  One I only knew by name ;
He had loved the one now sleeping,
  And for him was softly weeping ;
Now he came and sat by me,
  Took my children on his knee,
Whispered words that seemed a prayer,
  As they thrilled the saddened air !

And from out the winter skies
  Something seemed to fall on me.
Something touched my burning eyes
  Till the tears flowed soft and free ;
O those tears ! They washed away
  The stern sorrow of that day !
O those tears ! They made me whole,
  Healed my broken, widowed soul !

Still he to the children spoke,
  Words of praise and words of prayer,
Till the mother in me woke
  And I took the cross of care ;
Took it with a reverent hand,
  Saddest mother in the land,
And I said, amidst my tears,
  " They will brighten future years."

Still he held the children dear,
  Still he spoke in sweet, low tone;
And from out my heart stole fear,
  And I felt no more alone,
" These my comforts now will be !
  O my Father, I thank Thee
That I have this cross of care ;
  All I ask is strength to bear;
Strength to bear all thou dost send,
  Strength to bear unto the end ! "

Years have come, and years have fled,
  Since I mourned the early dead,
Since that friend came there to me,
  Took my children on his knee,
And such words of comfort spoke
  That the mother in me woke,
That the sorrow grew so still
  I was strong to do God's will !

Precious friend ! In all this land
  Lives no dearer one to me,
And I give you heart and hand
  In tender, reverent memory !
In memory of the day you came,
  When I only knew your name;
Came unto my house of woe,
  Came amidst the drifting snow,
Took my children on your knee,
  Whispered words that strenghened me,
Words of comfort, words of prayer,
  Words that thrilled like music rare !

I see you now, my friend so dear,
  See you 'midst a falling tear,
Little children on your knee !
  Sweet, O sweet this memory !
It will ever stay with me—
  A tender, reverent memory !

That Mrs. Soule could say this of him is no small
praise. And who shall claim that it was not all merited ?

CHAPTER X.

For so easy and voluminous a writer as Mr. Balch it can not be claimed for him that the number of his published sermons was great. His thought was never to get himself noticed by parading himself or any effort of his, before the public, and preaching extemporaneously, with fewer reporters in earlier days, his sermons were not made ready for the hands of the printer. He wrote more as duty seemed to impel, or admonish him to do so : and hence what he wrote was generally of a somewhat grave and consequential character. Among the most notable of his sermons, are : "Universalism : Its Rise and Progress in this Country; What It Has Done, and Is Doing to Liberalize the World." "What Jesus Taught"; "What of the Future Life"; "Are there Creeds and Sects in Heaven?" "Forty Years in the Ministry"; "The Pastor's Duty"; "Brotherly Admonition." "A Sermon for Professed Christians."

Most of the texts are quite suggestive. "Forty Years in the Ministry," the text is, "And thou shalt remember all the way which the Lord thy God led thee these forty years in the wilderness, to humble thee, and prove thee; to know what is in thy heart, whether thou wouldst keep his commandments or no."

164

From three or four of them I am selecting the
most important parts, which is nearly equivalent to
giving the substance of them.

The first of the above mentioned, preached before
the Illinois State Convention in the last years of 70,
has this text, "Everyone that hath this hope in him
purifieth himself even as he (Jesus) is pure." He starts
out with a statement as to what Universalism is:

"The most distinct and common idea of Universalism
is a belief in the final salvation of all men. This def-
inition is correct, if it be understood to include all the
means by which that most desirable end is to be attained. None but those who would purposely mis-
represent, would for a moment think any reasonable
men would assert or entertain a thought that such a
result could be attained without the adequate means
and methods to produce it. Universalists accept and
emphatically assert the fact that, "without holiness no
man shall see the Lord." They know that sin involves
punishment, and they believe that so long as sin exists
punishment will, of necessity, be inflicted; that only
where "sin is finished, transgression ended and everlasting righteousness brought in" will sin and sorrow
cease and the world be saved. They believe God desired, purposed, planned, willed such a result, and sanctified and sent his Son into the world not to condemn
it, but to save it; that he gave him all power in heaven
and on earth adequate to finish that work and be for
salvation to the ends of the earth; that he shall see of
the travail of his soul and be satisfied; destroy death
and him that had the power of death and deliver all
who through fear of death were subject to bondage;
will draw all men unto himself and deliver the kingdom to the Father, who subjected all things unto him,
that God may be all in all.

"That a great change has taken place in the doctrines, principles, feeling and practices in most churches within a century, every observer must admit. Doctrines which were thought permanent, fundamental, essential to salvation, have been loosened, are tottering and fast crumbling away; and broader, better and more rational and consistent principles are being substituted in their stead. As yet the fullness of these changes are not clearly manifest; but enough is known to sustain the position that I take in claiming for those called Universalists a large share, under God, in this great and glorious work. We have but to ask a contrast of the opinions, feelings, and more Christian and fraternal conduct of the present, with the past of a hundred or fifty years ago, to make plain what I assume in our own behalf.

"But the question I propose to discuss is: Has the advocacy of Universalism done any good in the world, or has it been an injury?

"This question cannot be answered correctly without ascertaining what it has done, and what it proposes to do. This information I shall not be able to give you in its fullness, in a single discourse. But I may be able to indicate some facts which will help the thoughtful to a clearer apprehension of what is embraced as essential principles in the formation of a true Christian character, and obtainment of a good hope.

" Although Universalism was hotly opposed and wickedly misrepresented, it advanced with astonishing rapidity and made many conquests. But its growth and extension can not be determined by its numbers and outside showing, as with the Methodists and other sects. Its chief work is in the mind, in the heart, warming and expanding the affections, liberalizing the views, inspiring confidence and hope in God, and, by gradual growth, enlarging the sphere of action, reconciling differences, and making paramount the love of God and man over all minor considerations. This has been the field of its chief operations. The improved feeling

of the churches, the more fraternal greetings among
professors ; the more united efforts to reform and save
the world from vices and miseries; the brighter hopes ;
the firmer faith; the kindlier feeling among all the people,
testify, in part, the great value of the universal principles we have preached, and to some extent practiced,
in our day and generation.

" The products of these labors have not ripened into
a full harvest. Prejudices still exist and selfishness
prevents the free extension of universal love in complete reconciliation to God, and peace and good will
among men. It is impossible, therefore, to calculate
what the harvest shall be in coming years—in quantity;
it is plain what it must be in kind, for love works no
ill, but seeks the good, the happiness, the salvation of all.

" We confess our work is but begun, and so far very
imperfectly done. We are in the world of human
influences and aspirations, too much controlled by its
forms and fashions, errors, and too ready to adopt the
machinery invented by men to carry on the work of
God. We do not appreciate enough our opportunities,
feel our personal responsibilities, and employ the means
at our command to enrich our souls in the love and
knowledge of God, in studying his laws as unfolded to
the thoughtful and devout in every department of his
government. We do not learn of Jesus the lessons of
true living and loving; how to possess our vessels in
honor and secure the blessings promised to reward the
well doers. The world and its fashions have a too
powerful control over us, making slaves where there
should be freemen, and keeping us back from the kingdom we seek and hope to find. Universalists must
assert their freedom from such control, and walk in the
light of their faith and hope, before they can demonstrate the great value of the principles they profess
and enter into the full enjoyment of the great salvation.

" Some may demand a more distinct statement of the

changes wrought by the ministry of Universalism,
that a more correct estimate may be set upon the value
of its labors. I will answer briefly as I can such
demand:

"1. Universalism has taught, and pretty thoroughly
established the doctrine that God is the father of all
men;

"2. The acceptance of the Universal Fatherhood of
God necessarily compelled the admission that all men
are brethren and under mutual obligations to love one
another.

"3. The relation of God to man, as revealed through
Jesus Christ, in the plan of salvation was clearly and
rationally made to consist in repentance— a complete
forsaking of sin, ceasing to do evil and learning to do
well; reconciliation to God; purity of heart and life.
and love and good-will to all men.

" Universalists, who are true to their principles, must
be among the best. the truest of men. and always strive
to be better still. ever reaching forward, and aspiring
towards the absolute and eternal good, and always
studious to adorn the doctrines of God our Saviour by
well ordered lives and a godly conversation, always
confiding in God their heavenly Father, and ever preparing to meet and live with the pure, the good, the
holy, and all kindred, in realms of light and love immortal.

" What is grander, nobler. more worthy of God, more
honorable to Jesus, or more desired by good men of all
names than the salvation of all men from sin, ignorance
and error, their purity, holiness and happiness in the
immortal life brought to light in the Gospel?"

This doctrine of the impartial benevolence of God,
is of all others the most favorable to the growth of
charitable and benevolent feelings. And the heart
that cherishes it sincerely, is a most fit and prolific soil
whence all   the noblest aspirations of the soul
spring spontaneously and abundantly, for it directs us

to copy the example of the merciful Father of mankind, who "causes His sun to rise on the evil and the
good, and sends his rain upon the just and the unjust."
It bids us cherish kind and benevolent dispositions toward the unthankful and the evil, and to do good to
all men as we are afforded the opportunity.

The Universalist is the one who has the principle
of universal love dwelling richly in him, so that he
loves all men, deals justly with all, acts mercifully toward all, lives peaceably with all, and hates and injures
none. In what a glorious condition would the world
be, if all could accept these views, not professedly, but
genuinely and practically. Strange that any rational
being should fear to have such sentiments prevail far
and wide till all shall embrace them, and obey their
heavenly and benign influence, and be governed by
universal and impartial love. If to believe that God is
our friend; that he is ever watchful over our lives, and
our happiness, making all the purposes of his moral
government work together for our good; if this is calculated to weaken the ties of virtue, then is the religion
of Jesus a failure. But how can this be, if "love is the
fulfilling of the law," or the goodness of God is what
leads to repentance? No—"He that hath this hope in
him purifieth himself, even as he is pure."

"THE PASTOR'S DUTY,"

is a plain lesson to Pastors of which I may give text,
and somewhat liberal extracts:

" Preach the word; be instant in season, out of season; reprove,
rebuke, exhort, with all long suffering and doctrine.
II. Tim. iv.: 2.

" By the *word* which Timothy is charged to preach
is signified, very evidently, the doctrine of the gospel.
It is so used in numerous cases. 'Receive with meekness the ingrafted *word*, which is able to save your
souls' (James i.: 21).

"To you is the *word* of this salvation sent (Acts xiii.: 27). Hence the phrases *word of life, the word of the gospel*, &c. In its extended sense, it is applied to the whole revelation of God, including the scriptures of the Old and New Testaments.

"The whole object of preaching is to make people better, more honest in their dealings, more virtuous in their conduct, more affectionate in their families, more peaceable in society, more humble and sincere in their devotions to God, and more engaged in the service and duties of religion. Particular doctrines are good for nothing, any further than they have a tendency to produce these effects. That doctrine is best which has the most wholesome influence upon the moral health and prosperity of the community.

"In preaching the *word* the minister of glad tidings, must take a bold and independent stand, and clearly state, and fearlessly defend those sentiments, which, in his opinion, derive support from the oracles of truth, and, in their operations, are calculated to promote the happiness of all who receive them.

"The natural tendency of the gospel is to produce great joy, peace and good-will among men. Hence it is evident that a doctrine which creates divisions in families, in churches, and in society, animosity among brethren, ill-will towards one another, cannot be the true doctrine. A pure fountain doth not send forth bitter water; neither doth a good tree bring forth evil fruit.

"When called to sympathize with the afflicted, he must preach the *word* with all that energy necessary to produce reverence in the bereaved, by teaching them humility and submission to the wise providence of God. There is nothing more admirably adapted to its end than the Gospel to meet the wants of mankind. It reveals every dark mystery, in the order of divine government, and unfolds the reason of human suffering. It assures us, beyond a doubt, that *good* is the leading object in all the works of God. Its language is, " Though grief may endure for a night yet joy cometh in the morning; that our light afflictions which are but for a moment shall work out for us a far more exceeding and eternal weight of glory; that though no chastening for the present seemeth joyous but grievous nevertheless, afterwards, it yieldeth the peaceable fruits of righteousness unto them that are exercised thereby." Especially when the mind is distressed with the cares and perplexities of life, or is wearied with over-much sorrow, the Gospel imparts its benign influence, which entirely dissipates the gathering gloom which seemed to threaten an overthrow of all earthly felicity. It whispers peace to the returning penitent under the assurance of forgiven sins. It breathes comfort to the mourner under a hope in a resurrection from the dead, and a re-union of souls in a state of immortal beatitude. Though it denounces the sorest punishment against all transgressions, it does not force the sinner to despair, by annihilating all hope of acceptance with God ; but it proclaims the simple method of salvation—by ceasing to do evil and learning to do well; by dealing justly, loving mercy and walking humbly with God : by doing unto others as we wish others to do unto us. How simple are its requirements, and yet how rich its reward ! Strange that any should attempt to walk by the wisdom of this world, when that which is from above is far more simple.

" Not only is the faithful minister called to preach the word at stated times, but he is also commanded to be 'instant in season, and out of season.' On all fit occasions he should strive to convince sinners of the error of their ways, and instil into their minds those sublime sentiments which naturally inspire the soul with ardent love to God, and subdue the unhallowed affections of the heart. The awful consequences of sin — the loss of character, the bitterness of spirit, the anguish of mind, and all the ten-thousand miseries it

brings upon its deluded votaries—should be portrayed
in living colors before them. He should cause them
to contrast the peaceable fruits of righteousness with
the unavoidable consequences of transgression, and
see how that by well-doing we shall be happy, and
by a neglect of duty we must be miserable."

"Let sinners know the advantages of a well-ordered
life, and they will sin no more. Let mourners feel
the comforts of the Gospel, and they will mourn no
more.

"These are duties, which, being productive of the
happiest consequences, may be pleasurable to the
preacher, and gratifying to the hearer, and increase
a mutual attachment between both. But there are
other duties inculcated in the text, which, though
more unpleasant, are not less important. To them
the faithful minister in the discharge of his holy calling, must also give attention. Paul not only charges
Timothy to preach the word in season and out of
season, but also to *reprove and rebuke.*

"These terms convey nearly the same ideas. Taken
in connection they carry with them a force not easily
resisted. They refer not only to the moral conduct
of the professor, but also to his belief. Paul so uses
them in his letter to Titus. Speaking of the Cretians
he says, 'Rebuke them sharply that they may be
sound in the faith.'

"The effectual preacher must at all times act for
the good of them to whom he preaches.

"He should adopt a course which to him appears
most consistent and best calculated to gain the object
in view, to wit: the glory of God in the salvation of
sinners. Wherever he discovers vice with all its attend-
ant enormities stalking abroad amongst men, he must
declaim against it with all the eloquence he can command. He must denounce iniquity of every kind, under
every circumstance without fear or favor.

"Sin is his antagonist, against which he must fearlessly contend, and wherever he finds it encamped, among the high or the low, the rich or the poor, the honored or despised, there he must bring his whole artillery to bear, nor cease the warfare, till he has demolished its strongholds, completely routed this enemy of all happiness, and forced it to retreat in deep disgrace to the abodes of dark oblivion whence it came. He must know no distinctions save between virtue and vice. Like an ancient prophet he must 'cry aloud and spare not, but lift up his voice like a trumpet and show the people their transgressions, and the house of Jacob their sins.'

"Not only must he oppose sin as a common enemy, but in contending ' earnestly for the faith once delivered to the saints,' he must *reprove and rebuke* those errors and false doctrines which reflect dishonor on God and promote misery among men. With them he must have no fellowship.

"All these reproofs, rebukes, and exortations should be made with all *long suffering and doctrine*. Charity suffereth long and is kind. Therefore *charity* should be the reigning principle, and leading impulse to the fulfillment of all these duties, and when compelled to specify the errors, or correct the faults of others, it should be done in the spirit of mildness, meekness, charity, with a view to reform and bring about the greatest good of those concerned. Every thing should be done in a plain, simple and unostentious manner, so that all may comprehend the length and breadth, the height and depth of all that is said. Mystery belongs not to the Gospel, nor dark sayings to the preacher of it."

WHAT OF THE FUTURE LIFE?

A SERMON PREACHED IN ELGIN, ILL., DECEMBER 10, 1871, AND PUBLISHED IN THE UNIVERSALIST BY SPECIAL REQUEST.

Then shall I know even as also I am known.—I. Cor. xiii: 12.

"From the connection we learn that St. Paul refers this language to a future life. He contrasts the highest
12

attainments here with the perfections of the blessed hereafter. In his best estate he confessed his imperfectness; that he had not apprehended all truth, nor reached the perfection to which he aspired; that the best gifts should cease and knowledge vanish away; that we know in part, and prophesy in part, but *when* that which is perfect is come, *then* that which is in part shall be done away. He then compares the progress of the soul to growth from childhood to manhood; for '*now* we see through a glass darkly, but *then* face to face; *now* I know in part, but *then* shall I know even as also I am known.'

"Man's future and final destiny is a matter of deep and solemn concern to all of us. We are conscious of our mortality. Death's doings are all about us. No thoughtful person doubts, for a moment, the fact that earth is not his home. He confesses that he cannot long inhabit this tabernacle made with hands. He knows that he must soon pass through the valley and shadow of death, and enter upon the realities of the great unknown:—if there be for him any realities beyond this present time, that *if*, he would have explained and removed if possible. It is that which perplexes and troubles him. His doubts congeal about it, his hopes are clouded and his heart is sad.

Is there no light to shine on this darkness? No voice to speak to us and break the awful silence?

What is revealed of that immortal life? What makes it an object of strong desire, of ardent hope? What is seen, in the clear light of Jesus' resurrection from the dead, which a rational faith can accept and hope lay hold upon? What does the voice utter which speaks from the sullen darkness, from the silence and mystery of the Spirit Land, entrancing by its sweetness, and ravishing with its exquisite harmony, which vibrates with the purest and holiest and noblest desires of the human heart?

In sober earnest, what convictions what affections,

what ideas, what hopes, what conditions do we associate with a future life, as brought to light in the Gospel?
Is it the paradise of the heathen, where human passions
still live, and hatred is not forgotten? Where the odious
distinctions of this life are magnified into infinite differences? Where ambition climbs, selfishness predomi-
nates, pretention triumphs, and honesty and humanity
aud virtue toil in vain? Is it the Indian heaven, where
indulgence comes to all earth desired, and the strifes of
time are triumphs for eternity? Are our ideas, our
hopes of the better land crudely formed, tinged with
the remembrance of the ills, the wrongs and sorrows
of the present life? Or are they based upon a radical
change in man's moral nature by a transition so sudden
and complete that no recognition of the past, of which
we have been, will remain?

Two doctrines have been preached as parts of
Christianity which seem to me radically wrong. Both
maintain that there will be a sudden and complete
change at death, by the act of God, which will entirely
disrupt and destroy the *moral* order and responsibility
of the present life. One teaches that, for other considerations than moral goodness or even love of God,
the souls of the elect and favored which have accepted
certain dogmas, obeyed certain authorities, once performed prescribed duties which are not necessarily connected with moral feeling or right conduct, will never
be punished for their sins, but will certainly obtain the
reward of immortal blessedness; while others, morally
more honest, more sincere, more benevolent, more
generous, more trustworthy—in everything better for
the domestic, social, intellectual and political welfare
of themselves and fellowmen, and even more sincere
and devout in their thoughts and feelings towards the
God and Father of all, and more in union, love and forbearance towards mankind, shall never be rewarded
for their good deeds, but are rejected, shut out of
heaven, cast down to hell, and be made miserable for-

ever. Read the history of the church in proof of this.
What else divides the sects of to-day?

The other teaches that no memory of the present
moral and social life and character will remain, but
man will become a new creation in all the attributes
of his being, retaining nothing of what he has been
and done. To me this is virtual annihilation. What
is a future life to *me* if no consciousness of *myself* remains? The lamp of this life may as well be extinguished at once and forever. There is for *me* no immortality. The particles of this body may molder,
separate and mingle with their primordial dust and be
absorbed into vegetables — a plant. a shrub, or tree,
and be as much in my body, as that the mind, its properties and principles, may be constructed into a being
unconscious of what I have been and done, no matter
how ethereal, pure, and angelic; it will be nothing to
me, with the ME left out. This at most is no more than
transmigration, after the heathen notion. Does Christianity present no surer hope, no sweeter comfort than
this? It is then of little worth as a comforter in sorrow, and illy sustains the spirit and promises of its
Founder.

Little is said, I admit, by Jesus or His apostles, about
the precise conditions of a future life. But much may
be learned from what is said, and inferred from what is
not said, which accords with the purest desires, the
soundest reason, and the best philosophy, viz. : that each
person will exist in his own proper identity and "know
as even also he is known." Jesus says, "In my Father's house are many mansions; if it were *not* so, I
would have told you. I go to prepare a place for you,
that where I am there ye may be also." Much is to be
learned from what is *not* said, to contradict what lives
spontaneously in the heart and is essential to its existence and happiness. It being already there, it only
needs proper culture to secure for it all that can be
enjoyed. Jesus came into the world for that purpose,

not to create, but to "bear witness to the truth," that we might have life, and have it more abundantly, and be comforted with the full assurance of hope, that where He is there we may be also.

Every promise is made to man *personally*, and every blessing is bestowed on individual ability to accept and enjoy. God deals with us morally, not in the aggregate, but as persons. To him we are held primarily, directly and personally responsible to answer for ourselves and not for others, except in our social capacity. And it seems to me a plain, necessary and most valuable truth, that we shall all remain the same identical beings in the future life that we are in this. As much as the youth was the child, and the man the youth, we there shall advance upon what we were here, retaining the several links which connect our earliest consciousness with an endless chain of being. I can think of immortality in no other way.

Life is a progress, a growth, a succession or accumulation of ideas, facts, feelings, enjoyments. These become real, what they should be, as we advance from the gross to the refined, from the material to the spiritual, from the mortal to the immortal, from the human to the divine. Through these preparatory steps we are, like children, growing into our real manhood, rising out of our low, imperfect state, and maturing for eternity, advancing towards the perfection and glory of the Infinite Father, where, "face to face, we shall know even as also we are known."

This answers the objection which perplexes some minds, that if we retain our personal identity and a consciousness of all we have been and done, we shall be made miserable by a review of our conduct and character in the light of God. Why so? No more than manhood is troubled by the memories of youth, or childhood by the foibles of infancy. On the contrary, the Gospel plan is founded upon the wisdom and goodness of God in saving from imperfection, sin and death. "The creature was made subject to vanity by reason of Him who hath subjected the same in hope." Our sweetest joys are kindled by the love of God in the forgiveness of our sins and gift of eternal life. "The wages of sin is death, but the gift of God is eternal life." Did not the Prodigal love as never before when freely and lovingly embraced by his Father? Remember Jesus' words, as He sat in the house of Simon, who disapproved the loving and grateful deed of one who had been wicked; but the odor of her pious offering filled all the house. I once witnessed a recognition of two old men who had parted in bitter anger many years before,

"Nursing their wrath to keep it warm,"

for a long time. Long years had passed; better principles had prevailed. They met and embraced. They recounted many scenes and events, away back to their youthful days; but neither alluded to difficulties which had parted them. The spirit of forgiveness was in both their hearts. Goodness had prevailed. The love of God had weaned them from sin and selfishness, and reconciled them to truth and right, and to God. They had repented, and they loved as sincerely as if never deceived by error or cheated by selfishness—as if they had never hated. An angel's presence was there; and there was joy in heaven. Immortal bliss is not made up of self gratulations, in boasting of what *we have done.* Jesus has some claim, and God deserves some praise. "Not unto us, but unto thy name be all the glory." "They sing the song of redeeming grace—of Moses and the Lamb," but give to God the glory. There we shall look upon the past, upon all life's thoughts, feelings and desires, not in the light of pride and self-interest as now, but in the light of God's love and truth, and grace; for we shall "know even as also we are known."

One fact more seems properly connected with our

subject, the recognition of friends in the future life. This follows of necessity from the premises accepted as true. It shall be no more difficult to recognize those we know in *part* and love, than to know ourselves in the spirit world. Wakened from the slumbers of degradation in ignorance and vice—a moral death—and transported to the home of purity, wisdom and elegant refinement, one would sooner recognize himself by the presence of friends than by a view of himself in conditions so changed, and so utterly unknown and unthought of. And then what would heaven be without a friend? How dreary! how sad! how unbearable! We can scarcely endure the loneliness of short separations in this life from those we love. What must heaven be with an eternal separation? What a sadness mingles with our joys in every scene of life when the heart is bereft of the affection of those we love to have near us. The finest views in nature, the grandest works of art, the most splendid representations of talent are doubly enhanced by their presence, and half the joy is lost when they are not with us to be happy also.

We are sometimes told by stoic theorists that we must not think of earthly friendships, the ties of love when contemplating the future state, the glories of heaven—everything will be so changed there—we must be willing to surrender our dearest kindred with unconcern for their welfare, when entered into the bliss of heaven, be willing to know they are lost—to be miserable infinitely and forever. What a doctrine to be baptized in the name of Christ? Think of heaven and hope for it without friends! Immortal blessedness without love! Impossible! There is no heaven where they are not. There can be none. Souls that hate are miserable. Bereft of those we love we can not be happy. I knew a mother once who was so utterly miserable at the death of her little child, that she caused its cold body to be dug twice from its grave

that she might embrace it and wail over it, for she believed God had no mercy on it. She afterward became
insane. Do you wonder?

How different the prospect to those who accept the
testimony of God's love and truth as revealed in the
heart and in the Word; who believe in the fulfillment
of his promises, the execution of his plan of grace—
salvation from sin, ignorance and death; that death
shall be swallowed up in victory, and there shall be no
more death, sorrow, nor crying, nor any more pain;
but former things be passed away, and all things be
made new—all things be of God, that God may be all
in all!

*   *   *   *   *   *   *

I have failed to mention an

OCCASIONAL SERMON.

DELIVERED BEFORE THE ILLINOIS UNIVERSALIST STATE CONVENTION
IN ELGIN, OCTOBER 20, 1868.

What shall we do that we may work the works of God.—
JOHN vi: 28.

There is an intimate connection between God and
all good works. He reigns everywhere. His laws are
permanent and universal. They are established in wisdom for the good of all men. He is good—nothing
evil can come from Him. He is perfect—He can never
change. He is almighty—none can escape His judgments. He rewards the righteous, the well-doers,
sends blessings upon all who remember His commandments to do them. He punishes the wicked, all evil-
doers, who live not according to His laws in the conditions of their being. He renders to every man according to his works. In every nation, he that fears Him
and works righteousness, is accepted of Him, while in
the nature of things, the way of the transgressor is
hard, and there is no peace to the wicked. Nothing is
plainer in revelation, philosophy and fact, and nothing

is safer as a foundation of moral action in the social relations of life.

Theories have been devised, altered, changed, reconstructed; rules have been decreed; rewards have been offered; punishments have been inflicted and severer ones threatened, yet the world has not worked the work of God, and has but slowly improved—some say not at all—in the great chief work of moral progress and personal perfection.

There is little cause for marvel why so many serious, thoughtful, honest, philanthropic, excellent people stray outside the pale of religious organizations, seeming to avoid the direct work of God, while they really love the principles of Christianity, and devoutly desire their universal prevalence. They do not see exemplified in the methods of sectarian work, the wisdom, spirit and moral excellence; the breadth and power and purity they have found in the Gospel, and felt to be, in some degree, in their own hearts. They do not find a witness to correspond with the narrow and selfish devices, the proud ambition, the bigoted adhesion to names, sects, and parties which have characterized the history of the church. They look into the humanities — the charities and benevolent workings outside the churches, and find moral reforms going on successfully, though neglected, and often frowned upon by professed Christians, and actually doing more good for the race, and approaching nearer to their convictions of what is the work of God. They ask, " Why are the churches so bound up in their own aggrandizement — building and adorning splendid structures for the rich and fashionable, sustaining arrogant and exclusive ministries, gathering in large revenues for sectarian colleges, publications, and missionaries; remodeling, patching, repairing and interpreting old, worn, torn, shattered, threadbare, rotten, dogmatic creeds, fit only for the moles and the bats while all around vice festers, dishonesty thrives, drunkenness revels, crime increases, industry struggles, fashion flouts insult in the face of honesty; good men suffer; pure men are disowned; sin luxuriates, and the poor perish without the Gospel?"

Who will answer them? Who will tell the reason of this long delay, of this weary wandering to find a way to the high altar of true worship and the work of God? Or, is it so, that Christianity is to remain an everlasting puzzle, and the work of God an involved problem for quacks to experiment on, philosophers to gaze at, sectarists to quarrel over, enthusiasts to talk about, and good men and honest to attempt in vain? It cannot be. There must be some solution of the difficulty — some way out of this wilderness — some highway of holiness for the humble seeker after truth; the follower after righteousness; for the honest, the faithful and the good — the true light that is to enlighten every man, and guide to the open entrance into the kingdom of God, which Jesus came to establish on earth. Let us seek that way in the light of God. It may be His good Spirit will help our infirmities and guide us right, that we may walk in the way, know the truth, enjoy the life, and work the work of God.

Jesus answers the question in our text by saying to those who put it: "This is the work of God, that ye believe on him whom he hath sent."

Faith is the true basis of all right work. Without it no man can work the work of God. Men do not work earnestly, heartily, cheerfully, in anything where they feel no desire, expect no good, take no interest, see no success, and have no faith. They must not only desire to have, but they must believe, to possess and enjoy, and then they will work for it. The heart of the soldier is roused to deeds of noble daring, and his arm is made strong in battle so long as victory is before him. Destroy his faith and he is powerless. The farmer will not sow where he sees no harvest. The mechanic will not ply his tools where he expects no rec-

ompense. The merchant carries on his traffic in kind
when he believes it will be most remunerative. The
fortune seeker hunts for gold in the mountains, and
digs where he believes it may be found. The speculator invests in lands, stocks and rents, where he thinks
to realize the largest profits. Fast men add excitement
to risk and expect gain at the stakes of the race or the
gaming table. The politician believes there is for him,
or his friends or party, a place of honor, profit or
power, and he buckles close his armor for the fray.

No man works without a motive, an object, an end.
That is always before him—a thing of faith. Where
he sees, or thinks he sees a way open, he pursues it.
Sometimes his vision is dim, and it is very dark, and
he stumbles and fails for lack of sight, which faith
alone supplies. Often false lights are held out by the
designing, who would decoy him into false channels
and make him a wreck for their own gain. More frequently he is deceived by his own selfishness—drawn
away of his own lust and enticed, and in making haste
to be rich or to enjoy, he fails of the real good desired.
Sometimes men become so fallen, so lost, so bereft of
their manhood and reason, that they act not from any
distinct motive ; have no fixed purpose, no settled desire, but are propelled by forces and outside pressure ;
driven by necessity, chased by a hated " creature of
circumstance."

Now as faith is the basis of all work, the work will be
in kind and character like the faith which produces it ;
just as certainly as the effect will be like the cause, the
stream like the fountain, or the fruit like the tree.
There is a natural and inseparable unity between the
two that makes both one, so that works can not exist
without faith, and faith is dead without works. It
can not live, being alone, any more than the body can
survive the departure of the spirit. Both must live
together, and dwell in harmony. Faith must precede
work, and work must correspond with, or be the ex-

pression of faith. Each plays, in turn, upon the other.
Together they constitute the real man.

There is no light, no life, no love, no soundness, no
joy, where faith is not. The difficulty under which the
world labors is the weakness, the imperfection or the
error of faith. Of them it can not be said, in any final
sense, that they worked the works of God.

The people, as in our day, were expecting a brighter
light to arise, a clearer revelation to be made, a mightier
power to be given for the guide of life. None were
satisfied with what they had, with what they knew,
with what they believed, with what they enjoyed. All
had higher ideals and nobler aspirations. They were
looking, they were waiting, they were praying, as millions of souls are praying to-day, all over the world, for
God to bring a true witness, a living light, a full conviction, a joyous hope, a great deliverance, a peaceful
rest, "the desire of all nations."

Jesus came. He began His work—the great refor-
mation, the salvation of the world. Multitudes were
drawn to Him. They looked, they heard, they thought,
but as yet they did not *believe* and *feel*. His first works
done in humility, His first words spoken in simplicity,
all pertaining to daily life and duty, surprised, but did
not satisfy them. They saw the blessings multipled
for them : they ate, but did not believe. They had no
clear conviction of the great purpose of His mission.
They comprehended not the lessons He gave them.
Their thoughts grasped not the idea of spiritual life, of
moral power, the kingdom of heaven in earth, the reign
of God in the affections, Christ formed in them the
hope of glory and destined to universal dominion.

They asked seriously, and earnestly, no doubt, "What
shall we do to work the works of God." He answers
promptly, and plainly, that the first great act, the
preparation for all true work, is to believe on Him
whom God had sent to teach and guide, and bless, and
save the world.

This first act, the basis of all the rest in the Christian life and work, is to believe in Jesus Christ as the appointed teacher of God, duly qualified and commissioned to save the world.   On this depends everything else pertaining to the Gospel scheme of redemption; to deny this is to reject the whole.

Had Christians always heeded the instructions, obeyed the precepts, imbibed the spirit, felt the humility, followed the example of Jesus, as one in whom they believed, in whom they had full confidence as Teacher, Guide and Savior, the Way, the Truth, and the Life His church would not now be rent and wrangling in a thousand sects, in bitter enmity, in hostile array, selfish, proud, arrogant, covetous, domineering.

The history of the church is a striking proof of its want of faith in Jesus Christ.   Almost every other means but that revealed by Him, have been employed to promote its prosperity and gain for it prominence and power.   The wisdom of the world, the artifices of crafty and designing men, the abuse of confidence, privilege and powers have been preferred to the "wisdom that is from above, which is pure, peaceable, gentle, easy to be entreated, full of mercy and good fruits without partiality and without hypocrisy."   Honesty, justice, loving-kindness, good-will among men, personal holiness, universal love, justice and right do not stand prominent on its records meddling with the affairs of state, the rights of conscience, the liberties of the people, to control, oppress and alienate by keeping in ignorance the masses of men.

Who that has read ecclesiastical history, or observed the proceedings of the churches, so narrow, exclusive, sectarian, can wonder that so many of the best men, profoundest thinkers, truest philosophers, wisest statesmen, noblest philanthropists—*real Christians*—have hesitated and refused to be numbered with believers, though they have worked the work of God, loved and labored for the good of mankind?

"Jesus revealed a system of religion, true in its doctrines, practical in its spirit, and every way adapted to the conditions and sufficient for the wants of all men, in all time. The human mind can conceive of none grander; logicians can prove none truer; the human heart can desire none better. It is sufficient to all things, having promise of the life that now is, and that which is to come. The wisdom of the world has contrived nothing to excel or equal it. The skill and learning of none have been able to improve or destroy it. It is now the same it was from the beginning—pure, truthful, sufficient, glorious. Like the diamond neglected, lost, buried beneath the accumulation of errors and wrongs of ages, when dug out and the rubbish is all cleared away, it is found to possess its primitive brilliancy and value. It is beautiful in every setting. It is the adornment alike of kings on their thrones, prisoners in their cells, beggars in the streets, statesmen in council, toilers in the fields of industry, humanity struggling everywhere. It is the brightest light of science, the profoundest axiom of philosophy, the sweetest charm of poetry, the truest friend, the safest counsellor, the crown of life, the hope, comfort and joy of the dying. It is truth, light, life, victory, immortality. It is the wisdom of God, and the power of God. Jesus taught it, lived it, embodied it.

"They do not accept Christianity as an institution of God, established for the moral government of responsible beings. They tell us it has been tried and failed; forgetting to distinguish its true principles from the gross and monstrous corruptions and errors which have been surreptitiously fastened upon it by the pride and ambition of wicked and ignorant men. They judge it in the disguises of worldly wisdom and power, where it has been foisted into high places of authority and splendor, and not as it is in fact among the humble, in the homes of the lowly. "The pure in heart see God." Jesus rules his kingdom by the moral law. He accepts not the cunning strategy of ambitious managers, the formal ceremonies of pretentious priests, the revered superstitions of ignorant enthusiasts, in the place of honest, earnest and intelligent devotion to truth, to virtue and to God. He promised, and he sent the Holy Spirit to guide his followers into all truth. As many as are led by the Spirit of God, they are the sons of God.

" Ours, my brethren, is a special work, for we live in a wonderful age.

" It is not ours to rebuild, patch, or prop the old ; but to use whatever is found sound and suitable in the construction of the new.

" We need organization—thorough, compact, voluntary. Now work means more than organization, it means that and more too. We include victory and the fruits of victory—the arts of peace. Others labored and we have entered into their labors. We are to carry forward the work and help finish what they so well began. We are to cultivate the fields their valor won.

" Ours is the ministry of reconciliation. We are ambassadors for Christ. In his name—in the faith, spirit and power of his religion, we persuade men to be reconciled to God. We are called to work the work of God—not of man, nor by man—to seek and to save them that are lost; to restore them to the fold of God, in the faith and love of Jesus Christ, that there may be one fold and one shepherd.

" Our first chief work is with our own hearts and lives, that our affections, our wills, our whole souls be deeply imbued with the Holy Spirit, that we be " lively stones—not dead weights—built up a spiritual house, an holy priesthood,"—every one of us—" to offer up spiritual sacrifices, acceptable to God by Jesus Christ." It is not the number, or the cunning of the craftsmen, so much as the fidelity, constancy and perseverance of those professedly engaged in his service, that shall promote the cause of truth and make it triumphant.

"The cause requires good men and true, pure men and humble, reverent of God and in love with mankind, whose daily prayer is, " Thy kingdom come ; Thy will be done on earth as it is in heaven ;" preachers, editors, writers ; men, women and children, who attach importance and a value to their religion, and make it *second* to nothing else; who will swerve not, nor waver in the fiercest conflict with error and vice for the sake of personal ease, wealth, enjoyment or renown ; but who, every day, and everywhere, are true to their convictions, resolute in the defense of truth, never terrified by their adversaries, always hopeful, joyous, happy, forgiving and full of true and kind words, letting their "light so shine before men that others may glorify our Father in heaven."

"As a denomination, with a great work before us, and full opportunity, we need more work and less legislation, more doing and less planning ; better workers and fewer managers. We need moral culture and spiritual growth ; personal piety and home religion ; love of God and faith in Jesus. Without such training any organization will be imperfect and incapable. It may count large numbers, make a fine show and attract much admiration, but for any practical work it will prove a splendid failure. It is not parade, but votes that will elect a President.

"Religion is personal ; its home is the heart. It must live there or it does not really live at all. It communicates with the world, but does not flourish in crowds, where the atmosphere becomes impure. It leads the soul apart, to commune with God in the closet, that it may grow strong, and then go out into the active world and receive its reward openly—"not yours, but you."

"The great lack of the church in other days was a want of faith in Jesus Christ as the Savior of the world. They did not believe he would do what he had undertaken. They distrusted the means and method of his working. They believed and taught the defeat and disaster of his cause, the failure of his mission.

" When was the world so ready for the truth, and so ripe for the sickle as to-day? The harvest is plenty. The reapers are few. Let us pray the Lord of the harvest to send more and better reapers into His field.

" What we need most, brethren, as I view it, is more self-consecration — more faith in Jesus Christ, and less confidence in human wisdom ; more love of God and less self-esteem ; more love for mankind, and less desire of personal and party preferment ; pure hearts, holier lives; more of the attractive forces of truth and love to draw into a warm-hearted, devoted, zealous. working brotherhood, that alone and together we may work the work of God. We believe in the universal love of God ; let us prove it by working after the pattern of Jesus — loving. and seeking, and suffering for the good of mankind. We believe in the salvation of all men — let us reject none from our tender sympathy and constant concern. We believe in the Universal Brotherhood ; let us love as brethren, even our enemies, and them that hate and persecute us.

" We do not believe in party schemes, private jealousies and personal rivalries ; let us avoid them. We do not believe in endless sin, hate and misery ; let us overcome evil with good. We do not believe in popes, priests, bishops, immense ecclesiastical properties and church domination over personal freedom ; let us never sink into them. We do not believe in money to buy the gifts of the Holy Ghost; let our hearts, and souls, and bodies be sanctified to God, with all our substance for His most glorious work.

" Our name is a good one. It was wisely chosen at the baptism of our denomination. A better I cannot conceive. It has a common center — UNITY — and a positive declaration—one God and Father of all; one

13

Lord, the Savior of all ; one brotherhood, one fold. It
has a boundless circumference, it accepts all truth,
embraces all goodness, rewards all virtue, punishes
all vice, saves and blesses all men. It overcomes all
evil, corrects all error, removes all wrong, reconciles
all hearts to God. It is universal. It cannot be confined or restrained to become narrow, selfish, sectarian,
without perverting and destroying its meaning and
intent. I love it; I admire it; I praise it; it is so like
God in all His works; so like Jesus in the Gospel; so
like the spirit of truth,and power of love everywhere. I
was ordained to preach it, to honor it, to defend it from
all personal pride, and party prejudice; working under it
for the conversion of sinners, the joy of hearts, the salvation of men. To me it is the synonymn of all that is
true, and pure, and good, and holy, and beautiful, and
lovely, and noble, and glorious in God, in man, and in
all the world. It comprehends all perfection, is all
light, life love and immortality. It banishes to eternal
oblivion whatever is opposed to God and human happiness: all wrath, enmity, hatred, variance, everything
impure, false, hateful, all sins, sorrows, suffering, death
and corruption. It fills the soul with all love, peace,
good-will, joy, and attunes the heart to the praise of
God. It embraces the faith of Jesus, and works the
work of God. Beautiful, harmonious, significant word
— UNIVERSALISM! May it always live in its spirit, be
honored in its true meaning and never be disgraced by
any who accept it, so long as names shall be needed to
distinguish principles and ideas — the faith, hope and
characters of mortal men."

     #   #   #   #   #   #   #

There are still other sermons from which we may
make less generous extracts; among them "Creeds and
Sects in Heaven;" and "What Jesus Taught." Of
the former of these we find him saying, that "Jesus
bore witness to the truth in its highest and grandest

revelation, for the purification, elevation, perfection, salvation of man.

"He taught that by 'doing the will of God we should know of the doctrine,' that we should know the truth and that the truth should make us free.

"His was not truth in the abstract, founded on statements, proposition, problems, and formed into theories and systems by curious contrivance. It was truth in the concrete, issuing from the Fountain of Life itself, and glowing in the warmth of purified affections, holy desires, in light and love, permeating the whole heart, elevating all thought, and consecrating every power to personal holiness and universal good. As such the Gospel contains truth of the highest importance to all men; acceptable to all who love righteousness, rejected by none who seek the moral devotion, purity and happiness of mankind.

"Who shall take up the letter of a creed or habit of a sect, and lay it as a stumbling block in his brother's way?

"The terms of Christian fellowship are plainly and explicitly stated by its Divine Author. None need misunderstand them, none should limit or misapply them. They are given in language intelligible to all. They accord precisely with the purest and holiest affections, and noblest aspirations of every soul. They need but be read without note or comment, to be intelligible to all. They interpret themselves, and waken an echo in every heart. The philosopher may be too busy with his speculations, the scientist with his theories, the artist with his imaginings, the sectarian dawdling with his creeds and forms and rules, the man of the world with the hum and bustle of business and love of gain, to listen and consider, but for all and to all who have ears to hear and hearts to feel, it speaks but one language—love, righteousness, truth, blessedness perfect, universal, immortal.

"Right here comes in the mistake which does all the

mischief in the churches. Instead of 'speaking the truth in love'—exhibiting such truth as we think we have in the loving spirit of the Lord, we assert it dogmatically as the absolute and ultimate truth, and in language others may not understand precisely as we do, and make it the basis of fellowship in the church of God which is the fullness of Him who filleth all in all. Or rather we form what we regard as truth into a creed, and not able to explain it so that others may know it to be the truth, we demand their assent to it by faith, till they shall find it to be truth. In so doing we reverse the order of things, and pervert the teaching of the word, by making faith the basis by dogmatic statement, preceding the reception of the spirit and practice of Christianity."

"What scene is grander, more beautiful, more like heaven than an assembly differing in name, thought, creed, and character, gathering in that one Name which is above every name, before the throne of the common Father, there to invoke his blessing alike upon all men, and eat and drink in memory of his beloved son, our Lord and Savior, as brethren and sisters of a common household! Forgetting all differences, all distinctions; each humbly and devoutly seeking the influence of love, the guidance of the spirit of truth, that he may be an accepted follower of Jesus, and live in love and peace with all mankind!

"Precisely what shall be the condition, character, and employment of the heavenly state none can pretend to know. 'Eye hath not seen nor ear heard, neither hath entered into the heart of man the things which God has prepared for those that love him.' Our ideas of the future are colored, deeply shaded by our knowledge, opinions and desires in the present life. The two are connected by a continuous chain whose links are fastened so close and strong, that in thought it is difficult to separate them.

"What we think of, hope for, call heaven, contains

no element of evil, no shadow of imperfection, and affords no occasion for strife and contention. The very atmosphere is purity, light, life, love, bliss immortal. There is no night there—no darkness at all. Therefore there can be no desire nor deed of evil; no rivalry, no pride, no hatred, no malice, no lust, no misery ; every one shall see as he is seen, and know. as he is known. They shall be like Jesus ; ' for they shall see him as he is,'—shall be changed into the same glory—from glory to glory by the spirit of the Lord ; and God shall be all in all.

"There may be difference there ; but no dissensions. Some will be no more than babes in Christ, but an open field for endless progress in knowledge and goodness will be for all. Comparatively all shall be reckoned so ; for between the finite and the infinite there is an eternity for growth in knowledge and perfection. Each with a cup full and running over shall be happy in his sphere, being good and doing good. Like a well-appointed school of pure-hearted, noble, earnest minded scholars, all anxious to learn, waiting to receive, ready to impart, loving, true and faithful ; no envy, no jealousy, no rivalry, no hazing of new-comers, each devoted to the other, and all laboring together in love for the good of all. Such are our ideas of heaven and of what the church on earth should be. Jesus the great Teacher, the lover and Savior of the world is Head over all to the Church, which is his body, the fullness of him that filleth all in all.

"Or, Heaven is like the happy home, where love flows freely from parent hearts and reaches and rules in the hearts of all the children. No distinctions are felt between oldest and youngest, richest and poorest, wisest and simplest. One spirit pervades all hearts, one desire moves all hands, to do all the good they can, to make all pleasant and happy. Over all preside loving father and mother, noting the difference which, like colors and forms in a landscape, give beauty by

variety, and watching with intense satisfaction, the
order, harmony and happiness which reign in all the
household."

*   *   *   *   *   *   *

Of the teaching of Jesus we may say, that a few
great central, simple faiths, or beliefs, truths which
were lying at the heart of Christianity, constituted all
there was of his gospel.

"WHAT DID JESUS TEACH?

"The answer to this question would be easily found,
plain, positive, direct and satisfactory, were it not for
the obscurity cast over the teaching of Jesus by the innumerable diverse and contradictory interpretations.
commentaries. paraphrases and perversions of preachers,
professors and writers, whose eyes are dimmed by prejudice; whose ears are dull or itching; whose judgments are biassed by a superstitious adhesion to creeds,
names, forms and fashions ; whose souls are too sluggish,
too worldly to think and examine carefully ; whose reason is too restricted by the decrees of councils and conventicles. or who are shorn of their personal liberty and
feeling of responsibility by a tame and perhaps unconscious submission to usurped ecclesiastical authority
over them by men no wiser, no more honest or reverent; no better than themselves.

"Jesus did not teach his disciples that they must submit blindly to old authorities because they were old,
but to embrace truth, because it is truth ; and do right,
because it is right. He reminded them of what had
been taught by them in old time, by priests and poten-
tates; but he did not teach them to obey their commands, right or wrong. He gave them a higher standard, raised them above the traditions and authority of
the elders. He brought them face to face with God,
that in his light they might of themselves judge what is
right. 'The pure in heart shall see God.' In his light,

shining through their reason, and instructed by Jesus
they could see more clearly and judge more wisely than
the ancients. He did not teach them to prefer the wisdom of men to · the wisdom that is from above, which
is first pure, then peaceable, gentle, easy to be entreated full of mercy and good fruits, without partiality and without hypocrisy.' He did not teach them
to follow the fashions of the world, or the church, to
covet the high places of wealth, position, or power.

"Jesus gave us lessons that are eminently fit and
needful for all to learn. His advice is to attend to the
duties of to-day and not be worried about the fate of
to-morrow; to seek first the kingdom of heaven—
righteousness, peace and joy, in the holy spirit; to
obey the physical, moral and spiritual laws; to do to
others as they would be done by; to be just and generous; to let their good works testify the goodness of
their hearts, the correctness of their principles, the
reality of their religion; in short, to adopt ·and practice the soundest, plainest, truest, most positive and
most needed principles of true philosophy, moral
science and sincere piety, all of which were taught in
the lessons and exemplified in the conduct of Jesus.

" What more or better could Jesus teach than he has
taught? What more does the world need to save it
from sin and sorrow than to learn and obey what Jesus
taught? What could God do more to save and help
his children? What more is required of man than to
love God and his neighbor as himself? On what surer
foundation can we rest our hopes than the love of God
shed abroad in our hearts, to prepare us for the duties
and conditions of this life under all circumstances, for
happiness here and hereafter, now and forever? Is it
not easy to see what such thought, feeling, action and
purpose, such confidence in God, in Christ, in truth
and love, would produce in the religious, moral, social,
business and political world? What a conquering
power for good Christianity would have over the sins

and errors, the crimes, the follies, the miseries, the meanness and littleness now so prevalent in the world, and not all outside the churches! Who believes the world can be saved, the work of Jesus be complete and all men holy and happy in any other way? Why is it, then, that the professed followers of Jesus will not yield their prejudices, crucify their selfishness, cease their contentions, bury the creeds invented by men and supported by sects, and learn of the Great Teacher how they ought to live—how they must live, feel and act, like brethren, children of one father, redeemed by one Savior, and commanded to cherish the same spirit, and to love one another?

He forewarned men of the strong temptations that come from high places more than from low; from secret insinuations, the love of money, and the influence of those who are the lovers of pleasure more than the lovers of God; of those who seek honor without merit, happiness without virtue, and heaven by pretension. He indicated that it was easier to say Lord, Lord than it was to do the will of the Father in heaven. For some it seems easier to quarrel than it is to keep the peace.

"While Jesus mingled with the humble and neglected, it was not to approve their conduct or condition, but to teach those who were willing to be taught by Him. The scribes and Pharisees, the rich, the great, the proud, the self-righteous would not listen to learn. Therefore his rebukes fell on them, and His labors were more especially bestowed on such as were willing to be convinced and converted.

"His work was to reform and save, not to destroy. He came to seek and to save what was lost, but worth saving. He taught not theory without practice, but to do the will of God, and so know the doctrine whether of God or men. He did not formulate a creed, write a systematic body of divinity, nor establish a hierarchy to overrule the consciences of men. He taught them to break off their sins by righteousness,

and sin no more; to be humble and virtuous; to lead
quiet and peaceable lives in all godliness and honesty,
that their sins might be blotted out, and a time of refreshing come from the presence of the Lord, such as
was in the house of the father when the prodigal came
home. He made the path of duty plainer, the motives
to right living stronger, and the assurance of hope
brighter than ever taught by priest, philosopher, poet
or potentate who had preceded him.

" The preaching of Jesus and His deeds of mercy,
wrought without respect of social distinction, soon
attracted much attention as He went about the cities
of Galilee, and multitudes followed Him to hear His
words and see His works. They had never heard of
such wonderful things before. Doubtless curiosity first
drew them about Him. The more thoughtful Jews were
expecting some special manifestation in behalf of their
nation about that time. Their prophets had foretold
the coming of a Messiah who should redeem Israel
from foreign servitude. They wondered if Jesus was
not the promised Deliverer. Greeks and Romans and
others, dwelling in that lovely region, became also
interested and anxious to learn whereunto these things
might come.

" We must know the truth before we can enjoy
its freedom. We must find the right way before
we can walk in it. We must have faith in the object sought, or we shall never find it. We must prepare our hearts for the blessings we desire, or there
will not be room to receive them. Error does not
bring freedom. Sin inflicts misery. Doubt brings
darkness and despair. Unbelief clouds the souls and
shuts out light and truth and love; it withers affection, blights hope and stretches on a bed of perpetual
unrest. Ignorance is night. Indifference is procras-
tination. Jesus is the Way, the Truth and the Life —
the light of the world. It is safe to follow Him."

It is not important that I refer to a large number
of Mr. Balch's written articles and addresses, which
his fertile pen has ever been furnishing the public.
They are on a great variety of subjects, too numerous
to more than barely mention a very few of them.

"The changed condition of thought and feeling,
demanding a change of action," was an address delivered at the Elgin Ministerial Conference, designed to
show that we were to cultivate, not creeds, differences
of opinion, or pride of condition, but the seeds of
humility, forbearance, fraternity, by "endeavoring to
keep the unity of the spirit in the bonds of peace."
He was sure that if nominal Christians of every name
would adopt and follow the standard of Jesus — "By
this shall all men know that ye are my disciples, if ye
have love one to another" —it would be an easy task to
convert the world. But "in biting and devouring one
another there was no other alternative but to be con-
sumed one of another." Sects and dogmas were and
always had been hindrances, and not helps in the work
of human redemption. Christians were to follow the
counsels by which they were to "grow up into Him
who was the head in all things, till they should all
come in the unity of the faith, and the knowledge of
the Son of God unto a perfect man, unto the measure
of the stature of the fulness of Christ." Let them
make the teaching and example of Jesus their model,
and there would be no division among them. He
thought it "one thing to help build a sect, and another
to help save the world. It was ours to 'take up our
cross and follow the Savior' among the lowly, the
common people, into the by-ways and hedges; to teach

comfort and inspire hope and assurance, of success in
the way of well-doing, and to reprove, rebuke and
exhort, with all long-suffering and doctrine, to humility
purity, meekness, good-will and good works towards
all men.'

We learn from him that it had "always been his·
aim in preaching and writing, and in all he did, to 'follow after the things that made for peace, and things
whereby one might edify another,' and he hoped ever
to keep clear of the spirit of division and contention,
and labor in the broad field of impartial love and benevolence." It was not far from the period of Brother
Balch's entrance into the ministry that the breaking off
of the party known as the Restorationists occurred, and
as partisan feeling ran high, the attempt was made to
draw him into the controversy that ensued, but he
never could be induced to take sides. He deemed it a
movement that was destined to soon spend itself, and
it was because he refused to mix with it that he was
called to be the successor at Providence, R. I., of David
Pickering, who was one of the malcontents. He did
not stop to speculate about any of these things. He
believed "sin would be punished adequately, for it involved punishment as something inhering in it. In the
event of a man's sinning he taught that he must suffer,
or be punished, for he must take the consequences of
his sins, and he should never flatter himself that he
could do wrong and find peace in it, for 'there was no
peace to the wicked.' Sin punished itself, as a man
takes coals of fire in his bosom and is burned by them."
He did not believe in any other punishment than the
consciousness which is inseparable from a wrong intent,

and thought it enough for us to believe that "so long as we are sinful we shall be miserable, and that the sure road to happiness is the road to virtue and holiness. Mankind were to suffer punishment until they ceased to do evil and learned to do well; but no longer, for there was 'no condemnation to them who were in Christ Jesus, who walked not after the flesh but after the spirit; for the law of the spirit of life in Christ Jesus had made them free from the law of sin and death.' If a man sinned through eternity he would be punished through eternity." It was sin that was the worst thing; it was the hell of the universe; as holiness was the best thing; the heaven of God and eternity.

He tells us for what God punished the sinner, that it was " for the purpose of reclaiming and benefiting him ; never to gratify a malignant disposition ; and for this reason it made no great difference whether the punishment continued for a longer or shorter time, since it was to bring about the accomplishment of a glorious design." And in view of this he remarks: " We see no cause of controversy upon the subject of future punishment viewed in this light. If we think all are punished enough in this life, or if we think some ought to have more hereafter, we can see no good reason for quarreling about it. Better do our duty here and now. Labor and toil for the true honor and happiness of ourselves and fellow-men, and leave the event with the *Judge of all the earth, for He will do right.*"

* * * * * * *

In an article, "The Future of Humanity: An Open Letter to Brothers T. J. Sawyer and A. A. Miner," he treats of the origin of sin, and the change of this life to the life that is hereafter. "Sin originated in the earth" he says, "in the imperfection and weakness of human nature. The Bible everywhere treats it as belonging to, and inhering in the natural,animal,mortal,earthly nature of reasonable, responsible man. It keeps a plain distinction between the corruptible and incorruptible, the dishonorable and glorious, the weak and powerful,the natural and spiritual. the first Adam and the last Adam, the earthly and the heavenly : and positively asserts the great change wrought by the resurrection from one condition to the other. Natural death was the end of man's earthly being—the house made with hands. The resurrection was into a spiritual state, a house not made with hands, eternal in the heavens."

Of the change from this to the future, he believed that "all would enter that world as they left this, but not to continue in an unchanged state, but to be molded and fashioned into some higher order of being and blessedness." He asks the question :

"In what degree of spiritual or moral advancement does the soul enter the future state? We have no direct revelation by word to give in answer. But it would be a consistent and safe conclusion, that it enters that world in a degree of spiritual attainment, as it leaves this; that the future is to the 'inner man' a continuation of the present life in immortality. With the weaknesses, imperfectness, and infirmities of the fleshly earth-mind, left in earth, where sin originated and dwelt, the soul, disrobed of all that belonged to time and sense, like a slave set free, starts on a new career with light and love, purity and peace, joy and rejoicing, in all its surroundings. He sees himself as he is, and knows himself as God and the pure of heart know him. With his desires all pure, and mental faculties quickened, like the child entering a graded school, he humbly and cheerfully surrenders his will, himself, his all, to the direction of the loved ones who recognize and gather about him in purest love and devotion, to help him on the upward, progressive course of endless growth in knowlege, love and worship, toward the absolute, the infinite, the impartial, the all-perfect, the all-Father, whom to know is life immortal."

He has many articles, such as "On the Situation," "Denominational Policy," "The Profession of Belief," " How to Advance the Church," "The True Object of Religious Organization," etc., etc. He has one " Fifty Years Ago and Now," an address read at a session of the Illinois State Convention," and " To Whom is Universalism Acceptable?" I make brief quotations from each of these; from the first :

" We have, of late, followed too closely the wisdom of the world and the methods of other churches. We have departed from the simplicity, zeal, humility and patient working of fifty years ago. We do not live in the love of God, nor follow the example of Jesus. We do not dwell in love, and God does not dwell in us, nor is His love perfected in us. It is, therefore, not fitting that we should boast, or expect to prosper and triumph more than others. Nor should we pretend to be like them, seeing there is a radical difference in doctrine. In spirit and essentials we may agree; in doctrine there is a positive and eternal antagonism. Truth is still to be sought and its spirit to be cultivated by all believers. But we have reason to be thankful to God, and take courage from what has been accomplished by the feeble labors of the past; even that other men are entered into them and are reaping their fruits. When we look upon the changed condition of the churches and note the broadening and more liberal views and kindly feelings prevailing in them, and in the minds of the people generally, comparing fifty years ago with to-day,

we do rejoice, and we will rejoice as Paul did, that the
Gospel of love is preached, and is doing its work, by
breaking down partition walls, letting in the light of
God, and setting at liberty them that were bound.
Were we to indulge a speck of pride, we might find
mingled in the causes, if not prominent among them,
the labors of the bold and earnest advocates of the universal love of God and of the ultimate salvation of the
race. We would claim no more than justice can grant.
To God be the glory. All may not be aware of the
secret permeating influences of the truths they defended, nor be willing to bestow honor where honor is
due, not having traced the motions of the spirit: while
many look with scorn upon those led by it, as Scribes
and Pharisees did upon the lowly man of Nazareth and
the fishermen of Galilee. Such forget that God sometimes 'chooses the foolish things of the world to con-
found the wise, the weak things of the world to con-
found the mighty, and things despised, and things that
are not, to bring to nought the things that are."

*　　*　　*　　*　　*　　*　　*

TO WHOM IS UNIVERSALISM ACCEPTABLE?

"It is plain enough to all sober, thinking people that
the doctrine of universal love, righteousness and salvation can be acceptable only to those of broad views and
generous hearts, who wish well to their fellow-men.
Narrow, prejudiced, bigoted minds cannot comprehend
it. The simple statement of its principles, object and
ultimate triumph, meet a ready and affirmative response
in all free souls not blinded by selfishness and false education, by worldly wisdom and ecclesiastical authorities.
The highest attainments of reason, and the purest affections and holiest desires of humble and uncorrupted
hearts, at once and gladly embrace it, and fondly cherish the bright hope it inspires. 'The common people
heard Jesus and rejoiced.'

"Allow me to quote briefly as I can three incidents

in my experience which serve to illustrate very clearly
the great value of the principles Universalists are ordained to advocate and exemplify, when presented to
minds never prejudiced against them by false teaching
and misrepresentation.

" One beautiful Sunday morning in August, 1852, a
young man came to my chamber, where I sat reading
the bold prophecies and grand descriptions of Isaiah,
glancing now and then at the clear white summit of
Mount Blanc, and the sublime scenery spread out in
front and on either hand.   He said the landlord, a Ger-
man, desired me to preach in the little chapel connected
with his hotel.   I answered I could not preach in Ger-
man, French, Italian or the patois of Chamouny.   Soon
after he returned, saying it was not expected; but as
many English and Americans were in the village the
service was desired for them, and as no other preacher
was present, I consented, without any time for preparation.

" Some sixty or seventy were gathered in the chapel,
all but a few entire strangers to me.   A Bible and
prayer-book lay on the desk.   I did not know how to
handle the latter.   As I rose most of the audience rose
also.   Recalling the form of Protestant worship in
France, I offered a brief invocation, and then proceeded
in our usual form.   Fortunately I had just read Isaiah ii :
2, 'It shall come to pass in the last day that the mountain of the Lord's house shall be established in the top
of the mountains, and shall be exalted above the hills,
and all nations shall flow unto it.'   I took it for a text.
The illustrations were near at hand, clear and forcible.
The leading thought was, Christianity, pure and simple,
is above *everything* else, and, like the sun, gives light,
heat and life, where nothing selfish and worldly inter-
cepts its influence.   *All distinctions*, like morning
shadows disappear before the light and love of God.
Then the last clause, '*all nations shall flow unto* (into)
it.'   Things flow downward, because the attraction is

below. Place the magnet *above* the needle, it just as naturally flows to it. Jesus has a name above every name; He has gone before, is risen, ascended up on high, and when the Father's love penetrates the heart, the knee bends in deep humility, and the tongue confesses Jesus to be Lord to the glory of God the Father. And thus in the Divine plan Jesus shall reign until all things are subdued, and all hearts are reconciled and drawn unto Him. All nations shall flow into the house — the church of the living God, the fullness of Him who filleth all in all.

" On retiring a gentleman lingered at the door. As I was about to pass he gave me his hand, saying, ' I want to thank you for your sermon; it is what all men ought to hear ; it would level all distinctions but those of merit, end all wars and controversies, and cause peace. love, good-will and happiness to abound everywhere.' He continued, 'I give you my card and extend to you a most cordial invitation to come to my castle and make it your home while in England.' The next day we started for the circuit of Mt. Blanc. We met his lordship at some distance. He beckoned me to stop, descended from his carriage and came and desired me to dismount — from my mule — and be introduced to his lady ! She said she was happy to meet a man whose sermon yesterday had made so deep an impression on the mind of his lordship ; that he had not ceased to speak of it, and the need of such a doctrine to convert the world. She heartily joined in his invitation to be at home in their castle. I need not add that I was glad the truth, simply presented, had made an impression on a nobleman ; but I was more pleased to know that its power is the same on all who receive it.

" On the Arabian Desert one Christmas eve it was proposed by some of our pilgrims to have a religious service. Being the only preacher present I was urged to hold one. Quite a congregation could he gathered

14

from a camp near by—over fifty in all.   I preached to
them Jesus, the Saviour of the world, who came to show
all men their Father, to teach all how to live in love,
peace and good-will, to do no wrong, to restrain all evil
thoughts and desires, to obey the Lord and hope and
strive to become pure, holy and happy, and prepare for
the kingdom the Good Father has prepared for all His
children, where there shall be one fold and one shepherd.   I talked slowly, and the dragomen interpreted to
those about them.   The next day, and every day after,
when I met them, the Moslems and others would drop
one knee and hold out their right hand that I might
lay my left in it and allow them to kiss the back of it
in token of their deep reverence of me as a Santon
(*saint*) of Allah.   Those I met after my return from
the Upper Nile showed the same respect.   I admired
their devotion to the few flashes of light that dawned
on their darkness, but I pitied them, shut up in the
confines of ignorance and superstition.

   " Six months after my return to New York, one who
heard me, our cook, came to my house in his Syrian
costume, and after kneeling and kissing my hand, said,
' I have come to America to learn more of that blessed
doctrine you preached on the desert, that I may tell it
to my people.'   I embraced him, and bade him never,
in this land, bend his knee to any but his God, and
know that he was a man among men.

   " The last incident I will name, though many more
might be, occurred last winter in Mexico.   Our party
who had ladies was invited to a dinner by the Nestor
of the Mexican press, a man of liberal thought, clear
understanding and eminent character.   He had been
twice banished and once imprisoned by the priestly
party, when in power, in that oft-disturbed country,
but is now esteemed as one of the most excellent men
in the land.   After dinner we were shown through his
extensive establishment, his pleasant residence, one
room in which is adorned with leading men of Europe

and America, and finally into his editorial sanctum, where some time was spent in conversation. He gave cards to our party, and most of them went out upon the veranda to look at the flowers and birds. Turning to his son, who was learning French (our Spanish interpreter had gone out), he told him to ask me if I was a merchant. I answered I was not, but a preacher (*pasteur*), which the lad interpreted into *padre*. A deep scowl swept over his countenance, and he was about to turn away. Comprehending the cause, I said to the boy, 'Tell your father I am not a priest, but a preacher of glad tidings for all men ; that I believe and teach there is one God the Father of all, one brotherhood of all men and all nations, and that I hope, in the Father's good time, and by means in His power, all will be guided onward through an endless life in continual progress, in ever increasing knowledge, purity, goodness and happiness towards the infinite and absolute goodness and truth and love constituting immortal blessedness.' I said it slowly, and he translated so his father understood it, for his countenance changed and grew brighter, until all was aglow with joy. He grasped my hand, and told his son to say, '*Je suis ton frère*'—'I am your brother.' We spent some time together, answering his questions as well as I could through his son. He gave me his portrait, engraved in Spain while in banishment, another card, on which he expressed his gratitude in knowing there were souls broad and free as his own, and desiring correspondence. He also asked for my photograph, and sent his son with me to our hotel to obtain it."

CHAPTER XI.

BROTHER Balch had a wide reputation as a writer, and there is found among his writings some of the finest gems of thought in our whole literature. There was such a manifest degree of ease, and a racy, flowing style or diction, together with the purest of sentiment, that one felt that he was taken possession of, and no other impulse was so strong, as to be hastened on in the reading that he might gain the utmost of the thought that was being expressed. One of our ripest thinkers writes me, that he "always read whatever he saw from his pen, not alone because his style was pleasing, but usually the substance was interesting. There were few persons who had equal observing powers, joined with equal judgment, and still further, few have had equal facility of language to detail what they saw." The letters written on his journeys, and especially during his tour in Europe, in the years 1852–53 display an uncommon power of narration and description, a talent which has earned for him distinguished reputation in a province of literary effort. Containing as they do many highly graphic sketches of eminent individuals, and remarkable places of natural scenery and works of art, a high degree of interest attaches to them altogether distinct from their personal associations. Of themselves they must have been read, and with greatest pleasure, by any intelligent person, however, indifferent to the name and character of the writer.'

Brother Weaver is the author of the following:

" When a youth just converted to Universalism, I read his letters from abroad, in a Universalist paper published in New York, and they interested me intensely. It was my first taste of anything of the kind. I could hardly wait from week to week for them. They were read in the family, and we all talked over them. I thought them over and over as I worked in the field. The reality of the great outside world came to me then, as it had not before. The name of W. S. Balch came to be a kind of hallowed thing with me. He was a Universalist minister; he was traveling in the old countries; he was writing home weekly letters that had the charm of revelations to me. Had I known that he was born and reared within fifteen miles of me, I should have felt even more stirred. And had I dreamed that I should ever know him personally, associate with him as a brother, eat at his table and join with him in public service, I should have thought that the dream related to heaven, and not to earth. I am certain that he was one of the men that waked me up in my youth. He seemed to me a wonderful man, and after his return home I read everything from his pen with greatest interest. When long years after I came to get acquainted with him, I was surprised to find him a common, humble man, just the equal associate of all of us, and particularly genial and sympathetic."

Brother Balch's letters and correspondence alone, would fill many books; but not many of these have fallen under my own eye. He held a large correspondence with a person in Providence, R. I., and for a large number of years, but I have not gained access to it.

He always remembered friends with a great deal of
cordiality, and warmth of attachment, and found himself writing them often. He made a practice of finish-
ing up his correspondence each year as it drew near
its close, and more than a single letter of his begins in
the following manner: "My Dear Friend; As the
year draws to a close I continue my invariable custom
and settle with myself, and pay all debts if I owe
any, and try and commence the new year square with
the world. No debt can be more sacred than that of
friendship. That can never be all paid, more than the
interest."

I find another of these letters, "Dear Friends of
Old and of Now," which starts off in this way: " I am
(some think) too apt to moralize. It is near the end of
the year, when all accounts should be settled truly and
honestly before God, especially with ourselves. New
Year's day has been for me an important day since I
was sixteen, a day of personal settlement with myself,
in which belongs both the material and spiritual, to find
what the debt and credit should be in this critical time.
In sight of eighty I am more than ever concerned about
the balance sheet; how it shall be when the year shall
be gone." He keeps up this manner till within a month
of his death, for November 27, 1887, he begins a letter,
" Dear Friends; Sitting alone in the house this Sunday
morning, Mrs. Balch and the girl gone to church, I begin thinking of old friends in Vermont, and thoughts
center on you and yours as among the best. So here I
am communing."

He begins one of his letters, " My Dear Bro. of Old
and Always;" calls it "An Old Clergyman's Moralizing

to a Friend," and tells us that it is to an "Octogenarian
Believer;" and another to a "Boy Friend," which I
conclude is the same, and the form of address is, "My
Dear Old Crony." I am tempted to transcribe extracts
from both of these letters, as well from the character
of them, as from the fact of having received a letter
from this same octogenarian, of Andover, Vt.,
signed Geo. W. Stickney, containing many reminiscences, looking back over an acquaintance, and steadfast friendship of almost eighty years. This letter I
give here on account of its general interest, and because it paves the way for the others to follow in a
kind of joint relationship. It reads as follows:

"DEAR BROTHER:—Your request for contributions to
the biography of Rev. Wm. S. Balch has recently come
to my notice. From our earliest childhood William
and I were playmates. He was born on the farm adjoining on the west, and the family moved a year or so
later to the farm on the northeast of that to which my
father came from New Hampshire when I was a year
and a half old, and on which I still reside. Through
all our long lives we have been warm friends. He and
I spent many hours at the forks of the roads leading
to our homes, before separating after being out together
from home. We were always interested in talking
over and investigating the affairs of life, politics, morals, religion and trade. We spent a good deal of time
in discussing John Calvin's doctrines and the false conceptions of God and religion which they involved.
We boys thought them horrible, even while we regarded them as taught in the Bible. I always thought
we were about equal in our studies in school, but when
we left our boyhood he left me far behind, as I plodded
along in the beaten path of the fathers, while he
started through the wilderness of life, and made his

way alone to fame, and his track is a beacon light, and a mariner's compass for all young people to follow. Wm. S. Balch, without a college diploma, early advantages of wealth, or an ancestry of great statesmen, divines, or noted jurists, has made for himself a name unaided, except by his genius, and determined will to do something for the good of mankind, and grandly has he succeeded.

"He was always fond of finding out the source of everything for himself. When he was quite young, in making sugar with his brother on the hill, he climbed a tree so he could see as he thought the source of West River. This was the make of the man. He would ascertain the cause and origin if possible of everything that came under his observation. Though separated from each other, we were alike pioneers in the temperance, and anti-slavery cause. Afterwards in the Legislature together, I remember that he understood every measure that came up. Those which agreed with his views of right and expediency he supported with argument and vote, and those which did not he opposed as strongly. No laws were enacted that escaped his notice.

"Mr. Balch lectured in Montpelier on his travels, one evening, and a Judge Wilder and myself persuaded all the members of the Legislature that we could to hear him. There was a dramatic company from Boston in town the same night which drew many, but those who heard the lecture were delighted. A member from Norwich said 'I had no idea that we had such a man in Vermont.'

"I am more than pleased that the biography of my dear old friend is to be written.

"Yours very truly,
"GEORGE W. STICKNEY."

It was to this friend that the following letters were inscribed. The one written last, in July, 1887, I give first. It was addressed,

"My Dear Old Friend of the long ago:—Sitting here alone, and wandering over the days of my boyhood and since, I thought of that spruce tree at the forks of the roads, where we used to sit often, and talk over the affairs of the world, and our business in it. You were wiser than I, and older, and I deferred to you. We used to talk of Elder Manning's sermons about religion, conversion, and political matters as well, and things too numerous to mention.

"Well, we are very nearly through with it; having done our work, borne our crosses, enjoyed our rewards, received our honors, and must, not long hence, bid it farewell, and go to our long home, to continue our journey there, relieved of the burdens of the flesh, and with keener spiritual powers, in spiritual bodies, progress forever in the higher, holier realm of light, purity and beauty, towards the Unseen and Unknown, but the Infinite, the Absolute, the Immortal. It is a consoling, joyous thought, a bright and glorious hope, that hereafter ' we shall know as we are known,' and forever rejoice in perfect happiness with a world redeemed and glorified. In such thoughts I have found relief in all troubles, strength in all weakness, and a light above all darkness. How then can we lament or fear to pass through the dark valley to the more shining shore, where is fulness of joy, and the life that is forever. We of course, cannot ; for so long as we hope in God, our souls are quieted within us, and darkness and fear fly away. 'Even now are we the children of God, and it doth not yet appear what we shall be ; but we know that when he shall appear we shall be like him, for we shall see him as he is. And every one that hath this hope in him purifieth himself, even as he is pure.' Blessed saying, joyous hope is this. I would all men had it. To it I have given the best thoughts and labors of my life, that they might have it. Although my labors have been feeble, there come echoes from the

long past — from sixty years ago and sweet assurances
all the way to the present from the souls who have
listened and learned and hoped through my ministrations. It is a rich comfort in my afternoon medita-
tions, worth more to me than the proudest honors and
the greatest wealth the world could bestow.

"Let us rejoice my brother, that our final salvation is
nearer than when we first believed. The world is
behind, heaven within and before us. Amen.

"There, I have spun these thoughts as rapidly as
our mothers and sisters spun their threads when we
were boys. I hope you can read them and respond.

" I suppose you are in the work-field as when we last
met, and I wish I was able to be there with you. My
health is fairly good, except my chronic complaint for
which doctors know no cure. Were I comfortably
well as last year I would now be in Vermont. I hope
to hear from you soon. Regards to family and
friends.

" Fraternally,
" W. S. Balch."

In another of these letters he follows up this strain
somewhat. His mind is called to the death of a
daughter many years before, and he writes:

" It brought back memories of our long past, and
stirred me so deeply that I catch up my pen to express
the kindly feelings which have survived all changes of
time and place for more than half a century, and live
still, fresh and vital as ever. Is there not found in
such a continuance of the purest, best and noblest
affections, a ground of hope that they will continue and
increase through all future changes—rising and aspiring and progressing, on and onward, forever toward
the perfect, constituting personal, mutual and eternal
happiness.

" Unlike the lower order of beings, man is never
satisfied with what he he is, or what he has, or what

he does. His desires reach for something more. Neither is the individual, nor the race content to stop thinking, desiring or progressing. If there is for him no future for progress and improvement, he is a failure in the works of creation—the greatest and saddest that can be conceived. Every other creature manifestly finishes his work, makes no improvement, unless taught by man, but dies satisfied, hoping for and preparing for nothing more for itself or those to come after. It is not so with man. When a work is done he looks at it, and sees how it could be improved. Thus he improves, and thus he advances, but never finds an end. The generation coming after takes up the unfinished and carries it forward. Are these unceasing desires, immortal capacities and unfinished works to fail when the body dies? The instruments may be impaired or changed, through which the mind and heart communicate their hidden powers to mortal eyes and ears. The mind lives while the body sleeps. When the soul enters the 'house not made with hands,' 'the spiritual body, such as God shall give it—to every seed his own body,' it shall be revived with superior powers and better opportunities, with no hindrances of the earthly body to prevent the spiritual faculties from running the race set before it. Bearing 'the image of the heavenly' it shall seek after and enjoy heavenly things, entering anew upon a course of endless progress and immortal happiness. Can the soul of man be satisfied, or the will and work of God be complete, with anything short of such a destiny? Such a hope can never be disappointed. Let us cherish it."

The letter to which I referred, commencing "My Dear Old Crony," reads as follows:

"It has been a rule of my life, ever since I was a boy, to look over my little affairs at the close of each year and settle with myself, and find how I stood in relation to things about and within me. As I have heeded the instruction, 'Owe no man anything, but to love one another,' it has been a short and easy work to square all accounts financially. The difficult part has been to heed the latter clause, so as to settle with myself morally, socially, religiously. In this it has not been so difficult to find what I have done as what I have neglected to do. It is easy to see how much better it would have been had I done differently. I did not see it then. I suppose it is so with all men. This year is near its close, and I have reduced my pile of unanswered letters to three. This morning must clear the deck for future action.

"We were boys together, you some months the older. We are now old men and not together. A thousand miles separate our bodies, not our minds, nor our hearts. Space and time can not divide them, and conditions should not fetter them. As you say, our ways through life have led in directions divergent, not wholly so, only in the outward life and living. The inner, spirit life, is not controlled by outward circumstance or condition. It abides the same. It may be shrouded at times like sunshine in storms, and perverted by selfishness and pride, but the clouds blown away, the sky is clearer and the sun warmer, and the evening more beautiful than ever.

"You have remained quiet in your rural mountain home, amid the romantic scenes of our childhood. I have been drifted hither and thither about the world. I may have seen more of the outward distinctions among men, the vast differences between the dead past and the living present; while you have nourished the elements of social rural life. You may have thought it your misfortune that you have not seen more of the toiling, striving, clashing outside world, and had more knowledge of men and things in their vast varieties and striking contrasts. I have seen too much of them, until the deep convicted soul refuses to be comforted until the valleys of vice and degradation are filled up, the hills of pride and oppression are digged down, the crooked ways of sin and selfishness are straightened by virtue and philanthropy, and the rough places of social, political and religious life are made smooth, and all flesh see the salvation of God. It is my misfortune that I have seen too much of the world as it was and is, which, like mountain barriers whose dark sides rise so high as to obscure the light and glory of what is beyond. Your sympathy has not been so heavily taxed by the sight of the ruined, oppressed, neglected, downtrodden sons and daughters of our common humanity, nor your wrath been kindled at the display of selfishness and pride, clothed in the robes of royalty and wrong, sitting on thrones of ease and luxury in state or church, or scheming in the highway of traffic for more gain.

"You and I grew up where none were rich, and none were poor, and every sign of pride or assumed superiority was shamed into humility or silence. If a man desired an office, it was fatal to let it be known. If he wanted friends he must be friendly. Aristocrats were rare, and when seen, were shunned. All naturally desire to see and know, but when they come to feel, the better sentiments are stirred, and 'a change comes o'er the spirit of our dreams,' and stern realities confront us at every step, and 'we are compelled to admit that where ignorance is bliss 'tis folly to be wise.' The ways of God's government are not so unequal as some imagine. He renders to every man according to what he is and does, and not to what he pretends. Every man receives what he deserves, or God is not just.

"We are neither rich nor great, as men decide it. What of it? We used to read in our lesson—

A competence is all we can enjoy;   .
Oh, be content where heaven can give no more.

"That has been a motto of my life. I am glad I am not a millionare, or have many thousands to be

troubled with. I was once offered $200,000 to take
care of a rich man's business five years, until his son
could manage it. It was a strong temptation; but I
respectfully declined it. I knew a man made crazy by
drawing a lottery prize of $20,000. What could I do
with ten times that amount? You on your hill farm,
and I in my cozy home and garden, are free from the
cares and anxieties of the rich and fashionable. Wealth
spoils many; the strife to get it many more.

"Well, brother, we are nearing the bank of the
river all must cross or sink! To me it looks bright and
beautiful on the other shore. Those I have loved beckon
me to them, and sweet voices sing

> Welcome to all; 'tis free, and fresh, and fair.

"When the angel comes, I'll take the proffered
hand, shut my eyes on all that is not good and pure
and true and holy and cheerfully launch into the
placid stream, not doubting the angels of God's mercy
will land me safe on the shore of the immortal, to meet
and mingle with all the beloved—the redeemed of the
Lord, in a bliss that shall never cloy. I hope you have
an equal faith and hope that we shall meet there and
be happy forever more."

There are several letters to his old friend Havemeyer, of New York City, one of which was penned
when past the seventy-seventh year of his age, and in
which he tells him:

" We are in good health, all of the family, and comfortable, and being all the spring, fixing in a quiet humble way, in doors and out, my mind and body have been
kept in a good condition. I am satisfied, and more than
satisfied, in seeing all looking nicely in garden
orchard and lawn. I have climbed oaks forty and fifty
feet, to prune into a more living condition by removing

dead branches. Neighbors say I am reckless, but carefulness gives safety even in old age. I am asked what I have to do without a parish? I will answer that I am comfortably situated, and am fairly content in contemplating the past, still busy with the present, and hopeful of a happy and immortal future."

You will understand that Brother Balch has now left his parish in Dubuque, and was never settled after it, but he is cheery, and just as anxious for the cause as when he first assumed to work for it. After this he is away in California, and Brother Tuttle is away, and meeting him in San Francisco, writes back that he heard him sigh as vigorously as any young apostle of the ministry could have done, over the depressed condition of our cause in that city, and seemed as anxious to enter the work of resuscitating it. "Let us" said he "call the friends together at some place and talk with them." He found him preaching as usual in Doctor Hamilton's pulpit.

He continues to tell us. "The world has gone well with me on the whole, and I have tried to go well with it. The Lord has blessed me, and for fifty-five years I have been prosperous beyond all I deserved or dared to hope. I have always found an open field, and work enough and good friends, both as a settled pastor and outside worker. So gracious and bountiful is the good Father to honest, patient and earnest endeavor."

Speaking of his being no longer under bonds to serve a particular parish, he says:

"I never was much fettered in my freedom, but always religiously observant to ful-

fill all obligations. Time wears away, and age
steals on, but God and love and truth and goodness are forever the same, unchanged and everlasting.
I now have it in my heart to accept an invitation to be in
New York a Sabbath or two, and at a wedding the 6th
of June. I am proposing to revisit some of the fields
and scences of my former labors. Alas, how changed
all will appear. Sad will it be to be gazed at by
strangers, where good friends and co-laborers once
lived, and to hear them whisper, 'What old man is
that? Do you know him?' and to ask for this and
that playmate of childhood, and strong friends in ma-
ture years, and be told 'Gone to the better land,' 'removed to a distant part of the country' 'old' 'decrepit' 'ready to go farther over the river to the
house not made with hands.' Ah, me, but so it is;
and we must become familiar by faith and hope with
what is to be. Let us be thankful and enjoy what we
have while we may, and trust in God for the rest.
There is sufficient provided for all needs, in all conditions of life. But in absence from friends we are deprived of the blessings of social life, one of the chief
sources of happiness, second only to the inward peace
that comes from the consciousness of having cultivated
right principles and affections, and done the duties appointed us by the loving Father. I have tried to live so
that others might have confidence in me, to deserve
their confidence if I did not receive it. Looking back
over seventy years of responsibility, I am grateful in
believing that others have bestowed upon me as a
whole all I deserved. What more could I claim? Yet
we are all indebted, the payment of which will constitute an element in the joy of heaven.

"So much prose" he says "by way of introduction."

But we have his confession. "It does seem a little
strange to me to be without a regular round of duty to
follow, day after day, year in and year out, as I have

done for more than half a century. Active as I have
been—like Martha, 'careful about many things'—I do
feel somewhat lost to be a boarder in my own house;
but I am not so desperately situated that I have nothing to do. As ever, I am thinking and working, according to opportunity, to help convert and save the world.
I find it is not saved, nor very safe. As I go about,
and look and learn, I find there is much work to be
done in all departments, in the church and out of it, before the earth will be full of ' righteousness, peace and
joy.' "

Brother Balch is writing the friend who, he says,
heard the second sermon that he ever preached (that
is, the first sermon out of his study I take it, and the
man I conclude from whom he received the first money
that was ever paid him, $4,) and says:

" I am no longer a settled pastor, but preach as
opportunity, offers among all the denominations;
always my Universalism, in the true and broad, not
the sectarian sense. I find I am more complimented
for preaching the principles of universal love, brotherhood, holiness and happiness among them, than among
our own. To them they are fresher, more attractive,
inspiring better hopes than they have dared cherish.
We are too indifferent, too neglectful of our great
opportunities, and value not our blessings as we should.
Are we not responsible? Every day I am more and
more convinced that the Gospel presented in a plain
and simple manner without human fixtures and adornments, theological dictum or ecclesiastical authorities,
is needed, and is of sufficient power to unite the church
and save the world. There is but little doubt that sectarianism, in its chamelion hues, is one of the chief
hindrances to the union, prosperity and speedy triumph
of the Christian church. How much better it is to have

15

good hearts in the people, and to teach mankind that an honest endeavor to gain the good and the true is preferable to any amount of creed we may elaborate. It is not through human creeds or sectarian names that the Kingdom of Heaven is seen coming. When will we come to think thus, and act accordingly ? "

A Brother Pierce, of Providence, furnishes a good example of this. He tells of meeting Brother Balch in Florida, and as the Baptist church had been some-time without a pastor he took occasion to recommend to a Deacon Walker of that church that he procure the services of this man as a distinguished preacher who had been settled in New York for quite a number of years. And so the Deacon called upon him effecting the arrangement, and the word was sent out to all the region round about. When the Sunday came it was pleasant, and a large congregation gathered to hear the new preacher. Dr. Balch was at his best, and went gracefully into the pulpit, and after the reading and singing a hymn, a fervent prayer was rendered, and then another hymn, when he took for his text " God is love," and for a full hour all eyes and ears were fixed upon him, and the words he gave forth. He seemed to hold the audience spell-bound, the most perfect silence reigning throughout the congregation. When church was dismissed he was surronuded by a large number of hand-shakers for the longest time. The next day he was waited upon by Deacon Walker to see if he could be had for further supply, or for a settle-ment, when Brother Balch informed him that he was a Universalist minister, and had preached that doctrine for more than fifty years. The good deacon was dumbfounded, and dropping his head for a half a minute he said, " Well, that was a good sermon yesterday, anyhow," and retired.

It must be said for Brother Balch that he has helped to win for his denomination a self-merited recognition. The truth is, everybody loves Universalism just as soon as it is brought to them in its beauty and purity. It is a word that is nigh to us all. It is in our mouths, and in our hearts; that is, the word of faith which we preach. How often has it welcomed our Brother to the pulpits of those of the contrary part, and what a work has it done for us in helping to disabuse the general public of their erroneous opinions of the Gospel of " the grace of God which bringeth salvation to all men, and teaches us that denying ungodliness and worldly lusts we should live soberly, righteously and godly in this present world."

I can not but think of him as having been raised up for a peculiar work, and we may properly revere the wisdom he displayed in adapting himself to the age and events amidst which he was called to act. No doubt the circumstances and time together with the natural goodness of his heart, had much to do in making him what he was, and we would not here indulge in the language of indiscriminate eulogy, since the parts assigned men in the same work are widely diverse, and their stations are fixed at different epochs in its progress. The fathers in the ministry may have done, each and all nobly the work of their generation, and so far we should emulate their praiseworthy lives, and catch their elevated spirit; but that God, as did the times, called for our Brother, is sufficiently evinced by the fact of his coming when most needed.   No man, I suppose, could commence at its close and live his own life over.   The world can never have a second Ballou, or Channing, for the conjunction of circumstances in which each acted can never recur.   The only niche in the temple of history fitted for such a man as Mr. Balch is filled, and the record or chapter sealed up.

I find where he has written letters and essays of a great variety of character, and on a great variety of subjects.   He has a letter to "The Mayor of Providence," "To the Governor of the State of Rhode Island,' "The President of the United States," "The People of the United States," and "The Pope of Rome."

CHAPTER XII

MR. BALCH was a great admirer of nature, and loved the hills and valleys of his native State. He had a heart to appreciate the ever varying grandeur and loveliness which nature constantly lavishes upon her beholder, and it made him delight in travel where his soul could be feasted with landscape and beauty. He, himself, tells us that " Reared among rural scenes, with but few books, and little time to read, he early learned to love natural scenery." Mountains and valleys, meadows and forests, were always before him in his youthful days. At school, geography, we are told, was his favorite study, and books of travel he devoured with keenest relish. No doubt his desire for travel was induced in a measure, at least, by the beauty and sublimity of some of the finest scenery on the earth's surface, and in the midst of which he had his birth. And then, too, he informs us that reading the Bible his soul was stirred with sacred story so poetically described, and a desire to go and see, and live and learn, became a leading object in all his thoughts and dreams.

I may quote him where he says:

" In my youthful days I lived among the romantic mountains of my native State. My father's dwelling was

situated on a hillside, with a deep valley opening towards
the southeast, down which ran a babbling brook, while
along the west, a mile distant, was stretched a frowning
ridge of mountains.   From the window of my chamber
I could look far down that valley, and, in a clear day,
see the grand Monadnock, at a distance of fifty miles,
towering, in proud and solitary majesty, high above
all surrounding objects.   In spring and summer I used
to see the sun rise from behind it, and I wondered
where it came from.   Close by its base lived maternal
grandfather, who, during his patriarchal visits, often
told us about that mountain, and the magnificent
scenery presented to the view of one still farther away
upon its summit.   While listening to him my young
heart burned with a desire to stand upon the top of
that mountain and gaze over all the world, which I
thought could be easily done from a position so
lofty."

Ile tells us further, " I wanted to go into the world
and see it.   Every hill and tree and rock and rill and
leafy blossom, had become familiar to me, and I longed
for something more, and that which should seem to be
new.   With what profound attention I listened to the
stories of those who had been about the world, when
they talked with my father, and detailed what they
had seen."

Ile had learned to love the religion of the great
Teacher. Jesus, and the passion had grown with him
that he must visit that land of Judea and Galilee, and
view the places where the Saviour stood, and made
ever memorable by His words of truth and love.   It
was his fondest dream from early boyhood.   " To me,"
he says, " the most interesting portions of the earth
were Greece and Rome and the Holy Land.   Around the

last were clustered the memories and feelings awakened
by a perusal of my mother's Bible. Ever since I could
read the Holy Book I have longed to go and see the
places where were performed the sacred dramas described in its pages; to climb over Lebanon, and rest
in the shadow of its cedars; to wander through the
valley of Esdraelon, and among the hills of Samaria;
to wet my feet in the dews of Hermon, and bathe in
the floods of Jordan; to eat fish on the shores of Ge-
nesareth, and drink water from Jacob's well; to repose
in the cave of Elijah, and gather roses on the plains of
Sharon; to stand upon Olivet, and look upon the joy
of the whole earth; to go through Jerusalem, along
the Via Dolorosa to Calvary and the tomb of Arima-
thea. I have studied hard to understand its descriptive language, that I might rejoice in the blessed
truths of the Bible. To see or to touch these objects
and find them realities would remove the last doubt,
and every description would become plain and forcible,
and seal its truth upon the heart.

"Nor was my young ambition confined to the
scenes of Jewry, rich as they are in the records of
startling events, for my reading led me to classic
Greece and the world-conquering Rome, around whose
histories there circles a vagueness like that which has
fallen on the land of miracles—the scene of man's redemption. As one reads, he desires to see, and I
longed to visit Mars Hill and the pass of Thermopylæ;
to see the ruins of the Eternal City and its living monu-
ments; to cross the Alps at St. Bernard and hear Mass
in St. Peter's. The more modern nations likewise have
their attractions—their temples of pride, their galleries

of art, their museums of curiosities, their libraries of
printed knowledge, their old feudal castles, the working of aristocratic institutions upon the condition of the
masses of the people. These and a thousand other considerations whetted my ambition and led me to form a
plan to visit the old world, which became the study of
my days and the dream of my nights."

* * * * * * *

Mr. Balch was an observing traveler. He had an
eye for seeing, and it did seem as though never anything escaped his notice. He liked to quote the passage of Scripture, "The eye is never satisfied with
seeing, nor the ear with hearing." And his descriptive powers being large, he could tell you all about
scenes he visited, and make you see them frequently
better than your own eyes would have served you for
such a purpose.

He had a style of expressing himself of great clearness and force, as well as of directness and earnestness.
The writings of such a man are all valuable. As com-
positions alone there are few better specimens in the
language, and their sentiment is always pure and elevating. A moral healthfulness distinguished all he
wrote. It does us good always to read what inspires
us with right sentiments, and he, with his enthusiastic
love of truth and goodness, which runs through all his
writings as a very high excellence, forever inspired these
in the hearts of others. It need not surprise us, his being
so wonderfully interesting in conversation, and in his
lectures upon travel, there were so many incidents to
relate of a pleasurable character that his keen perception had caught. How many will tell you of having

heard some one of these lectures, or of reading them
when published, and the pleasure thus given them; or
how they have been charmed and strengthened by his
marvelous utterances. Chancing to meet a friend who
had heard Mr. Balch tell on a single occasion of his
Oriental experiences, he declared that "his descriptive
powers were such as to leave him without a peer on
any platform of orators."

He had witnessed his "holding an assembly two
whole hours in rapt attention, and they had listened
with bated breath to his graphic illustrations, and
singularly felicitous descriptions of scenery." He
averred that "he would take a scene from Scripture
history, such as for instance the going up to Jerusalem;
or Christ before Pilate; or bearing His cross to the
place of execution; and draw a word-picture with such
vividness as to make his audience see it as plainly as
though an artist had taken his brush and drawn it upon
canvas." It was the remark of Doctor Cantwell that
"Brother Balch might leave Chicago in the morning to
go to Detroit. arriving there in the middle of the afternoon, when it should be announced that he would
lecture on that same evening in some place provided
for him, giving a description of the many scenes and
incidents transpiring by the way, and he would be most
likely to collect a crowd of hearers who would listen
with the greatest delight." There are numberless persons who have sat for hours and listened with marvelous interest to his brilliant talks of the ruined cities
of the old world, and the causes of their overthrow and
decay. with the lessons thence to be derived for the instruction and warning of modern cities and nations, till

they have imagined themselves on the spot, seeing everything just as he had looked upon them with his natural eyes.

Prof. J. S. Lee, of Canton, N. Y., describing a scene which he witnessed many years ago, after the close of the annual session of the Vermont State Convention of Universalists holden at Stowe, says : " The members of the convention and others, to the number of some 2,000 climbed to the summit of Mansfield Mountain, one of the highest peaks of the Green Mountain range. Brother Balch being present was invited to address them, and accepted the invitation, proposing to indulge in some casual remarks. But some of the friends urged that he should take a text, and preach them a sermon. This he was reluctant to do, but upon being further importuned he said he would gratify them, and announced as his text Isaiah xi : 9 : ' Get thee up into the mountain,' and for an hour he poured out a volume of eloquence, mingling instruction, anecdote, moral application, appeal, description and amusing detail, which delighted, entranced and uplifted his audience to the highest pitch of enthusiasm. They descended that lofty height not simply filled with the wonders of that wide and grand stretch of natural scenery which had been spread out before them, but with admiration inspired by the orator's noble sentiments, and matchless beauty of style.

"In the course of his address he compared the view as witnessed from the summit of Mount Tabor over the fields of Palestine, with the scene as witnessed from the spot where we were standing, and presented such a picture as shall never be effaced from my memory.

From that hour may be dated my love for the mountain scenery of the Holy Land which afterwards led me thither."

He also tells that on another occasion, when there had been a meeting of this same State Convention " the ministers met at a private house, and listened to his familiar talk on the Holy Land. He was in one of his best moods, and he painted in glowing colors his observations and his adventures. We were all intensely interested. We sat there in mute astonishment and admiration far into the night, and did not feel the least weariness over his fascinating talk. I have scarcely ever in my life spent a more delightful evening, or been so highly entertained by the conversation of a human being. When he got into his subject he was full of enthusiasm, and his soul glowed as with poetic fire, and he poured forth a matchless stream of inspiring description, and generous sentiment which held his hearers spell-bound."

Such is the expression of so many who have delighted to follow him in sermon and story and travel. A minister of the denomination, (himself an author) writes me, " I was surprised a short time since as I talked with him about his foreign travels, and his knowledge of men and things abroad. It seemed that like a Bayard Taylor, or a Humboldt, nothing could have escaped him which could be a matter of interest to any thoughtful person. And in all matters pertaining to his profession he was equally proficient. While sometimes adhering to special opinions more persistently than others might have done, he combined the philosopher with the theologian in a most remarkable degree."

Such then is our traveler, who goes abroad and visits also every part of his own country, to see and to learn as he tells us, and to be better prepared for usefulness in his profession. "I go" he says, "neither as a philosopher, sage or poet, but simply as a plain man, curious to see, and anxious to learn all I can in a given time; not to see large countries, long rivers, and vast mountain ranges. These we have at home in their proudest splendors, save perhaps the glaciered Alps. I go to see what mind and toil and ages have done; to trace the footsteps of humanity, as they come along down from the infant of days, rising and stumbling, and falling, and rising to stumble and fall again.

In speaking of what it might become him to say or think of foreign countries, he remarks:

"Of course I must measure everything by such standard as I have formed, and pronounce my own judgment upon it. I have not gone from home to ape the manners of others, or to change my own notions and habits that they may conform to those abroad; to be pleased with everything foreign, and dissatisfied with the plain, homespun habits of my own country. Neither am I to carry a bigoted attachment to the customs and institutions under which I was reared. I should go without prejudice, and under the influence of a principle broad and deep, which recognizes kings as companions, beggars as equals, and all men as brethren. I ought to carry with me a disposition to study the true, approve the good, honor the honorable, and admire the beautiful.

"That I love my own country and its liberal institutions, and more and more as I see those of others, I will not deny, but that does not impair my judgment, nor blind my sense of justice to these other lands. Is it not the dictate of Christianity to rise above all local and national distinctions in our estimate of right and wrong, of good and evil? Is not such the dictate of our higher nature? I must be pardoned for any freedom I may use in expressing my opinions. If I write at all, I must write as I think. I must express what I feel, and describe what I see."

*   *   *   *   *   *   *

Mr. Balch's first considerable journeying from home was in a visit paid with his old friend and intimate companion, Mr. Havemeyer, of the city of New York to the then Western country, in 1842. In speaking of this Mr. Havemeyer says, "I again traveled with him in 1848, the period of revolution on the continent of Europe, and arranged to visit Palestine for a short period, but was prevented by the troubles of that year, which made it difficult to go further than Rome." It was on his return, after spending considerable time in Great Britain, and Ireland especially, that his work "Ireland as I saw It" was written; a book of real merit, and full of the most interesting scenes, giving a correct view of the character of the people, and the causes of their poverty and wretchedness. Another in reviewing this work says, " He is very severe in his strictures upon the English Government, and the priesthood, and the landlords. The scenes of poverty described are heartrending, and we should suppose would call forth sympathy enough from the English Nation to have something done for the improvement of the condition of the people. The author recommends measures for educating the people, and is confident that if all were educated, Ireland would rise from its degradation.

There are several things brought forward in this

work too valuable to be passed over in silence.   He
shows what vast hordes of human beings, the children
of the same Father of himself, and brothers of the
same great family, are doomed to the most abject servitude by the working of a system of wrong from
which there is no escape but by expatiating themselves
to seek an asylum in a foreign country.   He thinks it
fortunate that they have no homes, no loved domestic
hearths to leave behind as they skulk away, for they
hate their miserable cabins, and the lords who oppress
them.   He is sure that there is not a link to attach
them to their native shores, as they flee like captives
escaped from cruel bondage, cheered for the briefest
period it may be by the fancied prospect before them
of comfort and competence, from which they are so
liable to awaken in the dark, dirty lanes and base-
ments of our cities, sorely disappointed and discouraged
for a life-time.   His remedy for it all is, that " right be
respected, industry encouraged, innocence protected,
and prosperity and happiness be suffered to prevail in
all parts of the kingdom."   He claims that "the teachers of religion are under a fearful responsibility—and
who shall escape?   He prays that the Lord may give
grace and mercy."

He preaches to the people, marveling that they
should be able to do as well as they do, but tells them
that " they must learn to help themselves.   They must
abjure their own clannishness, repudiate their bigotry,
and be willing to conform like good citizens, to the req-
uisitions of free, liberal and equitable institutions.   He
admonishes that the practical doctrines and precepts of
Christianity be brought before the people, and their

perfect and beautiful adaptedness to all the affairs and
conditions of men be shown, remembering that Christ
came to establish a kingdom of holiness and virtue
among men; that with Him the distinctions of earth are
nothing; that each and all are held directly and personally responsible to God for every act and word and
thought; that the poor oppressed and outcast have a
friend and defender in Him whose cause He will plead,
and whose wrongs He will avenge; that He abhors the
forms and fashions of religion which disguise the
truth, corrupt the heart and deceive the world; that
He requires righteousness in the inward parts, purity of
soul, and a perfect life. Could these things be understood and felt, he ventures to prophesy that a most
favorable result might be expected."

But then he does not forget that the chief cause of
Ireland's insufferable misery and shame was found
lying in another direction. "It had never risen from
its crushed condition. The lion's paw was laid heavily
upon it, and it writhed in agony. If it showed the
least disposition to turn itself in order to be relieved of
its painful attitude, the old lion growled and showed
its teeth all sharp for destruction, and the poor decrepit
creature laid down as quietly as it could, and licked the
foot of its oppressor, burying deeper its miseries which
gnawed still further into the very heart of its existence."
There are those in England, he reminds them, " who
would tear the whole carcass in pieces at once, and destroy it forever, making the Emerald Isle a province
into which they might introduce colonies of their own
wretched population. But heaven has reserved this
country for some other end, if not for freedom and

honor, to be as at present the manufactory of a race which is spreading itself like the old Teutons, among all the nations of the earth, for some purpose which shall be hereafter made manifest. But while waiting for their destiny, their very looks, dejected and heart-broken, indicate their unhappiness, their filth and rags their poverty. Numbers of them are seen everywhere idle, because there is nothing for them to do. Beggars are met at every turn, who promise liberally in heaven's name for the smallest pittance bestowed upon them."

"Talk of Southern slavery," he exclaims. "In practice it is not a thousandth part as wrong, as cruel, and abominable as the tenant system of Ireland. The slaveholder is obliged to treat his slaves mercifully, to provide for them in sickness and old age, and always give them enough to eat. But in Ireland, if the rent is not paid the constable is called in, and the tenant dis-trained, and if he cannot pay he is evicted, wife and children turned penniless upon the world to dig a shel-ter in a bog, or build one by the stone wall, and get his food as best he can. He is hunted out of his miser-able hovel as if he were a rat, and the land refuses him so much as a hole for a shelter. The workhouse is full, and the jail is a relief; but with the slave-master it is his interest that the slave shall have so much care and quiet as shall make him healthy for his task, and render him both profitable and marketable. I abom-inate the American slave system from the bottom of my soul. What then must be my feelings in the midst of such scenes of wrong and suffering as abounds in all parts of this ill-fated country. They are indescribable.

' Oh England, thou boasted land of freedom and

justice, of philosophy and nobleness, of religion and
philanthropy, English laws the models of Christian
jurisprudence, British honor and magnanimity, spirit
of Blackstone and Wilberforce, speeches of Peel and
Russell, glory of Wellington, himself an Irishman,
pride and extravagance of Victoria! What meaneth
these roofless huts, these starved stomachs, cadaverous
faces, naked limbs, and scattered corpses? Have ye
compassion for the well-fed, laughing, singing, shining
black men of sorrowful fate? It is well. But remember, charity begins at home. When you have purged
away the wrongs and miseries of your own sea-girt
isles, then come to our relief. But till then stand
mute in shame.

Mr. Balch says of all this, "I own that I have
touched upon some delicate points, trenched upon opinions by some held sacred, and described things which
might have been let alone, for which some will condemn, and nobody praise me. It is all the same to
me if I have told the truth. Facts will remain, and
my opinions go for what they are worth. I gazed with
astonishment and admiration on much I saw, and my
heart yearned deeply over the wrongs, oppressions, ignorance and misery I beheld. I saw more to approve
in the character of the people than I expected ; more
to lament in their condition, and more to condemn in
the operation of aristocratic institutions. My sympathies have ever been with the common people, and for
their sakes I ask to be heard. I commenced my journey among them with a determination to pay particular attention to the condition of the masses—to keep
along the side-hill of life, so as to see below as well as

16

above me, and calculate the chances for the improvement of the one, and to amuse myself with the proud
displays of the other. I have done both—looked on
kings and queens in their palaces; eaten stirabout
with cottiers on the banks of the Shannon ; butterbrod
with the peasantry of Deutschland, and green figs with
the lazzaroni of Italy, and I have formed my estimate
of things as they appeared to me, and in writing them
tried to be so minute in details that others might see
what I saw, and feel as I have felt." In this he shows
himself in full sympathy with the righting of the
wrongs that are forever oppressing the feebler classes.
His whole heart went out for the abatement of every
kind of evil, for did he not have an ear for the social
abuses of our times, and of all times?

If I might enter a word here in regard to Mr.
Balch's political opinions, I would say that he could
hardly be said to have had any politics in the usual
sense of the word, of being allied to a party, to be
bound by the party tactics. We may claim for him that
he was about the freest from policy or contrivance of
any man you often meet. It is true that he was a politician, as one being versed in the science of government, and the proper administration of national or public affairs. He was indeed politic, in the better sense
of being sagacious and judicious in the counseling of
those who were seeking to manage the affairs of state
and society, or country. But his politics (if he may be
said to have had any) was righteousness, in its application to the principles of governing and advancing the
welfare of a people, for which he was greatly concerned.

Some have said to the writer that he was a democrat. And so he was a democrat, in always advocating and defending a government of the people, by the people, and for the people, in the spirit and principles of democracy and republicanism both. He believed in a republic, in a representative form of popular government in which the sovereign power should be lodged in the hands of the people, and the people bearing rule, rather than their representatives. We can remember when there were those to proclaim that most unrighteous principle, "Our country right or wrong," but no such fealty to partisan warfare was ever acknowledged by Mr. Balch. He would scorn to have uttered a sentiment like that. He was opposed to all centralized power taken from the hands of the many to be transferred to the hands of the few, for them to abuse and to lord it over whomsoever they might choose to. It is noticeable that everything told of Mr. Balch points in one direction, showing that he was the people's man, loved and honored by the masses. With all his respect for the few, the distinguished few, he thought more of the many, the toiling and producing multitudes, whether theirs was the labor of the hands or of the head. Did any one in listening to Mr. Balch ever hear him voice a principle in politics or religion that did not do honor to his heart?

Speaking of the "Dangers of Our Republic, in an Oration delivered in Chester, Vt., July 4, 1857," he says:

"Our real danger is in the haughty spirit of ambition for place and parade and preferment, creating rivalries among veriest friends; producing a daring spirit of speculation to obtain wealth without industry, honor without honesty, fame without merit. It is in the blind adhesion to party, names and dictation, to the utter disregard of the principles of natural right, equal justice, the convictions of conscience and the true interests and honor of mankind. It is in the willing departure from the great truths asserted in the declaration of American independence, upon which our forefathers planted the standard of liberty, and sought to achieve the greatest good for their country and the world. It is in the substitution of a pretended for a real love and admiration for the institutions of liberty and right, on the part of gambling politicians, by which the unsuspicious are deceived and betrayed into the support of vicious measures. It is in the rapid and constant tendency to centralization, by the increase of political dishonesty and chicanery by which office-seekers and their helpers appeal to the lowest and basest passions to promote their selfish ends. It is in the low state of political sentiment among the people generally, or a habit of carelessness, in reference to the questions which concern the stability and development of our democratic form of government. It is in this that is our great and crying danger; a gross offense against the memories of our forefathers. We have not heeded their wise precepts, nor followed their good examples. We have departed from their simple, honest, earnest mode of life, and preferred the vanities and follies of a growing profligacy. Foreign fashions and flummeries have been imported, and exotic customs, and almost every species of extravagance have made a rapid growth in our exuberant love of apishness and aristocracy."

In preaching a Thanksgiving sermon in the city of New York, in 1844, subject "Political and Social Economy," he tells us that "True governments never seek to enrich and aggrandize a few ambitious men who are too indolent to be useful and too destitute of moral principle to care for anybody but self. Christianity unfolds the true system of government, wisely and condescendingly adapted to man's estate, and admirably suited to reform, redeem and exalt humanity. It is purely democratic in all its principles (using this word in its legitimate, not in its party sense), giving equal rights and privileges to all who embrace it. It levels the false distinctions of earth, and gives honor and praise to excellence wherever found. It humbles the proud and exalts the humble. It denounces vice revelling in a palace, and encourages virtue though dwelling in a hut. It says nothing of royal blood, noble birth, vested rights and tinselled dignity. It makes righteousness the standard of character, and commands truth and virtue as the sure avenue of true success, honor and greatness. Such," he tells us, "are my political principles. My father taught them to me, and maturer years have confirmed me in their truth and importance."

You find him saying, " What do our politicians but seek for party promotions in utter disregard of the principles on which our nation was founded—equal rights and common justice. Watch the doings of Congress and Legislatures and even courts of pretended justice, and see how much regard is paid to equality. Money is voted by thousands, obtained from the taxes of the people, directly or indirectly drawn from labor, the only wealth of any nation, and given for what? Favoritism, position; not for services rendered, such as all actual laborers are obliged to give before receiving pay. No; it is to sustain the dignity of the station. From presidents downward such is the order of the day; and such may be well if there is no God in heaven demanding justice and fraternity on earth. One may well doubt if such a Power is thought of during the session, though His presence be invoked in cold unlistening formality at each opening."

Mr. Balch, in writing to a friend who was afterward the democratic mayor of the city of New York, says, "Our democrats must learn what democracy means, and make practical the principles involved in the genius of our government. They must not get bewildered and lost in human plans and policies for personal party gains, or proceed in the wake of great monopolies, and financial splendors, but remember that the people are the basis of power, and that labor is the wealth of the nation. Enlightened as our people are in their natural, political and social rights, they will not submit long, as in Ireland, to be overridden and oppressed by those who live in and plunder on their millions, while digging in mines, toiling in shops and mills, sweating in the fields, or working anywhere at an average of wages that failed to keep soul and body together. Communism will grow out of such conditions, and we can not constrain the people as in Europe. Our soldiers are the people, and where is our safety in such a crisis? The party that shall live must correct, reform and avert this danger." He then adds, "You see that I am at my old hobby, but I will not bother you to help tame the giddy beast." This is what he calls the democratic party, "the giddy beast." He writes from Iowa, "The country all this way looks splendid. The signs indicate abundance. The people are hopeful, but party newspapers are glum, doubting more than hoping. I do not read them enough to have a mind on what they say. I know what I should like to see in the nation — less party, and more principle. When shall it be?"

The chief politics of Brother Balch was in being opposed to aristocracy, and he was ever seeking to defeat the plans of those who oppressed God's humbler children to advance their own selfish interests. There are a thousand ways in which we may belie our principles of religious equality, and he would let no differences of outward distinction hide from him the pure image of God stamped upon every soul of the race, but would honor all men as His immortal offspring. And seeing in the poorest and most despised his own brethren and kindred, he was ready to aid the feeble, resisting all wronging of them; remembering that inasmuch as he did good to the least of his brethren, he could be counted as doing it to Him who was the friend and brother of all men. Rooted and grounded in the truth that man as man, man universal, man everywhere was his brother, to be counted and honored as a brother, in all laws, and all governments, he essayed to respect him as such in all those relations and capacities in which he was called to act toward him, regarding the rights which others had to whatsoever aid his hand could afford, as sacred and inalienable.

In this was seen one of the prime excellencies of Brother Balch, and never did he appear to better advantage than when pleading for rules and regulations which were based in good, and to be used for the people's sake, and in educating and lifting up the mass of mind. It does not appear to whom he is writing, nor does it matter, so long as the sentiment is what it is, that "None are to be loved and respected more truly than the humble, patient laborers, who, under God, produce what they possess, to work their own way through life, and to be the architects of their own fortunes. No matter whether they are high or low, rich or poor in pelf, conspicuous or humble in position ; they are surely the upper circles in the order of nature, whatever the factitious distinctions of society, fashionable or unfashionable, may decree. There may be those to clutch and call their own, what rightfully is not theirs, and wrench the hard earnings of sacrifice and self denial; and so manage and monopolize these to themselves, while others are prevented, though vastly more worthy, from shaping the richer bounties of the beneficient Father. The history of the world, sacred and profane, is full of facts, illustrations and commandments, teaching such things. Ruins scattered all over the old world, demonstrate the need of right views and right conduct by the rich and the poor, the strong and the weak, the wise and the simple, in church and State, and in social and domestic life. He is a fortnnate man who heeds not the unbrotherly distinctions of the world, who envies not the rich, nor neglects the poor; who covets not promotion without merit, nor approves of indolence, worthlessness and wickedness anywhere, but in whose pure and liberal soul dwells the love of God and man to guide in the regulation of conduct, and the formation of character. He alone is the happy man who lives a good and useful life, in humility, peace and good will to all men. Is there not work enough to be done in such a cause? Most is to be done among the rich, the great, the noble—as they are called, and too often think themselves more highly than they ought to think—the wrongers and oppressors of their fellow-men."

He asks in one of his letters to an unknown person, "By what means do some become so immensely rich and powerful in so short a time, and lifted up above their fellows? Are they wiser and better, or more industrious and economical than others? Or are they wickeder, more cunning, crafty, unscrupulous and pretentious, than plain, honest toilers, who are willing to live among men, and let others live with them on terms of equality and fraternity. Thank God, such can eat with no more relish, sleep no more soundly, nor enjoy the world to any better advantage." He then adds, after very much more of the same general character:

"I did not start to write so serious a letter, but these thoughts flowed into my mind, and now it is written. I have concluded that I will not throw it away, but let you have it as it is. It will enable you to know some of the things I am thinking about. What I have seen in my travels, and all the way as I have gone along, is a too strong confirmation of the evils complained of by so many. Persons who twenty years ago were so honorably employed, have swollen into millionaires, twenty to forty million strong, and live in half-million palaces that outpass in splendor, most of those of the princes of Europe."

He brings this all home very closely to us, by speaking of the great city of New York, where he tells us he spent seventeen years of his manhood life, and had watched its changes and growth of pride and luxury

since 1825. We have his estimate of town and country
life. He says: "I am no admirer of large and crowded
cities. I believe they exist and flourish in derogation
of a sound philosophy, and the will of God. The whole
manner of city life is becoming little else than a system
of false pretenses from highest to lowest, with its
gambling houses, billiard saloons, grog-shops and broth-
els, which drum for customers to the lowest pits of vice,
poverty and degradation, which fester in the damp cel-
lars, dark lanes, rear buildings and horrid purlieus of
all large cities. Where are decencies and proprieties of
life so outraged as in our cities and large towns?
Where are mobs, murders, riots, thefts, drunkenness,
harlotry and lawless living, most common? Where are
reforms most difficult, crimes most successful, vice
most unblushing, and virtue least courted? The
adage is, 'God made the country, but men made the
town.' It may be said productive labor dwells in the
country, while traffic is confined to the towns; though
such remark is not literally true, for there is much productive labor in the great city, and not a little traffic
in the country. It is a plain truth that the source of
all true increase is in labor.

Trade really produces nothing but an exchange of
commodities. He who buys property for a particular
sum, and sells for ten times as much, may be called
lucky, but he adds nothing to the amount of wealth-
But he who buys a piece of land and makes it produce
ten times as much by his own labor, has so enriched the
world by nine. He who digs from the mine a piece of iron,
takes from the forest a tree, and makes therefrom an
article of use, comfort, or even beauty, has added in

the same way to the sum of human enjoyment. But he who only handles the earnings of others, and that often only in imagination, may enrich himself sometimes very rapidly, but he impoverishes others to do it. He puts nothing in the common fund.

New York has lived and thrived on commerce. The few have grown immensely rich, the many terribly poor. The proportion holds good, for the law of production and increase is inflexible. Those who keep in small dark rooms in Wall street, and traffic in trade, make fortunes most rapidly. They can show no visible, tangible substance, but grow rich (and become poor) on fancies. What do they to enhance the good of mankind? Thus, from the humblest producer in the rudest way, to the most refined and arch speculator, even on the prospective results of other's labor, there is a gradation regulated by a law just as marked and sure as can be found in any other department of social life. It is a happy consideration that here, as everywhere, God bears rule, for although merit may seem sometimes to be unrewarded, while fraud triumphs, yet the judgment comes at last. The law of compensation is not suspended. Each shall find his due. " The wrath of man shall praise Him.

"A terrible illustration of these simple but sadly neglected truths is in the process of completion in New York to-day. The blow has fallen first and heaviest on those who trafficked off their *integrity*, selling the small commodities they had of manly principles to secure the favor of barterers south. They now taste the bitter results of their mistaken deeds. Is not God just? And such as participated with them have not

escaped. Such, too, is the law of trade. Credit based
on paper, and the exhibit of names is not a sure support in time of trial. It is going to heaven by proxy.
Principal and proxy both rejected.

"In one sense it is sad to look on the dissolutions of
men's fortunes—hopes all destroyed, prospects all dark,
courage clean gone. It is like a sweeping scourge.
But the "curse causeless does not come." It is the
remedy for evils grown chronic, and he must be a
poor scholar who will not profit thereby. I wander
the streets as I do through the chambers of a hospital.
All are sick—some growing worse, a few improving,
but all anxious for the crisis. Those recovered may be
as imprudent as ever, though now they promise better
fashions. The evil is malarious and contagious, vac-
cination is not a sure remedy. A full return to a
legitimate business, honestly and honorably pursued,
not the sacrifice of every thing to "make haste to be
rich," but a steady, gradual increase to acquire a
competence for a comfortable life and a fair generos-
ity—not a princely palace and all extravagant luxuries—this will, in due time, remove the evil, and lay the
foundation of personal and general prosperity. Let
the wise take heed and triumph."

After so much we can scarcely fail to understand
how it was in perfect accord with the character of Mr.
Balch, having imbibed the principles of personal liberty, social equality and mutual responsibility, so far
as both religious and political rights were concerned,
to identify himself in the affairs of Rhode Island with
what was known as the "People's Movement." Bound
up with the affections of the masses, how could he be

otherwise than interested in sympathizing with them
in their trials and deprivations. There could scarcely
be a more unrighteous thing than the Charter, or Grant
of King Charles II., requiring a real estate qualifi
cation to become a citizen and voter. It is put forth
by Mr. Balch in " A Brief Account of the Cause, and
the Methods Adopted to Obtain a Republican Constitution for the State of Rhode Island," that " A man
might be worth a million dollars of personal property,
and be one of the best, wisest, and most patriotic of
inhabitants, but he was not a free man any more for
it. He tells us that " the price of freedom at the time
to which reference points was $134 of landed estate.
With that a man, and his eldest son could vote,
but without such qualifications no man could vote, hold,
office, sit on a jury, be tried by a jury of his peers, or
collect a debt without a landholder to back his writ,
and yet was compelled to pay taxes equal to others,
and do military duty without his consent. The ratio
of representation was wholly arbitrary, and it wrought
the disfranchisement of three-fifths of the American
citizens residing in the State. A man could be a citizen of the nation, but not of Rhode Island, without
buying the right. None were born free but the first
son. All others were aliens — political nobodies."
Such were some of the anti-republican principles and
disabilities which the people of Rhode Island were
laboring under at the time their troubles were brought
on, and yet entitled to a republican form of government, according to the Constitution of the United
States, and as much guaranteed to them as to any
other State in the Union. He asks the question, "Why

should the provisions of a charter, granted by a British King, which of course ceased to exist from the time the Constitution went into operation, defeat all the rights of the people? He wished it to be remembered that up to 1841 Rhode Island had no sort of constitution to alter, amend or abolish. The supreme power, till the colonies broke away from Great Britain, was in the King. And the abstract question when stripped of all mystification and misinterpretation he tells them " is simply whether the sovereignty itself, which is no longer with the king of England, resides in the Legislature, or does it go to the people to be exercised through its delegates? "

Brother Balch was of the revolutionists' opinion, and stood nearly alone of all the ministers of Providence, combating any opposite idea. "The principles contended for and sought to be established by the citizens of that State, the right of the people to rule, and determine what the government under which they lived should be, was the fundamental doctrine," he tells us, upon which the national existence was based. Everybody but anarchists and aristocrats admitted this fact. Deny it, and we had nothing left to characterize us from the governments of Europe, nothing worth the blood and treasure spent to liberate our country from foreign dominion." Rhode Island was under a landed aristocracy, and how to obtain the advantage of having their liberties guaranteed to them, became the great question seeking a solution.

Their cause, therefore, was legitimate, and peaceful, as well. Brother Balch at least was a peace man from principle, opposed to war under all circumstances.

He was a man of peace, as he was a man of God, and with the war spirit he had nothing to do but to rebuke it. He taught that war was not only a calamity, but a crime ; and the whole tendency of his ministry was to bring it into merited and lasting disgrace. He believed in the doctrine of O'Connel, the great Irish barrister and reformer, that " No change whatever was worth a single drop of blood." He was opposed to war, to capital punishment, and every engine of cruelty and oppression, as being opposed to the spirit of the age. as well as to the instructions of Christ and His apostles, who taught that we were to bless those that curse us, and do good to those that hate us, that we might be the children of our Father which is in heaven, not being "overcome of evil, but overcoming evil with good." He had no favor for any of these wrongs of society, and it seemed to him that they ought not to be tolerated in a civilized community. He ever taught that patience would better accomplish the cure of any evil, than the commission of a wrong. A strong government with him was not an unjust and tyrannical government, but one fostering liberty and conscience, rather than soul-tyranny. It never should exist but with a high degree of freedom. He looked forward to a day when love should emerge from passion and hate, and kindness be recognized as the sovereign of power ; when the graceful forms of humanity should have arrested victory from the dominions of ignorance and barbarism, when affection should occupy the throne of fear, the arts of peace 'become the business of life, and fraternity the watchword of joyous nations." We can then understand how it should be told us that "he had a great abhorrence of lawsuits tending to keep men at variance with each other, and that he was instrumental in settling several suits of long standing while preaching to his parish in Ludlow, Vt."

No one could ever suppose that there was anything in the life of Mr. Balch to encourage litigation, or a military spirit, and when the authorities of Rhode Island grew alarmed at the mad spirit that was rife in their midst, he was pleaded with, and had to be called in to quell the rashness and violence which their own misconduct had evoked. The people were gathered largely in a hall in Providence under the greatest excitement, and all parties came to him to urge him to go and see he could not quiet the agitation. To this he consented after much importuning, telling them that they had to submit to be ruled by a minority, as they could not hope to resist the whole military force of the nation in its guarantee to assist in the overthrow of the people's constitution. In hearing that some were proposing physical resistance, he assured them that he " would rather such weapons were sunk to the bottom of the Narragansett than to be used in such a cause." His advice was, " Continue to pursue a peaceful, persuasive course as they had done from the beginning, pleading their natural and inalienable rights, and they would triumph at last. The fairer minds would see the justice and righteousness of their cause, and history would finally do them honor."

There was no other course for them to pursue, with the opposition controlling all the machinery of the Government, and having all the prestige of authority and power. And more than all, Mr. Balch was a moralist,

and not a politician, and he could not forget his vocation. It may be said of him that he has always had
certain great principles of right to which he has adhered
independently of party considerations, and he has been
too firm in his judgment of men and measures, and
what was right, to conciliate politicians.

Mr. Balch, in concluding an oration given in Pawtucket, R. I., July 4, 1839, the subject of it, "Individual
Freedom the Foundation of a Democratic Government,"
utters such sentiments as these:

"The true value of our republican institutions
will be fully known: their rich blessings will completely unfold themselves and be duly appreciated
as soon as men become lovers of God, truth and
principle, more than lovers of pleasure, self and
party. When all our citizens will return to the patriot-
ism of our fathers, and be willing to let the majority
rule without a clamorous denunciation of every man,
and every measure which does not tally precisely with
their own infallible right to dictate; when the minority
will labor to correct abuses, not by denunciation, in-
trigue, or stratagem, but by an open exhibition of correct principles and superior wisdom and virtue; when
in short, goodness and truth shall receive the just meed
of honor, and the love of self, the love of sect, the love
of party, be merged in the love of country, and the greatest good of all, then will the banner of liberty wave its
rich folds over all the nations, giving peace and freedom
to all. No foul stain of party slander, or factional discord, will then dim the fair fame of the nation of the
free. Violence will no more be heard in the land, nor
wasting and destruction be in our borders. The East,
the West, the North, the South shall be enfolded in one
warm embrace. Men of virtue and intelligence, of
quality and decision, the chosen of the free, shall sit
in state, and rule in righteousness, enjoying the respect

17

of each and of all. Our country will rise to the acme of its true glory, and sit enthroned in the respect and praises of the whole earth."

I will, of course, be accredited with having rambled widely from my subject, which began with Mr. Balch's first visit to Europe in 1848. But in 1852 he was asked by two men, not of his church, with whom a third afterward joined, to go abroad if he wished, with his pulpit supplied at home, and full permission and means to journey as far, and remain as long as he pleased. He was wise enough to accept the generous offer, and traveled extensively in Europe, extending his journey to Palestine, across the desert and through Egypt to Nubia. The person accompanying him in his first tour to the old country, tells us that "In the month of June he set sail on the steamer Arctic, with several young men under his charge, and entrusted to his care, as guide, tutor and protector'.'

It was in setting out upon his former journey to the Old World that his reflections were made known to us as being of the following character:

"My favored time has come at last; the preparation has been made, and my ship, the 'Siddons', is floating on the bay, waiting for wind and tide to carry her out to sea. The last words have been spoken; the last look, the last signal given. I am leaving wife, children, friends, church, country, duty; no, I will not confess that, for it is the better to discharge duty that I have essayed to make real the dream of my life; to see and touch the places and things made sacred by the transactions recorded in the Holy Book. I am wanting to see and learn all I can, to gratify my long-desired wish, and to refresh my memory in these after years of the things which I read in my childhood life."

So now, in his "Notes of a Pilgrimage through Europe, to Egypt and the Holy Land," he is not without his reflections. His letter on the Arctic at sea, opens with the words:

"It is over, home is behind me again, and the country of my hope and desire before me. I am both sad and happy at parting, but expect to return better qualified for my arduous professional duties. I shall no doubt see and experience much, and it will be an eventful year, and may God spare my life and bless me in giving me a joyful return. But before all that shall be, what deeply interesting scenes are to pass before my eyes, beautiful, romantic, grand, beyond any pen to describe."

As he continues to write after arriving in the Old World, he is left to wonder that any one "should depreciate the blessings of republican liberty, and wish to live under a monarchy, that they might have an established aristocracy, a court, a born nobility, and ranks and grades to keep down the rabble."

He leaves the reader to sketch in his own mind the scenes in Ireland which he had passed over four years before, and says he "looks for nothing of special interest in that direction." Of Scotland the limits of this book do not permit me to more than mention it briefly. He says:

"It has its peculiarities, its attractions, its faults. In scenery it is beautiful, romantic, in a certain degree grand. Its heathery hills, tumbled together carelessly and in great disorder, skirted about their bases with sweet sylvan lakes, or gorged by deep glens and almost insuperable passes, afford a novelty and va riety at once pleasant and astonishing. But it has more of beauty than of grandeur, more to please than to astonish. And one feels more of quiet and contentment than when roving among the Alps.

"The fault of Scotland is its bigotry. In religion, in politics, in social life, there is a looking to the past for a standard, while materially and physically everything is steaming forward. In enterprise it does not lack at all since the days of Watt and Bell. But in loyalty to kings and creeds it is wofully behind. Bereft of their own nationality, reduced to being the province of a haughty rival, Scotchmen have forgotten the past, and learned to love the government that has conquered them. This may be well, for thereby the feuds and fights which hinder the progress of the world are removed; the expense of one royal family saved, and a chance given for the pursuit of the arts, peace and social prosperity. I can not object to that, but rather honor those who yield a king and court. But when they look at these things and say, ' no further,' they mistake, for the wrongs, the misrule, the oppressions of an established aristocracy, a native, a foreign, a born nobility, can not abide forever. The day of redemption draweth nigh, when the old shall pass away and the new be come in ; when stars and epaulets, crowns and garters, shall no longer entitle a man without merit to 10,000 acres of God's earth, while the honest, toiling laborer plods a whole life-time for a poor and precarious livelihood. In this respect I had rather hear the shout, "God bless the people," than hear them sing, 'God save the Queen.' The learned, the free in thought, the active in enterprise, are generally on the side of freedom, and hence there is hope. The large soul brooks no restraint. It will be free. I wonder at Scotland lying back so far from the reforms of the day. It may not in reality, but it does in pretense. The theology of John Knox, with all its iron incrustations, its chains and back straps, is still abiding, though few in fact do really wear its fetters. Still there is this fault; to adjure that faith is to enlist hostility and pass into the ranks of infidelity. So truly is this the case many suppose that to doubt, where they can not understand, is to be actually infidel. Hereby great injury is done to the truth, and thousands are kept back from the blessed light, hope and bliss of Christianity, because they can not see it as Calvin and Knox did."

Mr. Balch makes his way hastily along, mentioning places of note, arriving and departing from London and Amsterdam, across the channel, landing at Dover, and thence to Ostend, and a ride to Antwerp, and afterward to Brussels and to Rotterdam. He thinks it hardly to be expected that he should be detained to mention numerous places by the way, and even Germany and Switzerland are cast in the shade by the Holy Land, which is now the chief object of interest. He more than mentions some of the places through which he is passing, such as Milan, Leipsic, Hamburg, Berlin, Dresden, Vienna, Trieste, Venice, etc., and stops to make reflections upon the griefs and burdens of the people. "I confess my confidence in men is almost daily weakened," he says. "I am sorry it is so. But what can we do with the examples piled up before us? Can we turn from them? They meet us on every side. The past is full of them, and the present has its quota. I have wished a thousand times that I could shut my eyes to them, and be joyful and happy as others; that I could see no errors, no cause of complaint, but all bright, and fair and hopeful in the present and future of my race, it would be such a relief, so pleasant, so perfectly delightful. I have tried to look on the fair, and bright and beautiful. I have traversed fine cities, gazed on the grand in architecture, admired the beautiful in art, and consulted the wisdom of sages. What does it all avail so long as the myriads of God's children live in hovels, half starved in the rags of misery, and ignorant of the truth that maketh free indeed?

"Deem not that I am all sad or discouraged. I am not, but hopeful as ever. Cheered by the light of that blessed faith which sees in God a universal Father, in humanity a common brotherhood, in heaven a final home of freedom, love and bliss, I look upon this deathly stillness, upon these rustling commotions, and secret sighs, as one gazes from the mountain top upon the hills and valleys below him. Providence employs means which often seem strange to us — sometimes totaly inadequate."

He ever thought thus, and still would grow tired of looking upon all gorgeous scenes, and thinking how it was with the people, what were their conditions and prospects, and how they fared in body and soul.

*   *   *   *   *   *   *

In crossing the Adriatic on the steamer Germania, bound for the Orient, they first touched Corfu, passing along the coast of Arcadia, and were next in Athens, the ancient capital of art, of eloquence and oratory. Hurrying on they leave Athens after the shortest stay, making for Smyrna and Constantinople, and soon are at Beirut, in Syria.

"At length my feet," he says, "have trod the soil of Terre Sante, and wild and confused thoughts run through my brain. Another dream of my life has become reality. I could not sleep last night. I rose at one, and again at four, and watched for the day, till soft glimmerings of the earliest dawn stole through

the valleys, which indent the summit of the loftiest
range which seemed to rise directly from the sea. I
hoped to see the sun climb up its pathway in oriental
skies, resplendent in all its glory. But as the stars
grew pale, dark clouds stretched a thick veil along the
horizon and spoiled the grandeur of the scene.

"Another day and I have sat under the shadows of
the cedars of Lebanon, and, starting some minutes in
advance of the rest, I have ascended the last rise of
Lebanon alone, and the view is magnificent, sufficient
to repay my toil. Later, and I have been at Nazareth,
to the top of Tabor, and to Tiberias, bathed in the sea,
eaten fish from its pure waters, walked where Jesus
walked, and taught and blessed its inhabitants. Oh,
could I feel as He felt, live pure as he lived, and in all
things say 'Thy will be done!' If there is any spot in
nature beautiful—grandly, harmoniously beautiful—it is
from Nazareth by Tabor, along the sea of Galilee.
What more delightful spot as fit for the transfiguration,
than the top of this mountain? Nazareth is one of
the largest ruins of Syria, next to Beirut and Jerusalem.
The land is all very well. It is a goodly land as of
yore. But the people—there lies the fault. I looked
on the barrenness of soil. In this I am disappointed.
There is vastly more cultivation than I expected; but
the people are more ignorant and debased; more neglectful of all the arts and improvements, and comforts
of civilized life than I thought it possible for any corner of the earth to be. Poor deceived humanity, the
Lord have mercy upon it !

"But I must sleep and rouse myself early for tomor-
row, for my eyes are to behold Mount Zion and 'the joy

of the whole earth.' I am to enter the gates of Jerusalem, and look upon places of all others dear and sacred
to the Christian. I will not anticipate impressions,
but sleep and dream, and awake to behold what my·
eyes have long desired to see. One great fact ·has
been settled in my mind since wandering through
Palestine—its capacity to maintain the large population said to have once lived in it. It is indeed a beautiful and wonderful land. The soil is everywhere very
rich, and singularly adapted to serve man's comfort.
The sky is so serene and pure that one beholds a beauty
which Italy can not equal. I have never seen a spot
of earth more charming, more perfectly beautiful,
than about the sea of Gallilee. Standing upon the
summit of Mount Tabor. a panorama, vast and splendid,
is presented to the eye, which no spot on earth can
equal. The scene is so perfectly harmonious that one
can not wish it improved. It is not so majestically
grand as places in Switzerland. It is not so vast as
our prairies of the West. But all is beautifully combined.

"But Jerusalem. what shall I say of it? Here,
after all, is the spot most sacred and memorable of any
on earth. Sacred, yet it is not sacred. The desolations of 1,800 years, the present poverty, ignorance and
misery proves it is not sacred. But it is hallowed by the
deepest affection, by the highest hopes, by the proudest
triumphs the earth has ever witnessed. It must be
ever dear in the memory of all believers. Nobody in
the least familiar with its history can pass through its
streets unmoved. I sit and think, and in my sadness
I almost wish I had not come here; that I had never

looked on this desolation, darkness, death; that I had
never known so much of the mystery of iniquity which
works by monkish superstitions upon the poor credulity
of the simple-hearted—to palm upon them studied de-
ceptions, to keep them enslaved in the manacles of
error and ignorance, and hold back, if possible, the
world from its progress toward the high destiny to
which Heaven has appointed it. It is so sad to see,
here, in this city of our God, where Jesus taught and
suffered, and died to save the world from deception,
error and sin, and restore it to purity and perfection,
so many evidences of a people cheated of those excellent lessons; to see here the curse of sectarian rivalry,
put forth in all its strength and subtlety by the inter-
ference of a Moslem civil power averse to all Christian
ethics.

"Let not the believer be anxious to visit this land;
or let him come here and look at the real condition of
the people, and feel a twinge for the wrongs of
humanity, and then set about an inquiry into the causes
of this backwardness in everything, this look of dejec-
tion and poverty that stares one in the face at every
turn, and he will find, not in the soil, not in the
climate, not in the naturally indolent constitution of
the people, the reason for this state of things, but in
the selfishness, pride and arrogance of the church, by
which even the State is controlled. It is as men are
taught to think, that they are.

"There are sights one sees which he can not describe.
There are thoughts stirring the depths of the soul which
can not be uttered. But a feeling of sadness comes
over one, occasioned in part by the disappointment that

is met with everywhere. But I am glad to have been
here, that I have looked on the desolations of this naturally beautiful land. Nay, I rejoice at the very ruin
I see, and more, that scarce a spot can be identified so
as to become sacred. The Moslem has his Mecca, the
Jew his Jerusalem, but the doctrine and spirit of
Christianity is universal. It is neither in Gerizim nor
Jerusalem that men must go to worship, for 'God is
a Spirit, and they that worship Him must worship Him
in spirit and truth,' and 'In every nation he that
feareth Him and worketh righteousness is accepted of
Him.' Neither God nor Christianity can be localized.
A shudder runs over me when I look on attempts in
churches and galleries to represent the Universal
Father. A similar feeling is awakened when I visit places
claimed to be sacred. To see none of these did I come
to Jerusalem. But I did expect other emotions than
those I feel, and so I am disappointed. 'The Jerusalem that now is, is in bondage with her children,' and
how can a soul that has tasted 'the liberty where-
with Christ hath made it free,' be thrilled with
joy at the near view of such a bondage. No,
the spirit of God and Christ is not in any one place,
it is not in any temple human hands may rear, but
in every true, honest, Christian heart. It is in all
the earth. I weep to see men and women, and children, kneel and bow and kiss a stone, a fragment
of cloth, or a piece of wood. All these things are painful to me; I can not endure them. I turn and go away
in pity, almost in disgust. But I see in Christianity, as
taught by the great Master, a power that is to correct
all this. My faith grows stronger every day, and I am

more than ever thankful for the broad and comprehensive views revealed to us in the Gospel, and more
than ever impressed with the necessity of presenting
them among men. A more liberal spirit is to go
abroad in all the earth. The world must be civilized;
it must be Christianized and redeemed. All fetters
must fall off. The prison doors are all to burst open,
and the captives to be set free. It will come. In God's
time it will come, and that will be soon enough. Amen
—let it come. But I must go."

* * * * * * *

And he now sets out for his home, unable to sup-
press his emotions as he gazes for the last time upon
the scene he is leaving behind. He could not tell why,
but it was so that he wept, as if parting with the dearest friend. As he went on his way, his heart beating
heavily, he was in a mood for poetizing, and he writes
the following :

CROSSING THE DESERT.

A special doggerel, written on the back of a camel, while
crossing the desert from Palestine to Egypt, and read to the party at
an evening encampment:

Travelers from my native land,
Pilgrims o'er this burning sand,
To kill the tedium of the day,
And while the hours move swift away,
I sing to you this jolting lay,
Poor scribbling of a shaking hand.

With Arabs for a guaranty,
Of Hadjis any quantity,
Fifteen in our own merry band
From Britain and the Yankee-land,
We make a splendid caravan
Of wandering humanity.

We've doctors, lawyers, pastors here,
Of danger who has need to fear?

A Wolverine of gold to tell,
Three youngsters who can buy and sell,
Three dames, and four *chere demoiselles*
To keep us all in right good cheer.

Of camels we have forty four,
And horses six or seven more,
Eight tents, with beds and stools and dishes
For soups and prunes, for rice and fishes,
(Who cares for poverty and riches?)
With a desert for a floor.

So far there has been no contention,
Tho' some have murmured at detention;
With dragomen we're well supplied,
And cooks whose talents have been tried
On kids and chickens, baked and fried,
And plates too numerous to mention.

Here no one has satiety,
Nor bother and anxiety,
Of traveler's woes the bitterest dreg
But cakes and kids and chicks and eggs,
And scorpions of forty legs,
To add to the variety.

All ranged, we slowly pass along,
A moodish, merry, motley throng;
Some read, some chat, and some are thinking,
Some scold, some eat, and some are drinking,
The young, may be, at others blinking,
Or join the loud and laughing song.

Then he tells us something of

DESERT LIFE.

A life on the desert is no life for me;
The wild wastes so barren there's nothing to see;
The sun shines too brilliant, too constantly bright:
There's no hour of comfort but the dark hour of night.
Yet the desert has lessons by which to improve—
There's misery below, bliss and beauty above.
While passing through one and bearing the bother,
'Tis best to be patient, and hope for the other.
A few days' endurance and all will be o'er,
The desert behind us, the sweet Nile before;
The lone land of Bed'weens, and Jackalls' alarms.
Exchanged for green fields and the shadow of palms.
So when done with the ills, temptations and strife,
Which throng on our paths in the desert of life,
May me meet in that world where no sorrow is found;
But love, joy and praise immortal abound.

It was while here that they held a Christmas service, and sung

A CHRISTMAS HYMN.

Which had been suggested by seeing the Morning Star rise over Bethlehem.

A star shone bright o'er Bethlehem's plains,
    Blessed herald of Immortal birth !
And angels sang in heavenly strains,
    Good-will to men and peace on earth.

From that lone star a Light went forth
    To banish sin, a world to save;
To scatter blessings south and north,
    And burst the barriers of the grave.

The blind have seen, the deaf have heard,
    The sick been healed, the lost been found,
The dead been raised, the sad been cheered,
    And blessings spread the world around.

Shine forth, bright Star, disperse the clouds !
    That shadow still this sinning earth !
Let men arise, come forth in crowds,
    And glory in immortal truth!

During the last few years of his life, having now given up the care of a parish, and with a wonderful love of travel, as also in the way of health-seeking, he made several visits from home to California in 1880, to Mexico in 1881, to Colorado in 1882, and to Florida in 1882, 1884, and 1887, besides other visits paid to New England and the Middle and Southern States.

Of Mexico he says: "We have seen and learned much, and enjoyed considerable. Few of the comforts of travel enjoyed in our country, we may say, are found here. The traveler who would be wise and profit by what he sees must make up his mind to take things as he finds them, and not complain because they differ from the comforts and customs of home, else he may make himself and all about him, needlessly miserable.

As he can not control the world, it is wiser to resolve to make the best of everything, a doctrine not very inappropriate anywhere.

"The City of Mexico is decidedly one of the most romantically situated of any I have ever seen, Naples, Constantinople and Damascus not excepted. To jot down all one sees and hears and learns, so unlike any in our own country, would be a long and laborious task. To one familiar with cities and customs of the Old World, all is plainer and more easily comprehended. Mexico is not an American city in its characteristics. It is an exotic, imported from Spain, and bears a near resemblance to its Moorish relations. The visitor sees and feels at every turn that he is in a foreign land. Very few things will remind him of his own country. The look and language of the people, the streets and houses, churches and state buildings, carriages and horses—everything is to him unique and strange. The cookery and service is as unsatisfactory as anything he encounters. To describe the condition, character and manners of the people would be no easy tasks.

"The gathered multitudes in the market, in the streets, in the churches, in the plaza, anywhere and everywhere, present pictures of variety from the extremest poverty and almost nakedness, to the richest attire and gaudiest display seen in the richest adornments of the churches and decorations of the officiating priests, the latter surpassing Rome itself. Men are seen staggering under heavy burdens borne upon their shoulders — wardrobes, bureaus, counters of stores, square blocks of stone for buildings, large jugs of water laid upon their hips, held by broad straps around their foreheads, with another smaller jug hanging in front from the main strap as it passes by the neck; bales and boxes of goods, and women with baskets and bundles on their heads, showing there are two-legged, as well as four-legged beasts of burden. But after all,

Mexico is a fine city, and the most grandly situated in its surroundings of almost any I ever saw. Short interviews with the more intelligent confirmed me in the faith that Mexico is started on the high road of permanent advancement. It will take a long time and much effort, to bring this singular compound of humanit into the full enjoyment of equal rights and universal liberty and fraternity. It may be a long and hard road to travel, but it is confidently hoped they will reach it ere long, and together share all the safety and blessings that belong to a true democratic republic."

Of Florida he has this to say : " It is Florida, and not much else. It is not a paradise, nor a very near approach to it. It boasts of its climate, which is indeed very delightful for comfortable invalids, and for those who would escape the rough winters of the North. Facts prove that it is more sought for pleasure than for health, and most for profit by those who come to settle. Orange orchards are the rage, and those who have patience to bide their time, and learn the business well, reap handsome profits afterward. On the whole, Florida has many advantages to satisfy the emigrant who would make it his home. It has a fine climate, cheap lands, good timber and water ; and for the prudent liver and worker, a fair chance for good health and comfort. But it is flat, has many sluggish rivers, much poor land, large swamps, and of course is subject to billious diseases, fevers, etc., where the people are imprudent. It is a delightful region for winter residence. Hotels of first quality and highest prices, and lodging houses are numerous, and some very excellent. Having tried both, I am confident that for health and quiet comfort, Florida is superior to Italy. It has not the scenery, antiquities and works of art found there, yet there is a uniqueness and wierdness of romance here that is found no where else.

CHAPTER XIII.

HOME LIFE AND VARIED EMPLOYMENTS.

Mr. Balch was happily married twice—in the years of 1829 and 1856. His first wife was Adeline C. Capron, who was born in Winchester, N. H., and his second, Mary A. Waterhouse, born in New York City, both of them estimable women. The number of his children born to him in all, was eleven, eight by his first wife, and three by his last, only six of the former wife's surviving at the time of his death, and two of the latter's, Clarence dying in 1864, Charles in 1872, and Elena in 1876. He had also eleven grandchildren, and two great grandchildren, neither of which he ever saw, the first being born only a few short weeks, and the latter coming as a little stranger to be telegraphed to him, but three days before his death. He had a frugal, but welcome home, and a ready sympathy with all worthy virtues, and all good energies. I will not intrude into the most sacred and intimate of his domestic relations, since silence and imagination can alone picture his fidelity there, but I may be permitted to refer to the singular faithfulness and persevering exactitude with which he ever performed the duties of a father and careful provider, being kind, thoughtful, tender, affectionate, indulgent, doing everything possible for his family, and cherished and loved by them as we can not tell.

He was a great favorite of the children of his home, and of children generally, participating in all their little sports and amusements ; and there was no limit to the ingenuity, variety and ease with which he sought to give them pleasure. He seemed to always keep young and playful with them, frequently catching them up and swinging them over his head, and running up and down stairs with them, which made him the best of company with the young as well as the old. He knew nothing more holy than the heart of an innocent child, and loved the gush of its guileless glee. How else shall we account for the following poetical effusion, written off-hand, at a time when his afternoon nap had been disturbed by the prattling of an infant grandchild which had been born into the home, and was with its mother in the room above him ?

There is a baby in the house, I ween,
As bright, as sweet, as ever yet was seen;
I hear it laugh ; I hear it play.
It chirps, and prattles all the day ;
And helps to drive dull care away,
That home is happy now.

The mother's heart, though young, is full of joy;
The father's glad to find a new employ;
Both cheery with their new-born love ;
An angel sent them from above,
Delight in duty's path to move,
For life is real now.

That heart is sad indeed which never felt,
Tight drawn the silken strands which form the belt
Of social life, and help to bind,
The noblest passions of the mind,
A happier state on earth to find,
A universe of love.

As rays of light that center in the sun,
As drops in rills that to the ocean run,
So all that is, or was begun,

18

Shall, when the perfect work is done,
Unite, and happy be in one,
In the great God above.

He believed that we commit not only an error, but a most grievous moral wrong, when we check the child in its glow of natural playfulness. The thing was to see that this exuberance, or outburst, was guided aright. He was always glad at their gladness, and enjoyed spending days in giving them cheer, and assisting to make them happy.

I shall never forget a circumstance that transpired at the dedication of the church at Scotland, Windham County, Conn. Bro. Balch was brought on from New York City to preach the sermon, and the church was filled to its fullest capacity, clear to the entrance way. A woman with a babe in her arms was at the very center of the crowd, with no chance to gain an exit, and just as the sermon was proceeding in its best vein, her child set up crying at a terrible rate. The woman, greatly disturbed, could find no way to still it, and she knew not what to do. There she was with the painful situation confronting her. As soon as Bro. Balch's attention was drawn to the anxiety of the mother, he stopped, remarking that he never saw the time when he would not much rather hear a child cry than to listen to the piping of the most musical hand organ he ever heard in his life. In turning his attention in the direction where the child was, it seemed to take in the situation and stop crying, as though itself had been spoken to, and was comprehending the full purport of the words. The mother was so grateful to Bro. Balch as to wait (though a perfect stranger) till the crowd had dispersed, that she might meet him and thank him as she passed out at the door.

With his views of childhood the Sunday school picnic was made pleasant to him, and he made it a point to be always present at such gatherings of the children. You never would know but he enjoyed it as much as they did. Many of us have witnessed him running and laughing and playing like a boy. He indeed sought to give pleasure to everybody, adapting himself to all kinds of society.

I find our Bro. Eddy referring to this after the following manner:

"I remember him as very accessible to children and very much loved by them. His interest in the Sunday-school is well remembered, and to him I think we are indebted for what is now known as the Sunday-school Concert, originally called the Sunday-school Exhibition; the first of which was given in Providence, R. I., during the pastorate of Mr. Balch, about forty-eight years ago. It was then regarded as a great, if not dangerous innovation, and was denounced by the so-called orthodox as introducing the theatre into the church. About the same time Mr. Balch arranged an excursion and a picnic for the Sunday-school, which was probably the first attempt at what is now so popular in all the sects; it was then looked upon as a very vicious thing, a frivolous use of precious time."

It was about this time, in 1839, that he prepared and published his Sunday-school Manual, the first of the kind ever given to the public. The history of its origin I learn was this: He was to exchange with Hosea Ballou Second, and was told that he would have to lead the prayer of the Sunday-school, or write a prayer

for the superintendent to read, and out of it came this
publication. He wrote it while in Providence, and was
discouraged by brethren from ever publishing it, but
afterwards did publish 30,000. It contains about all
that any of the later manuals have brought out. It
can not be denied that Mr. Balch always loved children,
and that there was always a sensitiveness with him
about being supposed to grow old. He intended to
keep himself always young in spirit, as the years should
come and go.

Towards the close of his life he had repeated family
gatherings; and on the occasion of his seventy-fifth
birthday, not only the various members of his immediate family, but other kindred and friends were collected,
to nearly a hundred, and never was he made more
happy than on such occasions, for his heart was full of
filial and fraternal affection. If presents were not considered generally in order at such festivities, this event
was seized upon to make him the recipient of a valuable gold watch from Elgin friends, and at the banquet
given him in Chicago five years later, at his eightieth
birthday, a gold-headed cane.

*   *   *   *   *   *

We have marked him as a man of varied employments, and great versatility of talent. We have no
one in mind, and are quite sure we have never known
the person, with a greater variety of gifts, capable of
being made available in so many different ways. He
was constantly forming new plans, and engaging in
new duties, which bore almost uniformly the character
of usefulness. His life was full of striking incidents;
and in this way has he built for himself a monument of

enduring praise. Unceasing activity was one of his
chief characteristics, and it was impossible to meet
him without feeling his earnestness of purpose, and his
determination to work, hour by hour, and day by day,
to accomplish all the good he could. His habits of industry and perseverance were simply marvelous. Call
upon him when you would, you would always find
him doing something in the way of cultivating his
grounds or making repairs about the premises, or he
was reading a book, preparing a sermon, or writing an
article for publication which he wanted to show you;
ready to turn aside for a social call, and entertain you
as interestingly as though he had never anything else
to do.

He was certainly a busy man in his home. There
was no spark of idleness in his nature. It could be
said of his life that it was full of work; that it was
busy all through it, and that he was alert on some duty,
and in spurring others to duty. His advice to his students was, Always keep the barrel full, and then when
you tap it it will be sure and run out.

It did seem as though he knew how to do everything of the common kind, as well as the best. He
could tell you in what way to cook a meal of victuals,
and accomplish all kinds of out-door and in-door matters,
from the making of a book-jack to the repairing of a
watch, and the regulating of a steam engine; but he
sought most of all to cultivate the activities which find
expression in doing needful things.

He was never the man that wanted to be waited
upon. If anything needed to be done, he knew no
other way than to go right about it and do it; always
willing to do more than his part in everything.

He found greatest delight in reading and meditation. He had but little time for desultory or promiscuous reading, but perused with deep satisfaction all useful and profitable works that came within his reach, as promising to add to his information; to suggest thought, or to elevate and ennoble his mind. His aim was to discharge every duty that would aid his fellow men, as far as circumstances would allow, and never lose an opportunity of doing good.

There are very many traits of character for which Brother Balch was distinguished, without some mention of which any sketch of him would be singularly incomplete. Of course we can be expected to mention only a small part of these, and multiply them as much as we will, there would be still those to say: We could have told you of many more. To let one who was invited to his bedside during his last illness, as also to speak words of commendation and comfort at the last parting farewell, give expression to his own thought of his general mental and moral characteristics, it would be to say, " I have regarded him as a clear writer, an eloquent preacher, a faithful pastor, and a most careful observer of men and things, and events. He was simple in his tastes ; modest in his demeanor ; honest in all his dealings with his fellow men ; catholic in his spirit, and consecrated to the mission of making men better. Wherever he found grace of character he greeted it warmly, and applauded it. His esteem for manhood and womanhood, transcended all sectarian limits. The real breadth of good which he achieved cannot be easily measured." Another puts his estimate in this way: " He was a good man :

a great preacher; a zealous Christian, a broad thinker,
a friend to all humanity, a leader in every good word
and work. He exhibited a clearness of mind, a
soundness of judgment, and an acquaintance with all
the great subjects of thought and interest that are
commending themselves to the respect of the wise and
the good." And without assuming the office of counsellor or advisor. or appearing to know that he had the
capacity for imparting information, or of especially exerting influence in any direction, he was constantly
dropping precious words, and useful hints. conveyed in
varied manner and thus helping others to help themselves. He was frequently applied to by young and old,
as one possessing admirable wisdom ; inspiration. information. insight. and ripeness of soul. And by
virtue of these he knew how to admonish, and did not
hesitate (in deeming it necessary) to reprove. He was
ever thinking how to do good, and in what way his
ministrations could be made most useful. In this he
displayed the same excellent traits which distinguished
him in every field in which he wrought.

It is no small compliment to him to say, that while
he was a good preacher, he was also a good hearer ;
that he was equally as good a parishioner as pastor.
We might presume it a somewhat difficult thing for
an aged minister, after preaching many years. and retiring from the office of preacher and pastor, not to
assume superiority among the people, from his long
and varied experience. The force of habit. the consciousness of an unimpaired interest in his work, and
the continued esteem and confidence of friends who
remain as cordially attached to him as ever. all con-

spire to make him reluctant to leave the field in which
he has so delightfully labored. To be willing to re-
sign the place to another, and that, too, gracefully,
with commendable meekness, is evidence of a
right religious temper. But all who have known Mr.
Balch will bear witness that he left the pulpit for the
pew in a way to command respect, and set a bright
example to all others. I may quote here the words of
Brother Alcott, the Elgin pastor, given at the time of
Brother Balch's Memorial Service appointed for the
Fox River association. His words are:

"It has not always been found an easy matter, after
a man has been a good and eminent pastor and
preacher to become, when his work is done, also an
eminently good parishioner. This latter character implies other and additional rare qualities. It implies an
utter absence of self-conceit. It implies a disposition
to help in the best possible way a fellow-workman. It
proves an enlightened and exquisite sense of all fine
proprieties and courtesies of such a situation and such
a relation.

　　*　　　*　　　*　　　*　　　*　　　*

"The first time I ever met him on coming into this
field, I felt that I had met a noble, royal soul. I never
had the slightest reason or occasion for modifying in any
adverse respect this opinion. On the contrary, many
things transpired to confirm, to strengthen it. I had
no fear of him. At his hand I met with the heartiest
kind of a welcome. He impressed me at once as having, not a selfish, but an unselfish nature; as having,
not a cold, but a warm heart; as having, not a narrow,
but a broad mind.

　　*　　　*　　　*　　　*　　　*　　　*

"What kind of a parishioner was Dr. Balch? A
model one; a grand one; one who was trusted and

honored and loved; and one whose matured views
were most helpful on the many and varied subjects of
work and doctrine. His pastor, whoever he might be,
could feel that back of all his earnest, honest efforts in
the work of the parish he would find this father in
Israel, encouraging, approving, helping, saying a good
word—always! His was no lukewarmness, no indifference, but his were ever the heartiest of wishes and
helps. His pastor could never have a suspicion of
whispers by him behind his back, and he would never
happen on any traces of words spoken to his disad-
vantage in his absence. He could never feel that this
distinguished preacher, and practicer of the gospel as
well, was capable of this; but would feel that himself
and his interests were as secure in the hands of this
true friend as in his own. This is rare merit. Or, if it
be not rare it is at any rate glorious merit."

We account for this in part by saying that he had
none of the airs of superiority. He never sought for
prominent positions among his brethren, or to take any
high seat in the synagogue. You never thought of
him as putting on airs, or doing anything for effect.
Try and conceive of him as making a display of himself in any role in which he might appear to his fellowmen, and you will discover at once its impossibility.
He was always just what he seemed to be. There was
no ostentation in anything he ever did. He gave the lie
forever to all false pride, refusing to tolerate anything
of pompousness or parade. If he was ever ambitious,
his ambition had in it no taint of envy. Had he been
a proud man he would have coveted honors, but he was
a plain man without anything of pretension, and may
be considered as having had a perfect horror of everything artificial, of all show, and sham of every charac-

ter. With all his splendid gifts, it will not be said that
he ever sought to shine. He looked upon a large share
of the fashions and foibles, as well as the glitter and
glamour of the world, as the things that were gone
into to please a false taste, and he had to think of them
as heartless mummery.

It was this simplicity of character that made you
feel perfectly at ease in his presence, introducing him,
and making him welcome in all classes of society. He
would come into your home, and it would seem as if
you had been acquainted with him for years. And it
was this also that gave him his aversion to all high-
sounding names, and titles of honor and distinction,
which so illy comported with the primitive equality of
souls, and the common brotherhood of believers, and
which partook more of the spirit and distinctions of
the world than the humble spirit of Jesus; and the
honor which comes from men more than the honor
which comes from God. He was of the opinion that
plain " Mister " was the best possible designation which
Christians could properly employ as a title of honor or
respect, with but one exception—that of " Brother."

It was the Institution at Canton that bestowed on
Brother Balch what is considered the honorary degree
of D. D., the first ever conferred upon any one by it, in
recognition of his valuable services rendered in behalf
of the Institution and the church; but it was never by
any understanding with himself, and he never accepted
it. It was a thing that, could regard have been paid
to his feelings, would never have been. I find in his
scrap-book where the D. D. has been attached to articles
sent for publication, and in preserving these it has been

erased, or crossed out with pencil mark. One of the
two or three last sentences he caused to be written, is
the following : Calling his wife to his bedside, he re-
quested her to pen among other things for the benefit
of his brethren, the words, " Suppose the Popes, Cardi-
nals, Archbishops, Bishops, Lord Bishops, and all the
retinue of Clergy, in their richest and gayest robes of
attire, had appeared at the Last Supper on Mount Zion,
would Jesus have accepted them approvingly, and bestowed upon them the heavenly bendiction ?" He was
sure he would not, till they were first denuded of some
of their trappings, and had become of a very different
spirit.

I had started out at one time to make a chapter of
his miscellaneous poetry, but found that while he wrote
with greatest ease, and gave evidence of abundant
poetic talent, and had written more or less of good
poetry, yet for some reason, either that prose was more
suited to his original taste, and he conceived less pleasure in poetic composition, or he had not the time for
weaving his words into rhymes, and marshalling them
in a manner that they might be made to jingle; for
these or other reasons, his talent for versification had
not flourished equal to his zeal for many other things.
and instead of a department for his museful flights, his
lyrical indulgences have been scattered throughout the
volume to do service wherever they might. It will be
acknowledged that, for the most part, Brother Balch
wrote practically, but never prosaically, even when
treating of the gravest of matters. He could not ex-
cuse himself in what was liable to be regarded as an
attempt at display. His effort from his earliest years

had been to devote himself to schemes of usefulness; to spread goodness and happiness everywhere around him, and to leave in every community in which he might reside the impress of a most rare influence, doing service to his kind in all natural, easy and helpful ways.

It has seemed to me that the true manliness of Brother Balch's character has stood very largely in the naturalness, and simplicity of his demeanor, together with a disinterestedness and fraternity of feeling, such as are rarely found combined in any one person to the same extent.

I am not presuming that many have ever thought of Mr. Balch as a diffident man, and yet I must tell the reader, that, with my large acquaintance with him, I have often wondered if he was not thus; especially when it came to estimating the value of his own abilities and labors, a thing which he never got entirely over in his long life. I have always observed, when praising some effort of his, that he was almost sure to laugh away the point of my criticism, and he would not leave the subject till he had depreciated himself and his effort to the last degree. Not that he shrunk from the performance of any duty, when it came to be viewed in that light; but, meeting him in public, he never impressed you as a bold person, or as possessing a self-satisfied confidence ; but there was a kind of natural reserve, a retiring and unassuming modesty, often a hesitating, and waiting to be relieved, and letting others say the thing which was required to be said, if they would. Making the inquiry of his companion more recently respecting this, to know if I was right in it, she assured me that I was, though con-

vinced that it was in part a concealed aversion to
flattery, which was liable to be mixed with the praise
that was bestowed, and for which he had nothing but
the most utter detestation. We may all have a desire
to be thought well of; and most persons who have
lived long and well, and labored arduously in building
up a character for themselves, find it pleasurable to be
had in grateful recollection as we may presume, and
wish to be loved for their work's sake; but we can
hardly think of Brother Balch as ever having sought
adulatory honors. His reputation was a matter of
greatest worth, but always came to him by merit,
without any seeking of his own. He never went after
it, and was singularly chary of the language of vague
eulogy, as he would have been of an overweening
effort or straining for applause.

But without an opinionated self-confidence he was
capable of knowing what the actual labors of his life
had been. We have from his pen a partial summing
up of his work. He ventures to tell some things he
has done the first forty years of his ministry, and
shows that he has been a pretty hard-working and
poorly-paid preacher. "I have preached," he says,
"7,149 sermons, 25 at the dedication of new churches,
19 at ordinations, and 215 at public bodies. I have attended 1,372 funerals, sometimes as many as ten in a
single week, and three on Sunday. I have married
1,258 persons, and prepared 23 young men, in a poor
way, for the ministry. Nor have my labors been confined to my own societies. Never neglecting them, I have
traveled abroad into other fields where work was
needed for the upbuilding of the cause, and no matter

where I have gone, I have carried the same broad, truth-loving principles of Christianity. I have traveled and preached from Canada to North Carolina, from Cape Cod to St. Louis and Minneapolis, under the shadow of the Alps, and on the desert of Arabia. Outside of the ministry, but in keeping with its spirit and intentions, I have lectured in many of the states, giving 11 Fourth of July orations, 1,259 lectures, besides agricultural addresses, temperance, anti-capital punishment, political, war, benevolent and other speeches without number. I have traveled twice over Europe, allowing no object of interest to escape me, from the West of Ireland, North of Scotland and Denmark, to Damascus and the Cataract of the Nile. So far as I have kept the account, outside the ordinary movements about home, the sum is over 150,000 miles. One scarce knows what he has done till he counts up the sum. I have found and proved the truth of the Scripture, 'Life is full of labor.' It is also full of wonder. Without its doings it were little in fact, and less in worth.

"In addition to what is here narrated I have done no little service in actual work for the denomination and for humanity, devoting much time, thought, care and labor for years to establish our theological school in Canton, and make the Christian Ambassador, of New York, a denominational paper. For twelve years I was engrossed in its management, planning and carrying it forward to a sound financial basis, which, starting only with borrowed capital, redeemed itself in eight years and paid 7 per cent on the investment."

We have a more full account of this in another connection, where he tells us that "finding the Ambassador embarrassed and burdened with debt, under the fostering care of a devoted brother (Philo Price), and various attempts having been made to enlist the press in its defense on a free, broad basis, without success, while it was yet struggling for life, and was about to be transported to Boston, that good brother, O. A. Skinner, came to me with a proposition that we join hands to save it. After some hesitation I consented, on the condition that money should be raised to pay for it, and that no debt should be incurred to carry it on, so it could never fail. We succeeded far beyond our expectations. It sustained itself and afforded a small revenue. Brother Skinner removing to Boston, Brothers Hallock and Lyon became partners with us, and principal managers. Brother Hallock wearying of the burden from ill-health, a joint stock company was formed to purchase the concern, with the express condition that whenever the original price and 7 per cent. interest were offered the shareholders we should surrender it to the State Convention. In eight years it paid for itself and went into the hands of the denomination, with cash and subscriptions due amounting to over $10,000. It had bought up the Magazine and Advocate, a paper in Rochester, another in Pennsylvania, and paid for them."

But few are aware how much he did in this way, in the earlier days of the demonstration ; and yet, besides it all, he says, "I have done some work with my pen in religious, secular, and literary publications, with a view to the defense of truth, and increase of knowledge, and been engaged in works of reform and phil-

anthropy all my life, to some small benefit, I trust, to
suffering humanity. My old friends must pardon me
this egotism, as my most direct way of stating the
truth. I am growing old, and I have a right to be a
little fogy and garrulous."

This, recollect, in 1867; but at the time of his death,
twenty years later, as he states it himself, he had attended 2,671 funerals and solemnized 1,438 weddings,
for you have to remember that he is speaking of the
first forty years of his ministry, and he lived to do active service for a large part of twenty years after;
and it is safe to say that the number of his sermons and lectures alone could not have fallen much
short of 10,000 or 12,000. It was impossible to keep
an exact account of all these in the later years of his
life, as he had commenced to do earlier; for he would
be called to go to numberless places, here and there, on
excursions, and visiting friends, and would be expected
frequently to lecture and preach a half dozen times,
which he would fail to note at the instant, and then on
returning home the number had been borne from his
mind, and so he abandoned the thought of keeping
them, for what he could not do well he would not do
at all. On leaving his home simply to spend a night,
there would be more or less of those who would think
that they ought to have a sermon from him. Go
where he would, he was just about sure to get into
somebody's pulpit and be found preaching the glorious
Gospel of the blessed God, when many other ministers
would receive no such attention, and would be at a loss
to understand how it came about. There was no way
of knowing, only as he had come to have such a wide

reputation, having friends in all parts of the country, and they all eager to hear him preach, or to listen to one of his inimitable lectures.

A most remarkable circumstance of his life, was his being called to such distances to attend funerals and weddings, the former especially, to the Eastern, Middle and Southern States, seven times over 300 miles, five times a thousand, and once 1,700. Nor must we forget that in addition to all this arduous labor, besides his books to which reference has already been made, and, not to mention other publications, his orations alone are full twenty in number, upon such subjects as "Political and Social Equality," "Popular Liberty and Equal Rights," "Individual Freedom the Foundation of Democratic Government," "Romanism and Republicanism Incompatible" (a lecture delivered in the Broadway Tabernacle, April 5, 1852, in Review of the Catholic Chapter in the History of the United States, as written by the Rev. John Hughes, D. D., Archbishop, of New York). Besides all these he was expected to find time to give everybody a portion of his society.

We have his declaration as follows:—

"A review of these forty years has proved to me that such labor is not in vain. Go where I will I am pretty sure to meet glad hearts who, with a smile, tell me that my poor persuasions have led them to think, examine, and, by the grace of God, to believe and rejoice in the great salvation. This is my abundant reward.

"In all these years God has not forgotten me, but been gracious unto me, above all I had a right to expect. Though the compensation for regular preach-

19

ing has never supported me and the large family God
has given me, yet I have had enough of worldly goods
and tokens of affection to make me grateful to my
friends; and enough of strength and privilege to work
outside, and earn and lay by for future needs, without
impairing my usefulness or wronging any man in name
or property. I have sought to be strict, but fair and
kind in all my intercourse with the brethren, keeping
no cloak for any sin short of repentence, but always
ready to forgive and love.

"The love of God, as revealed by Jesus Ohrist, has
been the great theme, the central idea around which
all my thoughts and purposes have revolved, embracing
all truth and goodness, and encouraging every reform
which seeks the elevation of mankind to the level of a
common brotherhood, emancipating from all evil, and
the establishment of universal holiness, peace and happiness in subjection to the will of God.

" I have always looked to One as my Master, and
tried to teach his religion of love, peace and salvation,
free for all men ; I have sought to cherish good will
towards all men, and to do good, reprove and rebuke,
where it seemed needful, with all long suffering and
doctrine. To me the blessed truth, committed in some
sort to our keeping and defence, is more precious than
ever before. I have seen its blessed fruits so often and
so abundant in meeting and relieving the wants of
mankind, that it pains me to see any deviations by
following the rudiments of this world, to gain for it
popularity, or to gratify the pride of human hearts.
There is something so sweet and beautiful, so com-
forting and joyous in the meekness and simplicity of
Christianity, that the adornments of pride and power of
man's wisdom does but mar it, bestowed in any form,
or in any measure. Let us "hold fast the profession of
our faith without wavering."

A rare commendation may be claimed for him, that
he did not seem to abate his activity with the coming

on of age, as so many do. He sought to keep up his
acquaintance with passing events till the last, and was
even familiar with all the new modes of modern thought
and feeling of the day. He kept all his faculties bright,
and was ready to respond to every call, so far as he
could, to the last. He was not the kind of man to lie
down and rust out, so long as there was any spark of
original vitality in reserve to draw upon. There were
so many pressing duties lying near his heart, that he
might be said to live for, and which his existence was
bound up in, that to retire from activity with any stock
of vitality unexpended, seemed to him ungracious and
reprehensible. His was such an all-absorbing purpose,
that it was with sorrowful regret that he could lay
down his toil, and wait his mysterious transit, even
while he must have known that the larger work of his
life was done.

It may be said that such was the generous devotion
with which Bro. Balch gave himself to his work of
whatever character, and the enthusiasm he would
awaken in its behalf, eminently adapting him to arouse
the slumbering energies of the people, that important
trusts were ever confided to his care and management,
and he was always found fully equal to the demand
that was imposed upon him.

His success must have been particularly great in all
general matters for him to be able to say, " I never
set my heart on doing a thing without accomplishing
it," as he did on the Wednesday previous to his death,
which occurred on the following Sunday. And in view·
of this, what could be more beautiful than a congrat-
ulatory telegram, sent to his home in Elgin by a daugh-

ter then living in Brattleboro, Vt., received and read while celebrating the 75th anniversary of his birth, a quotation from words spoken by the prophet Hezekiah. " In every work he begun in the service of the house of God, and in the law, and in the comandments to seek his God, he did it with all his heart and prospered." If he entered upon a thing he carried it out to the end. Almost to the same effect is a testimonial from the pen of Bro. Francis. " I recall how glad I was when I heard that Bro. Balch was chosen as agent in raising the funds for our first Theological school, for I said to myself, now I am certain of its successful establishment, as the event afterwards proved."

Perhaps his great work was his financial achievements in the part he contributed to found and endow St. Lawrence University. Bro. Atwood, writing to the committee for the getting up of the reception given to Bro. Balch in 1886, says, " We do not forget that he occupies a foremost place in the group of honored brethren and fathers whose foresight and industry established the Canton Theological School, and made possible the St. Lawrence University. And Dr. Adams, in his " Fifty Notable Years," tells us how completely the " business capacity of our brother was evinced in his raising funds for that institution, taking charge of the location, as well as the plan and rearing of the buildings, and selection of the Principal to preside over it." He moreover gives the account of his "afterwards completing the raising of a large fund for the institution, obtaining also $10,000 for the library and securing the valuable libraries of Dr. Credner and Rev. F. C. Loveland."

I find where he tells us about this himself; how the work was started. and carried forward to its completion. He says:

" It fell to my lot to do much work for the school. The thought was to provide the means for the better preparation of young men for the ministry of the great salvation—not to build a sect after the fashion of the churches, or to cramp the mind into a creed or form after man's construction, to make a part appear greater than the whole. I secured the title to the land, twenty acres, that students might present their bodies a 'living sacrifice, holy and acceptable unto God. a reasonable service,' according to the terms of subscription of Mr. Greeley and others. I drew the plan and specifications of the building, made nine journeys, all but one without expense, to see that all was done right. When completed. on the recommendation of Hosea Ballou Second. I procured the appointment of Rev. Ebenezer Fisher for Principal."

He does not fail to remind us of some of " the sad disadvantages and discouragements under which he labored. and that no one but himself and his God ever knew what he endured when so few of his brethren came to his help." But his thought was to " resolutely do his duty, putting in all his strength against delays and hindrances. determined that the enterprise should carry if it was a possible thing." The offer was made to him of ten per cent. of what he should raise for a part of his work, if he would but assist to relieve the institution in its later embarrassment, but as he had formerly accepted of no compensation, and only a part of his real expenses, deeming it wrong to make merchandise of work in such a cause; so now he resolved to enter the field and do the best he could, agreeing

upon no terms of payment, only receiving for all his
arduous labors and trials what he actually paid out,
" the sum of 304 or 403 dollars."

Dr. Lee, of the University, writes the committee in-
viting him to attend the reception given in honor of
Brother Balch in Chicago, " I was glad to hear of the
reception, and to receive your invitation to attend it.
I am profoundly grateful to him, for he did more than
any other individual to establish, and permanently endow our Theoligical School. The school, during its
twenty-eight years of life, has sent out hundreds of
ministers well equipped for their work, and for this we
are largely indebted to him, and I wish, through you,
to present to him our grateful acknowledgements."

To this he adds in a later communication :

" He toiled amid opposition, indifference and oblo-
quy ; but succeeded in raising money sufficient to keep
it in successful operation ; and with the assistance of
other friends of the school laid plans for securing funds
to meet its future necessities, so that its existence and usefulness were made permanent ; and for this he received
the hearty thanks of Dr. Fisher, the first president of
the school, and others, professors and students, who
were aware of his labors in its behalf, and the sacrifices which he made to sustain it. It may safely be
said that had it not been for William S. Balch, this
Theological school would not now be in existence."

He continues :   .

" In June, 1884, Dr. Balch and Mr. F. C. Havemeyer, who constituted the committee that located the
school nearly thirty years before, were present at the
annual exercises, and took an active interest in the dedication of Fisher Memorial Hall, which transpired
June 28, 1883. Mr. Balch was then seventy-seven
years old, but spoke feelingly and eloquently, with all

the animation and enthusiasm of his youthful days, concerning the early history of the institution, its progress, its influence and present needs."

My heart has impelled me to say more at this point than I otherwise would have done, as there are those to feel that full justice had never been done Mr. Balch in this regard.

Such, then, was the varied working talent of our Brother. But few men in any generation have performed a greater number of useful labors. or won the sincere regard of more hearts than he. And still, what I have chronicled gives but a feeble view of his wonderful fertility of conception, and the manifold incidents of his busy life, or of the great variety and amount of his achievements and productions. All will have to agree in this, that his life has been one of great faithfulness; that he has emphatically lived to the end of serving humanity as best he could: and that he has only left the world for his works to praise him, and his conduct to define his character. He has gained a reputation for practical wisdom, genuine goodness and helpfulness in every varied field of human effort which the proudest of his kind might well envy.

CHAPTER XV.

Mr. Balch was of a most unselfish spirit, always sacrificing for others, and endeavoring to do something to make them comfortable and happy. His thoughts were for others first, and for himself afterward, if at all. Even when doing for himself he did for others. Unlike too many who husband their gains to have a goodly sum to bequeath at their death, he gave liberally while he lived, and as calls came for him to be helpful, desiring to be his own executor, and enjoy the pleasure of dispensing his gifts with his own free, open hand. We need not complain of others, especially when so many do even in this way acknowledge God's claim upon a portion of their abundance with which He has blessed them, but the subject of this notice has gone through the world with the true heart of giving, himself his own best sacrifice, "not letting his left hand know what his right hand did," sacrificing without a regret promising opportunities of gain; succeeding as but few have ever succeeded; asking no favors that he did not merit, and yet distributing them all about him on every side. By careful economy, and exemplary self denial, he regularly spared a generous portion of his income, and returned it as a free-will offering to the cause which he served, and

"So lived not for himself alone,
Nor joined the selfish few,
But prized much more than all things else
The good that he could do."

His was the unselfish success of an untiring life, and shows how much a devout, earnest and self-forgetting person by his own energies, unaided except from above, consecrated to one great object, can accomplish. He has left a priceless memory as benefactor, friend and brother; toiling for the ignorant, the neglected, the destitute, the old in error and sin, and the young in innocence and peril. To make others happier, and the world better, seemed to be the desire most prominent with him. As a man, a minister, a reformer, an enthusiastic traveler in foreign lands; as a true patriot, both at home and abroad, he has found it his delight to do what he could. For nothing was he distinguished more than for his strong and deep sympathy for the weak and tempted, the sorrowful and oppressed of his fellows; so that he never shrunk from espousing their cause. We shall never half know of the blessings he has dispensed in this direction, so diligent was he in seeking out and relieving want and distress on the part of those who with slender resources were overtaken by illness or misfortune. So unstintedly generous was he in ministering to their necessities, and the delicacy with which he rendered his aid, that it were in vain the attempt at doing him justice in this regard ; and I am aware that I must fail in the presentation of this portion of his life. It is evident that he valued wealth chiefly for its humane and Christian uses. He was accustomed to complain that women were so generally underpaid, and would often give them more than they asked. He was not the person to ever bid down on prices ; nor, like thousands of others, could he be induced to think that he had achieved a triumph when he made for himself as purchaser, some paltry gain to the loss and discomfort of the seller. He would sooner return and pay extra for what he thought had been sold to him too cheaply.

And it was in his preaching as in everything else. He would go at every call of his brethren, ready to spend and be spent, regarding it as a blessed thing if he was but invited to continue his going. The compensation of his services was frequently in his being able to obtain an audience who were willing to listen to his messages, and that he could thus assist to plant the religion which was the salvation, and glory, and blessedness of the world. The period had been when he was very grateful, as he tells us, at beholding an occasional new face among his hearers. And it was in answering some such appeals of a disinterested character that he frequently brought harm to himself, for though he would be told that his health was of first importance, and that he was unable to leave home, to attend upon his preaching, his reply would be that he "had been sent for, and he must go." He was of the number who always found his greatest pleasure in obliging his friends, and his spirit of accommodation was evinced in his willingness to serve them at whatever hazard.

It was a fixed principle with him through life to regard the raising of money a secondary matter, and to make it his first concern to spread information, and lay the foundation of a steady support of all good causes by awakening an intelligent understanding of the demands of Christianity, and giving permanency and system to the benevolent impulses of our natures.

He did not believe in any mere fiscal, or monetary organization, or a gathering of the people where every agitator went to quarrel for his peculiar resolutions; but where Christian brethren met to mingle in holy sympathies, and through the presence and anointing of the spirit of God and his Christ, their hearts were to be renewed, and larger effort was to be made to give vitality to men's professions, and unconquerable energy to their efforts for enlarging, and building up, and strengthening the enclosures of the Masters fold. In this way would the money flow freely into the treasury of the Lord, through the quickening of the religious life, and every rich blessing accrue to the worshiper, as a matter of course.

A peculiarity of Brother Balch was, that he never came to believe in large salaries for ministers, never set a price on his preaching, to say that he must have any certain amount or sum of money to go anywhere to labor in the vineyard of his Master. He never made it a matter of agreement to be paid for a funeral or a wedding service, or the delivery of a temperance or other lecture of a moral or religious character. He felt himself a debtor to the cause, to supply the spiritual wants of the people, and they in supply of his temporal wants have given him what they felt they could, or were pleased to do. Finding an opening outside of his parish, he has tried to occupy it, sowing the seeds of truth irrespective of being paid for it; and I doubt not that there have been some whole years in which he has preached more sermons, receiving nothing for them, than there are Sundays or weeks in a year. When he was leaving Providence in 1841 to go to New York City, they thought at first to give him $1,200 a year, but then it was said he could not live on it, and they made it $1,500.

Brother Balch writes to an old friend in New York City, after preaching forty-five years:

"My pay is not great, nor very prompt, but I live and do not suffer. We have not all we could wish; Who has? We have enough to make us grateful, and keep us humble. What more could we have?"

I have found the man who paid Brother Balch the first money he ever received for preaching. He says his "father invited him to come and preach a sermon in their school-house, which he did, and he was afterwards made the bearer of the only compensation made for his services, and the amount was just four dollars." Brother Balch tells us of his first experience in going to a place after his ordination. He says, "After service many crowded around to be introduced, and to urge me to stop and preach there. Some even went so far as to ask me what I should charge. This astonished me, for I had been brought up where the minister pretended that it was wicked to have a fixed salary, to be a hireling. And then on Sunday to make such a proposition — bargain about preaching? But we get hardened by long and familiar experience to many things, at first strange."

He is particularly severe on those young men who enter the ministry because they discover no easier road open to them. "With little knowledge of men," he tells us, "and the trials and struggles of active life, they enter our schools and live on gratuities, with no care but to spend, careless of the very means which

are to fit them for the positions of after life. They
have never learned the Scripture, 'It is good for a man
to bear the yoke in his youth.'" He regrets that
preaching is so worldly in our times, and says:

"My advice to young men looking towards the ministry is: 1. Examine yourself; see that your heart is
full of love to God and man ; that you are impressed
with a deep conviction that you can do most good by
preaching the Gospel; that you have an 'aptness to
teach,' and are willing to make sacrifices to fit yourself
for such a work, and to take the position wherein you
can be most useful. Do not think of yourself, of ease
or honor, but of God and duty. Make it a serious,
solemn matter of high moral consideration, a thing not
to be trifled with. Don't rely on the charity of others.
It will take the life, the spirit, the manhood out of
you. Be self-reliant on God and his promised grace,
that you may stand square up with your fellow men
and avoid the conscious degradation of eating others'
bread. If you have not the means at your command,
nor the confidence of immediate success to aid you, do
as our most successful men have done; go to work and
earn the means, and not feel crushed and benumbed in
conscience.

"You need to develop a character that will fit you
for all hard work; a self-denial and consecration that
will take you out of self, and swallow you up in a
grand purpose of serving others. You need not ask
Societies what they are going to give their preachers ?
Probably nothing to mere adventurers, who are selfish
enough to propound such a question. Shame on such
a spirit, wherever it is found. Go into the vineyard
and work; no matter about the hour, or the penny.
The Lord of the harvest will do right. Don't lust
after the flesh pots of Egypt, but follow the example
of the early Christians, early Universalists, early
Methodists, the early and faithful of all good causes.

"Several of our early preachers were shoemakers, some clothiers, more farmers and teachers ; none poor dependents on charity. Those who borrowed were less successful—they were few.

"In Canton there is land enough, properly tilled,to feed the theoligical students, and a portion of the funds were given on the express condition that students should be required to labor two hours a day. Who has done it, except at croquet and base-ball? Horace Greeley started that idea, and the committee provided the means to carry it out, with every arrangement for convenience and fair comfort—not too much self-denial—quite equal to early Christians and students in former years. It is not good for students of the gospel to live in luxury, and get ready to marry before earning an honest living. If such institutions are thought too severe for a gospel minister, he had better seek some other vocation where he will be less likely to suffer disappointment.

"One thing more : The close-closeted student who has devoted his whole thought to theories and methods, ancient and modern, and neglected to study men and manners, the ways and means of daily life, is poorly fitted to mix and mingle as a preacher should with people in all conditions, poor as well as rich, ignorant as well as wise. good, bad and indifferent—with humanity as he finds it, and feel sympathy and interest in all, ready to serve them as they need by leading them in the way of salvation, reproving. admonishing, encouraging as they need. The people demand more than fine essays on nonsense, sound logic on dogmas, exact descriptions of old errors, corruptions and superstitions, the sins of Babylon, and idolatry in Egypt. Ours is a practical age, and the world needs practical Christianity, practically taught and correctly exemplified, by living, plain. practical preachers who shall be 'ensamples in all things.' The true preacher seeks to edify the church, convert sinners, comfort the afflicted and help save the world."

He is telling what kind of preachers the West is needing, and says:

"The West needs live preachers whose souls are in the work, who are fitted to preach the gospel intelligently, practically, forcibly, and to adorn it by well-ordered lives and a godly conversation; who are willing to sow before they reap, to spend and be spent, without worrying their souls about to-morrow, and pining into worthlessness because they cannot get as large a salary as somebody else who can preach no better than they think they can. Let them learn humility and resolve in earnest to be prepared unto every good word and work, to enter any door that opens into the field of labor, to hunt the lost sheep until they find it. They shall not fail of a full reward, for God is just, and gracious too. They must deserve before they can expect to have. An hundred gates stand wide open, and thousands of anxious souls await the coming of such preachers of the Everlasting Gospel. Let preachers come west as early emigrants came, resolved to work and wait, as young preachers did in years gone by, and they need not hunt long before they will hear of scattered believers everywhere who desire to be gathered into the true fold. The fields are already white with the harvest. Many are seeking homes in other flocks, and not a few preachers of other names are leading them in pastures much greener, and to waters more calm than could be found a few years ago. There never was a more accepted time, or the Macedonian cry more plainly and oftener heard, than to-day, and in the West. 'Tramps are not wanted—men always seeking work but never working. Men apt to teach, not by fine essays and pretty sermons in stilted phrases, but plain, practical, humble, honest, earnest, true men, who love the truth and their fellowmen more than filthy lucre, and the praise of God more than the pride and flattery of the world. Such, and such only, can long endure the climate of the West."

He is discussing different sorts of ministers, and among them the "right sort," and makes the inquiry. " What sort is that?" and the answer is :

"Not the lazy, fashionable, fustian young men, who wear patent-leather boots, and dare not step off a flagged sidewalk for fear of soiling them. Not the would-be *literary* men who have read all the fashion-able novels and dream-books in print to make them-selves acquainted with *fine words*, and beautiful tropes and sentences, to the neglect of everything like sub-stantial knowledge, good common sense, and a familiar acquaintance with the old Bible. Not the proud and ambitious men, who, because they cannot obtain a large, wealthy and liberal Society, and a large salary, will turn off, or turn back from the work of the minis-try or abandon it altogether, to run into every new-fangled folly that knocks at the door of their credulity and love of notoriety.

" I had almost forgotten the object of this epistle, which is to inquire of the brethren, what means can be employed to re-awaken a new and growing interest in our cause, and call into the field of public labor a class of young men who would give themselves to the work of the ministry — men who will study the Master, learn his doctrine, and follow his examples : men who will devote their energies to the establishment of the truth — Gospel truth — and will not abandon the work be-cause they cannot be indulged in every whim that may take them, and gratify their vanity by a peacock dis-play of their own diminutive capacities.

" We very much need—never more—a large number of devoted young men of honest purpose, humble spir-it, and fair talents — no matter how great — who will come into the vast field of labor, already ripe to the harvest, and *work*. Never were there such inducements as now exist.

" Why do they not come forth to our help? Why do

so many delay? I can think of but two reasons: the defection of those who have been with us, and the— what shall I call it?—indolence? pride? ambition?—I have no precise word at command. I mean those who *blow up* here, and *burst up* there, or *run down* in some other place,—simply because they ran up *too fast* and *too high*,—who are grumbling about the ingratitude, want of zeal, stinginess of Societies, moving here and moving there, to find a people willing to praise their poor old sermons, instead of studying new and more interesting ones. I have no patience with these clerical loafers—minister vagabonds—who go about killing Societies by their inattention to the real duties of their vocation, as faithful ministers of the New Testament— and then try to shirk a merited condemnation by finding fault with Societies.

" With such a country as ours, and in such an age as this, there is no need of this state of things. There is not, and never was—I trust there never will be—any occasion, any justification, for a good, capable, faithful preacher of Universalism, to be idle, out of employ— to sink into the cities to beg their way through life.— There are hundreds of places to-day where men, duly qualified, could find abundant encouragement, to sustain themselves and families. Yes, a thousand, more desirable than those into which most of our preachers, twenty years ago, entered when they commenced their missions. New England and New York could support twice as many as they have,—the Western States four times,—and the Southern States ten times as many. All that is wanting is men of the right stamp. For want of them our cause languishes. 'Pray the Lord to send more laborers into the field.'"

He declares that " clergymen are solemnly ordained to a specific work. Thereafter they have vowed unto God to live and work for the ministry; to persuade men unto holiness ; to comfort those in affliction, and

20

do good as they have opportunity. Whenever any
worldly object or interest comes between them and the
duties of their vocation. they act unworthily, and on
no good ground of fairness can they pretend to belong
to the ministry. He who becomes worldly, and pre-
fers business. honor. pleasure. to that of godliness, deserves not to retain his standing."

CHAPTER XV.

Brother Balch naturally had a hardy constitution, and was descended from a family of more than ordinary length of life. And yet most of the early years of his ministry were darkened by a terrible struggle with painful disease, induced by over-study and unacquaintance of the laws of health, to be borne with most marked submission; and his preaching during all this time was kept beautifully radiant with the hopes and joys of the Gospel. I remember him in some of those years in which he calls himself "a poor, nervous, shadowy dyspeptic, and a wonder to himself, till he learned to use the world as not abusing it, and then doing as well as knowing, despite fashions, luxuries and habits." His disease would frequently come upon him with great violence, and he would suffer for weeks beyond description.

I find in a published sermon of his, "Forty Years in the Ministry," in which he says:

"For the first twenty years of my ministry, I suffered much from disease, induced by ignorance of God's holy law written all over and through my being. Over-taxing the brain, restraining the body by sedentary habits, regardless of diet, and abusing a naturally strong constitution, I passed through all the horrors of a miserable dyspeptic, made worse by medical ignorance prevailing at the time in such cases. During

303

those twenty years I scarce knew a comfortable night's rest, or a decent meal. How I lived I know not. Nothing but sovereign grace preserved me from all the nostrums, regular and irregular, blisters and bran-bread, calomel, cayenne, and cold water. But somehow I did live through it all, and, for twenty years, by a fair and strict regard to the laws of my being, I have enjoyed very excellent health. During this time, many friends and brethren, who, in their robust health, pitied me in my sufferings, have gone over the river before me. I am to-day in as good health as at any period of my life — could not ask for better."

Indeed, for nearly twenty years after the time here noted (1867), he claimed that his health was nearly perfect, and he capable of endurance almost as in his youth, except as at times he would greatly suffer from his long-standing, chronic affliction, which toward the last became severely telling upon him, and as he went from home to different places to fill appointments, gave to all sad premonitions of his approaching departure, and added to the solemnity of the occasion and the force of the words to which he gave utterance.

His last sickness, which brought him to his death, was not very protracted. When the physician who attended him was first called to see him, he felt confident that his chances to recover were indeed very slight. But at the end of a week there had been what seemed a somewhat favorable change, that made him conjecture that possibly after all he might rally for a brief space of time. This, however, Brother Balch did not think. He was of the opinion that he knew himself better. He felt almost from the moment he was compelled to take his bed, that it was his last illness, and that he never would rise from it a well man. And it thus proved that the symptoms were disappointing, for he commenced almost immediately from that hour to fail, and in two or three days he was entirely given up by all the household friends, after which he sank very rapidly, so that his death seemed sudden at last. It was best that it should be so, for he had greatly feared from the complicated nature of his disease that he would have to experience a lingering, painful illness, till he should pray to be relieved from intolerable suffering.

It was at this juncture that Brother Reed of Rockford and myself, were called to his bedside, only four days previous to his death, that he might counsel with us and make known his wishes respecting his funeral obsequies, and other matters, as they were agitating his mind; and it was no common satisfaction to listen to his talk, his mind so unclouded and vigorous, that he seemed helped by the All-helpful One. While his voice was feeble his intellect was in nothing dimmed, and he went on relating with wonderful minuteness the circumstances to which he would direct our attention.

In these last solemn moments of his life, when he was getting ready to bid adieu to all its joys and sorrows, its hopes and its fears, it was most refreshing to find him so tranquil and composed, as one who lays himself down to a peaceful sleep after the toils of a wearisome day; holding himself as cheerful through all the long hours we conversed with him, as in his more hale and halcyon days, showing that he could calmly practice the submission he had so long preached as a

Christian duty. Brother Reed, in referring to this on the day of his burial, said: "His intellect was as vigorous, his memory as vivid and minute, his smile as genial, and his sensitiveness as keen as at any previous moment of his life." And why should not this be so, the contemplation of his going as peaceful as the bosom of a summer sea; for was he not resting in the joy of a constant faith and holy hope that all lost ones from earth were to be gathered to the higher and better home, and a ransomed universe to be blest with the fulness of God's illimitable and unchangeable love? He had a faith that saw the future clear, and everything beyond this dim earth seemed to him bright and beautiful. What other possibility was there for him, now that he was hastening to that beautiful shore to which he had pointed so many dear ones that had gone before. Was it not the only approriate thing for him, that he should now be wishing to die, for could he not say, " I am weary, let me go; lay me low, my work is done"?

It so happened that his last hours were painless, for he fell into an insensible condition on Christmas day and remained unconscious from the early hours of morning till the time of his death,, rousing from it but once, and then only to ask if the day was breaking. Upon receiving the reply he remained silent after it.

And so death took him; transferring him from his sufferings here on the earth to his rest and joy in the great hereafter. And it was a grand ending of a grand life; to pass away from earth on Christmas day, the birthday of the world's Redeemer; our second birthday into the realms of glory; the birthday of love and peace, and joy and hope, deeper than all the fountains

of human misery shall ever quench. And we yield him
to a tenderer care than the homes of earth could afford
him. He has put on a new garniture of grace and
glory, and has gone forward into other scenes, and a
grander discipline, connecting these years of our earthly
pilgrimage with the years of eternity.

And shall we not give joyous assent to the breath-
ings of the beautiful hymn which says,

> "Thou art gone to the grave, but we will not deplore thee,
> Since God was thy refuge, thy guardian, thy guide;
> He gave thee, He took thee, and He will restore thee,
> And death hath no sting since the Saviour hath died."

We can but appreciate how changed are all the affairs of her who stood closest to him, and other changes
to follow, she cannot know how many, nor when, nor
what; yet she will find much consolation in the reflection, that

> "As a bird to its nest,
> When the storm is abroad,
> He has gone to his rest
> In the bosom of God."

She could not but let him go from so much of in-
firmity, and sickness, and pain, and did so with the
feeling, that

> The saddest of all was the sad refrain,
> That she never would look on his like again

*   *   *   *   *   *   *   *   *   *   *

Our brother had no fear of death, which was to
dismiss him into some new and higher development.
He dreaded a helpless life much more. It was to him a
glorious thing to pass away from earth, and go at the
Heavenly Father's call to be with those who preceded
him in the celestial mansions. His was the faith that
assured him that death was a step forward in that life

which knows no cessation; a doorway through which we pass as we go onward and upward forever. It was through death that he was expecting to cast off, or lay down his weakness, his infirmities and diseases, that he himself might rise up to another and more glorious life. He felt that he was to cease in all that is frail and decaying; cease to be human (if so) that he might advance to the glory and blessedness of the angel throng.

He always claimed for himself the most cheerful views of his departure, and the eternity lying beyond it; for how but they must hold an appropriate and beneficent place in the divine economy? It was in the likeness of a spiritual birth, and a necessary stage in human progress, to be passed as we would pass from childhood to youth, and from youth to manhood, and with the same consciousness of an ever unfolding nature. Under this view it was no dreaded power; but a part of the great plan, or course of nature; an appointment of God as much as life itself; a wise and good appointment, to be met as such, with submission, calmness and trust.

It seemed to him a most mistaken view, that in our exit from this world we are lying down in all our powers and facilities to die; and so are to go out of being eternally, to be extinguished as a soul and a spirit; and not rather that we are to leap forward into a higher existence, and into conditions more favorable than those we are experiencing here, and in which we are to measure on in the forward march that is lying before us, and which we are still to pass, from knowledge to knowledge; from wisdom to wisdom; increasing forever and forever. The demand in human nature for to-morrow, and for life to be continued indefinitely, he was sure was stronger than and every other, and so what was to the materialist the extinction of all being, became to him the gateway to an endless life; a going forward from lower to higher; the goodly prospect ever enlarging, each preparing for the one that was to come after.

Life on this earth seemed to him too brief to develop the full estate of that idea which God has expressed in the creation of man; and from its very incompleteness he argued its continuance, that it might be given the opportunity of unfolding itself to the utmost of its capacity; of attaining whatever of knowledge, of virtue and holiness its powers would admit of. This was at least ground for strong presumption that there was some further progress; some sequel yet to be enacted. It was so that he had the feeling that a good and true life ought to be immortal, since to strike off the future beyond this sublunary existence, the noble life especially becomes a sadly unfinished thing. There are no completed lives or characters in this short period of existence: and it was the insight and suggestion of his moral reason that these unfinished beginnings that pass under our observation, must relate to perfection elsewhere. If we went not beyond the present with our imperfections, our ignorance and trials clinging to us, how were man other than a failure? The end of his existence would not be answered, and indeed could not be. All lives would be wasted lives, and every death would be premature.

With such a view it will be readily perceived that death is no catastrophe. It is appalling, we know, in certain phases of it, when its change comes over loved

ones only a little before radiant with life, and filled
with animation and beauty. As such we stand aghast
at it. But still our Brother stood ready to affirm that,
let it come when it would come, in whatever manner,
and to whomsoever it might, it never came as a calamity or punishment; never as a final end, out of which
nothing of good was suffered to spriug, but generally
as a relief, and always as a stepping-stone to progress
hereafter.

Now it was in this continued existence of his being,
after the manner we have described, that Mr. Balch
could scarcely be said to entertain a doubt. He believed it with all the force of assent which a reflecting
mind is capable of giving to any subject not resting
upon absolute demonstration. He believed it, because
without it, as I said, this life appeared to him a perfectly unfinished plan.

Not to dwell at this point, I find my thoughts turning back to December 26th, 1887, when after a short
service at the residence of the deceased there was gathered at the Baptist church a large assemblage of his
fellow citizens and friends to pay once again the tribute
of loving respect, when a brief eulogy was pronounced
by the writer of this, and a very cogent inferential
argument for immortality, filled with the spirit of
abiding faith and trust, was given in an address by the
Rev. Dr. Reed, after which, proceeding to the cemetery,
the remains borne by the sons and sons-in-law, an appropriate and impressive service was spoken, and an
affecting farewell taken. And as we left our trusted
friend, brother, husband, father, to sleep as it were in
honored dust, we felt to say, " Peace to thy ashes, and

respect to thy memory," with the humble prayer that it might be hallowed, as it never can be hallowed or made sacred in the printed page.

To supply the place of the memorial of such a man requires more than the set facts of a biography, for the dates and details presumably at one's command form but a feeble clue to a character which it seems presumptuous to attempt to analyze. Anything we might say of our brother would be too slight and imperfect a tribute to one who has added such honor to the name he bore; who has so adorned the sacred literature of his country, setting a deep impress of his mind and character upon the hearts of such vast multitudes, and as a friend being lamented, as in this world of imperfect relations but few have ever been lamented.

How should we indeed be able to fully appreciate the labors of one so grand and true, bearing himself manfully in an eminently useful career which has placed him in the sacred role of noble and excellent characters; one who has done so much to give our church a standing in the world, serving it with a most singular devotion, that shall cause his name and character to shine with an ever-brightening lustre. But few names have ever deserved to be, or will be, more cherished in grateful remembrance than that of Wm. S. Balch. But few have known the honored space he has filled for more than an entire generation, as generations are reckoned, and among the fathers of our ministry; or the general regard, respect and deference in which he has been holden as an enduring monument of his faithfulness.

Our church has never had within its borders a per-

son more consecrated to the one purpose of making the
race loving and happy ; for has he not given his all to
human needs and welfare? Of the impression he has
made upon all our hearts, and of his world-wide influence, we shall only come to know better and better as
the years go by. Of how many lives can it ever be
told, so well rounded out into completeness and usefulness ; so grown up into genuine, Christian manhood,
rightly developed by the divine life of goodness in every
faculty of his being. Has he not been a sort of " living
epistle known and read of all men," in having been a
leader, a vital force and concrete power unto salvation to every one that believeth? and though dead, will
he not yet speak to us by an example such as goes
preaching on with persuasive power long after the lips
are silent, and the eloquence of speech forgotten, the
example of a good, true and noble life ?

Aye, he has lived long and nobly, fulfilling faithfully
his appointed years of service, doing what he could do
to recall the attention of men from their creeds and
dogmas of speculative faith, from their forms and ceremonies, and fastings and outward observances, to the
exercise of a real, genuine love to God and man, such
as will prompt to the performance of the great practical duties of life. He has taught that religion is something more than the assent of the mind to a system ;
something more than the exercise of devotional feelings, and emotions in the heart: that it is love and
mercy and forgiveness to man: ;and that its fruits are
the fruits of peace. joy, long-suffering, gentleness, goodness, truth and benevolence ; such as is approved in the
sight of all honest principle, and before God and the
Father, as the primary Author of the Christian system.

In truth he believed, that the only all-important concern of a man was to be good and do good; to seek
for the best, and do for the best, now to-day, to-morrow
and always. His faith led him to respect all good
men; not religious men in the accepted sense of the
word particularly, but men of virtuous lives, true to
their integrity, useful, kind-hearted men, above a mean,
sordid action. It led him to detest all cant, all mere
professions and sanctimoniousness. He thought far
less of the outward signs and forms of religion than
most men; but it was because he honored the real
spirit of religion the more. He was not content, like
thousands of others, to pass away from earth, leaving
no trace of good behind him; but would do something
for the cause of virtue and the happiness of his fellow
men, and so made his life one of good motives and
good deeds; of usefulness, honesty, integrity and truth-
fulness.

The number of persons is never large, who will give
their entire lives to the doing of good. And we do
pray for the appearance of other such, as the world-
wide want of our natures, to be consecrated to the
cause which had his whole heart. Every person who
has known our brother is the better and happier for it.
And oh, to make others happier, and the world better,
what so grateful a service. I trust it may be our privilege to remember him as having had largely to do
with all the manifold interests interwoven with the
life of society, and working for the common good.
May we look back upon him as upon the loss of a
leader whom it is our greatest excellence and honor to
cherish, and whom we have never seen but to be made

glad. If I have succeeded in presenting only a tolerably faithful picture of him, I shall be sure of his holding a high place in the enrollment of the many worthies that have done honor to our cause. We trust that the young men for whom the work was planned by Mr. Balch himself, that it might do them a much-needed service, may learn from it the strength and beauty of a consecrated life.

It is a welcome thought that the hearts of so many have been moved by him, and that he has been made the theme of numerous discourses, giving more or less full accounts of his life and labors, as one who has been greatly loved, honored and trusted.

Among the first to speak of him outside of the local home press, was the organ of the denomination for the Western Branch of the Publishing House, in its forthcoming issue, and after remarking that the event was unexpected to the general public, and that it was yet without particulars as to the cause of his death, it gave forth the following utterance: "Dr. Balch descends to the grave in the impressive figure of the Scriptures, "as a shock of corn fully ripe." His history is indissolubly connected with that of Universalism in the New England, the Middle, and the Western States. Wherever Universalism is known as an organized body of Christian believers, William S. Balch was known. Intelligence of his death will find mourners all over our Zion. He was highly honored for his steadfast adherence to the principles of our faith as a minister for over sixty years. And we may add that the man was also widely eteemed for solid and attractive qualities, which linked many friends to him as with hooks of

REV. WILLIAM STEVENS BALCH.

steel. He now leaves these earthly scenes in which he was so conspicuous a figure, even in a venerable old age, and there are many outside a large and devoted family circle, who will mourn his departure."

A paper from Dubuque, Iowa, but echoes the sentiment of multitudes of others from various parts of the land, in saying. "The death of Doctor Balch is a personal bereavement to a large circle of friends scattered from Maine to California, and will bring sorrow to the hearts of the membership of the Universalist church throughout the country."

As soon as it was known of his death, there came letters of condolence to Mrs. Balch from many sympathizing friends. As a specimen character of some of these I present the following. Rev. H. D. L. Webster wrote. "The loss seems a personal one to us all. We esteemed him as one so rich in experience, so learned in the lore that adds lustre to the clerical profession, that we were glad to call him our leader. No one of our many popular and great men in the ministry will be more missed."

Dr. Tuttle proffered tenderest sympathy in a missive in which he said, "Brother Balch wrote me so kindly in my sad bereavement that I cannot but be mindful of you in your sore trial, and please accept my every assurance of esteem."

The words of Dr. Rexford were, "You will not need that I should tell you of my sorrow at the death of Brother Balch. for I had great esteem and love for him, and have been made stronger because of him; and I would desire that what help may be in a brother's sympathy, and a most heartfelt wish, may be taken from my heart by one who is so stricken by the event of his death."

Also Brother Manley W. Tabor. "He has earned his release from service. A noble, valiant soldier in truth's army has he been, and no small factor in the bringing to pass the success, the honor, the high estate which the Universalist church rejoices in to-day. His standing protest against narrowness in thinking and believing; against all assumption of ecclesiastical authority; were a fitting close of a life's work, written in the name of liberty and reform. It is with thankfulness and pride that I think of his manly Christian position, and his unswerving loyalty to principle. It has not been in vain, for as leaven is it working in our midst, and will work till all shall be leavened."

A brother minister who shall be nameless, wrote Mrs. Balch, "He is the only man whom I ever really loved, and it is my sincere and deep affection for him that causes me at this time to intrude upon you. He was more to me in his interest in what I am attempting to do; in his kindly criticism and forbearance than my father ever has been; and in my heart, since I came to know and appreciate him for what he was, he has held the first place. Thus to me it has been as a son's loss to his father, rather than the going away from sight and touch of a friend."

As I sent out proposals for this Memoir, I can hardly tell you of the many good words and testimonials of warmest personal regard that came pouring in to me, some of which I have included in previous chapters of the work, and will proceed to give other portions of these here. There were those to ask it

as a favor that they might be permitted to pen some
word of affection and commendation of a life that had
been an inspiration to them, and whose personal
friendship they counted as one of their choicest treas-
ures. I was made the recipient of numerous letters
from old and young, scattered widely over the country,
telling me in more than a single instance of their being
taught in their earliest childhood to reverence the man
who had blessed so many. Miss Eva J. Stickney, of
Sioux Falls, Dakota, wrote to inform me that her
father and Mr. Balch were boys together, and laid their
plans of life together; and "as children they were
taught to regard Mr. Balch with the utmost veneration
and esteem; a feeling that had been strengthened by
the closer acquaintance of later years." A niece of
Rev. Otis A. Skinner sent me a line from Kansas,
giving reminiscences of her mother in the eighty-fourth
year of her age, in which incidents are related of
Brothers Skinner and Balch having studied together,
with Rev. Samuel C. Loveland, and the love and tenderness with which they regarded each other as being
characteristically beautiful of the hearts of both. She
is at pains to relate the following: "The last time my
mother saw Brother Balch was in his calling upon her,
on the eve of our departure from our eastern home in
Vermont, to the State of Wisconsin. Placing his hand
affectionately on her shoulder, he said, ' God bless you,
Martha,' for they were such tried and trusted friends
that they always clung to the familiar way of addressing
each other by their Christian names." This was Brother
Balch's custom : always so free-hearted and simple-
mannered, that no one could help greatly loving him.

21

Of the many letters that have come to my hands. I may make extracts from but very few, which are a fair sample of the whole number. In responding promptly to a letter of my own, Brother Dinsmore wrote:

"You ask me to give something out of my memory regarding our good brother. What can I say? I seldom saw him except at public gatherings, and then but a few times in my life. But I learned to prize and honor him above many, and indeed most of the ministers I have known. I think of him somehow as I imagine the second generation of Christians at Ephesus, as the first hundred years of the church were declining to a close, must have thought of the Apostle John. They thought of him as the last who had seen the Lord. I thought of Father Balch as the last who had seen the early days of the church which I so loved. He was the last who had been called to pass through the deep waters for the precious faith. I revered him for his strong and noble spirit, and his broad understanding of the work of the ministry. I loved him for the kindness and peace of his character. He was a strong, but a peaceful soul. He was above doubt and dismay. I dare not attempt an analysis of his character; but this much I may say, 'He was great in his simplicity, his transparent heart and soul. He is gone, and his works will follow him.'"

In a line from Brother Francis, he tells us:

"My remembrance of Dr. Balch reaches back to the time when he was the Universalist minister of Watertown, Mass., about 1830. I went with my father one Sunday afternoon to hear him preach; and the impression of earnestness, sincerity and devotedness lingers yet in my mind. Years went by and I became personally acquainted with him. After I engaged in the ministry, I always received his kindly greetings and words of encouragement, whenever we chanced to meet, as later in life we frequently did. He was ever the same warm-hearted brother and friend."

In a somewhat different, but a more eulogistic strain, Brother Shrigley speaks:

"Nearly sixty years have passed since I heard Brother Balch preach in Putney, Vt., and although his testimony was in accord with my previous religious convictions, I could have shouted for joy at the good words he uttered. It was the first sermon in defence of the final triumph of the good and true over all evil I ever heard from human lips; and never can I forget how precious to me was that testimony. It was the period of the opening chapter of Universalism in this country, and our good Brother Balch was one of the most prominent figures in that generation, strong in his arguments, and so simple in his words, and in the construction of his sentences, that even a child would have no difficulty in understanding him. Few were more happy in illustrating and defending the Gospel of peace and love, and as an efficient public speaker he was scarcely second to any other speaker from any platform. We may say of him that he has lived a life of spotless integrity; sound in his religious opinions, loved best by those who knew him best, and one of the ablest preachers on the American continent. This is saying very much of him; but none too much; for it is every word true. It seemed often to me, in listening to him, as if he was unable to check the hopeful words that fell from his lips. They rolled out and on in such perfect torrents of sacred eloquence, as completely astonished all who heard him. And what changes our brother had witnessed during his long and eventful life, and how much he had done to bring about those changes which are now visible in almost every church creed in the land. I do not know the man that has done more for our cause, and no one certainly has been more faithful."

Judge Adams of Dubuque, Iowa, tells of paying a visit to the East in the summer of 1887, and passing by Brother Balch's home in Andover, Vermont. It had been sixty years since he lived there; and he says: " Seeing a man not far from the wayside I stopped and said. Do you know Dr. Balch? And the answer came, Perfectly. Every one knows him about here, and respects him, too. And when I told him I lived neighbor to him—which in the West was only about a hundred and fifty miles—that was enough; I needed no other introduction."

Prof. Lee, of the St. Lawrence University, had asked on a former occasion to be allowed to relate a personal incident, and gave what follows: " When I was ten years old I heard Universalism preached for the first time from his lips. Little did he think on that occasion, in an obscure village of Vermont, in that five o'clock Sunday afternoon service, he was awakening in that boy's mind a deep interest in that faith, then so despised, now so honored, which has done so much to enlighten the world."

Dr. Sawyer, whom I must especially mention with favor, as having indulged me in quite a correspondence, and assured me that if I wished any information from him I had only to ask any question I pleased, and he would answer as well as he could, has this, in addition to other matters distributed throughout the work :

" Through three-quarters of his life it has been my privilege to enjoy his acquaintance and friendship. Though his senior by two years and a quarter, he was in the ministry a year or two before me, and our lives have been in many ways connected; and it affords me peculiar satisfaction to acknowledge my obligations to him for financial aid when leaving college burdened with debt, and also with advice and assistance in entering the ministry. He was my theological tutor, and instrumental in getting me ordained. Thus, you see, that Brother Balch was a kind of godfather to me. For many years we were yoke-fellows in the neighboring parishes in New York City, at a time when our faith had not only more, but more zealous opponents than now, and our lives were little else than a strife with those of the contrary part. I thank God for his long life, and for the faithful service he has done our church and the great cause for which it stands."

It was his pen that drew the series of resolutions passed by the ministers' meeting of Boston and vicinity, in which they speak of "the high endowments of his mind and heart; of his long and active life, and the many-handed and eminent services he has rendered to our church, and the best interests of society at large; of the benign and lasting influences he has exerted upon his day and generation, and the untarnished Christian character he has maintained through a public ministry of sixty years."

This body was followed by others, and notably by the Chicago Ministerial Association convened March 19, 1888.

" WHEREAS, Our much honored brother, William S. Balch, has been called away from his home on earth to the higher and better spirit life, and to brighter, more joyous, and active scenes of happiness, and we are to meet him no more in the family circle and in the social gathering, and are to have his counsel, his assistance and coöperation no more in society and the church ; therefore,

" *Resolved*, that it is a most willing duty we perform,

to express our high regard for him who has passed on before us ; to recall the many excellent traits of character for which he was distinguished, and the many good deeds which he cheerfully performed, as well as the great work he has done for enlightened and liberal Christianity, and which has given him such potent sway over all our hearts.

"*Resolved*, That while our bosoms have been thrilled and rapt with delight in listening to his many golden thoughts and his most eloquent appeals, yet we revere his memory in nothing so much as for his beneficent gifts, and his benignly wrought influences by which his name and fame have so marked him as a pattern for us to follow, and which made him so worthy the love and esteem of all men everywhere.

"*Resolved*, That we look upon him as having been a clear, strong thinker; a guide, a teacher and leader, a devoted, affectionate and faithful working pastor; under whose ministrations, replete with instruction, the cause of God has been greatly blessed, and the shackles removed from many imprisoned minds and hearts.

"*Resolved*, That he having proved such a champion for the cause, in valiant services done for truth and righteousness, and won such life-long friends and friendships, by efforts never to die in their consequences, we are proud to do him this honor of paying humble tribute to his worth, and in standing by the side of him who has toiled so earnestly and diligently all these years.

"*Resolved*, That we but too feebly express the sorrow of our hearts at this link of his life being broken, while we send our sincere "God bless you" to the dear ones left behind, asking that Heaven's choicest favor may be with all who were allied to him in closest bonds of family and filial attachment, though not grieving for him whose life was so worn and oppressed with disease and pain, for here was no room for tears.

> " For when his arm grew palsied, and his eye
> Dark with the mists of age, it was his time to die."

Commemorative services were held also, and resolutions passed by nearly all of the several churches over which he had been settled as pastor. They would together form quite a list, testifying to the faithful services he has rendered our Zion. The last of these, the church at Dubuque, was the first to speak, and then followed others till they had gone the round of the different churches that were included in this category. The church at Dubuque did not feel that they could well over-estimate the good results of his presence and labors in behalf of the cause in their midst. In a memorial service Judge Adams, with several others speaking, gave expression to the general feeling and sentiment in this wise. " The Universalist denomination, from the Atlantic to the Pacific, takes notice of his death, and mourns his loss. The denomintion, it is true, contains other great and good men, but it contains no other Dr. Balch, and never can. He is identified with its history in a peculiar manner, and will be remembered as its fitting representative beyond that of any other now remaining in our midst. Others perhaps have done a great work in controversial theology, but no man stands as a better exemplification of all that is most beautiful and lovely in the religion which he professed."

At the annual meeting of the Universalist church in Elgin, after attending to other business of the meeting, the following resolutions were offered by the trustees, and unanimously adopted :

" The memory of a good man is the heritage of the world. The Rev. W. S. Balch, who lately died in our midst, has added to the word's heritage a legacy of memory and of blessing such as few men ever leave.

His sixty years of public ministration have been of a character such as only a noble, cultivated mind and a pure and lofty spirit could give. His social life has been pure, peaceable and just. Here he has set an example which to follow would place the crown of happiness upon home. As pastor to this people he ever was leading toward the best ideals in life, and seeking to mould the minds and spirits of his flock into the kindly affection, the brotherly love and the exalted nobility in which he had a supreme confidence. As a friend he was steadfast, sincere and noble. As a counselor he was wise, discreet and safe. His work in the world was always stamped by the broad and independent character of the man. He wrought not by ordinary methods ; his own strength was always that upon which it was turned, and his ideals were so perfect and so faithfully followed that when his work was done it presented the finish of his master mind. Mr. Balch was impatient with creeds. He refused to set any limit to the power and love of God, and his ideal was the perfect manhood of the perfect man. The full ripened grain has been gathered. We rejoice in the harvest, knowing that in the garner is a store of example of courageous and exalted living that we can safely copy. The ways of life have been trod by no man more manly than he. The work of no one life has been rounded up and made complete in a more gracious symmetry than was the life work of our friend at the close of his more than four score years. The end is not—his eloquent tongue yet speaks—the waves of influence from his revered memory are ever widening and broadening, bearing their blessings. Time can but add to their richness and eternity only can disclose all their wealth.

" We hereby resolve to place this tribute to his memory upon the records of our church."

But no more glowing tribute has been paid to any one in our denomination, than was the testimonial

Reception and Banquet given him by the Ministerial Association in Chicago, April 12. 1886, upon the eightieth anniversary of his birth. It was an occasion of great interest, and a fit recognition of the worth of the man. How could there be any more remarkable success in doing him honor, when as it was thought there were nearly three hundred present, and from several States, to offer their congratulations and pay their respects to the guest of the evening.

It were well if the memory of the just was always so blest in the hearts of the living. How many unbidden tears have been caused to flow as a tribute to his memory we shall never know, for we do not know the measure of a long and valued life of usefulness. There was something divinely beautiful in his unaffected, genial companionship, leading men into the light of truth and the love and practice of goodness, to cause him to linger long in our thoughts, giving him an honored place among us, and making the world proud to be his friend.

In letting this work go from our hands, may we not ask what is the whole simple message that such a life, such a death, and such a memory bears to us? Is not the one all-surpassing truth that beams out from it this: the supreme worth of goodness? Here is certainly testimony to its value. Here is an instance of its triumph, and a pledge of its immortality. Can we not say that nothing reaches so far, nothing tells so mightily, and nothing so spreads the glory of heaven over the common places of earth as the plain, good man, or good woman? Let us try and learn this great moral lesson which we derive from the review of this good man's life, which is that of usefulness, practical good will, the promotion of industry, order, virtue, social progress and social happiness, developing all the resources God has placed at our disposal.

Some one has asked that, when they shall rear the marble column that is to mark the resting place of Rev. Wm. S. S. Balch, there shall be inscribed upon it the words which tell the whole story of his life, "He loved his fellow men." But he himself has expressed in as choice a form of words as can be, the following: "When a few more years are past, and my earthly form is laid to its final rest, I have sometimes dared to hope that some whom I have sought to instruct, comfort and bless, will gather at my grave, and in their deep soul's feeling say of me, "He did not live and labor in vain."